WORST IN SHOW

ANNA E. COLLINS

T0281991

FOREVER

New York   Boston

Copyright © 2024 by Anna E. Collins

Cover design and illustration by Sarah Congdon
Cover copyright © 2024 by Hachette Book Group, Inc.

Forever
Hachette Book Group
1290 Avenue of the Americas, New York, NY 10104
read-forever.com
@readforeverpub

First Edition: August 2024

Forever is an imprint of Grand Central Publishing. The Forever name and logo are registered trademarks of Hachette Book Group, Inc.

The publisher is not responsible for websites (or their content) that are not owned by the publisher.

The Hachette Speakers Bureau provides a wide range of authors for speaking events. To find out more, go to hachettespeakersbureau.com or email HachetteSpeakers@hbgusa.com.

Forever books may be purchased in bulk for business, educational, or promotional use. For information, please contact your local bookseller or the Hachette Book Group Special Markets Department at special.markets@hbgusa.com.

Print book interior design by Taylor Navis

Library of Congress Cataloging-in-Publication Data
Names: Collins, Anna E., author.
Title: Worst in show / Anna E. Collins.
Description: First edition. | New York : Forever, 2024.
Identifiers: LCCN 2023056565 | ISBN 9781538742280 (trade paperback) |
    ISBN 9781538742303 (ebook)
Subjects: LCGFT: Romance fiction. | Novels.
Classification: LCC PS3603.O4525 W67 2024 | DDC 813/.6—dc23/eng/20231214
LC record available at https://lccn.loc.gov/2023056565

ISBN: 9781538742280 (trade paperback), 9781538742303 (ebook)

Printed in the United States of America

LSC

Printing 1, 2024

To all dogs, but especially to Archie

1

I have dog kibble in my bra. Again. I wish I could say it was on purpose—some kind of genius obedience training technique perhaps—but what really happened was that the thirty-pound bag I was attempting to hoist onto a high shelf in the storage room of my grandpa's pet store, Happy Paws, burst at the seam at the most inopportune moment.

I should have known what kind of morning I was in for as soon as I got up. The stop button on the toaster in my apartment doesn't work, so to save my breakfast, I have to unplug the whole thing and fish out my slice at the exact right moment. Today I missed my window, and instead of heeding the sign that I'd be better off going back to bed, I proceeded as if nothing was amiss.

Hence, here I am, ankle-deep in freeze-dried beef and regret.

I shake out my sweater to clear the pet food from my decolletage and take a couple of crunchy steps to the side, but that's all I have time for before two dervishes come barreling into the room, surrounding me with gleeful barks.

"Good morning, monsters," I coo, crouching to their level to block them from the heap of tempting nuggets. Cholula, our Chihuahua mix, jumps up and slobbers a wet one across my nose. Her aim is off due to an extensive underbite, but no one can fault her enthusiasm. Cap waits patiently until she's done, and I reward him with some extra ear scratches for the effort. He's the oldest of our three remaining shelter dogs—some sort of beagle-terrier combo with a few other breeds peppered in as evidenced by his short brown coat and boxy face. "Did you have breakfast yet?" I ask him, receiving only heavy panting in response.

"Morning, Pop," I call up the stairs to the small space above the store that my grandpa Harvey had converted from office to apartment after my grandma passed a few years ago.

He appears at the landing above, mug in hand. "Morning, Cora. They ate. Would you like some coffee?"

I free myself of my backpack by the counter and smile at him. "You've known me almost twenty-eight years, and you still have to ask?"

He shrugs and heads back into his space. I follow.

"So, what's on the docket today?" I ask once we're seated at his small table and the first hit of caffeine has done its thing. I eye the English muffin in front of him. Softening butter and a wedge of hard cheese sit off to the side.

Harvey consults his planner and runs a curled finger down the page. "A couple of deliveries. We'll have to move the rest of those bully sticks and the pigs' ears to the front. Two for one I think as we phase them out."

"One pallet was already delivered. I brought in the bags."

"That's what the ruckus was?"

"Minor snafu. Don't worry, I'll clean it up. Are you replacing the chewies with anything else?"

"Those cookies we sold last year did well. I'll call the vendor to see if she still makes them."

My stomach growls loudly. *Mmm, cookies.* "Can I have one of those?" I point to his plate.

"In the pantry."

While I butter the crumbly goodness, I say, "It's almost October. Maybe I'll make some more pet costumes? They were pretty popular. And I posted in that online forum on Flockify this morning to see if anyone is looking to have something made, too. Look." I show him the post.

Living History Illinois Flockify Post, Period Dress Channel

SingerQueen Tuesday 06:53 AM
Hi all, it's about that time. I've got a few spots open for costume commissions—first come basis. Holler at me.

"You're this 'SingerQueen'?" Harvey asks, peering up at me above his readers.

"It's my username. Because my sewing machine is a Singer."

"Ah. Yes, all good ideas, kiddo."

That boosts me even more than the coffee and carbs. There are always themed events popping up closer to the holidays, so I should be able to pick up a commissioned outfit or two from the historical reenactment folks online, and I know exactly what I'm going to make for our pet clientele. I scored a stack of vintage fabrics at a flea market this past summer, and I'm thinking a line of literary-inspired get-ups—Sherlock Holmes, Mr. Darcy, Scarlett O'Hara, Laura Ingalls...Our customers will love that. If they can be persuaded to spread the word, too, maybe the end-of-month bills downstairs will seem less nefarious.

I finish my food in a rush and get up to put my mug away, but as I do, my foot catches on something soft that sends me stumbling ungracefully for the remaining steps to the counter. Dregs of coffee end up across my chest in a Rorschach pattern that looks like a smiling *T. rex.* I shake dark droplets off my hand as I straighten. "Come on, Boris. Not again."

The wolfhound lifts his head and looks in my general direction. I'll never understand how it's possible for an aging, blind behemoth to move around that quietly.

"Aw, he can't help it." Harvey pats his leg to get Boris to move. The two of them snuggle close for a moment before Boris sinks onto the floor again.

Technically, Boris, Cholula, and Cap are still available for adoption, but when my grandma died, and the shelter part of the business along with her, Harvey stopped trying to find them new homes. "Who'd want them more than me?" he said once when I asked him about it. And it's true—I can't picture the store without them.

I rinse off my mug and my hands and then grab Harvey's mug, too. "Do you have a T-shirt I can borrow?"

He nods toward the corner that harbors his alcove bed and a robust closet. Then he looks at his watch and stretches. "Today's going to be a good day," he says, like he always does. "I can feel it in my bones."

"If you say so, Pop." I go to find a new top and holler to him, "I'll be down in a minute."

His footsteps are already receding, so I take to rummaging through his clothes. The closet smells like soap and cedar with a faint old-person undertone. Familiar and safe. In the back, there's a bag of my grandma's things, and in it, I find a soft denim shirt that must be decades old but also, somehow, once again fashionable. I pull my stained top off, and then out of habit, I glance out the window. I'm too high up for anyone to be able to see me, but I duck down regardless at the sight of activity across the street. No Tuesday morning peep show here. What are they doing over there anyway? Did someone finally lease the empty space?

Cholula's beady eyes watch me from the doorway, her tongue flopping limply out the side of her mouth. She really is the ugliest little cutie pie. I dig in my waistband for lingering pieces of kibble, and she comes scampering closer.

"Here you go." I hold my hand low enough for her to find the straggling goodie that had been stuck near my belly button and then stand to redo the messy bun on top of my head.

"Who cares what we look like, am I right?"

Cholula sits, anticipating another snack, but this time I've got nothing.

"Come on, Cho." I scoop her up and head down to the store.

"Do you know what they're doing over there?" I ask Harvey after setting Cholula down. I nod toward the street.

"Huh?" He blinks at me.

There's an envelope stamped FINAL NOTICE in his hand that makes my stomach tighten. I thought I had tucked the late notices at the bottom of the pile when I brought in the mail, but clearly that wasn't enough. What makes the situation even worse is that I moved back out here to Batavia three years ago to help him with the store, and all signs so far point to failure. Online retail chains obviously make it hard for small mom-and-pop shops like ours to stand out, but still. We're well established, so I don't know what we're doing wrong.

"Across the street?" I point. "Looks like someone's moving in."

Harvey walks to the front and squints out the window. "I think you might be right." A grin spreads across his lips. "Exactly what we need. Another store means more foot traffic, more commerce. New customers!" He slaps his thigh, which immediately sets the two smaller dogs running toward him. Boris only lifts his head from the ray of sunlight where he's currently lounging.

"Fingers crossed."

"That reminds me. End of month." Harvey opens the till and pulls out an envelope. "Your paycheck."

It's tempting. My piggybank has seen as little action as I have this past year, but I just can't. "I think you already paid me." I look away and pretend to focus on Cap waddling toward me like a bowlegged cowboy. When I glance up again, Harvey has something soft in his eyes.

"You found Martha's shirt," he says, resting his hand on the counter.

"You don't mind, do you?"

"No, it suits you." He sighs and looks down at the envelope. "Don't think I don't know what you're doing." He opens the till, extracts a few bills, and presses them into my palm. "You need some for rent at the very least. Normally, I'd insist you take what's owed, but since I had to get the car fixed last month, I put off the phone company, and it can't wait any longer or they'll cut the line and the internet."

"Pop, it's fine. I'm fine." I put on my most reassuring smile, pocketing the money. "We're going to have a great fall. I'll start making more clothes tonight, so we'll have some ready by this weekend. How's that?"

"Yes, excellent, excellent."

Harvey is a young eighty-four. He and my grandma tried to

retire twenty years ago, but that lasted only about as long as one of Cholula's peanut butter treats when she's hungry. Which is always. My grandpa is what the twinkly eyed ladies at the senior rec center call *spry*, but he shouldn't still be working at his age. Unfortunately, he won't even entertain the idea of slowing down. "Even if I didn't have the dogs to care for, I refuse to be a charity case," he always says. If only I could find a way to make us profitable enough that he could get some real help in here. Then I might...

No. I shake my head. Daydreaming doesn't put food on the table, and this isn't the worst place to be. There are a lot of memories here. The maple shelves have darkened with age, but this store mostly looks like it always did. I used to crawl into one of the big crates in the corner with a book when I was little. I found my first zit in the latticed mirror behind the cat toys. And I've stacked hundreds if not thousands of cans of food into humble pyramids on the tartan-covered display tables. Grandma looks down at me from a framed photo behind the counter. She's grinning wide, holding up a blue first place rosette ribbon next to a lanky dalmatian mix in a Santa hat. It was taken when I was around twelve years old at the annual Winter Fest's Amateur Dog Show. Patch was the only rescue ever to take her all the way. If I remember correctly, he found his forever home shortly after. That didn't stop Grandma from participating year after year, though, just for "a bit of holiday frivolity."

"Put that check away, Pop," I say. "Time to open."

"Fine." He rubs his hands together. "I'm ready, are you ready?" As if we have a long line of customers outside in a frenzy over two-for-one bully sticks.

I chuckle. "I'll set out the A-frame. Then I'll take the dogs for a walk."

He waves me off and starts arranging the bandanna display next to the register.

The late September air is still warm, the sun on its way to turn this into another beautiful day, but in the park down the street the tips of the trees are turning, slowly but surely. I don't mind—fall is my favorite season. Sweaters and warm drinks all the way. I make sure our sale sign reflects our current specials and say hi to a few morning walkers. Then I take a deep breath and turn my face to the blue sky. Whatever Harvey needs me to do, I'll do. So what if the pet store isn't my dream?

I'm about to set off when the squeak of the scissor lift across the street stops me in my tracks. It's coming down, revealing the name of our brand-new neighbor. I shade my eyes as the shiny letters come into view.

Canine King

I blink and read it again. And again.

"Well, fuck me," I mutter as the implication sinks in.

We've got competition.

2

Because it's a Tuesday and school is in session, the park and Riverwalk aren't crowded. There are a few other dog walkers out, a couple of moms with rambunctious toddlers, and a group of teens who surely should be in a classroom right now, but that's it. The benches overlooking the water where I like to sit are occupied by an older couple and a guy with a pretty Australian shepherd, so my posse and I loop back at a slow pace. The sun warms my shoulders and lights up the leaves above us in a spectacular way, and I'm deep in thought over this morning's complication when we pass the playground, not paying attention. One second is all it takes, and Cholula has escaped.

A moment later, a piercing shriek carries through the air. "My ice cream! My ice cream! The monster took it!"

Cholula comes shooting out from beneath the play structure with a waffle cone the size of her head lodged in her jaws. She's pursued by one of the little boys, but his mom grabs his arm before he can take off after her.

Crap. "Cholula! Bad dog!" With Boris's leash in one hand and Cap's in the other, I stumble across the lawn after Cho, and suddenly there's a fourth dog in the mix. Where the heck did it come from?

"Mom, is it a gremlin?" the kid cries behind me.

I didn't know kids still knew what gremlins were, but I suppose I can't fault anyone for mistaking Cholula for one. I should have been paying better attention, but that Canine King sign has thrown off my whole morning. Besides, why are kids eating ice cream at the park at nine thirty? Isn't that poor parenting? Cho did the kid a favor.

"Sorry," I call over my shoulder to the mom, who's trying to console her deprived little one.

Cholula and the other dog are chasing each other back and forth, having the time of their lives while I make my way toward the water. Boris is our weakest link, and no matter how I coax, we make slow progress.

"Tilly, here!"

The guy I saw on the bench earlier, presumably the owner of the Aussie playing tag with Cho, is closer to the dogs, and even in my stressed-out state, my dormant lady parts give a standing ovation at the way his gray fitted button-down hugs his arms. He must be new to the area.

"It that thing yours?" he calls to me in a deep baritone. His words have edges that knock me about. No doubt there's a glower behind those mirrored Ray-Bans.

Cholula stops for a moment and swings her head in his direction as if she understands the implication perfectly, but then the Aussie circles her and the two are off again. Cholula's leash trails her on the ground like a happy snake.

"Oh, come on," hot, snide guy says with exasperation. "Tilly, here!"

I finally reach their part of the park. "Seems like she's got better things to do." I smile. "Don't worry, Cholula only has another few minutes in her. They'll be back."

"You know, you really should keep your dogs in check." His shapely mouth puckers as he lets out a loud whistle.

"Excuse me?"

He gestures impatiently toward the frolicking dogs. "This is totally out of character for Tilly."

Ah, so he's one of those people. The deflecting kind. I purse my lips. "Maybe if you'd kept her on a leash…"

"Like I said, she always stays by me."

"Clearly not always."

This guy is getting under my skin. The air around him practically vibrates with impatience, and what is that scent stinging my nostrils? Is that…? Yep, I know Au de Snob when I smell it. From the cut of his clothes to the Patek on his wrist, I'd bet a million bucks he and his precious Tilly usually run in different circles. So what the heck is he doing here?

I sneak another sideways glance at hair the rich summery hue of ripe wheat. The ugly contents of his soul certainly got wrapped in shiny paper.

Cap tugs on his leash, wanting to join the play, but I keep it in a firm grasp. Boris has melted into his usual pile on the ground. Time to end this. "Cho-lu-la!" I try again. "Treat!"

"That's great—reward bad behavior," the guy mutters under his breath.

I spin toward him, my hands on my hips. "Do you want the dogs to come back or not?"

His face briefly goes blank as if he wasn't expecting the bite in my voice, and he takes a step back, palms forward. Unfortunately, that's where Boris is, and before I have time to yell *Timber*, the guy's majestic arms flail like the rotor blades of a runaway chopper, and he goes down.

He lets out an unintelligible shout on his way to the ground, and that, finally, is what gets the dogs' attention. Cholula and Tilly come bounding back, no doubt thinking they've got a new playmate, and cover him with kisses on the ground.

"No, come on." He puts his arms up for protection. "Tilly!"

His pathetic attempts at fending them off makes a laugh bubble up my chest. Serves him right. I hope those are expensive jeans.

"A little help," he pleads, stretching a hand my direction.

"I think you've got this." I smirk.

"Please."

I roll my eyes but give in. "Fine." I manage to put a foot on Cholula's leash. Then I lean forward to give him a hand while Cho jumps at my leg, the happiest I've ever seen the tiny beast.

The guy's hand is large and warm, his fingers closing tightly around mine as I pull him up, but he's only halfway off the ground when Cap sees his chance to get in on the action and jumps between us. I have no time to further ponder the sensation of actual male skin-to-skin contact before Tilly follows Cap, and Cholula circles behind us, pulling my legs from under me. It's a people and dog pile-up, and instead of helping the guy up, I end up using him as a cushion for my fall. Dogs bark, sunglasses go flying, and hands find purchase in unknown places.

"Oof," he grunts as we hit the ground, me on top of his (very solid) chest.

If this was one of my roommate-slash–best friend Micki's beloved Hallmark rom-coms, now would be when he'd look up at me, a twinkle in his sparkling eyes. My long, dark hair, loose from its bun, would be framing our faces. He'd reach up to place a hand against my cheek. We'd kiss—gently at first and then with more intent.

"Do you mind?" he says instead, jolting me back to the present moment.

There's no string quartet playing, and my hair is not so much cascading gracefully around us as it is smothering him. He wipes at his face to get my strands out of his mouth.

"Sorry," I grunt, trying to heave myself off him. "So sorry."

When we're finally free of each other, and all the dogs are accounted for, I brush off the sleeve of my grandma's shirt and peer up at him, expecting a stranger. Instead, I find a vaguely familiar face angled toward me. Somewhere in my distant memory, students cheer from packed bleachers as our team obliterates the competition thanks to the guy before me.

"Leo?"

He squints.

"You are Leo Salinger, right? Batavia High School?"

"Yeah?" He says it like he doesn't understand why I'm asking. Tilly pulls at her leash, but he tightens his grip on it and puts his sunglasses back on.

"You were a year ahead of me. I'm Cora Lewis. Go Bulldogs?" I try.

No reaction. So much for the old school spirit. I would have thought the guy who had been voted homecoming king three years in a row by his peers would have easy access to a smile and a friendly word, but I suppose a lot can happen in twelve years.

I swallow the sting and clear my throat. "Um, there's an off-leash dog park if you take Main Street west past Randall. They've actually gotten pretty strict about leashing your dogs here in town the past few years. I assume you've been elsewhere?"

He looks away and ignores my question. "Like I said before,

it wouldn't have been an issue if that thing hadn't gotten Tilly riled up."

Heat flushes through me, building pressure. On second thought, I didn't really know him in high school. Maybe he was always like this—kind of an asshole. Where does he get off? "This *thing* has a name. It's Cholula. And she wasn't anywhere near you when Tilly took off after her. They clearly like each other. They're dogs." Sure, I should have had a better grip on Cho's leash, but I have two other dogs, too, and ice cream is her catnip.

"Fine." He cuts his gaze between me and Cholula one more time. "What's wrong with her, anyway?"

"What's *wrong*?" I gape at him. I've had just about enough of this. "Not everyone is as perfect as you and yours, I suppose. Let's leave it at that and pretend this never happened. Have a fantastic day." With that, I turn on my heel and march back toward the store.

I'm sure my face still looks like a storm cloud as I escort my band of misfits through the door because Harvey takes only one look at me before he puts down the bag of kibble he's stacking and comes to relieve me.

"You look like you've been run over," he says, astute observer that he is. "What happened?" He squats to unleash the dogs, who set off upstairs to their water bowls and beds.

I lean against the counter and relay the incident in as few words as I can, leaving out that I recognized Leo. "He was such a jerk about it," I say to wrap things up. "Sweet dog, though." I rifle through my purse for some gum to calm myself with.

Harvey squints out the window. "An Aussie you say? And the young man, what did he look like?"

A freaking Calvin Klein ad. "I don't know. Tall, blond, chin dimple."

"Good looking you'd say?"

I frown at him. "What's that got to do with anything?"

"Like that?" He points out the window, and there across the street are Tilly and Leo looking up at the Canine King sign. He says something to the workers before pulling out a key and letting himself into the store.

You have got to be kidding me.

3

Living History Illinois Flockify DM, Wednesday
07:33 PM

AlCaponesGhost25: Moderator here. Your post got
flagged. If you are a registered company, you may
not promote it on the server.
SingerQueen: Not a company and it's been allowed
in the past. New here?
AlCaponesGhost25: Me or the rules? As long as you
are not a company, I'll allow it.
SingerQueen: So magnanimous...
AlCaponesGhost25: Lol. And yes, I'm new here.

Two days after my run-in with Leo in the park, the store across
the street is unrecognizable. Like all Canine Kings, the storefront framework has been painted black with the name con-
trasted in gold lettering to make sure no one misses the fact
that this is an *exclusive* boutique even though it is a chain. And
to think I used to enjoy visiting the downtown Chicago location
when I lived there.

I shoot icy glares through the window where I stand half

covered by the curtain, nursing a cup of coffee. From up here, I can see most of Leo's store—the new shelves and display tables, a fridge undoubtedly filled with fresh, organic dog food, and a large chalkboard leaning against the counter. Everything looks neat and organized, if not completely done yet. As I'm watching, Leo emerges from the back, Tilly at his feet. He's there all the time it seems—probably because they've moved into the apartment above the store. He studies something in his hands before placing a HELP WANTED sign in the window.

"Yeah, I *bet* you need help," I mutter.

As if he hears me, he looks up, skimming our facade before finding the window where I'm standing.

I take a quick step back and hold my breath.

When I peek a minute later, he's gone.

I've just put my mug in the sink when the bell at the front door downstairs jingles, announcing our first customer of the day. I peer through the railing to make sure Harvey's got it covered, and...it's him.

Leo looks around Happy Paws, and for a moment, I see it the way he might. A mishmash of cardboard cut-out animals in the window display, two old birdcages my grandma found at a flea market, stuffed dogs in cowboy costumes...I inhale the rich, musty smell of dry pet food as the radio plays faintly in the background. To me, it's homey, but Leo looks like all his senses have been assaulted by a dressed-up monkey banging cymbals together. He's above this, his flared nostrils say. His judgy nostrils.

But as I'm watching, Harvey steps out from behind the counter, and like that, Leo's pinched discomfort transforms into a pleasant smile. The deception force is strong with this one. I should remember that. Fool me once, etcetera.

"Hello, there," Harvey says in his usual jolly way. "How can I help you today?"

As quietly as I can, I squat lower to hear better. Leo looks around before stepping closer to Harvey. The dogs are resting near the bottom of the stairs. Cap and Boris ignore him, but Cholula lifts her head and growls at the uninvited visitor. *That's my girl.*

"No, that's no way to greet people," Harvey admonishes her.

Cholula quiets down but stays vigilant.

"Hi," Leo says, extending his hand toward my grandpa. "I wanted to stop in and introduce myself since we're new neighbors. I'm Leo Salinger."

"The Canine King." Harvey nods but leaves Leo hanging a moment before shaking his hand.

I suppress a giggle when Leo startles at the firmness of Harvey's grip. I've introduced a couple of boyfriends to him in the past, so I know this move.

"Harvey Morton," Pop says.

"Nice to meet you, Mr. Morton."

Pop shakes his head. "Harvey is fine. Is the store coming along all right? I see you've been busy."

"Slowly but surely." Leo smiles again, and my fingers clench tight at his self-assured tone. "I'm inviting all the neighbors to the soft launch next Friday. We'll have some drinks and appetizers, free samples, and live music. Hope you can make it." He spots the corner where we keep our hamster cages. Currently Muffin and Ham Solo are our only two residents, and that's fine by me. Cleaning out wood shavings was never my thing. Leo runs his palms down his shirt as if the mere sight of our facility makes him feel dirty.

How dare he insult Pop this way? I stand and grip the banister to propel myself downstairs. "You," I say, loudly.

Leo spins around, surprise and something else brighter flickering across his features.

"You've got a lot of nerve coming in here."

"My granddaughter, Cora," Harvey says. "This is Leo Salinger of the Canine King."

"Yeah, I know who he is." I point at Leo. "You should have told me you're the one opening that store when we met in the park. Seems a bit...wily...to keep that fact to yourself."

He blinks. "Wily? If my memory serves me right, there were no introductions made from your side, either. I didn't know who you were."

That's true. *Ugh.* "Whatever. Why are you here?"

"Um, I was inviting Mr. Morton—Harvey—to my opening next week."

The nerve. No doubt all he wants is to show off. *Look at my fancy store that makes yours look like a moth-eaten relic my sensitive nose can't handle.*

"You're welcome to come, too, of course." He shows me rows of pearly whites, and the star quarterback I once cheered on peeks out from behind the now more mature planes of his face. At least half the girls in my class had a crush on him at one point or another.

"We'll be busy," I growl. "As we are now. So, if you'll excuse us, that would be splendid."

To his credit, he flinches. His blue eyes look so innocent, but I know better. I know what these chain stores do. They eliminate the competition. What I don't know is why the hell *he* is opening a Canine King *here.*

"Now, now, Cora." Harvey puts a hand on my arm. "Manners."

I shrug him off. I'm twenty-seven, not ten. "It's not going to work, you know," I continue. "Everyone knows Harvey. Our customers are loyal."

Leo's pupils darken. "That's great," he says snidely. "Then you should have nothing to worry about." He clamps his jaw shut as soon as the words are out. Then he runs a hand through his hair and turns back to Harvey with the pleasant expression from earlier back in place. "What I meant was, I'm confident there are enough customers to go around."

"I'm sure, I'm sure," Harvey says.

"I guess we'll see, won't we?" I cross my arms.

Cholula lets out another growl as if to concur.

"I think that's my cue." Leo chuckles without any warmth. "Just wanted to be a good neighbor. Anyway, here's my card." He slides it across the counter like a smarmy salesman finishing his pitch.

Harvey picks it up with a nod, and for a moment, I think Leo is going to leave, but instead he glances down, a look of alarm coming over him. "What's wrong with your dog?"

This again? I'm about to lay into him about how differences should be celebrated when he crouches by Cap and looks up at me. "We've got to do something." His hand rests against Cap's shaking shoulders.

Crap. "No, he's fine. Don't touch him." I sit down next to Cap and lower my voice. "You're okay, buddy." He's stiff as a board and jerking like an animatronic puppet, but there's nothing to do but wait it out. Cholula and Boris lie down next to him. They know.

"He spaces out like that sometimes," Harvey says. "Probably had a head injury before he was rescued. But the vet says it's harmless."

Leo looks skeptical.

"Don't worry. It'll be over soon."

As soon as Pop says that, Cap shrugs as if a spell's been lifted and sits down.

"Good boy," I coo, petting his square brow. "All better?"

"Jeez. That was freaky." Leo runs a hand through those wheat-colored strands. "Well, hey, if you ever decide you want a, um, different sort of dog, I can talk to my aunt about reserving an Aussie from one of her litters. She breeds them. Super reliable, great lineage, you know exactly what you'll get."

I dig my nails into my palms. "I'm sure you're not suggesting we are looking to replace our dogs. Our *family members*?"

"Okay, okay." Harvey steps between us. "Leo, thanks for stopping by, but I think it's best if you…"

"Yeah, sure." He cuts his eyes between us. "I didn't… Yes."

My hands are shaking. *That's right. Take your broad shoulders and get lost.*

I turn to Harvey, who's watching me, displeased.

"What was that?" he asks.

"What was what?"

"I don't normally know you to be rude. What brought that on?"

"He was insulting Cap."

"I hardly think he meant it that way."

I don't like it when Pop scrutinizes me like this. Like he's trying to find my soul. "Well…" I fling a hand in the direction of Canine King. "Doesn't it bother you that he's opening one of those here? We're not exactly rolling in cash."

"So, it's about money?" Harvey blinks slowly. It's his I've-taught-you-better look.

I examine the cracks between the floorboards. "I just think it's a dick move."

"Ha! Is that the official terminology?"

A smile tugs at the corner of my mouth. "Should be."

He puts an arm around my shoulders and pulls me close. "Come now. We'll be fine. We've always been fine. Canine King has nothing on Happy Paws. We've been here forever; you said so yourself. If you think about it, he's the one who is the underdog, no pun intended."

"If you say so."

"That's the spirit. Now let's not mind Leo Salinger and what he's doing anymore. We have inventory and cleaning to do. And you were going to check your internet thingamajig for more work."

He's right. We do have enough going on without adding a stuck-up pretty boy to the list. After a fortifying breath, I open the browser on the old computer that sits on the counter and navigate to the Flockify server to check for responses to my post.

Welcome to Living History Illinois beams at me in bright blocky letters on the landing page. The column on the left lists the sub-channels—General Forum, Mobsters, Sports of Yore, Historical Foods, Illinois in the News, and, because the server apparently started as a project at another Chicago-land high school, several "class of" channels where former students can keep in touch with their dispersed friends. A Memes channel and a Quizzes channel have also been added since last I was here. The channels I most often frequent are Period Dress, Famous People, and Historical Reenactments, though. That's where the potential money is.

There are no responses to my original post in the Period Dress channel, so I head to Famous People where I repost it to create a wider net. Cross my fingers, hope to die.

I'm about to close out of it when the message before mine stops me. It's from yesterday and posted by that same guy who tried to moderate me before.

> **AlCaponesGhost25** Wednesday 10:22 PM
> *What's the legal term for when Al Capone goes camping?*

I let out an amused huff and lean closer. "Aren't we a contradiction?" I mumble.

"Something interesting?" Harvey asks.

"Someone posted a riddle." Curiosity piqued, I click on the avatar (a picture of the Colosseum in Rome) but there's not much information to be gleaned. He is indeed a moderator and also a verified user. His location status is set to "international," whatever that means.

Harvey chuckles. "Ah, your kryptonite."

Mine and my grandma's. When she was alive, we had whole text threads with riddles going back and forth. She was a master.

"Do you know it?" Harvey asks.

I tap my fingertips against the tabletop. "Give me a minute and I will." The rusted gears in my brain churn into motion. *Al Capone, camping, mob, crime, campfire, sleeping bag… Hmm…Got it!*

> **SingerQueen** Thursday 12:37 PM
> *Easy—Criminal intent.*

After a moment's deliberation, I decide to return his serve with one of my grandma's favorites.

SingerQueen Thursday 12:38 PM
But do you know who built King Arthur's round table?

Unfortunately, my momentary distraction from the threat across the street doesn't last long. All afternoon, hammering and clanging interrupts our calm at irregular intervals like some kind of water torture, and by the time we close up and I set off for home, my rage at Leo Salinger's presence has once again reached combustible levels.

4

I have never—and I mean *never*—met a guy who's so full of himself, who cares so little about the people around him, and, and…" I gesture toward the ceiling.

"Okay, take a deep breath and start from the beginning." Micki pulls her legs up under her on our couch and pops open a can of seltzer. She and her sister, Jaz, returned from their cousin's wedding hoopla in Barbados last night, and the apartment looks like a closet ate something bad and threw up.

"Yeah, who is this person?" Jaz asks. She's a few years younger than we are, graduated with a double major in English and theater arts but no plans. As far as I know, she's been working on the same screenplay since I first met her. "I need details, so I know where to direct my ire."

"His name is Leo, and he's a jerk," I say, the petulant child in me stomping her foot. I tell them about our run-in in the park and his visit to the store. "It's like he's dying to rub our faces in how he's going to steal our customers. Just, ugh!"

"Sounds stressful." Micki brushes her newly purple bob away from her heart-shaped face. She's a hairdresser at the salon next to Happy Paws and changes her look with the frequency others change their towels. "What does Harvey say?"

"You know him—always seeing the best in people. He called him 'a nice, young man.'" I roll my eyes.

"Really? Maybe you misjudged him then. You have only met the guy twice."

"Well…"

"Is he old? Young?" Jaz asks.

I twirl the tassels of my hoodie together and then untwirl them again. "I actually went to high school with him. Or, well, he was a year ahead of me."

"Wait, hold up." Micki straightens.

"You know him?" Jaz adds.

"It's not important." I don't like where this conversation is heading so I go for distraction instead and point to Micki's head. "I like the purple-gray fade thing you've got going on there."

"Nuh-uh, that's not going to work. Spill."

"I don't *know* him know him," I tell my captive audience. "More like I knew who he was because everyone did."

"Ooh, do I sense a confession of a youthful crush coming on?" Micki hoots.

I tsk. "Sorry to disappoint."

"Boo."

"But he remembers you?" Jaz asks.

I shake my head. "He'd have no reason to. I was a complete nobody. A younger-than-him, complete nobody."

"You should tell him you went to the same school," Micki says. "Maybe that'll chill him out a bit."

"I did. He could not have cared less. I believe his exact words were 'What's wrong with your dog?'"

"Seriously?" Micki's face contorts.

"Told you he's a jerk."

"Was he always?" Jaz asks.

An image of Leo with his peer buddy from the special educa-
tion program imposes itself in my mind, unbidden. They were
always huddled together in the high school cafeteria at lunch. I
know the peer coaching program was for credit, but if I'm being
honest, despite all his popularity, teenage Leo had seemed like a
pretty decent guy. So either I misjudged him back then or something's gotten stuck up his butt along the way.

"Who knows?" I ball up a few wrappers from our dinner and
tuck them in a paper bag. "But why did he have to open his stupid store right here?"

Micki pulls me into a sideways hug. "Aww. Maybe he'll fail
miserably. You've got this."

"Thanks."

"What you need is some pampering." She smiles and flips her
strands forward. "If you honestly do like my hair, you should let
Donna do yours, too."

I shake my head. My hair is a constant point of contention
between us. It's a rich, dark brown, thick and halfway to my
waist—the kind "everyone wants" according to Micki. But I
never do anything with it. It's either up in a bun or pulled back
in a sloppy braid, and by this point, she takes that as a personal
slight. "I'm good."

"One day," she mutters, gathering her trash and putting it in
the bin in our small galley kitchen.

"Never going to happen." Which reminds me…"Speaking
of rare events." I pull out the cash from Harvey and hand it to
Micki.

A grin spreads on her lips. "Rent!" She bats her lashes and
fans herself with the bills. "Oh, darling, you shouldn't have."

"I'm a little short, but we have overdue bills at the store, and
I couldn't take all of Pop's money when he's already in the hole.

I'll make it up to you. Breakfast in bed, foot massage…Oh, I can make you a new dress."

"Sell me your hair?"

My hand goes to my braid as if she's serious. "No."

Micki laughs. "Seriously, it's fine. Better than nothing. You've helped me out in the past. That's what friends do. Besides, I'm still using your Netflix daily and you're still going to help me study, right?" She recently went back to school to get a massage therapy license since the salon is expanding its services.

"Of course. And I promise I'll pay you back. But first I need to figure out how to make the store do better."

"Isn't your grandpa old?" Jaz asks. "Doesn't he want to retire?"

"He's too sentimental," Micki tells her. "Plus, he can't afford to, which is why Cora is stuck there even though it's not what she wants to do." She gestures toward my sewing machine that's tucked underneath our kitchen table, indicating where my true passion lies.

"Well, that sucks," Jaz says.

"It's not that bad," I say. "It's all he has left of my grandma. And if the store folds right now, the dogs will have nowhere to go. Harvey would end up moving, and he can't take care of them himself, this building doesn't allow pets, and the only other shelter around here isn't no-kill. What chances do you think any of them have of making it there?"

"Right, the dogs." Jaz nods as if she's thinking hard. Then her expression brightens. "Hey, there was a poster about some dog show at the grocery store. Maybe that's something?"

"The one at Winter Fest?" Micki asks, and Jaz confirms.

I shake my head. "The grand prize is only five hundred dollars. Not enough to make a difference. And I'm about to start on some new costumes for the shop and maybe some other stuff, too…" I gesture to my laptop that's sitting open to the Flockify server. No responses yet other than a few general hellos. No guesses from the Riddler either.

"Ah, well then." Micki smirks. "Practically living the dream."

"Really, it's fine. Not everyone gets to do exactly what they want."

"True. But I guess I believe everyone should at least get to try."

Her words grate at the back of my mind and prickle my throat when I look at the stack of soon-to-be tutus on the table. That's what I want. I want to design clothes, have my own line—only not for pets.

"Hey, I remember that Flockify server," Jaz says, interrupting my thoughts. She leans closer to my screen. "Ms. McInnis's class, junior year. God, she was so into it. We all had to post research and have discussions on there, but I spent most of my time perfecting my avatar. I think my username was *MrsShakespeare* or something else inane like that." She chuckles. "But why the heck are you on it?"

"It must have grown a lot bigger since you used it for school because there are thousands of members from all over the world now." I tell her about my sewing commissions while we clear the table, and once the topic is exhausted, Jaz and Micki commence their post-travel cleanup while I do the dishes.

Micki's words about living the dream echo in my mind, but I keep a steady hold on the pragmatic side of things. At least I still get to work with fabric from time to time—things could be worse for a college drop-out like me who hasn't managed to live up to any of the potential I was told I showed when I was younger. Besides, I'd have no idea how to run my own business. Not like Leo Salinger who practically oozes Ivy League business schools, ten-year life plans, and a trust fund to fall back on.

Before I get too far down that rabbit hole, my phone rings in my purse on the counter. I get to it at the last second and pick up.

"Coralynn? Coralynn are you there?" My mother's voice echoes as if she's in a cave.

Only my parents call me by my given name. I suppose I should be thankful they didn't go with the runner-up, Hildegarde, after my great-grandmother, but Coralynn still feels like a mouthful. It's not me.

"Mom, where are you?" I lean against the counter and cradle the phone to my ear. I haven't seen my parents since Christmas. Twelve years on the road now, all fifty states visited, and they're still all about that RV life. I don't know how they stand it, but they've never been happier.

"Montana!" Mom hollers. "We decided to chase the fall foliage this year. It's gorge."

"Is that Coralynn?" Dad says in the background. "Tell her I said hi."

"Hi, Dad," I mumble.

"Hello?" Mom shouts. "I don't think the reception is very good here."

"But you guys are doing well?" I walk over to the window and look down at the streetlights below. From behind the door to my left, I can hear Jaz's and Micki's muted voices.

"Never better. We saw an enormous herd of bison today. Frontier adventures! How's Dad doing?"

"Harvey is doing all ri—"

"Did I tell you your father is improving at his putting game? We stop at every golf course we pass. I go with him once in a while, but a drink on the green is my preference. You know how my back acts up. As luck would have it, we met this wonderful couple that…" And on and on she goes.

The windowpane is cool against my forehead while I listen, and my breath makes foggy circles on the glass until eventually Mom announces her phone is running out of battery and she needs to go. "I'll call you again from Wyoming or Colorado. Hugs and kisses." She hangs up.

I look at my phone and sigh. "I'm doing okay. Thanks for asking," I say out loud. "Bills to pay, places to be. You know."

"Talking to yourself again?" Micki asks from her doorway.

I turn and give her half a smile. "Something like that." I toss my phone onto the table and sit down at my sewing machine. The tutus are bestsellers, so my plan is to make a few more of those tonight and then move on to my first literary costume. Mrs. Keller's Scottish terrier would look fantastic as Sherlock Holmes.

"Hey, is it okay if Jaz crashes on the couch for a few days?" Micki heads toward the fridge.

"Another guy bites the dust?"

"Seems like it."

"Sure, no problem."

"Cool. Don't stay up too late."

I give her a noncommittal wave and dive back in.

5

Living History Illinois Flockify, Famous People Channel

AlCaponesGhost25 Friday 11:47 PM
I believe Sir Cumference was responsible for the round table.

SingerQueen Saturday 08:29 AM
*Took you a while, but I'll allow it. *winky face emoji**

AlCaponesGhost25 Saturday 10:17 AM
Believe it or not, I do have other responsibilities.

SingerQueen Saturday 11:40 AM
What could possibly be more important?

AlCaponesGhost25 Saturday 01:33 PM
Fair point. Henceforth, riddles it is. New career, here I come!

SingerQueen Saturday 01:45 PM
Who says "henceforth"? Wait, are you actually an old-timey ghost?

AlCaponesGhost25 Saturday 02:02 PM
zips lips

SingerQueen Saturday at 02:10 PM
shocked face emoji

W e're going out tonight," Jaz announces when Micki and I get home from work Saturday. "I finished another scene for my play this morning so it's celebration time!"

I share a look with Micki that tells me she, too, wants to argue with this logic, but then again, why shouldn't we let loose a little? O'Connor's on Main Street has six-dollar pints until seven on the weekends, something even I can afford.

We get ready, elbow to elbow in the small bathroom, while Jaz explains the scene she wrote and why it's necessary for the story. This play has changed directions more times than I can count, but she's fired up today until Micki asks for clarification on a plot point, and she struggles to give one.

"Shoot. I'll need to figure that out tomorrow," she says. "Oh well."

And so the story goes with her. At least she doesn't allow the challenges to weigh her down. I should be more like that. Be the duck with the water down its back or what have you.

I apply my reddest lipstick and fluff my hair in the mirror.

"I wish I could pull off color like you do," Jaz says, pulling her ash-brown waves into a high ponytail before leaning forward to tweak her signature cat-eye liner in the mirror.

Both she and Micki are in black jeans and dark tops, while I'm wearing my high-waisted red jeans and a long-sleeved yellow crop top. If I had a dollar for every time someone's described my style as *quirky* or *boho*, Happy Paws wouldn't be in such dire straits.

"There's nothing to it. You simply look at your black clothes and say 'no thank you.'" I wink at her, and she tightens her lips around a smile that's reminiscent of her sister's. They don't share many family traits, but this one they do.

"You ready?" Micki asks, reaching for her purse. "I could kill for some fish and chips right about now."

"Ready." I pull on my boots and open the door. "Let's go. No manslaughter tonight, please."

O'Connor's is your average suburban Irish pub complete with dark wood paneling, framed pictures of the Emerald Isle on the walls, shamrocks on the bathroom doors, two dart boards in the corner, and an endless supply of beer in thick glasses. It fills up nightly, but especially on weekends, and the only reason we snag a table is because another party decides to move to the bar.

We order two rounds of drinks and a sharable plate of food for the table. Jaz is on her phone, typing frenetically. Micki and I ignore her while we stuff ourselves with beer-battered cod, but all of a sudden, Jaz lets out a loud "Well that's fucking great!" and slams the phone down onto the table.

Micki jumps at the outburst, lager splashing onto her chin. She wipes it off with the back of her hand.

"What's wrong?" I ask.

"I got fired." Jaz pouts.

"You had a job?" Micki asks.

"Yeah." Jaz tips her head back and sighs. "Well, sort of. I was helping out at Javier's café part-time."

"Javier who you just broke up with?" Micki takes another, more careful, sip from her glass.

"Right. And now he says I don't have to bother coming back."

"Well, yeah…" Micki looks at her sister like she's an alien. "Because you broke up with him."

"I can still do the job."

Micki faces me. "I swear, sometimes I have no idea how we're related."

"Come on." I tut. "Sorry about that," I tell Jaz. "But it's probably for the best. Clean break, etcetera."

"I guess."

"Hey, didn't you say Leo needs help in his store?" Micki asks me.

I give her a death stare in response.

Jaz grabs a handful of fries and shoves them in her mouth. "He does?"

"I'm joking, sis. Although…" Micki gets something calculating in her features. "In a way, wouldn't it be…Hmm…"

I toss a burnt fry at her. "Finish the sentence, please."

Micki leans in over the table and lowers her voice, so Jaz and I are forced to do the same. "Say that you wanted to get a leg up on him—wouldn't it be sort of helpful to have a woman on the inside so to speak?"

"Ooh, that's not a bad idea," Jaz agrees.

They both turn their attention to me, and as much as I don't want anything to do with Canine King, I must admit that Micki might be onto something here. "Did you see the A-frame he put out today?" I ask. *"Talk to me about how I can fulfill your unmet canine needs."* My tongue curls around the words he'd written in blocky chalk lettering. "Happy Paws is literally right across the street. There are no *unmet* needs here. So basically, he's not just rude. He's rude and presumptuous."

I have a sip of beer and go to continue my rant when the front door opens to let in a few more patrons. Among them, a familiar blond head stands out. "Speak of the devil," I mumble.

"Where?" Micki and Jaz turn as one, and right then, Leo looks our way.

I can only imagine how we must appear—three deer in headlights ogling him. Of course, he's here. Invading all my spaces.

"That's him?" Micki asks.

"Mm-hmm."

"I'll take the job," Jaz says, still staring.

Micki slaps her on the arm. "Repeat after me: we do not get involved with our friends' enemies." She spins my way. "That said, you never told me he was hot. Like…" She bites her lip and nods in approval. "And isn't it interesting that you chose to leave that detail out while you've been bitching about him?"

"Hot people can be asses."

"Hot people have fine asses," she counters, eyes twinkling. "Why is your face turning red?"

It isn't, but her saying so makes me flush hot. She's infuriating.

"Leave Cora alone, Mick," Jaz says, before addressing me. "But seriously, I'll apply if you want me to. And I'll tell you any secrets I find out."

Leo and his friend have made it to the bar now. There's a lot of back slapping and laughter. I vaguely recognize the other guy from high school, too. His face and gut are fuller than I remember, but it must be Marcus Kapperling. He and Leo were the hottest commodity jocks back then. Good buds. Bros.

"Blech." I wrinkle my nose.

"What's that now?" Micki asks.

"Is this what it's going to be like from now on? Everywhere I go, *he'll* be there, ruining things?"

"You want to know what I think?" Jaz asks. "I think you

should let him know you can't be messed with. This is your pub. It doesn't bother you that he's here because you don't care. He means nothing."

"Yeah?"

"Yeah."

I look Leo's way again. Who wears a button-down and a sport coat to a pub? It's probably tailored to better fit those wide shoulders, too. His friend, who hasn't aged half as gracefully, is in a flannel and blue jeans. My attention returns to Leo, but this time he's watching me. He raises his beer in greeting and nods.

"Fuck." I sink lower in my seat and pretend to be searching for something in my purse, but then I stop. Jaz is right. If I back down now, he's already won.

"I'll be right back," I say, draining the rest of my glass.

Leo is facing the bar when I reach him. I tap him on the shoulder and clear my throat.

"Oh. Hey," he says.

"Why are you here?" I ask, not bothering with a greeting.

"Cora, was it? This is Marcus. Marcus, Cora."

Somewhere beneath the scruffy chin and receding hairline is the former captain of the lacrosse team. He regards me with interest. "With the dogs, right? I've seen you around. Moved here a couple of years ago?"

"Yes to the dogs, but I grew up here."

"Are you sure?"

"I was a year under you in high school."

He squints, looking me up and down. "Nah, I would have remembered you being *under* me."

Gross. I pretend I don't hear him and turn back to Leo, who to his credit mutters, "What the fuck, man?" and slaps Marcus on the shoulder.

"There are literally thousands of other places you could have chosen for Canine King," I say. "Why here?"

Leo crosses his arms. "We did our research. It's the best location for foot traffic in the fastest growing area. Plus there was an available apartment right above it."

"And what did your research say about there already being a pet store on the block? That can't be great for you."

Marcus is unable to take a hint and tilts his head forward. "Seriously, I can't place you at all. What did you say your name was?"

"Cora," Leo and I say together.

"Give us a minute," Leo tells him. Then he takes a few steps sideways toward the passage leading to the restrooms, indicating for me to follow. "Sorry about him."

"It's fine. I know how to handle myself."

"I never said you didn't."

We stare at each other for a long moment.

"Look," Leo says after a while, "it's not personal, it's business. And it's not like our target customers are the same."

"People with pets?"

"Canine King is exclusively for dogs. And unlike you guys, we curate the store for a specific clientele that—"

"Oh my God, do you even hear yourself?"

His expression hardens. "My point is our researchers didn't consider your little mom-and-pop shop an obstacle to Canine King's success. Either they'll both make it or they won't, but I expect Canine King will come out on top either way. Serious dog people want a serious retailer. I will carry the organic brands they seek, the right supplements, designer bowls and beds, and locally sourced treats. In my store, they will be able to get in and out, efficiently finding what they need—everything has its place and there's no superfluous clutter."

This must be what a kettle feels like at boiling. My neck is steaming beneath my hair. "And I suppose that's all that matters. You coming out on top. High school all over again, basically. Marcus is still the douchey flirt who can't hold his liquor, and you're still the entitled sportsball star–slash–homecoming king who never has to bother with common courtesies like thinking about other people because it's always *always* about what's in it for you." I'm sucking in a breath, relishing some slight satisfaction at the surprise on Leo's face when Micki grabs my elbow from behind and leans in close.

"Red alert. Sweaty Lips just entered the building."

"No." I look left and right, and then I spot him. We went on one blind date two years ago, where he called his mother to check in every half hour. And as if that wasn't enough, the image of his sloppy open mouth coming at me in the car after he drove me home is forever ingrained on my brain—hence the nickname. Unfortunately, he did not see the date for the failure it was and has pursued a second one with some regularity since, but now it's been over six months since I last saw him. I'd been so sure he moved. "Damn it," I mutter.

"What is it?" Leo scans the room.

"Hi, I'm Micki." She sticks her hand out to him.

"Um, Leo." He shakes her hand. "Something going on?"

"Just someone she'd rather not see," Micki volunteers.

I elbow her to silence. Leo doesn't need to know that. When I look again, Sweaty Lips has spotted me and is making his way through the crowd. "Shit, he's coming over. What do I do?"

"I'll stall him." Micki sets off.

Is there a place to hide? Bathrooms? Behind the bar? I look up at Leo and make a split-second decision. Good idea or not, I grab his arm. "Quick, act like you're into me." I step into his space, the crisp, clean scent of aftershave wafting around me.

He stills. "What?"

"Prove me wrong—that you can do something unselfish. Pretend we're on a date. You can't get enough of me." I let one hand slide inside his sport coat and around his waist. Taut muscle greets my palm. So that's what the proper surface is hiding. I allow myself a moment to be impressed.

"Um…okay." He remains immobile, staring down at me.

I sigh. "Put your hands on my ass. Pretend to whisper something in my ear." I nudge his sleeves to make him move. "You know—make believe."

Now he gets it.

Large palms settle on my hips, tentatively at first, then with more confidence. He bends down close to my neck. A pause and then a whisper: "Is this what you had in mind?" His breath is warm and humid against my ear, making the fine hairs on my arms rise.

"Yeah, that's good." I shift and tilt my head.

"You want me to tell you a joke?"

The giggle that bubbles up my chest is equal parts acting and a knee-jerk surprise at the ball of heat suddenly present at my core. His breath smells like malt and mint.

I twist a little to locate Sweaty Lips, and Leo's fingertips dig more firmly into my flesh. I shiver.

"He's to my left," he whispers. "He's watching." He straightens and pushes a strand of my hair back as if he's done it a million times before.

I take a deep breath and let my hands run up Leo's chest. He's still keeping tabs on the guy, so I grip his lapels. We have to make this convincing. Sweaty Lips's pursuit ends here. "Look at me," I mumble.

He does.

In the golden light from the bar, Leo's blue eyes turn the turquoise of tropical waters. They're bottomless, vibrant, and locked on me. I flinch when he lifts his hand and runs the back of his fingers along my jaw. It takes effort to keep my eyelids from fluttering closed.

This is very convincing. Was he in the school play back in high school?

Leo glances one more time to his left, and then he hooks his arm behind my waist and pulls me closer. From chest to knee, my skin tingles at the contact. My hips want to press harder even, but I'd never. Not for a million bucks. Especially not when I spot the glint of a challenge in his heavy-lidded gaze. He's enjoying this now. He thinks he has the upper hand. Well, two can play at that game.

"Is he still there?" I ask on a breath, slowly sliding one hand up to his neck and into his hair. It's soft and thick. God, what a waste on a man.

"Behind you. Moving. Ohh…" The last noise escapes him when I tug, ever so gently, on his strands. His gaze flashes hot to mine.

"Everything okay?" I say as innocently as I can. "Did he leave?" I turn to look, still in Leo's arms.

He inhales deeply before he lets go of me with a pinched, "Yeah."

"Did you just smell my hair?"

Micki waves to me from the door and shows a thumbs-up. Good. *Be gone, Sweaty Lips.*

"No."

"Huh. Could have sworn you did."

"Don't flatter yourself." He scoffs. "Just because you were in my face while I was breathing. Normally," he adds. He runs a finger beneath the collar of his shirt and straightens his sport coat.

"Okay, okay. No need to get your tighty-whities in a bunch." The noise level around us has risen, and the bar is two people deep now. I should get back to the table.

"So, did I do it?" Leo asks.

"Do what?"

"Prove you wrong. Unselfish deeds and all that. You're welcome by the way."

I press my lips together into a pout and pretend to think about it. "I do appreciate your service," I say, finally. "But I'm not sure about unselfish—that would imply you got nothing out of it."

"Well, I didn't."

I nod slowly, my gaze trailing down his torso to his crotch and back up. "Oh yeah?" I say. Then I turn and walk away.

Cora vs. Leo, 1–0.

6

Living History Illinois Flockify, Famous People Channel

NotOprah Sunday 07:14 PM
Oo fun. I've got one too. What happens when you touch Dwayne Johnson's butt? You hit rock bottom. ROFL

AlCaponesGhost25 Sunday 07:42 PM
@NotOprah You're not supposed to answer your own riddle. Watch and learn—What's the difference between Al Capone and Anakin Skywalker driving an Uber?

NotOprah Sunday 07:45 PM
I dunno what?

AlCaponesGhost25 Sunday 07:47 PM
No you're supposed to think about it.

NotOprah Sunday 07:50 PM
Fuck off

SingerQueen Sunday 10:20 PM
@AlCaponesGhost25 Making fast friends, I see.

AlCaponesGhost25 Monday 05:32 AM
They weren't following the rules

SingerQueen Monday 10:02 AM
I don't disagree

AlCaponesGhost25 Monday 12:10 PM
We need to maintain some riddle standards imo

SingerQueen Monday 12:45 PM
Yes, sir, Mr. Moderator!

My neck is shot, but I have two huge bags of costumes to bring in, having spent my days off sewing. The Scarlett O'Haras turned out amazing. I made three different sizes, and I know exactly how to display them. Literary scenes in the windows should catch people's attention. And in other good news, User4549 has requested a quote for a Cleopatra getup for Halloween in response to my post. It's an easy enough commission and hopefully just the beginning.

"Morning, Pop," I call, pushing open the door with my hip. "How was your weekend?" We still call it our weekend, even though, technically, we're closed Sundays and Mondays. I glance across the street and spot a faint outline of a ladder in Leo's store. The lights are on so he must be up and at it already. I shrug to rid myself of the annoyance that immediately bubbles up my chest. Couldn't he at least be a slacker?

"Morning, kiddo!" Harvey hollers from upstairs.

"Want me to put the costumes in the back?"

"You know it."

It's a good morning—three customers in the first hour, all of whom actually make purchases. Before lunch, while Harvey schmoozes a woman he knows from the senior center, I talk to a mom and her daughter about the Halloween costumes. They're specifically looking for something dragon-like for their golden to complement the girl's Sleeping Beauty dress.

"Good choice," I tell the girl. "Princesses are always a hit. I'm going to be Belle, and my dogs are going as Lumiere, Mrs. Potts, and Cogsworth."

She giggles, showing a gap-toothed grin.

"I can absolutely make you something," I tell the mom. "I'll just need measurements."

They leave, promising to bring their pooch in later in the week. Score!

No sooner have they left before the back door slams closed and Micki hollers, "I hope you fine people are in the mood for chili! Jaz made a huge batch yesterday." She rounds the corner holding up a container.

"Michaela!" Harvey greets her with a hug.

Micki never knew her grandparents, so she adopted Harvey as her own the first time they met. He didn't mind. I think he was always secretly sad my parents only had me, though he'd never say so to my face.

"Upstairs?" Micki asks me.

"Yes, let me put the sign up, and I'll be right there." At the door, I pause, distracted by movement across the street.

I hide behind the doorjamb and watch as Leo steps outside dressed in dark jeans, a gray button-down, and a tailored vest, cutting a figure *GQ* would be proud to feature. He looks up and down the street before adjusting the offending A-frame, making me wonder if he's had any takers on the whole "unmet needs" front. Before my blood starts to boil again, I turn on my heel. "Let's eat," I call upstairs.

Harvey and Micki have already dug in by the time I sit down.

"And it's very stylish, don't you think?" Harvey asks, tapping something on the table between them with a finger.

"Very," Micki agrees.

I pull out a chair. "What are we talking about?"

Micki slides a glossy card in gold and graphite in front of me. "Free drinks," she says, one eyebrow raised. "You should go."

"What is this?" I blow on a spoonful of chili and skim the cursive writing.

"Leo dropped it off," Harvey says. "It's for the launch on Friday. We need it to get in."

I stare at them both for a moment. "We need it to get in?" I repeat. "What?"

Harvey wipes his mouth. "Because it's not open to the public. An exclusive event. It sounds very fancy." He smiles. "Should be fun."

"Fun?" I turn to Micki, hoping for backup but getting none.

"You should give him a chance, kiddo," Pop continues. "The man is making big changes in his life from what I understand. He seems perfectly pleasant to me."

"That's what he wants you to think, and you're walking straight into his trap."

"But free drinks." Micki points to the invite.

"You, my friend, need to raise your standards."

"He is single," Harvey says, unprompted.

That shuts up both Micki and me.

"What's that got to do with anything?" I ask, eventually.

"Oh, nothing." Harvey's eyes widen with innocence. "Just saying."

Next to me, Micki giggles, so I kick her in the shin. "Don't," I warn her.

"What?"

"Did you know he also went to Batavia High?" Pop asks.

"I do, but since when do you?" In fact, my grandpa seems to know an awful lot about Leo Salinger all of a sudden.

"Met him at the park. We had a nice chat. Apparently, his grandma and my Martha knew each other. How about that? Small world. So, I thought…" He shrugs. "He's easy on the eyes—ask if he's single."

"Pop." I sigh. "This guy is currently conspiring with the forces of the universe to bring ruin to Happy Paws. It doesn't matter how hot he is, or if he's single, or filthy rich, or the last man on the planet. We should all steer clear of him."

Micki considers me for a long moment. "So, you do think he's hot. Gotcha."

I groan and dig back into my food.

"Well, I think we should go," Harvey says after a minute.

I scoff. "Yeah, right."

"You should listen to your elders," Micki says. "Maybe you can get some tips from him."

"You're a smart girl, Michaela." Harvey nods. "Leo does seem to have his act together."

"And we don't? No, don't answer that." Are they right? The invite to his soft launch is better put together than any promo material we've ever created.

Harvey scrapes a last spoonful from his bowl before standing. "That's it for me, but please tell your sister thank you. It was delicious. I'll open up. You ladies take your time."

Once Pop has descended the stairs, Micki turns in her chair so she's fully facing me. "You know I love you both, but you guys don't even have a website, not to mention any social media accounts." She squints. "Marketing 101—I suspect Fancy Pants over there is in the know." She jerks her head toward Canine King.

"Yeah?" I finish chewing and swallow.

"Yeah, babe. And it doesn't have to be for fun. You'll essentially be spying on him. There are trade secrets to be uncovered." She lowers her voice. "Fine men to bed…"

I roll my eyes. "If I go, will you give it a rest already?"

Micki just laughs, shoveling another piece of bread into her mouth. "No promises."

That evening, I have two DMs. One is from User4549 agreeing to my price, and the other from my new friend who seems to still be online.

> **AlCaponesGhost25:** So riddle me this—what's a sharp Freddie Mercury fan like yourself doing in an Illinois history forum?

I frown at the monitor as if it's a trick question. He must not remember me posting about costume commissions.

> **SingerQueen:** Freddie Mercury?
> **AlCaponesGhost25:** Your username.

It takes me a moment to figure out what he means. When I do, I don't correct him.

SingerQueen: Maybe I'm just looking to connect with fellow hotdog obsessed Lincoln fans

AlCaponesGhost25: You're obsessed with hotdogs?

SingerQueen: Sans ketchup.

AlCaponesGhost25: A true Chicagoan then.

SingerQueen: You?

AlCaponesGhost25: No I definitely need ketchup.

SingerQueen: Touché. I assume you're here for the mob channel.

AlCaponesGhost25: Possibly.

SingerQueen: And to force riddles down the throat of unsuspecting strangers of course.

AlCaponesGhost25: Of course. Can't help myself.

SingerQueen: I have the answer by the way.

AlCaponesGhost25: To life?!?! *surprised face emoji*

A laugh bubbles up my chest.

SingerQueen: I wish. No your Uber riddle. Al Capone = tax evader Anakin Skywalker = taxi Vader.

AlCaponesGhost25: *standing ovation*

SingerQueen: *takes a bow*

AlCaponesGhost25: I have met my match.

My face warms. I know it's stupid, but that just made my day. I start a message to tell him so but erase it. Too personal. Then I start typing a good night but erase that too. Finally, I just send a smiley face before I close my laptop and set it aside. I should get to sleep anyway.

7

pass right by the entry of Canine King Thursday morning on my way to the post office. In the process of simultaneously trying to make myself invisible and giraffing my neck to see through the open door, I almost trip on the curb. The store is coming together nicely. The counter has been wrapped in natural wood boards for a rustic look, the wall displays are up, and half the shelves are already stocked and organized by type and color. I hate to admit it, but it looks flawless.

"Finally stopping by to wish me welcome like the other neighbors?" a voice says behind me. His voice. "How do you like my window displays? I'm going for something less predictable, sort of bringing the outdoors inside."

Behind the glass, large potted plants in woven baskets mix with artificial turf, fence segments, and crates of exclusively white and brown toys. Very design-y.

"It's certainly unique for a pet store." *Some might even call it pretentious...*

"Dog boutique. No need to bombard customers with all the colors of the rainbow like some sort of carnival attraction."

I glance toward the colorful mishmash in Happy Paws' windows. "You mean like our store."

"Your words, not mi—"

Before he finishes his sentence, the electrician who's up on a ladder hanging light fixtures swears loudly.

Leo hurries past me. "Is there a problem?"

"You could say that." The man grunts as he makes his way down. "Those wires need to be replaced at the switch, all the way." He gestures across the ceiling.

"What do you mean? Why?"

"The fire code wasn't the same when this was built, and there's some signs of rodent activity."

Leo stiffens. "Rodents as in mice?"

"Yup." The guy folds up his tool kit. "Is it okay if I leave the ladder?"

"You're heading out? I thought you were finishing up today."

"I'll need another guy now if we're going to remove the ceiling panels."

"Remove? When? I'm opening tomorrow."

Maybe there is some poetic justice in the world after all.

"Best of luck!" I holler as Leo disappears into the depths of the store, but as I turn, a voice whispers my name from behind a display right inside the door.

"Psst, Cora." A red bob becomes visible. It takes me a moment to recognize Jaz. She's wearing a black apron emblazoned with *Canine King* in gold stitching.

"Why are you in a wig?"

She glances behind her as if to make sure no one's watching and whispers, "I got the job."

My face must betray my lack of preparation for this turn of events because Jaz steps through the doorway. "Don't worry, I have not switched sides. Still one hundred percent Team Cora. But a girl's gotta eat."

"In a wig?"

"I'm undercover. In case he spotted me with you at O'Connor's. You're not mad about it, right?"

"No, it's fine. I just didn't know you had applied."

She hikes her thumb toward the back where Leo and the electrician continue their squabble. "If it makes you feel any better, he was pretty desperate to get someone in here. The pay is actually decent for a clerk job."

"Well good for you."

"So, is there anything in particular you want me to snoop for?" Her eyes are round and eager.

"No, I don't—"

"Oh!" She cuts me off. "I did overhear him telling someone on the phone to 'keep it between them' in a scheming sort of way. Maybe there's something shady there like an illicit contract or a mob connection or something?"

Leo is at the counter with his back to us now. His neck is bent as he leafs through a stack of documents with short, precise movements. He's strung tightly, that's for sure, but who wouldn't be when on the brink of opening a new business. If he's anything at all like his high school self, I imagine perfection is what he's going for, and nothing else will be considered a success. "I highly doubt it," I say, adding, "but keep up the good work" when Jaz's enthusiastic grin wanes. "See you tomorrow at the launch?"

"Jaz, when you have a minute," Leo calls from inside in a bossy tone some might call sexy. Not me, though.

"I'll pour you an extra tall glass of wine." She winks at me. "Got to go."

I text Micki as soon as I'm out of sight. She knows her sister better than I do, and I need her to tell me this isn't the Most Terrible idea.

Of course, because he's Leo, he doesn't need luck to get the store ready in time. The electrical truck packs up and leaves by noon the following day—I pay close attention to the morning's developments from inside Happy Paws between stocking shelves and helping customers. I enjoy the view of Leo wiping drywall dust off the window display, and smile when Jaz mimics panic for my behalf behind his back. It's down to the wire for them, so I believe it.

"Blue tie or silver?" Harvey calls from the stairs.

"You're going, then?" I ask.

"As are you." Harvey examines the two options in his hands. "No, Martha preferred the blue one. I'll go with that."

"Um, I haven't decided yet. And I'm not exactly dressed for an *exclusive event.*" I look down at my floral skirt and red cable-knit sweater.

"You look perfectly presentable. Remember, we have trade secrets to uncover over there. Or so Michaela tells us." He winks.

Lord knows we need some. After another look through the window, I concede with a grunt. "Fine, but I'm not fixing my hair." No need to go overboard.

"That's my girl."

A few hours later, Canine King is filled with mingling people and a handful of pooches as we step through the door. A guy with a guitar sits in the back corner, his calm strumming setting the mood. All around me superlatives flow.

"This is wonderful," an older woman with two meticulously groomed Havanese comments as she browses the custom collar selection.

"I need to find out what kind of wine this is," says another.

Harvey is quickly pulled into a conversation with people he knows, so I take to exploring on my own. Every surface is so pristine that I want to throw up, but I've come prepared, juvenile though it may be. Since Leo is getting under my skin, I will now get under his with a small "gift" to show my appreciation for his presence.

As discreetly as I can, I tuck an old digital wristwatch from our lost-and-found box into one of the flowerpots in the window before I join the mingling crowd. It's a children's watch in the shape of a cat, and instead of beeping, it meows. I've set it to go off on the hour every hour. That should annoy him at least for a bit.

"Hi," Leo says at my side, startling me. "I didn't think you were going to make it." He's in a navy-blue suit for the occasion—a ridiculously expensive one if I'm to guess. The patterned tie and pocket square match in an international superstar kind of way. Men should not be allowed to be this pretty.

I step out of the way for a couple of people on the move and nod a "hello" to them. There are several familiar faces here actually, each one a stab in the back. "Honestly, I could use a drink," I tell Leo. "Figured I'd pop in."

If he's offended, he doesn't let on. "White or red?" He gestures for me to follow him to the counter where Jaz has taken on the role of bartender.

"What can I get you, miss," she says, staying in character as a complete stranger.

"A large glass of red, please."

"Of course. One second." She dives behind the makeshift bar for a slightly bigger glass than what everyone else is holding and proceeds to pour me a healthy helping. "There you go."

Leo frowns in my peripheral but doesn't have time to comment before a man in a Burberry coat pats him on the shoulder. "Great turnout, Leo. Everything looks flawless."

Leo flashes a smile. "Thank you." His gaze flicks upward past my head, then back.

Next to the glasses on the counter is a guest book, and as we're talking, guest after guest steps up to enter their names and email addresses. Why have we never done anything like that? The missed opportunity is so obvious when it's staring me in the face.

"Is Harvey here, too?" Leo asks. He glances above my head again, lips tightening briefly before returning to neutral.

What is he looking at?

I peer over my shoulder but don't see anything out of place. Only organized perfection and happy customers. I swallow the metaphorical sour grapes and then a mouthful of the liquefied ones. "Over there." I point. Pop is laughing and talking animatedly as if we're here on a social call.

"Looks like he's enjoying himself." Leo smiles, but it doesn't reach his eyes. "Hey, I'm really not here to ruin things for—"

"Hi, there." A tall woman with dark lashes and shoulder-length brown hair who looks vaguely familiar interrupts him. There's a curious glint in her eye as she smiles at me. "I don't think we've met. I'm Diane Kurtz, Leo's aunt."

"Cora Lewis." I shake her hand. I didn't know he still had relatives around here. His family used to own a big equestrian center outside of town, but they closed it and moved around the time his class graduated. Maybe they're all back, and that's why he's here?

"You must be Harvey and Martha's granddaughter." Diane gives Leo a look that suggests my name's come up. "Happy Paws, right?"

"That's right." *Has* he been talking about me?

"We were in the middle of something, actually," Leo tells Diane. "Maybe we can circle back?"

"Oh." Diane looks between us. "Of course. Sorry. But really quick, Dawn wanted me to tell you thanks for helping with that website thing of hers. It's made a big difference. I swear she was completely overwhelmed before." The message relayed, she flashes an apologetic smile and backs away.

"Tell her no problem. Happy to do it." Leo smiles indulgently as his aunt retreats. "Sorry about that. She wants to talk to everyone. She and her wife, Dawn, have been great to me this past year. I think they brought along at least twenty people tonight."

"That's nice. Is the rest of your family here, too?"

A shadow crosses his features. "No," he says.

I wait for him to elaborate but get nothing. *Okay, then.* I finish what's left of my wine in one fell swoop. *Pick a different topic.* "So, 'circle back,' huh?" I do bunny ears with my fingers. "What did you do before coming here? Something 'results-driven' no doubt, where you could 'build consensus' and follow 'best practices.' I know—corporate takeovers?"

He glances at the ceiling again, and now I see it. The farthest light above the counter is out, and it's driving him bananas.

Leo clears his throat. "Um, I worked in investment banking and financial risk management actually."

I let out a dry laugh. "Yeah, that tracks. A true capitalist. And now you're here…" I set my empty glass down on the display table closest to us. This was a mistake. I don't want to learn anything from him. "I think I'm going to go. Thanks for the wine." I wave to Harvey who's chatting with the troubadour, to let him know I'm heading out.

Leo doesn't try to stop me, and why should he? But when I've walked a few steps, I turn back around and find him still watching me.

"Forgot something?" he asks.

"Yeah, I meant to tell you…" I let my gaze rise higher and point. "You've got a broken light. Might want to fix it."

On the way out, my eyes land on his A-frame once more. *Talk to me about how I can meet your unmet canine needs.* Without thinking, I crouch down and erase part of the sentence from the board. I dig around in my pocket and find a chalk stump left from lettering Happy Paws' promotions this morning that I use to give the prompt a different ending. "Enjoy," I whisper, standing to admire my work.

Talk to me about our interpretive dance class for dogs.

8

I spend most of Saturday morning going over Happy Paws' financial records, and the tune playing in the back of my mind goes something like this: *Broken light notwithstanding, Leo's store is amazing. Ooh, ooh, baby.*

It's classy, organized, well-stocked, and, judging by the turn-out, clearly something the people want.

I hate it.

If I ever had doubts about what this would do to our business, they're now gone. Pet owners who've been loyal to us for years were at Leo's launch. I guess all it took for them to leave us was some glitz.

Our predicament is even clearer after Harvey brings in the mail and there's a second notice from the power company. We have enough money for next month's rent, but after that, it's looking dicey. To cover our expenses, we'd need to make October our strongest month in sales since... I skim the past year's records. Since June two years ago. At my feet, Boris lifts his sleepy head a couple of inches and sniffs the air. Then he puts it back down on top of my toes. Okay fine. The dogs need me. Pop needs me. Challenge accepted!

I spend my lunch break on internet searches like "how to make your business successful" and "make money fast."

"Finding anything?" Pop asks, stirring cream into a cup of coffee across from me.

"So far it seems our options are to donate plasma or start driving for a delivery service. If only I wasn't prone to anemia and didn't already have a full-time job…" I smirk.

"I'm sure we'll be fine, kiddo. We've always been fine."

I don't have the heart to tell him I don't share his conviction. "Maybe," I say instead, "but in the meantime, we really need to get Happy Paws online. We need a website, and at a very minimum, an Instagram account, too." After all these years, we don't even have a digital list of our customers. Everything is in Harvey's head. Why have I never questioned that?

I pull out an empty sheet of paper and start a new list. *Internet* goes on top and then *Sell more pet costumes*. I have an Etsy shop for my creations that I started a couple of years ago that I should revive to add to what we sell in store. It's the only added source of income that comes to mind for October. There's also our booth at Winter Fest, but we won't see that extra income until December. I may not be vying for the blue rosette in the amateur dog show, but we do sell well there since people come from all over with their dogs to compete.

"Any luck with the costume people?" Harvey asks.

"Let me check again." I open the Flockify server and click to my posts. "Only the Cleopatra so far."

One new DM awaits me, and I open it. It's from late Thursday night. I was too busy dealing with Leo's launch yesterday to check. I almost feel bad I've kept my new friend waiting.

AlCaponesGhost25: You never told me what fascinating aspect of Illinois history brings you here.

"Another riddle?" Harvey asks.

What do I tell the guy? If he's forgotten about me soliciting business, maybe bringing it up again would be a bad idea.

"Cora?"

I look up to find Harvey watching me, one eyebrow raised. "Huh?"

He chuckles. "Never mind." As he leaves the table, he mutters something that sounds like "Martha would be proud."

I return my attention to the screen.

SingerQueen: Would you believe me if I said all of it?

I only have to wait a moment for a response.

AlCaponesGhost25: Hot dog girl!

The weight of my to-do list slips off my shoulders, and I smile.

SingerQueen: Definitely not answering to that.
AlCaponesGhost25: Fair enough. What's up?

There's a brief impulse to tell him about the past few days, but I push it away. I'd rather keep the two worlds separate.

SingerQueen: Not much. Did you make it through the week without upsetting anyone else with your superior joke standards?

AlCaponesGhost25: You mean did anyone else tell me to eff off? No, but there are definitely people in my life who I'd like to teach a lesson or two in what constitutes a good joke.

SingerQueen: Yikes.

AlCaponesGhost25: Nah it's all good. They've got nothing on me. I have professional experience in dealing with opportunistic cheats.

SingerQueen: Let me guess—you run an underground gambling ring?

AlCaponesGhost25: I'm not actually Al Capone.

SingerQueen: Lol. Just his ghost. Maybe you should haunt these subpar jokesters.

AlCaponesGhost25: I will if I have to.

A shiver runs up my spine at his no-nonsense response. Something tells me I wouldn't want to be on the receiving end of whatever lessons he'd be doling out. I'm about to say so when another message appears.

AlCaponesGhost25: And no, I don't believe for a second you're into ALL history. No one is that nerdy. *winky face emoji*

SingerQueen: Spoken as the newbie to this forum he is.

AlCaponesGhost25: *wears innocence as a badge of pride*

SingerQueen: And yet somehow you're a moderator here?

AlCaponesGhost25: Doing someone a favor.

SingerQueen: Aren't you the altruist.

AlCaponesGhost25: Far from it.

I frown. This guy speaks in riddles even when he's not trying to. Maybe he, too, is compartmentalizing. If I want to know something real about him, I might have to take the plunge first, then.

> **SingerQueen:** Your question earlier…I'm actually here for costuming. I'm a clothing designer and sometimes people on here need my help. Not super into history if I'm being honest.
>
> **AlCaponesGhost25:** LOL knew it! Very sneaky.
>
> **SingerQueen:** *shrug emoji* But for you it's the mob stuff? Or mostly just to boss people around? Did you ever hear about that restaurant by the way—Al Capone's Hideaway?
>
> **AlCaponesGhost25:** Both and ate there lots of times when I was a kid. Good times. It's basically my only knowledge of IL history.

I stare at the screen. He used to live in the area? If he's twenty-five like his username suggests, Jaz might know who he is.

> **SingerQueen:** You grew up in Illinois? Where?
>
> **AlCaponesGhost25:** Yup. I've been away a long time though.

It doesn't escape my notice that he sidesteps my question. Then again, even a child knows not to share personal information with strangers online. I shouldn't have asked.

> **SingerQueen:** Away haunting people?
>
> **AlCaponesGhost25:** It's a tough job, but someone's gotta do it.

"When you're done with that, can you take Cho and Cap for a walk?" Harvey asks. "Otherwise, your next riddle may well be 'Why is the rug wet?'"

Pop is right. Where did time go? I hurry to sign off with a quick **Sry gotta go** and then stand and stretch.

"You seem pretty captivated by whatever that is?" Harvey peers at me as he gestures to the computer. "Good to see a smile on your face, kiddo."

"It's just this guy in the group. He's funny."

"A guy, you say?"

I tut at him. "Not local, so don't worry." I close the laptop and reach for the leashes beneath the counter. "Come on, pups. Let's go outside."

It's a busy Saturday afternoon on the Riverwalk, so I hold on extra tight to Cholula's leash just in case. Fortunately, Leo and Tilly are nowhere to be seen. We pass the playground, the snack stand, and a sign announcing the last farmer's market of the season coming up tomorrow. That's why I recognized Leo's aunt, I realize. She sometimes has a table there selling baked goods.

The thought brings me back to the launch and his curt response when I asked about his family. Maybe it's time to do a little research. I lead the dogs to the nearest bench where I sit down and pull out my phone. *Salinger + horses*, I type into the search engine. The first result in the list is a hit for Salinger and Sons Royal Equine in New York. The link takes me to a landing page with pictures of gorgeous horses and endless fields of green, and a quick survey of the About page reveals it is indeed Leo's family and that their business has been in operation since right after World War I. A picture of three older men in front of portraits of what must be their ancestors draws my attention as Leo bears a striking resemblance especially to one of them. "Hello, Leo's dad," I say.

I'm about to close the page when I land on a link in the top right corner. Canine King, it says.

"Of course," I mumble. Royal Equine, Canine King...So, he's in the family business. But didn't he say he used to be an investment banker? I click through to the canine side of the business and snoop around some more. Under locations, I enter my zip code, but only the downtown Chicago branch comes up. A site search for Leo's name similarly yields nothing.

"Huh?" I feel like I've stumbled upon something, but what exactly, I have no idea.

9

Living History Illinois Flockify DM, Monday 8:44 AM
@AlCaponesGhost25

SingerQueen: So if you could haunt anyone in the
world—who would you choose and why?

Canine King officially opened its doors today, and since Happy Paws is closed on Mondays, I've spent all day distracting myself with sewing. Piles of tutus, capes, and dog-sized vests on the table behind me bear witness to my productiveness, but now my fingers ache, and my neck is almost certainly growing a hump.

It's past 6:30 p.m., so Micki and Jaz should be home soon. I've started boiling water for our pasta, but while I wait, I check for the third time today to see if "Al" has responded to my question from this morning. And finally, he has.

AlCaponesGhost25: Hmm tricky. Surely there's a
whole slew of war criminals who could do with a bit
of poltergeisting.
SingerQueen: A diplomatic response. Snooze…

AlCaponesGhost25: Alright fine. I recently started a new job and there's this person—a real grouch—who really has it in for me for no reason. They're messing up my work and making things up about me. It's extremely frustrating.

SingerQueen: Let's send some chain rattling their way then! What a dick.

AlCaponesGhost25: Done. You?

SingerQueen: Must be something in the air. Also someone at work.

AlCaponesGhost25: Another designer?

Oh yeah, I forgot about that little lie...

SingerQueen: He's so full of himself. Thinks my clients will like his sketches better than mine, and he's always prancing around showing off.

AlCaponesGhost25: Can't stand people like that. How about I slam some of his cabinet doors around at night. Maybe make a dresser float across the room?

SingerQueen: Perfect.

The door to the apartment opens, and Micki and Jaz crowd in, kicking off shoes and hanging up jackets.

"God, I'm beat," Jaz says, pulling off her red wig.

I close my laptop. "Do I want to know?"

"No."

"Tell me anyway." I move to the stove and empty a box of spaghetti into the bubbling water.

"Let's see…"

"Tell her about the weird stuff first," Micki says from the couch. She's put her feet up on the table and is wiggling her toes back and forth.

"There was weird stuff?"

"Well first, I spent the morning chasing this meowing noise that was driving Tilly nuts. Leo said it was there all weekend, but he couldn't find the source. It was like *meow, meow, meow*, and then it would be quiet for a long time. I found it right away, of course. Ears like a bat. Turns out it was someone's watch. They must have dropped it during the launch on Friday."

Micki gives me a pointed look that I ignore, turning my back to them.

"Sounds annoying," I say, fully aware I'm going to have to make this up to Jaz.

"It was. And then lots of people kept asking when we're planning on starting the dance class. At first I thought they had the store mixed up with the studio down the street, but no—dance for dogs. Is that even a thing?"

I cover a snort with my hand as my spiteful revision of Leo's A-frame prompt comes back to me. I'd assumed Leo would catch and erase it right away, but maybe he was too busy tracking the meowing.

"And how did Leo handle that?" I ask as I stir the pot.

"What are you not telling us?" Micki asks. "I can hear you smiling from over here."

"Fine." I explain my impromptu sabotage and add to Jaz, "Sorry if it made for a frustrating day."

Jaz looks at me with admiration in her eyes. "Not at all. I found the watch right away, and I'd much rather talk to people about interpretive dance than dog biscuits. I met an eighty-year-old lady who used to be a Rockette! She had some *stories*."

"And Leo?"

"Doubt he's been a Rockette."

"Ha, ha."

"No, he was extremely confused. But God that guy is a good salesman. Almost everyone who came in asking about the dance still left having made a purchase."

"Oh."

"Sorry."

"No, that's fine." The timer for the food goes off, giving me a reason to disengage. It's not like I didn't know he'd have a good first day.

When I've cleared off my sewing stuff and we're seated at the table with bowlfuls of noodles and pesto from a jar, Micki points to me with her fork. "You should think of some other pranks you can pull on him."

"I should?"

"I think it will make you feel better. Small acts of resistance, you know."

I chew slowly. Maybe she's right.

"Does he ever mention his family?" I ask Jaz after a while.

"No, why?"

"If he does, will you let me know? I have questions."

"Any you care to share?" Micki slurps up a wayward noodle.

I think again about the fact that Leo's parents weren't at the launch and that his store isn't listed on their website. But maybe I'm making something out of nothing. "Not yet," I say.

"I can fish around," Jaz offers. "This is exciting stuff."

"You're writing about it, aren't you?" Micki asks.

Jaz looks offended. "Loosely inspired by. Which reminds me—Cora can I borrow your laptop tonight? I got the blue screen of death on mine, but everything's in the cloud."

"Sure." A brief twinge of regret follows my answer. I had hoped to chat more with "Al" before bed. My idiocy becomes clear as I'm brushing my teeth. There's an app. I've only ever accessed the server on the computer because I was so rarely on it, but now having access on my phone will be much more convenient.

I crawl under the covers and log in.

> **AlCaponesGhost25:** Ok my turn to ask a question
> **AlCaponesGhost25:** Hello?

A smile stretches across my lips as I scoot into a more comfortable position, propped against my headboard.

> **SingerQueen:** Sorry, got busy. Go ahead.
> **AlCaponesGhost25:** If I'm going to let you in on my haunting business, I feel like we need to know each other better.

He does, does he? Interesting.

> **SingerQueen:** Before this goes any further you should know my policy is NOT to end up as a case on Unsolved Mysteries.
> **AlCaponesGhost25:** Meaning?
> **SingerQueen:** I won't tell you my name or anything in the event you're a psychopath
> **AlCaponesGhost25:** Jeez that's dark. But agreed.
> **SingerQueen:** Ok then I'm game. What did you have in mind?
> **AlCaponesGhost25:** Rapid choice questions. We take turns. Ready?

SingerQueen: Ready.

AlCaponesGhost25: Spring or fall?

SingerQueen: Fall. Coffee or tea?

AlCaponesGhost25: Coffee. Cats or dogs?

SingerQueen: Dogs all the way. Night owl or morning person?

AlCaponesGhost25: Both? I don't like to sleep.

SingerQueen: What??? Who doesn't like to sleep? Psychopath meter just gave a reading . . .

AlCaponesGhost25: See also: love for coffee. *winky face emoji*

SingerQueen: Ok fine. Your turn.

AlCaponesGhost25: Sushi or burger?

SingerQueen: Burger. City or suburb?

AlCaponesGhost25: City. Thinker or doer?

SingerQueen: Thinker. Trying to be more of a doer.

AlCaponesGhost25: How so?

SingerQueen: Thinking only gets you so far. Love or friendship?

This time it takes a while before he responds. I almost think he's left the chat.

AlCaponesGhost25: You stumped me with that one. I was going to say love because everyone wants that, right? But with this new job and stuff, I guess I do need to figure out how to make some friends, too.

SingerQueen: It's definitely harder as an adult.

AlCaponesGhost25: Yeah how do people do it?

SingerQueen: Maybe they connect online?

AlCaponesGhost25: *grinning face emoji*

I smile at the screen, warmth spreading through my chest. This seems like a good place to end our conversation for tonight. Any further and I'm not sure where it will take us.

I sign off and then wrap myself tightly in the blankets and shut my eyes. *Doesn't like sleeping*, I think. *But it feels so good.* Hopefully, I get a solid night's shut-eye to get me ready for tomorrow. I've got clothes to sew, a store to keep afloat, and a foe to foil.

10

Different possible scenarios for how to keep sabotaging Leo's peace of mind play before me as I walk to work. Do I sign him up for a wake-up call service? Put fake bullet holes on his windows and cordon off the door?

I take out my key as I reach our street and approach the mailbox. Maybe a surprise confetti bomb would send the right message. I bite my lip, pondering this as I open the mail hatch, and I have my hand halfway there when I register what's in front of me.

"Gah! What the hell?" I recoil in horror at the sight of the enormous brown recluse guarding our mail. I freaking *hate* spiders.

Every hair on my body stands at attention as my mind struggles to compute. What do I do? Do we just never get mail again? No, that's probably not a viable option.

I squint at the eight long, pointy legs, and a ripple of phantom prickles runs up my arm as if my body already knows what it would feel like to have the creature use me as its personal runway. What I need is a stick or a can of elephant tranquilizer or a bazooka. I look around at the ground as if weapons of mass destruction will suddenly materialize, but as I run through my options, it occurs to some deep part of my consciousness that the arachnid in question didn't move when I opened the hatch. It also occurs to me that it's watching me a little too intently. Against my better judgment, I take a step closer.

"Nice spidey," I whisper.

Fishing through my purse, I find a pencil that's long enough to provide some distance and very, very carefully, I stick it into the mailbox and nudge my nightmare.

It stays exactly the same.

I nudge again, harder this time, and it tips over.

What? Finally, my shoulders relax, and I get close enough to see what I maybe should have guessed from the beginning. This is no ordinary recluse—it's fake.

I don't even have to think about it before I spin around to face Canine King, and there's Leo, bright red in the face and wiping tears from his eyes.

You should have seen yourself, he mimes.

All I can do is shake my head and shoot virtual daggers. Now he's just asking for it.

Grinding my teeth together, I pick up the rubber spider (I admit, it still makes me shudder) and the mail and storm inside.

"Good morning!" Harvey calls upon hearing the bell.

"Is it?" I mutter.

"Did you say something?"

"Nothing. Hi, Pop." I put the mail down and throw the spider in the garbage. This time I'm going to have to think of something epic.

"I'll be down in a bit. Will you put up the doorbuster sign?"

"Sure thing."

The deal this week is buy a collar, get a free toy, and I'm pretty proud of the poster I drew Saturday. It's one of my best ones yet, I think as I tape up the first corner, colorful with shaded lettering and a sweet pup off to the side.

Leo is doing the same inside Canine King, but about discounted dog food, and his sign has text only. He notices me a second later, and as soon as he does, he reenacts what I assume is supposed to be my reaction to the spider. He pretends to poke something in the air and jumps back, scrunching up his face with hilarity. In return, I pretend to crank up my middle finger, which makes his features return to RBF (resting brat face).

I finish taping up the poster, trying to get my irritation to recede, but when I look again, Leo has taken down his sign and is writing something on it. When done, he smacks it up against the pane, and even from where I'm standing, I can see what it says: BUY A COLLAR, GET TWO FREE TOYS!

He did not.

He raises his chin as if to say "Take that."

"Insufferable," I mutter. "Pop, can we do a different promo this week?" I call up to Harvey as I head toward storage. "Or add something to sweeten the deal?" Maybe we have some superfluous junk in there we can include to one-up Leo's offer. And balloons to embellish our sign.

There's no immediate response, so I yell louder, "Pop, did you hear me?"

"Hold your horses, I'm coming," he calls back, but before his voice has rung out, Cap lets out a loud bark upstairs, followed by a shout from Harvey, and then I hear a long string of dull thuds as something goes tumbling down the stairs.

For a split second, I can't move, but when the noise stops, the paralysis breaks, and I rush to the front. "Pop?"

Harvey is at the foot of the stairs, moaning. I crouch by him, my hands flitting across his shoulders. There's no blood, but he's obviously in pain. "Pop, can you hear me?"

"My leg," Harvey groans, his hand jerking to his right side.

Behind me, the bell jingles, and heavy steps reach us in a hurry.

"I've called 9-1-1," Leo says. "I saw him fall from my window." He surveys the length of my grandpa's supine body and leans closer. "Harvey, how are you doing? Stay with us, okay? An ambulance is on the way."

"I think it's his leg or hip."

"It's a pretty steep fall," Leo says, looking up.

I follow his gaze, and there's Boris at the top of the stairs. It doesn't take a genius to figure out what happened.

The five minutes it takes for the medics to show up are the longest of my life. Harvey is clasping my hand tight, so I know he's alert, but his face is greenish white with pain.

"Miss, are you coming?" one of the medics asks as they're loading Harvey into the ambulance.

I look from the gurney to the store. A knot forms in my throat as I check my watch. "We're supposed to open in...I'd have to lock up first."

"We're taking him to Delnor. You can follow us," the medic says, closing the doors.

"But I don't have a car."

Leo, who has been lingering off to the side, takes a step closer. "I can drive you. Do what you need to do here, and we'll follow them."

I look up at him. Analyze his face for ulterior motives. There is nothing but concern in his expression. "Are you sure? Aren't you busy?"

"This seems more important." To the medic he says, "We'll be there shortly."

After the ambulance leaves, Leo escorts me back into the store and tells me to come over when I'm ready.

I nod numbly, but not until Cap's black nose presses into my hand do I snap into action. The dogs, the store...

"One thing at a time, Cora," I say to myself. "What would Harvey do?" The store is eerily silent as if it knows not to encroach on my already strained mental state. "Okay, pups—up you go." I bring the dogs up to the apartment and make sure they have water. Boris is under the table, and he looks more miserable than usual, so I take a moment to reassure him it wasn't his fault. "I do think we need to put a bell on you though. Before you actually kill someone."

I put the gate up at the top of the stairs to keep them contained and double-check that the sign on the front door says we're closed before I hurry across the street. Outside Canine King, I pause for a moment. Inhale. Exhale. I can't see Leo inside, but Tilly watches me through the window, and maybe it's those kind, brown eyes that help me finally turn the handle.

Into the lion's den I go.

11

"You shouldn't bite your nails," Leo says at a stoplight.

I grunt a monosyllabic response.

"There's a plethora of bacteria under there. Gross habit."

I take in his profile. The sturdy, straight nose, sharp jawline, and lightly tan skin. He's at ease behind the wheel, relaxed. Despite his choice of words, I don't think he means to be rude. "Thanks. I'll take it under consideration." I pick up my phone to distract from the gnawing.

The rest of the ride to the hospital goes by in a blur. Leo makes a few more attempts at conversation, but all I can think about is Harvey, so he probably regrets offering up his driving services.

I assume Leo will drop me at the entrance and be on his way, but he parks and stays at my side as I walk into the ER. There's a shift in him when we step into the waiting room, a subtle tensing of the shoulders, but he doesn't say anything as he sits down next to me.

Thankfully, it's a quiet Tuesday morning in the emergency department, and a nurse comes to get us after only a brief wait.

"We've given him something for the pain so he's comfortable," she says, opening the door. "The doctor will be here shortly."

"Thanks," I say, my hands clutched tightly together.

Harvey has his eyes closed, but he blinks them open when I approach the bed.

"How are you, Pop?" I ask, leaning in to kiss his cheek.

"Doing good." Harvey smiles. "They've got quality drugs in this place. My hip is busted, they tell me, so now I'm going to be a bob—" He sighs. "A rob...robert." Another slow grin. "No, that's not my name."

I look to see if Leo understands what he's saying.

Leo takes a step closer to the bed. "Do you mean a robot, Harvey?"

"That's what I said," my grandpa mumbles.

"Because of the artificial hip," Leo clarifies to me as if I'm incapable of deductive reasoning. "Wow, he is pretty out of it."

"Am not, young man," Harvey says with more gusto.

"You remember Leo, right, Pop?" I ask. "He gave me a ride here."

"Leo. That's right." He gestures for me to come closer, and then says in what I assume is supposed to be a whisper but that falls far from the mark, "Your nemesis."

I shake my head and sigh before venturing a glance at Leo, who looks amused.

"Nemesis, huh?" He cocks a brow.

I ignore him and turn back to Harvey. "Okay, I think that's enough talking."

"He is a handsome fellow, though," Harvey says as if he didn't hear me. "Don't you think he's handsome?"

My face goes hot. Where are the doctors when I need them?

"I had blond hair like that when I was your age," Harvey says to Leo.

"Really?" He smiles.

I give him a warning glare not to encourage this, but he seems to be enjoying the conversation quite a bit.

"And I was a hit with the ladies." Harvey nods.

"I bet."

Please stop it, I mouth to Leo.

Stop what? he mouths back.

"Leo." Harvey pats the bed in an invitation to sit, which he does. "You'll take care of her, right? When I'm gone?"

"Um…" Leo finally looks like he's bitten off more than he can chew and blinks blankly at my grandpa.

This is mortifying.

A knock on the door saves us all, and the doctor strides in. "How are we doing, Mr. Morton?" she asks. "I'm the orthopedic surgeon who'll be fixing you up today."

"Did you hear that, Leo? She'll be 'fixing me up.'" Harvey winks.

"Pop, that is not appropriate." I cross my arms in front of me before apologizing to the doctor. "It's the painkillers. He's usually not like this."

She smiles. "No worries. It means they're working. And trust me, I've heard worse."

"So what happens next?"

"I take it you two are next of kin?"

"I am," I say. "I'm his granddaughter."

The doctor looks at Leo as if expecting him to justify his presence as well, but instead he backs away a step and turns to me. "Hey, how about I wait for you outside? Let you guys talk."

I nod. "If you don't mind."

Once he's gone, I focus all my attention on Harvey and the doctor. There are surgery details, recovery times, and assurances.

"Will you wait here?" the doctor asks. "It might be a while."

"No, she needs to get back to the dogs," Harvey says. "You can call her, right doc?"

"Of course."

"Are you sure?" I ask Harvey.

"As sure as sun follows rain."

I guess that settles it.

I take my leave and head to the waiting area, expecting to see Leo there but finding it empty. I walk through the sliding doors, and there he is on a bench, his head in his hands as if he got terrible news himself right now.

He startles when I say his name. "Sorry, I was just…" He stands. "How's Harvey? Everything okay?"

Did he get bad news? "I could ask you the same. You look like you've seen a ghost."

"Um no, I…" He inhales deeply. "It's just been a while since I was in a hospital. Ready to go?" A million more unspoken words filter through his expression, but I don't pry.

"Ready."

I stare out the side window until we're back on the main road. It feels wrong to go back to the store without Harvey, without knowing what they're doing to him right now.

"He's going to be all right," Leo says when I've almost managed to forget he's next to me. "Like new."

As if he's reading my thoughts.

It's annoying and presumptuous, and I want to be mad at him for it, but instead a lump forms in my throat. "Uh-huh," I manage.

"I'm serious. The doctors know what they're doing."

I stay turned away from him. "It's okay. You don't have to do that. I appreciate you driving me and everything, but you don't have to pretend like we're friends."

There's a long pause. "O-kay then."

When I look, his mouth is set tight. Like I've hurt him. "What do you expect? For me to simply ignore the fact that you're trying to shut down our store?"

"I'm not trying…" He sighs. "Like I said, it's not personal. To be successful at anything, you have to follow the metrics. The stats."

I gape at him. He truly thinks I'm the one being unreasonable in this situation. "I rest my case," I say, sinking back in my seat. When he tries to continue the argument, I put my hand up to stop him. If he hadn't raised the stakes for our doorbuster, I wouldn't have yelled for Harvey, and Harvey wouldn't have hurried and tripped. Some deep part of me knows that's faulty reasoning, but right now, I need a scapegoat. "Let's not. Thanks for the ride, and that's it."

It's a relief when he finally parks, and I'm allowed to flee back to my side of the street.

12

I make it into the store before the tears come. All the tension and worry from the past few hours are coiled tightly in my core and explode until I'm sobbing so hard I have to use the counter for support to stay upright.

The dogs' whining is what finally snaps me out of it. I wipe my face with the back of my hands while I go upstairs.

"Hi, guys," I say, moving the gate. "Everything is okay. Pop will be back before you know it." I say it as much for me as for them.

I sit down on the floor and let the dogs blanket me in their warm, heavy bodies.

What am I going to do? I don't know how to run the store—Harvey always calls the shots. I'm behind the scenes. The walls around me could not seem taller or more imposing. A million tasks float about my head like some sort of sharp-toothed sharknado. If I linger too long on any one thing, it'll bite me.

I might have stayed there on the floor the rest of the day if Boris wasn't the most flatulent dog I've ever met. Eventually, I'm forced to get up, if only to open a window, and once I'm up, I make the conscious decision not to sit back down.

"Start small," I say to myself. "Open the store, call Mom." Harvey is her dad after all, and I'm hoping she'll know better than me what to do.

With a steadying breath, I flip the OPEN sign and take my position behind the counter.

Mom picks up after two rings, and after I explain what's happened, she's quiet for a long moment.

"Oh, shoot," she says eventually, as if I've merely told her I missed the school bus. "Well, it was only a matter of time. He should have retired ages ago. Stubborn old fool."

That's helpful. I rub my brow.

"I suppose that means we should head that way for the holidays again," she says. "Your dad will be disappointed. He had his heart set on Arizona this year."

My hands pause their nervous sorting of the stack of mail from this morning. "You weren't even going to come back for Christmas?"

"Chicago is so cold and snowy."

I shake my head. I don't know what I was hoping for. Best to switch gears. "The social worker at the hospital told me the recovery can be lengthy. What should we do about rehab?"

"Well, I don't know, hon. I'm all the way over here."

"Mom!" The dogs' heads whip around to stare at me. "Please," I say in a softer voice. "He's your dad. I can't deal with the store and the hospital and the dogs by myself."

She's quiet for another beat. Then she clicks her tongue. "Fine. I'll make some calls."

I let out a long breath. "Thanks."

"But for God's sake, let the store fizzle, Coralynn. You must have enough saved up for grad school by now, and Dad should be enjoying his sunset days in a nice home."

I resist the urge to let out a loud cackle. She knows neither one of us.

The corner of a colorful brochure peeks out from the stack of envelopes in front of me, drawing my attention. I tug on it.

"That reminds me," Mom says. "The sunsets here are remarkable. You really should come. Perhaps you and Dad can join *us* for the holidays this year instead."

"Can't bring the dogs on a plane," I mumble as I scan the front of the brochure. It's about Winter Fest and the dog show, and the words I'm reading are not making sense.

ONE WINNER TAKES HOME...

The skin on my arms starts to tingle. That must be a typo. "You know what, Mom, I've got to go. Let me know what you find out, okay?"

"About what?"

I tilt my head back in a silent plea for strength. "Pop's care."

"Oh, right. Okay. Will do."

I put my phone away, squeeze my eyes shut, and then look at the brochure again. The first part reads the same as I remember from previous years. County fair, vendor sign-up, yada, yada, yada. Below that is the information about the dog show. While I've been at the fest every year, I haven't seen the show since Grandma passed. That was her thing. Every year she'd enter with one of the many rescues in the shelter, and adoptions always soared afterward. She loved that anyone was allowed to compete and that most of the contestants were in it for the fun experience, not the five-hundred-dollar prize.

Except, this year, the amount listed for first prize is a little more than that, if I'm to believe what I'm seeing.

I stare at the bold font on the page.

ONE WINNER TAKES HOME $15,000!
(Thank you to our generous sponsors.)

I drop the brochure on the counter. The peace of mind that amount of money would bring…I glance behind me at the photo of my grandma and Patch the dalmatian mix with their blue rosette. "Can you believe this?" I ask her. Of course, I get nothing but a sanguine smile in return.

My brain is churning. Is this even possible? And if so, which dog would I run in the show? There are two parts to the competition—an obstacle course and a talent show—and none of our mutts is a clear choice. I glance at the big wolf-hound at the bottom of the stairs. Well, it would have to be Cap or Cholula since Boris is an obvious no-go.

I open a browser and do a quick search of past winners. There was the bloodhound from Kenosha whose talent was finding all five peanut butter cups hidden in the audience within three minutes, the Yorkie who could climb his owner like a baby mountain goat, and the terrifying German shepherd who did impressions of famous movie dogs on command. (His Cujo scared the bejeezus out of half the audience.) But these were all dogs with agility experience and years of training. There's no chance I could compete with that.

My excitement dwindles as I browse the official page for the fest, but when I reach the sign-up page and see that the cutoff for registering is in less than a week, something snaps inside me.

I'm about to ask Pop what he thinks we should do before remembering the state of things. What was true this morning is suddenly false. I no longer have a boss; I am the boss. If vendors need to be paid or orders need to be placed, it's on me. I'll have to figure out our accounting system and our order status, not to mention whatever Harvey uses for regular bills. I can't go home tonight—or any night for the foreseeable future—because the dogs are here, and so I'll need to move in with them. Everything is upside down.

If I want to win $15,000 and save the store, I'm on my own.

Before I can change my mind, I sign up for both the booth and the competition, pay the fees, and then click the browser closed. Exhale. No looking back. I turn on music over the speakers and start bopping my head along to shed all worries. Boris joins me, and the beat does make me feel better.

"Come here," I tell the big dog, lifting his front paws up onto my shoulders. For a few measures we sway together—a fitting celebration of this next big step. Now all I have to do is discover Cap's and Cholula's secret talents, and we're set.

13

That evening, Micki helps me move my things from our place to the tiny store apartment. Cap and Cho circle our legs, but Boris stays away. If I didn't know better, I'd say he still feels guilty for sending Harvey summersaulting down the stairs.

"It's the end of an era," Micki mopes as we carry bags and boxes up the stairs.

"Three years—pretty short era. Plus, I'll be back."

She bumps my arm with her shoulder. "You know what I mean."

"I know. And I'm really sorry."

She shakes her head. "Don't be. Like you said, it's temporary, and Jaz was actually hoping to stay a bit longer, so I think this will work out okay. She can pay rent now that she has a job."

My vision clouds at the thought of Canine King. Despite what's happened, Leo hasn't taken down his competing door-buster. Showing his true colors.

"God, you have way too much fabric," Micki says after bringing the third box up and tucking it in a corner.

I didn't think I had that many belongings, but for this space, I have plenty. After I set up my sewing machine on the small table, fit my clothes next to Harvey's in the closet, and tuck a box of photos and books under the bed, I've run out of space. Anything else I don't immediately need will have to go into storage if Jaz wants it out of the way.

The doctor calls right as we finish. "I'll take it downstairs," I tell Micki. "Be right back."

To my great relief, everything's gone well, and Harvey is resting.

"We received a call from a Lynda Lewis earlier about transfer to Dalebrook once Mr. Morton is ready," the doctor says. "Are you aware of this?"

Thank God. Mom came through with a nursing home placement. "I know my mother was making arrangements. In your professional opinion, is that the right place for him? I want to be sure he'll receive exactly the care he needs to get better."

"Oh yes, Dalebrook is one of the best. He'll be in their rehab wing. I think you'll both be very happy."

That's the first piece of good news I've had today, and I thank the doctor and tell her I'll be by to see Harvey tomorrow during visiting hours. Then I hang up and take a deep breath. Everything will work out. Everything will be fine.

"Hey!" Micki hollers, peering down from upstairs. "Think Harv will mind if I have this ice cream in the freezer? I'm starving."

"I'm sure it's fine as long as you—"

A loud yelp cuts me off and makes Micki spin around.

"Did you leave the freezer open?" I ask, bolting up the stairs. "You never leave it open. Cholula gets her—"

"Shit." Micki covers her mouth in her hands. "Her tongue is stuck."

"Damn it, Cho." I crouch next to the little beast and pet her back. She peers up at me even as she tries to tug her tongue free of the built-up ice at the bottom of the freezer. "Get me a glass of water," I tell Micki. "Room temperature."

With the water applied, Cholula is soon free and not much worse for wear. She barks twice and starts zooming, up onto the bed, down around the table, back and forth. She finally skids to a stop by the bathroom door—or rather, the door stops her short—and promptly lies down and falls asleep.

"Man, dogs are so weird," Micki says. "Sorry about the tongue thing. Are you sure she's okay?"

"She's fine. You didn't know." I grab the paper towels and clean up the water that's leaked onto the floor. "She has a thing for cold stuff. In the winter, she's impossible to take for walks because she tries to eat all the snow. And I mean all of it." I stand and wipe my hands on my bell-bottom jeans. "Crisis averted."

"You've really got your hands full, don't you?" Micki looks at me with sympathy.

I can't do anything else but agree that I do.

After she leaves, I try to get settled in the alcove bed. The mattress has seen cushier days, so it's hard to get comfortable. An hour in, I give up and open my computer instead. I have a message from Al that he sent after I logged off last night. *Last night...* It feels like weeks ago.

AlCaponesGhost25: Do you have good friends? The kind you can count on no matter what?

I think about the day I've just had and Micki being there.

SingerQueen: I do. My best friend. Not sure what I'd do without her.

AlCaponesGhost25: You're lucky.

SingerQueen: You don't have anyone like that?

AlCaponesGhost25: Not really. I thought I did—people I worked with at my old job—but I left and they didn't last.

SingerQueen: You'll make new ones at your new job.

AlCaponesGhost25: Maybe.

SingerQueen: Just make sure their riddle standards are up to par. *winky face emoji*

AlCaponesGhost25: What if my standards are too high?

He's serious, I realize. He's grappling with something.

SingerQueen: It's not rocket science. If your standards are too high, you lower them. Perfection is overrated anyway.

AlCaponesGhost25: Is it though?

SingerQueen: 100%. If I needed all my seams to be straight, I'd never finish a single garment. Flaws can be charming. And they're human.

AlCaponesGhost25: I guess you're right. Did you always know you wanted to be a designer?

SingerQueen: Not always. I went to college for something else, but it wasn't right.

AlCaponesGhost25: I feel that. Your first choice not being the right one, I mean.

SingerQueen: Yeah.

AlCaponesGhost25: Cool job, though. Do you get to travel a lot? Meet tons of interesting people?

I swallow hard and then look around at where I am, at the sleeping dogs in the corner. Tomorrow, I'll open the store, work to up our sales, and find new ways to get the better of Leo so I can make Pop proud. Tomorrow and the next day and every day after that, too.

I push the thought away.

> **SingerQueen:** All the time.
> **AlCaponesGhost25:** Nice.

I nod to myself. Yes, I imagine it would be.

14

I spend the next couple of days getting my bearings with the back-end intricacies of the store, making sure Harvey is settled into the rehabilitation home, and calling agility centers. I find only one that has an affordable class with openings. While I am dedicated to this venture, there are limits to my commitment, and paying annual membership fees is a hard no.

On the flip side, I've started playing around with designing a website, and I've also set up a table in the storage room for my sewing machine, so at times when the store isn't busy, I'm working on filling commissioned orders. In addition to the Cleopatra getup, I'm in the process of making two haunted mansion costumes for a couple who runs the pumpkin patch two towns over. They've given me free rein, so it's proving to be a nice distraction.

That's where I am Thursday evening when my cell lights up with Mom's picture.

"I don't have long," she says in greeting. "Your father is waiting."

"Okay...What's going on?"

"I just talked to Dad. He'd like his green robe and a bag of those blue corn chips he loves, so if you could bring that to him tomorrow, that would be great."

I had this conversation with Harvey already. He knows I'll only be able to get out to Dalebrook when I can borrow Micki's car, and I tell Mom as much.

"Isn't Dad's car right there? Or did it break down again?"

"No, he had it fixed. But you know I don't drive stick."

"Pfft. Your grandpa needs you, Coralynn. I'm sure you'll figure it out." She says something to my dad on the other end before she comes back. "Your dad says it's easy. Break, clutch, shift, let up gently."

I'm pretty sure there's more to it. Harvey tried to teach me when I was in high school, and for a while I almost got it, but when I moved away for college, my brain had to make room for other information and promptly dumped everything I knew about manual transmissions.

"You can do it," Mom insists. "I've got to run. We're doing a guided tour at Yellowstone today. I'll send you pictures. Your dad spent a fortune on new hiking boots, so we'd better put them to use!"

At this reminder of my parents' decently flush bank accounts, I almost ask Mom for help. A small investment in the store, a loan even, to pull us out of the red. Except I know she'll say no. My parents are all about individual responsibility, and she's made clear more than once how she feels about Pop still working at his age.

"Okay, have fun," I say instead.

"And you'll bring Dad his things?" Mom asks.

"If I can get the car running."

We hang up, and with rising apprehension, I add to my list: learn to drive stick.

I get up early to give Harvey's car a try. It's an old, gray Ford Mustang that he's had as long as I can remember. It smells of pine air freshener and wet dog, but he's kept it meticulously clean throughout the years, and the seat hugs me like it wants me to be there.

"Okay, Pop," I mutter, inserting the key into the ignition. "Show me your ways."

I turn the key, and the car immediately rocks forward and dies. I grip the steering wheel tightly, my foot pressing down hard on the brake pedal. This feels familiar in all the wrong ways.

After two more unsuccessful attempts, I pull out my phone and search for a stick shift primer for dummies. "Make sure the car is in neutral," I read. It's not. Harvey has left it in first gear. "Press down on the clutch and keep it down while you start the car." Okay, here goes...

The engine thrums to life without issue. "Haha! Gotcha." I read on. "Move the gear shift into first gear. Gradually let up the clutch as you start driving." It's starting to come back to me, but that doesn't make me sweat any less. Here goes.

This time, I manage to get out of the parking space before the engine stalls again, and after two more tries, I realize there's such a thing as going too slowly. I'm going to have to be more deliberate with the gas pedal, no matter how much I don't want to die. I'm in charge now. I need to be able to drive myself places.

I do a few starts and stops around the parking lot, thanking all the gods no one else is out and about, and when I've managed this small feat, the next logical step is to venture around the block. The first turn is fine. I stop at the stop sign without incident, the engine still purring, but when I make a left onto the street that runs in front of the store, there's a truck parked in my lane and oncoming traffic in the other. Instantly, I forget the clutch, and the car stops in the middle of the street. Damn it! What order was it again? Brake, clutch, gas, shift? Clutch, shift, brake? Somewhere near me, a car honks, and that doesn't help my frazzled state.

I'm on the verge of tears when there's a knock on the passenger window. Leo gestures for me to open it.

"Is this part of your marketing strategy?" he asks. "Forcing customers to stop in front of the store? Because I don't think it's working."

As if wanting to emphasize the truth in his words, the car behind me honks again. "One sec!" Leo hollers to them. Then to me, "What's going on?"

The impulse to unbuckle and run away is overwhelming. How he must enjoy this. "I'm having some issues with the car," I say, not looking at him.

Out of the corner of my eye, I see him glance down at the center console and up to where I'm still holding on to the wheel for dear life.

"Is the issue that you don't know how to drive stick?" he asks.

"Maybe."

He taps both hands on the open window frame. "Okay, move over." He comes around to my side and opens my door.

"Why?"

"So we can get the car out of the street." The honking behind us intensifies. "Seems kind of like a priority, no?"

I'd protest, but he's not wrong. I crawl over to the passenger seat, and two minutes later, he's completed the lap around the block and parked us safely back in Harvey's spot.

Leo turns off the engine, and for a long moment, neither of us speaks.

"I think 'thank you' are the words you're looking for." He unbuckles his seat belt but doesn't get out.

Somehow, he's now come to my aid twice this week. It unnerves me, but at least he doesn't seem to be gloating about it.

"Thank you. I would have figured it out." It might have taken a while, but still...

"Of course you would. How's Harvey by the way?"

His eyes soften as he says Pop's name. Or maybe that's just in my imagination.

"He's moved from the hospital to the nursing home. He's fine. Just logistics, you know. Getting settled."

"Good." He smiles and reaches for the door handle. "I've got to get back to the store. Deliveries." Halfway out the door, he looks back at me. "You're not going to take off into traffic again as soon as I leave, are you?"

"Duh."

"Just making sure. Got to crawl before you walk."

Okay, wiseass. Problem is, I need to know how now. Harvey needs me tonight. The dog training starts tomorrow. There's no time for crawling.

Leo closes the door behind him, and the air around me quiets and stills as he walks away. The morning light illuminates a few stray specks of dust on the dash that I wipe off while I try to conjure a next step. As I move, the seat creaks beneath me, and the key chain swings gently from the ignition.

I reach over to grab it, and at that moment, the most terrible idea of the century strikes. My only explanation is that desperation tops pride.

I jump out of the car as Leo is approaching the corner and call his name.

He turns. "Yeah?"

"Any chance you could show me how to do it?"

He looks from me to the car. "You want me to…No, I don't think so. I've got a business to run as you know. Trying to stay competitive."

Okay, I deserve that. My mind scrambles for something to bargain with. Lord knows I have no money. "I'll mention your opening on our social media."

He starts walking again, but backward this time. "You're not on social media. Bye, Cora."

How does he know that? Has he been net stalking me? I don't have time to consider this further. He's getting away. "If not for me then for Harvey." It's a shot in the dark, but the two of them did seem to hit it off.

Leo slows. "Oh, that's playing dirty."

I take a couple of steps closer. "Please. I need a way to get to the nursing home or Pop will be all alone there. A few lessons are all I ask. It's not like I'm starting from scratch."

His expression says he begs to differ, but to his credit, he doesn't spell it out.

I go in for the kill. "Unless you don't trust your teaching skills, of course."

He squares his shoulders. "There's nothing wrong with my teaching skills. I'll have you driving that thing in no ti—" His eyes widen. "Ah, very clever, I see what you did there."

I smile. "So you'll help? He wants me to bring him a few things tonight."

Leo runs a hand through his hair and sighs. "Fine." He puts a finger up to stop me from responding. "On one condition."

My stomach dips. If he asks me to let Canine King best Happy Paws, I—

"Look, I know you're feeling a little territorial perhaps and protective of Harvey and his pet shop, but—"

I cross my arms. "With all due respect, you don't know anything about me."

He mimics my stance and considers me for a long moment. "Debate team, art club, volleyball…Parents' names are Martin and Lynda, and apparently you hold a twenty-year town record for most money made off a lemonade stand in one day."

I gape at him. "You looked me up?"

"You had the advantage of knowing me. It didn't seem fair. What was in that lemonade?"

"I'm getting light serial-killer vibes here."

"Well, being forced to listen to incessant meowing in the store for three days admittedly made me feel a little stabby." He raises an eyebrow.

I could deny it was me, but what's the point? "Okay, that's fair."

"Besides, it was hardly a deep dive into your personal vaults," he says. "I checked my yearbook and talked to my aunts. Over five hundred dollars in a day?"

"They knew about that?"

"They remember standing in line for it. Come on, tell me. What was your secret?" His eyes glitter as he tilts his head forward, all earnest and innocent.

To my dismay, it works. "It was 104 degrees that day, and my grandparents' house was on a busy corner. That's all. Sorry to disappoint."

"Still impressive."

I clear my throat. "You said you had a condition?"

"Yes." He lets his arms relax at his sides. "I'll teach you to drive stick if you agree to a truce. No more of this sabotage and prank business—it's below both of us. We're adults."

When he says it like that...

I blink up at him, weighing the pros and cons. Maybe I can be mad at him but still be civil. For Harvey. "Okay." I nod. "A truce."

He stares at me for a moment, something that looks almost like relief playing behind his eyes. Then he turns on his heels. "I close at six. I'll be over at six thirty."

15

I locked the front door," Leo says when I come down the stairs after closing. He's browsing the mishmash of our displays, and for the first time ever, I'm ashamed of what the place looks like. Compared to Canine King, we are the dumpy, backwater cousin.

"Thanks, must have forgotten." I grab my scarf from under the counter but avoid looking at the stack of red-stamped envelopes next to it. Got to shake it off. I have a plan. Sort of. "Okay, ready. Show me your manual transmission ways, master."

My word choice triggers a glint in his eyes. "Master, huh?"

I blush at my unfortunate choice of words. "Whatever. Come on."

Leo drives us out of town and narrates his moves as we go. "It's a flow—clutch, gear, release, clutch, gear, release. Once you're on the road and you're giving it enough gas, you'll have no issue. It's harder to start and drive slowly." He pulls into a pharmacy parking lot so we can switch seats.

"How'd you learn to drive stick anyway?" I warily wrap my fingers around the steering wheel.

He buckles into the passenger seat. "Started driving a tractor at twelve."

"You did not."

"We had horses and I helped in the stables when I could. Sometimes that included moving bales of hay from one end of the property to the other."

Royal Equine, I think. That makes sense. "So, not working the fields, then?"

He laughs, his whole face lighting up. The sound makes something long dormant flutter in my chest. I swallow to make it go away. He's only doing this for Harvey, I remind myself. It's an agreement, and no one wants it to be anything else. Not me, not Leo. Okay, maybe Micki, but inside this well-loved automobile, she doesn't count.

"No. Sorry to disappoint. So, you ready?"

"Yes." I nod once. "Walk me through it?"

He does, and I start the car.

"Now let up the clutch at the same time you give some gas."

The engine stalls out.

"Fucking thing." I'm starting to sweat, and there's a strand of hair stuck to my cheek. I push it behind my ear and pull the neckline of my sweater out to fan my skin. Ah, that's better.

"Relax." Leo's voice sounds oddly strangled. "You don't have to grip the knob so hard." He places his hand on top of mine to demonstrate a softer hold. It's gone before I can react, but the sensation lingers across my knuckles. "A little more gas this time."

I do what he asks and voilà! "I'm doing it." I laugh.

"See. It's not that difficult. Now stop at the stop sign. Stop!"

The car stalls again as I hit the brake hard. "Sorry, I got too excited."

"Sweet Jesus, you're going to kill me, aren't you?"

"Please, it wasn't that bad."

"Agree to disagree. Now try again, and let's obey the rules of the road this time."

I suppress a childish urge to stick my tongue out at him and instead do what he asks. And while I somehow manage to kill the engine at almost every traffic light, which makes the drive take twice as long as it should, eventually we make it to our destination.

I park in the Dalebrook parking lot and grin at Leo. "I did it."

He feigns exaggerated relief, which earns him a light slap on the shoulder.

"You know," he says when we're walking to the entrance, "I think I'm going to need you to say it out loud."

"Say what?"

"That I'm a good teacher."

He's trailing behind me, so I turn around. "Is that still bothering you? Wow, male egos...Fine. You're a good teacher."

Is it just me or does his back actually straighten at my words?

"Thank you." He slows his steps. "Hey, maybe I should wait in the car. If you two have stuff to chat about."

"Oh, um..." We do, but it's also cold out, and I have no idea how long this will take. Time to put that civility into play. "You don't have to. There's a TV. Plus, Pop likes you. Don't ask me why. I mean, unless you think coming with would be weird?"

I pause by the front door, deferring to him. He looks back toward the car and then reaches for the door handle. "After you."

Animated voices reach us in the hallway outside Harvey's room.

"I thought we'd get dim lights and sleeping elders," Leo says in a hushed voice.

I smile at him as a female voice calls out, "No way. The brunette, Marissa, suits him so much better."

"Is she the one with short hair or long hair?" Harvey asks as we step inside. He lights up at the sight of us. "Cora. And Leo?" His eyebrows jump.

"Are we interrupting something?" I ask, setting my bag down on a chair next to Harvey's bed.

"Sylvia is introducing me to *The Bachelor*. Have you seen it? It's a wild ride."

"I know what it is. Hi," I say to Sylvia.

Harvey makes introductions, and we learn that Sylvia is there visiting her brother Charles, Harvey's roommate, who's recovering from a stroke.

"You're looking better, Pop," I say after Sylvia excuses herself and leaves to go finish her show in the common room.

"I feel better. The staff here is great, the food's great—"

"I brought you your chips." I fish a bag out of my backpack. "And the robe is in that bag."

"Thanks, kiddo. How about you? Anything new?"

Leo excuses himself. "I'm going to go find a vending machine or something." He takes a step toward the door.

"Leo." Harvey says his name as if he'd forgotten he was there. "How was your first week?"

"Leo's helping me remember how to drive your car," I say.

"Is he now? Whoo boy. Not the easiest task." Harvey winks at Leo.

"Thanks a lot, Pop."

"I care too much about my life to confirm or deny," Leo says. "But the week has been good. Eventful." He turns to me with a smirk. "I'll be back in a bit."

Once Harvey and I are alone, I sit down next to him, and for a few minutes, we watch the muted screen in silence. I haven't been following this season's show, so I don't know who anyone is, but Harvey seems satisfied with the outcome of the rose ceremony.

"How are you really, kiddo?" he asks after turning off the TV. "You look tired."

I give a pointed glare to his bed. "You're asking me?"

"Well, it's not like I don't realize I've put you in a bit of a bind. Obviously, I have complete faith in you handling things like a champ, but I do feel bad."

I take his hand. "You just worry about healing. I actually got an order on Etsy two minutes after I posted one of my Scarlett O'Haras the other day."

I tell him about my costumes, and we talk about the Halloween decorations in storage and how I'm helping Micki study for her physiology exam.

"Oh, and I completely forgot. I've signed up for the booth *and* the dog show at Winter Fest this year." I lean in and lower my voice. "Pop, the grand prize is fifteen thousand dollars."

His eyes go round. "Is it really? The whole thing will be so much bigger then. People will come from out of state and—"

Leo pushes open the door. "Junior Mints anyone? Or Funyuns?" He holds up the packages. "Pickings were slim," he says to explain the mismatched loot.

And yet he was gone for over half an hour. He must have stayed away to give us time to talk.

"Everything okay?" Leo asks. "Did I interrupt something?"

"Um, no. It's nothing," I say. "We were just talking about Winter Fest."

"Oh yeah? What's that?" Leo rips open the snack bag. The pungent smell of fried onions fills the room.

"The county holiday extravaganza in December." I steal a quick glance at Harvey, who's adjusting the collar of his nightshirt. "Think flea market meets Santa's village meets carnival fair. People come from all over, and we always have a booth because of…" My voice trails off. *He doesn't need to know about the dog show, does he?*

"Cat got your tongue?" Leo nudges me with his elbow.

"Um, what? No. We do decent business there. That's all." I put a smile in place, hoping Pop won't see it necessary to amend my description. "Anyway, we should probably get going. It's getting late."

We drive the first five minutes of the way in silence. I stall the car only once, so a definite improvement. But the longer we're in the car, the bigger the risk of Leo bringing up Winter Fest again. I need to distract him until we're home.

"You're on social media, right?" I ask.

Leo frowns. "Sure. Why?"

"Do you get new customers that way? Like, is it worth it?" I glance at him. Is he taking my bait?

He tilts his head to the headrest. "It absolutely makes a difference. A website makes you more accessible, it makes you findable, and a social media account lets potential customers interact with you, get updates, get to know what you're about. Nowadays, your community isn't simply your immediate physical location but a much wider network. Who's to say you wouldn't get a follower who lives downtown, but because of something particular that you have to offer, they're willing to make the trek out here? I don't know, that's how I think of it."

I nod. This is more interesting than I thought. "I guess I'm a bit overwhelmed with it. Stuck in the 'olden days' as we are at Happy Paws." I cringe at my corny attempt at a joke. "Any-hoo. So, say I wanted to get on Instagram. What would I put on there?"

"Well…you need to stand out. What's something unique about Happy Paws that could make customers talk about you?"

I slow down and swivel the steering wheel a full three-sixty, pondering this. "That's actually helpful."

He smiles. "Guess I'm losing my edge, giving advice to the competition."

"You're finally willing to admit we're competitors, then?" I put the car in park.

"No. No, that's not what I meant. And you can't give me shit here because, if you didn't notice, you now drive stick. You're welcome."

I look around, noticing for the first time where we are. I've parked behind the store. How about that?

"See, I'm not evil incarnate." Behind the levity, there's a pleading look in his eyes. One I haven't seen before.

I look away. "I never said you were."

When the silence stretches, we both unbuckle and get out of the car, but for a moment, our eyes come together again across the roof. His lips part as if he's about to speak, but then he clamps them shut.

"I should head inside," I say.

"Yeah, me too." He starts walking.

I call his name, even though I'm not sure why. All I know is that this abrupt ending isn't right. "Thanks for tonight. I do appreciate it."

He must feel differently because he waves without turning around, and then he's gone.

16

Living History Illinois Flockify DM, Saturday 12:04 PM

AlCaponesGhost25: Want to tease some history nerds together?

SingerQueen: Always. How?

AlCaponesGhost25: I'm posting a poll for people to vote on the most important Illinoisan. The options are Henry Ford, Martin Luther King Jr, Clara Barton, and JFK

SingerQueen: But none of them are from Illinois.

AlCaponesGhost25: Exactly!

SingerQueen: LOL AlCaponesGHOUL is more like it.

AlCaponesGhost25: *devil emoji*

The day passes quickly with the distraction of spirited conversations online, but after work, I load the dogs up and head out of town. Cholula is restless with excitement in the back seat while Cap glares at me for stuffing him into this moving tin can.

"We'll get through this, bud," I tell him. "We've got to be more like Cho now, okay? Ready for adventure."

There are several other dog-human pairs already warming up when we arrive. Some are doing recall, others weaving between cones. All look like they've been taking classes forever. In the back of the property, there's a large hangar-like building, and in front of it, two fenced-in fields and a smattering of small buildings. I leave the dogs in the car and go up to the main one to check in.

As I reach for the handle, the door opens from within and a smiling Leo exits, Tilly at his side.

"Cora?" His expression falters at the edges. "What are you doing here?"

You have got to be kidding me. "What are *you* doing here?" I counter.

"I asked first."

I purse my lips. "If you must know, I'm training the dogs."

"Uh-huh." His eyes narrow. "Does it by any chance have something to do with the Winter Fest's dog show?"

My spine stiffens. "How do you know about that?"

"Well, no thanks to you. I went to check out the Winter Fest website after you mentioned it to see if I should get a booth there, too, and whaddaya know? You left out a small detail."

I glance at my car. Two curious faces are following my every move. "I don't know what you're talking about."

"Oh, come on. I don't blame you for not telling me about the contest, though technically one might say it skirts the agreement of our truce, but don't pretend you didn't know exactly what you were doing."

I cross my arms. He's so infuriating. "Fine. Maybe I didn't want more competition from you than I already have, so I chose not to tell you. Clearly, you're more than capable of figuring things out on your own."

He cocks his head. "Sure am. And if you ask me, that's the wrong attitude. Competition is what makes us better."

I scoff. "I take it you've signed up for the show, then?"

"From a marketing standpoint, it's a great opportunity. Lots of visibility. People tend to remember Tilly when they see her."

Tilly looks up upon hearing her name, intent on her owner.

I can't help it—a frustrated growl escapes me.

Leo chuckles. "Guess I'll see you inside. Good luck and may the best dog win."

Even his backside looks cocky as he walks toward the hangar. If I let down my guard in the car the other night, it is now firmly back in place. He's enjoying this way too much, and I can't say I'm looking forward to training Cho and Cap in front of him. They know the basic commands, but many dogs do. I'm sure Tilly is already show material.

I pay my fee and leash up the dogs. Cholula pulls like she's twelve pounds going on forty-eight while Cap moves at a more reasonable pace.

The space is divided into two rectangles—for large and small breeds—separated by temporary three-foot fencing. Leo is in the other enclosure, thankfully, so I'm going to do my best to pretend he's not here. I tie Cap up and start warming up Cho. Keeping her on a leash, I run her around the space a few times to let her get her zoomies out. Then I let her sniff the tunnel, cones, and seesaw at the edge of the space. She's all over that, happily walking up the tilting board without much prompting. Promising.

Next up is Cap. I do the same lap with him, but he only sniffs the end of the tunnel and then returns to me for another treat. "You have to go through it, silly," I coax. He doesn't move. I sure hope the woman with the brown lab isn't signing up for the contest because her dog knows all the tricks. She laps the course again and again, and all I hear is, "Well done, Boxley. Up and over. Yes!"

Leo is also watching them, his face mirroring the discouragement I'm sure is on mine. I can't see Tilly, but I do take heart at his seeming dismay. Maybe I was wrong. Maybe Tilly doesn't have all this down. She is still a puppy after all.

Behind me, Cholula barks for my attention, and after that everything happens too fast to follow. A pale blur flies out of the large breed enclosure, clearing the fencing with margin. It's Tilly, and she lets out a high bark, which sets Cholula off in an even more giddy fit. Before I can reach her, she's snapped the leash and is ready when Tilly reaches us. It's the park all over again. The two dogs circle each other as if they're long-lost besties finally reunited and take off.

"Tilly, here!" Leo calls from afar, but I've seen this before. No matter how purebred Tilly is or how well-behaved at home— Leo's got nothing on Cholula.

I chase after the two dogs to the fence, thinking I'll catch Cho there, but to my surprise, she also clears the obstacle, as small as she is. For a moment, I stop panicking and allow excitement in its place. The choice between Cho and Cap is clear. I've got my contestant. Unfortunately, the other dogs in the arena are getting in on the mayhem, and the shouts from other owners pull me out of my epiphany.

"Call your dog back," one man yells at Leo, who's jogging back and forth depending on what direction the pack is taking, Tilly's limp leash in his hands.

"You know, you really should keep your dog under better control," I tell him with a smirk when I reach him. This time it wasn't Cholula's fault, and I'm more than happy to feed him his own words in place of a humble pie.

"Ha, ha, very funny."

"I think it is. Oh, how the righteous fall. Maybe if you lie down on the ground they'll come back. Worked last time."

He looks down at the sawdust as if considering this.

"I'm joking. Wouldn't want to ruin that fancy leather jacket of yours." What was he thinking wearing that here?

"Then how will we get them back?"

Our eyes trail the romping canines, who clearly have no intention of stopping any time soon.

At that moment, the door opens and the teacher enters with one of the other patrons. She raises a whistle to her mouth and blows a long, high-pitched note. The dogs immediately stop in their tracks.

"Leash up," she calls. Then she looks at me and Leo. "And you two—I'd like to see you both in my office."

Leo and I gather our dogs and walk to the main building.

"Unbelievable," Leo says. "Called to the 'principal's office' like some…" He doesn't finish the sentence but keeps muttering under his breath.

I tug Cho and Cap along across the muddy grounds. "Why are you making such a big deal about this? She probably just wants to remind us of the rules."

"Well, I don't like it."

"Being in trouble? Does it hurt your feelings that someone thinks you fucked up?"

He doesn't respond, but the crease on his brow deepens. I must have hit a nerve.

Once inside, we stand shoulder to shoulder in front of the

matron in charge who's leveling us with the glare to end all glares.

"I am sure I made it clear when we spoke on the phone that we require our clients to have at least a basic level of control over their animals when they attend our classes."

"You did," Leo says.

I nod.

"And yet here we are."

Leo juts his chin out. "Tilly is usually well-behaved. But when she sees Cora's dog—"

I whip my head his way. "It's my fault now? Tilly started it this time."

The woman's ruddy cheeks puff up. "This has happened before?"

"Only once," Leo assures her. "And like I said, it's not typical."

I scoff. "You would blame me. You've disliked Cholula from the get-go. Just because she looks different and doesn't have a fancy pedigree doesn't mean you can throw her under the bus."

"I'm doing nothing of the sort."

"Be that as it may…" The woman demands our attention again. "We will not be inviting you back here."

What? I gape at her. "No, please. I need a place to train my dogs for Winter Fest. I promise this won't happen again. If his dog hadn't gotten loose—"

The woman raises her hand to stop me. "Unfortunately, we have zero tolerance for that sort of thing here. It's for everyone's safety. My hands are tied."

Her words leave a burning, stinging sensation across my skin as if she's slapped me. We're dismissed.

"But I…" My arms fall limply to my side.

The finality in her statement gives me no choice but to walk out of there. Leo is behind me, and halfway to the cars, I do a one-eighty on him. "Thanks a lot," I say. "Without this place, I can't train them, and we can't be in the show. Not only have you ruined my best chance of saving the store, but I'm also out fifty bucks for the registration fee."

"What do you mean 'saving the store'? Are you in trouble?"

Me and my big mouth. "That's none of your business."

"So we'll find a different place," he says, voice placating.

"I've called all of them. And while I'm sure you can afford to join any one of those fancy clubs, I can't." My voice cracks. *Fuck.*

His hand flutters across his hair, clearly uncomfortable. "I'm sorry, okay? I should have had a better hold on Tilly."

"That's right." I wipe my nose with the back of my hand. "And it wasn't Cholula's fault."

"Well, technically, if Cholula hadn't been there..."

I give him the iciest glare I can muster.

"Sure," he says. "It wasn't Cholula's fault."

Another infraction of his comes to mind. "*And* there's nothing wrong with her."

"If you're referring to our run-in in the park, I still think that was a justified question. She looked completely bananas with that ice cream cone in her mouth."

I hate that he's right, but I don't have the energy for this anymore. All I want is to go home and pull a blanket over me. I turn back toward my car.

"Are you going to be okay driving home?" Leo calls after me.

"Does it matter?" I ask.

To that he says nothing. Like I thought.

17

Living History Illinois Flockify DM, Saturday 08:08 PM

SingerQueen: What's your go-to pick-me-up song?

AlCaponesGhost25: Promise not to laugh

SingerQueen: No can do. Tell me anyway?

AlCaponesGhost25: I'm too sexy by Right Said Fred

SingerQueen: OMG LOL Please tell me you dance to it too.

AlCaponesGhost25: My lips are sealed.

SingerQueen: I'm putting it on now. Thank you!

AlCaponesGhost25: Much obliged.

It's a beautiful fall Sunday, cool but sunny, and the trees lining the street down to the park sport their prettiest colors. My first day off since Harvey's accident. I called the agility place back this morning, but they would not be persuaded to take us back. Thankfully, Right Said Fred has taken the edge off my disappointment. Al was right—it's a great mood booster. I'm determined to come up with a different solution because, if I'm certain of one thing, it's that I'll compete in that dog show no matter what. I will do whatever it takes to get Cho ready.

The dogs prance along unburdened by my conundrum, and for a while I try to be more like them—smell all the scents of fall, listen to the birds getting ready to migrate, breathe in the crisp air. I'm momentarily mesmerized by the way the water skips and sprays over the rocks in the Fox River when the calm is interrupted by rhythmic footfalls coming up behind us.

"There you are," Leo says once he reaches us, as if he's been looking for me. He's in track pants and a fitted T-shirt that enhances a muscled physique my palms still remember from the close encounter in the bar. "Great minds think alike."

"Don't think so." I gesture to his forehead. "Judging by how sweaty you are, I assume you're coming back from a run, and *my* great mind would never have such a self-flagellating idea."

To my surprise, he laughs, and I have to pull with all my might to keep Cholula from making a snack of his calf. She's surprisingly strong for such a small dog.

"Wow, you really are one of the prickliest people I've ever met. And I've worked on Wall Street so that's saying something. Were you always like this or is it reserved for me?"

"Just you." I press my lips together.

"You're funny," he says. "Any updates on Harvey?"

"I wasn't trying to be, and no, he has physical therapy right now, so I'll be calling him later." Squinting up at him, I'm briefly distracted by how his hair shimmers gold in the sunlight. Is that natural or does he get it colored? I wouldn't put it past him. I take a deep breath. I did agree to a truce. "But thanks for asking, I guess."

"You're welcome." He looks at me expectantly as if waiting for me to say something else.

I shift from one foot to the other, careful not to step on Boris.

"What can I do for you, Leo? I think I'm currently out of prospects for you to ruin." *Oops. Civility fail...*

"Funny again." He looks off into the distance. Then, after a beat, he says, "Well, basically, I feel really bad about yesterday."

"Yeah?"

"But I've had an idea that might fix it." He hesitates.

"I'm listening. Don't suppose you're closing the store and getting out of Dodge?"

"Ouch." He touches his chest. "Solid Western reference, but no. Um, I just got off the phone with my aunts. Their farm is only fifteen minutes farther than the agility place, and they have plenty of space, so I'm going to use one of their fields to train Tilly."

I scoff. It figures. "Way to rub it in."

"No, you don't get it." A flash of frustration. "I wanted to see if you'd be interested in training there, too. We'd have to get our own obstacle course equipment, but if I know my aunts, there are boards and barrels lying about for us to use." He looks serious and doesn't avert his eyes under my scrutiny.

"What's the catch?" I ask.

"No catch."

"No, I mean, what's in it for you? Why are you being helpful all of a sudden?"

He lets out an amused huff. "I promise there's nothing. I just thought... You need a place to train as much as I do, right? And we've called a truce. Consider it my way of saying sorry. Tilly was the instigator last night."

"Oh." I switch the leashes from one hand to the other and then back again. That *would* help a lot. The door that was almost closed in my mind blows open a little wider again. "Even though we're competing for the same prize?"

A crooked smile. "Like I said—a little competition never hurt anyone."

"Well…" I look straight into his eyes. "As long as you understand I intend to whoop your butt at the show."

"I would expect nothing less." He scans the park and starts jogging in place. "I'm going out there in a couple of hours, so if you've got nothing else planned…"

"Um, no…Yeah…I could probably do that," I hear myself saying. *I could?*

"Great!" He lights up. "Just come by around noon. Oh, and there'll be food." And with that he's off.

I stare after him, feeling as if a microburst just picked me up and set me down wrong side up. "Huh?" I say to no one in particular. This may well be an even worse idea than asking him to teach me how to drive stick.

18

I must be out of my mind agreeing to this. Driving together? Having Sunday lunch at his aunts' place? Training the dogs side by side? But I did say I'd stop at nothing to get Cho ready, and if it puts me back in the race for $15,000 ... I'm going to win this thing, and then I'm going to rub Leo's much-too-handsome face in it. In a civil way, of course.

"Isn't it going to be weird for your aunts that I'm coming along?" I ask in the car. All the dogs are hanging out in the back, and so far, there's been no circus. Well, no circus except Boris letting out melodic howls every time an old-school country song comes on. My grandma only listened to the likes of Loretta Lynn, Patsy Cline, and Dolly so we think he's singing along out of appreciation, but of course it could also be him trying to drown out the sound because he hates it. Tilly and Cholula are sleeping next to each other as if they're litter mates.

Leo drives with one hand, the other arm resting against the center console. He showered and changed out of his running clothes, but he's still dressed more casually than usual in jeans and a threadbare black Yale hoodie. He's pushed the sleeves up his arms, and the muscles in his forearm tense and relax beneath the skin when he shifts his grip. I try not to notice.

"They're looking forward to it." He glances at me, a smile crinkling the corners of his eyes. How is he so at ease in this situation? "The more people the merrier. But I should warn you, they're pretty nosy, so prepare for the third degree."

That makes me even more flustered. "Is it okay if I open a window?"

"Knock yourself out."

The cool air helps. "You should warn *them* they'll be disappointed. I'm not particularly interesting."

"You sure about that?" He looks at me again, longer this time. "Everyone has secrets."

I snort. "If I did, I wouldn't tell you. You're my opposition, remember? I'm not going to supply the ammunition."

"This again? I mean, I'm obviously going to win the fifteen grand, but I'm telling you, Canine King's existence doesn't mean an automatic eradication of Happy Paws."

He really believes it, I can tell. Wall Street must have messed him up. How do I make him see it the way I do? "Remember at the launch—there was a woman there with two black labs?" I ask.

"Sure."

"And that couple in matching parkas with the beagle?"

"Yeah?"

"And the lady with the tight gray perm who was talking to your aunt?"

"What's your point?"

"I know all of them." I rattle off their names as well as the names of their dogs. "They've been loyal to Harvey for years, and yet, there they were, in your store. So you'll have to forgive me if I have a slightly different take on this situation."

He looks like he's thinking hard. Did I finally get through his thick skull?

"I see what you're saying, but—"

I groan. Apparently not.

"No, no, hear me out." He switches hands on the wheel. "What you're saying is, you can only be successful if you get to keep doing things the way you've always done them, for the same customers you've always had with complete monopoly."

Successful might be a stretch…

He continues. "You're assuming because they've checked out Canine King that they'll deem it superior when what you should be doing is ensuring they won't. I'm the underdog here. You're already established."

I frown at him. Pop used the same term.

"Take the Winter Fest show—have you already decided you can't win?"

"No, I wouldn't be here if I had."

"Right. And yet you view the 'competition' between our stores as a done deal. Why?"

"There you go again, admitting we're competitors."

"No, I used air quotes. My point is, you're going to do your best to win first place at the dog show, why not do your best to be number one in business, too? You might find something positive will come of it."

Am I going nuts or is he making sense? The urge to argue is still there, but I'm having a hard time coming up with a rebuttal. "It wouldn't bother you if Happy Paws did better than Canine King?"

"Not at all. It would inspire me to keep up."

I shake my head and look away. "You're weird."

He lets out a hearty laugh that makes my cold, cold ticker warm at the edges. "I'll take it."

We drive the rest of the way in silence. Maybe change can be positive. Maybe all I have to do is give our customers reasons to stay loyal. It's like a lid has been lifted off my bucket of possibilities.

"We're here." Leo points out the side window toward a beautiful farmhouse at the end of a dirt road. There's a large barn behind the main house and a smaller outbuilding to the left. The property is lined by huge oak trees and surrounded by endless cornfields.

Three Australian shepherds come running to the edge of the fenced-in backyard when we park. Tilly starts whining the moment she sees them.

"Are you excited to see your siblings?" Leo asks.

"They're all beautiful," I say.

"You should tell Diane that. She'll love you forever."

I leash up my three mutts and follow Leo to the house. "Should I leave them outside?"

"It's up to you. It's a dog-friendly house, and Tilly is coming with me."

Inside it is. Cholula wouldn't stand for being separated from her new best friend.

"Hello, hello, I'm Dawn." The aunt I wasn't introduced to at the launch comes down the hallway, arms outstretched.

I try to remain in the background while Leo greets her, but he ushers me forward. "Cora Lewis from across the street."

"Of course. Oh, that's some gorgeous hair you have there. Like a forest nymph."

Never heard that one before.

"And who are these three charmers?" She stoops down to the dogs' level.

Cholula immediately starts licking her hand, Cap sits and lifts his front paw, and Boris lays down with his head on his front feet. I introduce them, and Dawn offers plenty of head scratches.

Diane comes out from what I assume is the kitchen. "Sorry, I had to check on the chicken. Hi!" She hugs Leo and then goes straight for me. "Welcome, welcome. I'm so glad this worked out."

I'm starting to feel like a celebrity.

"Wow, you guys have gone all out," Leo says when we enter the kitchen. "Are you expecting more people?"

In front of us on a large granite island is a spread of roast chicken, gravy, two veggie sides, bread rolls, a salad, and a pitcher of lemonade. The room itself is moderate in size but made bigger by a bay-windowed nook with a round table and four chairs. A tall plant sits in a woven pot in one corner, and on the walls hang framed art of varying sizes. Some are clearly made by children while others show defter skills.

"No, just us." Diane places a cork coaster on the counter for the homemade steak fries. "We just added a couple of sides after you texted earlier. No biggie."

"It's not always like this," Leo says to me. "I should bring you along more frequently."

"I think we'd all enjoy that," Dawn says with a wink.

Okay...

Leo glances my way. "Let's just eat, so we can get outside."

"Now, Cora," Diane says when we're all seated in front of loaded plates, "will this be your first time competing in a dog show?"

I finish chewing a mouthful of garlicky chicken and nod. "Yeah, I doubt our dogs would be allowed within fifty feet of a regular show." I look over my shoulder at Boris, Cho, and Cap. Cholula looks up, her tongue flopping sideways out her mouth like a tie set askew. "They're not exactly purebreds."

Diane keeps asking questions about how the dogs came to be in our care. I tell her the story of my grandma's shelter and how Pop had to downsize when she died.

"I always liked Martha," Diane says of my grandmother. "She and my mom were friends. You look a lot like her."

"I do?"

"She wore her hair in a braid like that, too. She could almost sit on it. I remember admiring it when I was little."

This is news to me. As long as I knew her, she wore her hair in a wavy, shoulder-length bob.

The conversation delves deeper into Diane's childhood, and I learn that she and Leo's mom, Annabeth, grew up right here in this house, and that it's been in their family for two generations before that. "We've had some work done to it, of course, but the general layout is the same," Diane says. "A good, old family homestead. What do your parents do, Cora?"

"They were dentists. They retired when I was in high school and sold the house so they could travel. I moved in with my grandparents."

"Wait, they left you?" Leo asks, frowning.

Dawn shares a look with Diane. "And you were okay with that?"

My parents told me the day the realtor came by to get the house ready for showings. They'd already talked to my grandparents and bought me an old Corolla so I'd be able to drive myself to school. Everything was taken care of. But, no, I wouldn't say I was okay with it. I was sixteen, and my parents were done being parents.

"It's not a big deal," I say, ignoring the sympathy suffusing the air. "They worked hard. They deserve to spend their time however they want." I move a piece of bread to the other side of my plate, grab my glass of lemonade, and then set it back down. No one's ever asked me to explain this before. "It's their life. Their choice."

Leo puts his silverware on the empty plate with a clang. "Enough with the third degree you two," he says as if sensing my need for a topic change. "How about some dessert?"

"Yes, good idea." Dawn gets out of her chair. "There's apple pie and ice cream."

I smile up at Leo, grateful for the diversion. It's not that I don't understand how my parents' decision might rub people the wrong way, but I'm not going to throw them under the bus. We were always like that; my parents did their thing, I did mine. I would have been more surprised if they had asked my opinion. "Sounds wonderful. As long as we keep it away from Boris. Apple is his favorite. I'll help clear the table."

"Sorry we're so nosy," Dawn says to me in the kitchen. "I get it. Families are complicated. I moved out at seventeen and never looked back."

"You did?"

"Yeah, but they were assholes. Not keen on me 'choosing' a life without a husband and kids." She nods at the framed wedding invitation next to the window.

"Ah." I skim the cursive writing that's framed by a garland of wildflowers:

Diane Kirtz & Dawn McInnis

July 10, 2014

Something stirs in my mind. *McInnis*—where have I heard that name before?

"Yeah, tradition before everything else. Kind of like Leo's dad."

My ears perk up, and I push the previous thought away. "How so?"

"John's a hard man." Dawn shakes her head. "Adores Annabeth like she's one of the seven wonders of the world, which I suppose is something, but he was always tough on those boys. They could do nothing right. And he only got worse after the accident."

Leo has a brother? What accident? There's so much I don't know.

"Poor Annabeth. Never been the same." Dawn sighs.

Just then, Leo comes around the corner. "What do you say we head out to the field?"

I tear my attention away from Dawn. That's right. That's what we're actually doing here.

My curiosity will have to wait. Time to get this training thing started.

19

Not without regret do I follow Leo outside. Part of me wants to stay in the kitchen and learn everything I can about him, but another knows I'm better off removing myself from the temptation.

"They like you," he says once we've let the dogs loose. Boris stays by our feet, but Cap, Cholula, Tilly, and her siblings are running laps. Cap with his bowed legs falls behind but still lets out happy barks every few yards. I throw him a stick, and he brings it straight back for a repeat.

"It's mutual. And I haven't had a meal like that in forever."

He grins. "Get used to it. If we're going to practice here, Diane will insist on feeding you."

He's standing close enough to me that I smell the minty floral notes of his aftershave.

"So, how are we going to work this?" I ask, putting another yard between us. "Cholula is going to need a lot of training, but I don't want to get in anyone's way."

"You've decided to run her in the show?"

"She's the fastest." Hardly a qualifying trait on its own, but I have to work with what I've got.

"I'll probably come out here a couple times during the week, plus the weekend." He looks away. "We can coordinate, or you can come alone. It's up to you."

He's different out here, his voice deeper, calmer. I glance at his profile as he laughs at something the dogs are doing. Could it be that I have judged him too harshly? "We may as well coordinate," I say. "Our schedules are pretty similar."

His perfect teeth gleam in the sun at that. "True. Okay cool."

This doesn't mean I'm letting my guard down again. If anything, it will give me a chance to gauge the competition—that's why I'm not putting up a fight. In case anyone was wondering. Keep your friends close and your enemies closer.

"Dawn said she put some cones outside the shed." He points and veers left. "Do you have a plan for what to start with or do you not want to say?"

I'm supposed to have a plan? "I don't. Do you?"

"Of course."

"Why am I not surprised?"

"There's nothing wrong with being prepared. How do you know what direction you're going or how to measure your progress if you don't have set goals?"

I stop and turn to the sniffing wolfhound who's making me fall behind. "Come on, Boris. Pick it up."

"Watch your step." Leo skirts a water-filled tire track.

"If Cholula does what I tell her, I'll know I've made progress. And my goal is for her to be the best."

"That's it? Personally, I prefer more detail." He pulls out a small notebook from his pocket and shows me the list of dates for the training sessions leading up to the contest and what he plans on working on each time.

"You are such a nerd." I laugh and grab the notebook from him. "Day one: recall." I look up. "Good choice. I think I'll be doing the same." I scan the rest of the page, tension brewing. "You're not playing around."

He takes the book back. "It's for a lot of money."

Ain't that the truth? I'm going to have to step up my game.

After the dogs get their zoomies out, Cholula, Cap, Boris, and I move to one end of the field, and Leo and Tilly to the other. Cholula and Tilly's love for each other works in our favor because every time we let them go, they run to each other, allowing us to call them back. I'm equally thrilled and surprised that Cholula does a lot better than Tilly, who could not care less about Leo's company while her tiny BFF is nearby.

"Would you mind if I stand on the same side as you?" Leo asks when we've been working for twenty minutes, and the dogs are getting a break. "Maybe she'll listen better."

"That's fine. I'm going to see what Cho thinks of the cones."

"Already?"

I like that he sounds impressed. "Too bad your schedule will only let you do recall today. Written in ink—pretty set in stone…" I give him a cheeky smile.

"That's hilarious," he says behind me as I head to the shed. "So funny."

"Tilly does kind of look like she needs the practice."

"Yeah, yeah. You're not wrong."

While Leo keeps working on getting Tilly to stay and come when he tells her, I lead Cholula on a leash through a set of eight cones, back and forth, spacing them closer and closer together to introduce a weave. Boris is sleeping, and Cap waddles around exploring the outskirts of the field, occasionally returning to check on us.

"How much longer do you think you'll be going?" Leo calls eventually. "I think Tilly is done."

"Cho, too." I let my soon-to-be champion off the leash and instantly she heads for Tilly. The two dogs bark with elation and take off.

"Looks like you made great progress." Leo picks up two of my cones and stacks them.

"Yeah, she's a quick learner. It's easy to underestimate her because of how she looks, but she's super smart." I reach for another cone, but Cap gets to it first. He's decided to help with cleanup, and the orange plastic wobbles between his jaws as he happily struts away. "No, you little stinker. Over here."

"I think he's jealous Cholula got to have all the fun," Leo says.

"Cap." I sharpen my voice. "That's not yours." I follow him, but he feints every time I get close. "Oh, you…" I straighten and put my hands on my hips. "Captain Spots von Puppington, get back here right now!"

Leo comes up next to me. "Now, that's a mouthful."

"Works, though. Look, he dropped it."

Cap stares at us, a string of drool still connecting his lips to the cone on the ground.

"Are you going to let me have it?" I ask, but as soon as I take a step in his direction, he shoves his whole head into the cone, and…it's stuck. He lifts his conehead in the air and makes a run for it, heading straight for the side of the barn, as blind as Boris.

"Shit." I take off after him, followed by Cholula and Tilly, who also want to be part of this new fun game. They dance around my legs, and I sense more than hear Leo yell out a warning before I trip and go flying headfirst into one of the muddy puddles. It's my loud "Aaaaah!" that finally makes Cap slow down—and right on time, too, or he'd have hit the barn wall head-on.

Leo reaches me a second later. "Are you okay?"

I roll over to sitting and shake out my mud-soaked sleeves. A laugh bubbles up my chest.

"What's so funny? You just fell. Your clothes are ruined."

"But he looked hysterical running. Poor thing must be terrified." When Leo remains unconvinced, I add, "I'm fine. Please go get the faceless unicorn over there before he takes off again."

Cap has plopped down on the ground, the cone swaying back and forth as if he's searching for a radio signal.

"On it." Leo leaves, and I heave myself off the ground. "Coming to help you, bud," he calls on approach.

The pant legs of my jeans slosh against each other as I join them. "What were you thinking, you goof?" I rub Cap's ears. "You could have gotten hurt."

"Here." Leo hands me a monogrammed handkerchief from his pocket, because of course he carries one of those around. "You have some…" He gestures to my face.

"Thanks." I try as best as I can to clean the splatters off my cheek. "Did I get it?"

"Let me see." He steps into my space, stirring up the air with faint traces of chilled leather. With a flick of his head, he prompts me to tilt my face up. "No, there's still— Hold on." He takes the handkerchief from me and then pauses, his hand inches from my chin. "May I?"

His jacket is open, and the zippered hem sticks out just enough to brush against my sweater. The jagged edge scratches the wool as if it wants to grab hold, a minuscule tug that makes my belly flop. I give him a small nod.

Very gently, he braces the right side of my jaw with his fingertips so that he can wipe my left cheek. His skin is cool, his touch steady as he adjusts his grip and tilts my head for better access. When his pinkie slips down to my throat, I feel it all the way up my scalp. The prickling sensation makes my eyelids heavy. It's very confusing.

"There," he says, finally. "Better."

"Thanks." I push my hair behind my ear and look up at him. He's still close. Too close? I take a step back.

"But it's hardly going to be enough." He smiles and shoves the muddy fabric back into his pocket. "You're soaked."

I look down at my abysmal figure. "I am, aren't I?"

His grin widens. "Come on." He nods toward the house. "Let's get you properly cleaned up."

Diane springs into action, offering a shower and a change of clothes, and I gratefully accept. I have a feeling Leo wouldn't let me back in his SUV if I didn't.

I emerge fifteen minutes later, freshly scrubbed and dressed in someone's old high school sweatshirt. *Go Falcons* it reads in maroon across my chest behind tangles of wet hair. The sweatpants are equally oversized and so comfortable. The dogs are resting in a heap in the foyer, and Leo and Diane are in her office with the French doors closed. I pause on the stairs at the serious expressions on their faces. Diane hands him something flat and white. A letter maybe? His shoulders slump.

"There you are." Dawn peeks out from the kitchen. "Everything go okay? I've put your clothes in the washer. They'll be ready for you next time."

I jog the last few steps down. "You didn't have to do that." I look at Leo again, and the question is out before I can stop it. "Do you know what they're talking about? He looks upset."

Dawn waves it away. "He's fine. Don't worry about it."

Leo sees me through the small windowpanes and straightens. He says something to Diane and opens the door. "I'll be right there. Ready to head out?"

"I'm ready."

He shoves whatever Diane gave him in his back pocket and kisses his aunt on the cheek. "I'll handle it," he says.

"Handle what?" I ask, innocently, when he joins me.

"Just some, um, paperwork. Nothing important."

Hmm...I believe I've found a new task for Jaz.

20

Living History Illinois Flockify DM, Sunday 11:10 PM

SingerQueen: Feeling philosophical. Do you think people deserve second chances?

AlCaponesGhost25: Is this a historical question? In that case no. I can think of a number of horrid megalomaniacs who shouldn't have gotten even a first chance.

SingerQueen: No, more like friends and family.

AlCaponesGhost25: Hmm. I guess it would depend on what they did. There are deal breakers.

SingerQueen: Such as?

AlCaponesGhost25: Well, there's the obvious triad— cheating, murder, and putting an empty milk carton back in the fridge.

SingerQueen: Ha!

AlCaponesGhost25: Where's this coming from?

nibble at my lip as I try to think of how to explain my confusion about today's events while keeping up my half-truth about working as a designer.

SingerQueen: Remember that guy at my work we were going to haunt?

AlCaponesGhost25: The showoff?

SingerQueen: Yeah.

AlCaponesGhost25: Is he still being annoying?

I think of the spider in the mailbox, Tilly and Cho getting us kicked out of agility, and Leo's irritatingly self-assured ways. But the image is shifting even as I do.

SingerQueen: He's a pain in my ass for sure, but the problem is, now he's sharing his portfolio with me, which is actually really helpful. It might even lead to a promotion if things work out.

AlCaponesGhost25: Hence your question.

SingerQueen: Maybe I judged him unfairly.

AlCaponesGhost25: You sound a bit like me. I tend to assume the worst of people.

SingerQueen: You do?

AlCaponesGhost25: Trying to do better.

SingerQueen: So I should give him a second chance?

AlCaponesGhost25: If he's worthy. How is his riddle game?

SingerQueen: Non-existent. Too buttoned-up.

AlCaponesGhost25: Phew. I won't get jealous then.

SingerQueen: …

AlCaponesGhost25: What?

SingerQueen: Are you flirting with me?

AlCaponesGhost25: Would never. *winky face emoji*

Thank goodness the store's closed on Mondays. Even though the dogs let me sleep until eight, I'm a zombie as I feed them and take them out. A sore zombie. I must have strained a few muscles in my muddy fall yesterday. I stretch in front of the window as I wait for my coffee to brew. The light is on in Leo's apartment. He's probably been up since six checking off his to-do list.

My snarky thought isn't followed by its usual pang of emotional acidity, possibly because today I have a to-do list of my own. As much as I hate to admit it, Leo's training plan is a good idea. I also want to organize the store better and finally start that Instagram account. What was it he said? I need to ensure my customers don't find Canine King superior.

I have about eight weeks left until the show. Say we train two times per week, that's sixteen sessions. I glance down at Cholula. That's plenty, right? If I focus on different obstacles each week, we should be ready. Of course, there's one other problem to solve—the talent part. Pretty sure "stealing food" doesn't count, and that's the only area where Cho is prodigious. I'll have to give this some thought.

I use a pencil to divide a sheet of paper into eight boxes and jot down what my training focus will be for each. Who knew there was such relief in taking all those loose thoughts from your head and organizing them on paper?

As soon as I'm done with breakfast, I hit the floor. I have three hours to make a dent in my list before I head out to Pop at Dalebrook, and I intend to put them to good use.

I'm even more sore when I walk into the nursing home after lunch. There's a kink in my back, and my hands are callused from hauling thirty-pound bags of kibble across the store all morning. Inspired by Leo, I decided to move the food to the back wall. It's our number one revenue maker, and after reading up on sales and marketing basics, I now know that, to optimize sales, we need to make customers pass all the other merchandise to get to the food. It's obvious once it stares you in the face.

To my surprise, Pop's bed is empty when I get there. His roommate looks like he's sleeping, but the TV is on. He's not in the bathroom either, and when I peer into the hallway, only a few nurses move in and out of the rooms.

I'm about to go look for him when a laugh trills up the corridor from the common area. A second later, Harvey and Sylvia come into view. He's leaning heavily on his walker, and she has her arm on his back, but they're giggling like two schoolchildren about something. Harvey is moving slowly, but other than that, he looks good.

"Hey, Pop," I say as they get closer.

He pauses and looks up. "Cora! Look at me." He grins.

Sylvia and I nod to each other in greeting.

"I saw your empty bed and thought you'd escaped," I say.

"Yep, Sylvia broke me out." He winks.

"The nurses say he needs to get up and move, and since Charles still sleeps a lot, I have nothing but time on my hands," Sylvia says. She has friendly pale eyes and a steel-gray pixie cut reminiscent of Jamie Lee Curtis. I have no doubt she was a knock-out in her younger days. Heck, just like JLC, she's a knockout even now.

"That's great," I say. "As long as you're not pushing yourself too hard, Pop."

He waves my concern away as he sits back down on his bed.

"I'm doing great. But tell me about you. How's the store? How's Leo?"

"Leo?" Why is he asking about him as if he's someone to me?

"Nice young man," he tells Sylvia. "You met him last time Cora was here."

"I remember. Is he your boyfriend?" Sylvia asks me.

"No!" It comes out a tad too emphatic. "He's just a friend. *Barely* a friend." My face warms.

"He opened a store across the street from ours," Harvey explains.

"A competing store," I add, willing the color out of my cheeks.

Sylvia's attention ping-pongs between us. "Ah."

"But no worries," I tell Harvey. "I have a plan."

"I'll give you guys some privacy," Sylvia says, drawing the curtain between the beds before she leaves the room again.

"Thanks again," Harvey calls to her.

"Anytime."

He beams. Oh boy, the ladies back home are about to have their hopes dashed.

I start laying out my agenda in detail, and he listens without interrupting. When I get to the show, his forehead creases.

"This sounds well and good, kiddo," he says when I'm done, "but it does pain me that you have to shoulder all this on your own. It's a big undertaking."

I don't have it in me to brush off his concern. It is a lot. But also... "I moved here to help, and I'm not about to give up now. As long as you and the dogs need me, I'm here. I probably can't win, but I'm going to try. But maybe you can help me think of a talent for Cho."

Harvey rests a pensive finger against his lower lip. "She climbs the furniture a lot. Could you do something with that?"

"We'll be on a stage. I don't think it's possible to turn it into a 'floor is lava' game where she jumps between tables, and shelves, and whatnot."

He shrugs. "A couple of chairs, a ladder maybe…Or what about Boris or Cap? Sometimes she sits on top of them."

I have seen that. And Cap's name is already on the registration since I hadn't yet decided which one of them to show. Could I train her to stand on Cap's back?

"She's so smart," Pop continues. "I bet you could teach her to balance on one of those big exercise balls."

"Now, that would be a real circus act."

Harvey takes my hand, squeezes it. "I believe in you, Cora. You can do anything you set your mind to. You'll win that grand prize; I can feel it in my bones. Best in Show."

More like *Worst in Show* at the rate I'm going. His confidence in me makes my throat tighten. I never told him I dropped out of college, that helping him at the store was only part of the reason I moved out here. No one but Micki knows. I'm very much aware that, if I mess this up, it won't be the first time I falter at the finish line.

"I'm going to do my best to be there to watch you win," he says with a determined nod. "The doctors are happy with my recovery so far."

I swallow against the lump in my throat. "Yeah, you show them. Rest, eat, do your physical therapy."

"Speaking of eating. Could you check if Charles still has his pudding from lunch?"

My mouth pops open. "Excuse me?"

"He doesn't eat it anyway. It's a waste."

"Pop…" I chuckle but go check, nevertheless. Sure enough,

there's a pudding cup on his roommate's side table. Charles doesn't move as I lean closer, but it feels as if he knows.

"I can't do it." I sit back on Harvey's bed. "You're as bad as Cholula."

He sighs with dramatic flair. "Guess I'll have to wait for Sylvia to come back, then."

Something tells me she'll be more than happy to oblige.

21

Living History Illinois Flockify DM, Monday 05:15 PM

RenaissanceMom: Desperately need a dress made for Lincoln Masquerade Ball on Halloween. Too late? Happy to pay double what you charged last time.

SingerQueen: Good to hear from you! Hope the Outlander gown worked out.

RenaissanceMom: So many compliments!!! *heart eyes emoji*

SingerQueen: Awesome. Same measurements? Inspo pics?

RenaissanceMom: I'll send a link to my Pinterest.

SingerQueen: Let me go check...

RenaissanceMom: What do you think?

SingerQueen: It'll be tight, but let's do it.

H ow is our Harv?" Micki asks later over pizza. "I miss him."
    I give her and Jaz a status report, and then I put my plate away. "You're going to have to talk to me while I sew tonight."

I consult the list I made this morning where checkmarks adorn most of the tasks I set for myself. "I have two more outfits to finish, and then I have to start the commission I picked up today. Plus…" I hold up my phone for her to see.

"You're on Insta?" Micki gapes. "Welcome to the twenty-first century. I've only been telling you to get on social media for a few years now."

"I only have the one post so far. Do you think it was silly to put Cho in a dress for the pic?"

"No, it's great. It's your brand." She beams at me and reads my caption out loud: *"Halloween is for everyone. Need ideas for your pets? Happy Paws can help."*

"I like it," Jaz says.

"What changed your mind?" Micki asks.

"I don't know." I replace the gray thread I used for a Sherlock-inspired tweed waistcoat earlier with a beige one. I'm working on Cogsworth's brown suit for Cap. I'm also planning on making Belle's yellow ballgown for myself. With three weeks until Halloween, I have my work cut out for me.

"Leo has a list of to-dos like that, too," Jaz says, unprompted. "He keeps a notebook by the register."

Micki stops chewing and taps her phone. Her lips curve into a smile at what she sees on the screen. "My ass you don't know."

I finish a seam before I look up.

"You're telling me this"—she holds up today's to-do list—"has nothing to do with a certain hunky store neighbor and his prolific social media presence. You're kicking up the competition!"

My pulse quickens. "Let me see that." I take the phone from her, and sure enough, she's found Leo's Canine King feed, which is somehow already full of artfully lit posts about the renovation, Tilly, and various product offerings. "He must be posting multiple times a day. How does he have time?"

Micki takes her phone back. "He probably uses a scheduling app. You should too."

"Yeah, it's easier to set aside a couple of hours once a week and schedule all your posts than to fit it in daily," Jaz agrees. "Trust me. We all made that mistake in the beginning."

"Not all of us."

Micki blows me a kiss. "The fact that you're almost twenty-eight and an Insta virgin is not something to brag about. Trust me on that, too."

She scrolls the feed while I return to my sewing. My heart is slowly settling back to its normal rhythm when she suddenly lets out a crescendoing "Whaaaat?"

The fabric runs amok beneath my fingers, creating a bulging seam. "What is it now?"

"Why are *you* in Leo's Insta feed?" Her eyebrows are halfway to her hairline. She shows me a picture from yesterday at the aunts' house. Its primary focus is Tilly, but yep, that's me and Cholula in the background. *Fuck.* I'm forced to explain everything, and I swear her eyes are heart-shaped at the end of it.

"He brought you home for Sunday lunch? This is moving faster than even I could have predicted."

"Like I said—he was making up for getting us kicked out of the agility place."

"But you agreed."

"I had no choice." I leave the table in a huff and busy myself with filling a glass with water.

"Oh, honey. There's always a choice."

"Fine, I made a professional choice. For Happy Paws. Is that better?"

"I think it's cool," Jaz says. "Sworn enemies working together. Gives me faith in humanity. Do you mind if I use that in my screenplay?"

"How is he with his aunts?" Micki asks. "I bet he's annoyingly sweet and does the dishes and shit."

I refuse to answer that. Micki hardly needs to know how on the nose that theory is.

"You should cut down on your Hallmark movie marathons," I say instead, taking my seat again. "It was basically work. We were working."

"Together…" she says in a sing-song voice.

"In the vicinity of one another." I grab my seam ripper and start undoing the mess she caused. Her gaze is still on me, but I pretend not to notice.

Very slowly, she reaches across the table, puts a finger on my to-do list, and drags it back to her side.

I know what's coming, so I brace myself.

"So, Mr. Professional's got you stepping up your game. I see, I see."

I lean back and rest my hands in my lap. "Is there something wrong with that? Maybe I don't want to give our customers reason to find Happy Paws subpar."

She smirks. "*Subpar*, even. Sounds like he's made quite an impression on you."

"Pfft. Whatever, dude. Yes, maybe Leo's inspired me to rethink how we're doing things and fix what's not working. And sure, he's not ugly, he's surprisingly helpful sometimes, he has a good relationship with his aunts, and is this…this business genius." Yikes, I'm trying to convince her why I'm not interested, right? "But I've known guys like him. They never stop working. Always want to be the best. Everything is about what's next."

A flashback intrudes of the phone call when Evan, my college boyfriend of two years, informed me that he'd been accepted to grad school at Harvard and would be leaving after finals. We'd been looking at apartments together as recently as the week before, but his mind was made up, his priorities clear. *Long-distance relationships never work out, babe.* I scratch my forehead as if that will erase his parting line. "Even if Leo wasn't my 'sworn enemy,' as Jaz so aptly described him, I don't need that energy in my life."

A look of studied innocence comes over Micki. "Then you wouldn't mind if I gave it a go?"

"Um…" Why would she do that? She's on at least two dating apps and has no problem getting dates. The images of Micki and Leo together that infiltrate my mind make my neck tense up. They're too different. A messy ending would be inevitable. Not that it'd be any of my busine—

"That's what I thought." Micki grabs her plate and brings it to the sink. "Don't worry, I was only kidding."

I want to argue with her, but I've run out of words. Instead, I settle for telling myself the relief I feel has to do with my good friend avoiding potential heartache. Men like Leo Salinger should come with a warning.

Which reminds me. "Hey, Jaz, I've got a job for you. Of the clandestine kind…"

"Finally." She leans forward. "You need something planted on his person? An anonymous threat called in to the store?"

"What? No." I explain what I overheard at the farm. "I want

to know what it is he has to 'handle.' See if you can find any-thing out."

"On it. And if I find the letter, I'll bring it to you ASAP."

Micki groans. "Come on, Jaz..."

"Again, no," I say, more gently. "No stealing. But if you see it, maybe peek at the sender or something."

She frowns. "You're definitely underutilizing my potential here."

"Maybe I shouldn't have asked."

"No," Jaz says in a hurry. "I'll do it. A girl can only inventory so many bully sticks..."

Micki has been tapping her phone some more, and now she shows me the screen. "He has a personal account, too. Maybe you'll find some clues there." She scrolls down the feed. "Goes way back. Damn, he fills out a suit."

"Stop it. I don't want to stalk him like that." I make her put her phone away, but just then mine chimes with a notification. @caninekingbatavia has followed me, and there's one new com-ment on my post:

Nice dress. Does it come in a men's size large? ;)

"Ha!" I clasp a hand over my mouth.

"You mean stalk him like he's stalking you?" Micki gives me a pointed look before getting up and turning to Jaz. "Come on, sis. We've got to go. I'm beat, and my first client is at seven thirty tomorrow."

After they're gone, I clean up, trying to ignore my phone, which is face down on the table. I'm not going to do it.

I'm not.

I'm really not.

I'm...Oh, who am I kidding?

When I flip the phone over, there's a notification for a message from Al, but tonight I have other things on my mind, so I swipe it away. Then I curl up in bed, take a deep breath, open Instagram again, and start scrolling.

Canine King's account is pretty but too promotional for what I'm after. I find Leo's personal one after a brief search, and right off the bat, it shows promise. His profile pic is a semi-casual portrait against a city backdrop. A small smile lingers as if the photographer said something funny, but the suit is all business, and Micki wasn't wrong. It hugs his broad shoulders in that way only tailored garments do. I nod slowly to myself as a small flame flickers on in my belly.

The posts from this year are mostly of Tilly as a tiny puppy, Diane's place, and selfies against sunlit cornstalks and barn walls. But going back to the beginning of the year, there's a shift. Something must have happened because earlier posts are of bars and restaurants, groups of business-clad people, and cityscapes. There's a close-up of a familiar Patek wristwatch at 1:50 a.m. with the caption *Midnight oil*, and another from Christmas two years ago of him on the phone in a red tie and Santa hat captioned *Business and pleasure*.

He used to do CrossFit (because of course he did), and I slow down my scrolling through those images to admire popping muscles I didn't know existed. The flame grows inside me, sending trickles of heat between my legs. "Well done, Leo," I whisper.

I go farther and farther back, his chiseled features flashing past in the feed, until I stop at a candid shot of him exiting a pool in some tropical location. The water drips off his tan skin, and the shorts cling to him in a way that makes me dig my teeth into my lower lip.

Without thinking, I slip my fingers underneath the elastic of my sweats and let them trail the hem of my panties. I sigh and scoot lower.

Leo's face is slightly turned away, one hand smoothing wet hair off his forehead. My gaze roams the curves of his biceps, the smattering of fair hair across his chest, a six-pack highlighted by adoring sunlight.

I go lower between my legs and find the fabric damp already. Pressure is building.

His hands would probably know exactly what to do. They're broad and strong, well-groomed, gentle. And he knows what he wants.

My eyelids flutter closed on a low moan, but as I relax into the fantasy, my phone slips, and I fumble it against my chest.

"Ah, no. Damn it." I get hold of it again, turn it over, and what I see is the most effective cold shower. A big red heart.

I've accidentally liked his photo.

22

unliked it right away," I tell Micki the next morning over the phone. "Will he still know?"

She's laughing so hard she can barely talk. "Yes," she wheezes. "Oh, this is too perfect."

"I told you I shouldn't be on social media." My cheeks are burning. How will I ever be able to look at him again?

"There are a few pool pics here," she says, still giggling. "Which one is it?"

"No, don't look at them!"

"But I want to know what did it for you. It's the one where he's stepping out, isn't it? Yeah, that's hot."

I lean my head into my free hand. "So hot, right? God, I'm mortified."

"Don't be. He's not going to say anything."

"How do you know?"

"Because he likes you. He wouldn't embarrass you like that."

"He tolerates me at best. Out of guilt."

"You keep telling yourself that. But um…" She pauses. "Shit. Hey, you didn't happen to look at the caption before your little *ménage à moi*, did you?"

"No. Why?"

"It says *Quality time with my baby*."

There's a mini-pinch in my chest, but I shrug it off. "It would be weirder if he'd never been in a relationship."

"Yeah, but…hashtag livinglavidaloca, hashtag brightfuture, hashtag *honeymoon*…"

The line is silent while I let that sink in. "He's married?"

"Or he was? Harvey said he's single, remember?"

The plot is thickening. "Either way, it doesn't matter to me. It's his life."

"You're not even a little curious?"

"Of course I am. But it's not like I can ask him about it." Especially not now that I've revealed myself to be the creepiest creeper ever. "I'm just going to forget about the whole thing. He could have a whole harem of wives, and that wouldn't change a thing. Or rather I'd feel bad for him. A harem would be freaking exhausting."

"Mm-hmm." Micki's blasé hum tells me she's done with this conversation now. If I'm not going to play along with her Hallmark-y fantasies, there's no point. "You let me know how that goes, okay? Are you training tonight?"

A new wave of shame washes over me. "Yes," I sigh. Fifteen thousand is worth it, I tell myself. Fifteen thousand and the satisfaction of beating his fine ass.

Despite my resolve to move on, my brain fails to conjure normal topics of conversation on our way to the farm. Leo is in a good mood, smiling and humming along to the music he has playing, but all my focus is spent trying not to blurt "sorry I accidentally liked your thirsty post."

"You're quiet today," he says when we're halfway there. "Something wrong?"

That smile again. He totally knows.

"Nope, all good."

He glances at me. "I liked the picture you posted of Cholula. How does it feel to officially join the modern world?"

Dear Lord, he's going there. "Fine."

"Let me know if you need any tips."

"Will do."

"Or if you have any questions…?"

I look at him, but his face is neutral, concentrating on the road. *I do,* I want to say. *I have So. Many. Questions.* "I can't stay out late tonight," I say instead. "I've got more work to do at the store."

"Do you ever just chill?"

"You're the one telling me to be 'number one in business.'"

That elicits a small smile from him. "That's a terrible impression of me. But I'm glad you were listening. I didn't think you would." He slows at a stoplight. "Does this mean you no longer consider me the human equivalent of the plague?"

I pretend to think about it. "I wouldn't go that far."

He touches his heart. "Ouch."

"But I'll concede you may have some valid points about how to run a business."

"*Some* valid points. I'm overwhelmed with this praise."

I slap him in the shoulder but can't fully suppress my laugh.

Now that the mood is lighter, I venture a question that's been on my mind. "So, Dawn tells me you have a brother?"

Leo's jaw clenches almost imperceptibly. "I do."

I hesitate. "Should I not ask about him?"

He glances at me. "Why do you say that?"

"You look all storm-cloudy all of a sudden."

"That's not a word." His chin juts out, but then he makes a visible effort to relax his features. "Our relationship is complicated," he says, finally.

"He's the handsomer, more successful one, right? Is that why you can't stand him?"

Leo shakes his head. "God, you're a pain. Fine. What do you want to know? Bennett is a year younger, definitely not as handsome, but yeah, a pretty successful lawyer."

He should have been in my year at school, then. I rack my brain for a Bennett Salinger but come up empty-handed. "Was he at Batavia High School, too? I don't remember him."

"No, he was a bit rowdy in middle school, so my parents sent him to Marmion. They figured a Catholic, all-boys high school would set him straight, and I guess they were right."

That would explain it. "So what's the complication?"

"You don't beat around the bush much, do you?" A sidelong glare. "Um...he and my father have opinions about me being out here. Let's leave it at that."

I don't want to leave it there at all. What kind of opinions? Does this have something to do with his lifestyle change around the holidays? But maybe I've already pushed my luck.

"Yeah, I'm really not looking forward to having him right up in my business," he continues.

"He's coming here?"

"The whole family. Diane says they always come out Halloween weekend. Apparently, the kids love trick-or-treating here in town."

"The kids?"

"Evie and Oscar, my niece and nephew. They're four and three. Love those kids to death. It'll be good to see them at least."

"Aw, that's cute. And now they can come trick-or-treat at your store. That'll be fun."

"At the store?" Leo looks at me.

I turn more fully his way. "All the businesses open for trick-or-treating that afternoon. It's a thing. Lots of people come. You didn't know?"

"Does everyone dress up? Do I have to?" He shudders. "Can't I just put out a bowl of candy by the front door?"

"Of course everybody dresses up. It's Halloween—the best holiday of the year. The stores go all out. Which reminds me— could we stop at the pumpkin farm on the way back on Friday? I need some pumpkins."

"Pumpkins plural?"

"Yeah."

"Why do you need several?"

"For decoration, obviously. You should get some too or Canine King will be the only storefront not decked out." I pretend to study my nails. "Unless you're aiming for standing out in a really scroogey way."

He huffs. "That analogy makes no sense. Last I checked, Scrooge was about Christmas."

"You get the gist. You'll be a party pooper. A Halloween pooper."

"I don't know. To me, dress-up is for kids. I sell dog supplies, not an immersive haunted house experience."

I bark a laugh at his self-importance. "Gotcha—Halloween is not 'on-brand' for you. Well, more foot traffic for me, then. Thank you kindly." I tip an invisible hat to him, and maybe it's my teasing tone or the thought of his Halloween aversion pushing customers away, but suddenly he squares his shoulders and raises his chin.

"I didn't say I wasn't going to participate. I simply hadn't thought about it. If you want to stop for pumpkins, we'll stop for pumpkins."

I look at him as we take the last turn off the road and come up to the farmhouse. "Really?"

"Sure." He stops the car and puts it in park. "In fact, I bet you I can make Canine King even more 'decked out' than Happy Paws."

"Not likely."

"You scared you're going to lose?" He smirks.

The nerve. "Fine, you're on. Best-decorated store wins. The loser has to wear the other store's swag for a day and post a picture of it to social media. How about that? I'm not scared. Are you?"

The light from an exterior lamp on the house reflects in his large pupils as he nods approvingly. "Okay. Okay. I see you, Cora Lewis. Didn't know you had it in you. Deal." He offers me his hand. Its grip is strong and assured—much like in the picture where he clutched the ladder to pull himself out of the water. The vision before me changes. *Blue skies and palm trees, sun-kissed skin. Leo, shaking his hair, spraying me with droplets as he tries to tug me into the glittering pool with him.*

"But my clothes will get wet," I say. It only takes a second for me to realize the words didn't stay in my head.

"What?" Leo squints on a smile.

I pull my hand out of his, my mind blank. "Uh...um... pumpkins."

"Wet clothes and pumpkins?" He stares at me. "Are you okay?"

I nod, slowly at first and then faster. My right hand massages my throat as if a logical explanation has gotten stuck there. "Sure, yeah." *Say something better. Now.* "Um, if it rains. Pumpkin-picking. It's muddy. Best to wear a rain jacket."

"Ah." He doesn't look convinced. "I will."

"Good. Wouldn't want you to get, um, wet." My chin slumps to my chest on a sigh. *Damn it, I did it again.* I've got to get out of here. I open the door but get tangled in the seat belt I've forgotten to unbuckle.

He reaches over to assist at the same time I go for the button, and again his warm skin brushes mine.

"I've got it," I say, more brusquely than I intend.

Finally free, I straighten and suck in a deep gulp of cool air to clear my head. "Thanks," I say. "Let's just…" I hike my thumb toward the field.

An amused frown lingers on his face. "Whatever you say. Pumpkin."

23

Living History Illinois Flockify DM, Thursday 10:30 PM

SingerQueen: Sorry I haven't been online much. Swamped!
AlCaponesGhost25: Seems to be a busy time of year for everyone.
SingerQueen: #holidayfun
AlCaponesGhost25: Travel plans?
SingerQueen: No, but I picked up a commission for a Lincoln masquerade ball costume. It's this annual Halloween party in downtown Chicago.
AlCaponesGhost25: I've heard of it. That's good. Congrats!
SingerQueen: Thx. It's a big job, so don't take it personally if I'm on here less for a bit.
AlCaponesGhost25: Whatever will I do?
SingerQueen: Shake your little tush on the catwalk? ♪♪
AlCaponesGhost25: Bah-ha-ha
SingerQueen: *blows kiss*

This is a shit-ton of pumpkins," Micki says upon entering the store Saturday before opening.

She's helping organize the crafting extravaganza I have planned as part of the two-week countdown to Halloween. I was prepared to do it inside the store, but because of the gorgeous blue skies, we'll be setting up a couple of tables outside.

"That's what Leo said, too. It's not that many." His exact words at the pumpkin patch were "The dogs are going to have to ride on the roof if you keep this up."

He was grossly exaggerating, of course. I have twelve full-sized pumpkins and ten smaller ones interspersed around the store and in the entryway, and I didn't even get all of them at the patch. I picked up a few more at the grocery store yesterday.

I'm balancing on top of a ladder by the window, stringing up leaf garlands I found in storage. It wobbles precariously beneath me. "All of those supplies need to be set up outside. Start with that." I point to bins of foam pumpkins, popsicle sticks, felt scraps, glitter glue, crayons, stickers, and googly eyes. I've posted to social media and put fliers up all over town. The idea is that families will stop by to make their own pumpkin to display in my window, and then people vote for their favorite. I'll announce the winner on Halloween, and they get a twenty-dollar gift card to the store.

Micki pulls out her phone and takes a picture of me. "For your Instagram. It's cute. Very Martha Stewart."

"Because that's the image I'm going for." I finish tying the garland and climb down.

"It's personable, and that's on-brand for Happy Paws." She shows me the photo. "See, you look pretty, too."

The morning light from the window hits my face like a diffused spotlight, and she's right, it does do me favors. Unlike some other candids she snapped of me this past week, I don't hate this one. "Okay, send it to me."

"So, do we not get to actually carve pumpkins?" Micki asks, tucking her phone back in her pocket.

"Maybe later. We can't have knives lying about with kids around."

"Because I'm freaking fabulous at pumpkin carving. Where do you want these?" She holds up an armful of cornstalks I got from Diane and Dawn.

I look around the store, and it's pretty darn festive already if I may say so myself. No way is Leo going to beat me at this. "How are things outside? Maybe put a few next to the door in the corner there. Can we tie some of them to the tables somehow?"

"If we trim them shorter maybe?"

We're trying to figure it out when Leo comes up behind us. "What's going on over here?" His gaze skims all my decorations, lingering on the stacked pumpkins framing the entry to Happy Paws.

"A small event I'm doing today."

"The pumpkin craft thing." He nods. "I saw your post."

"Yeah, our girl is rocking the interwebs these days," Micki says a little too loudly.

Our girl? I throw her a glare, but if Leo thinks she's being overly familiar, he doesn't show it.

"I'd like to make one," he says. "Or are you not open for business yet?"

"See, I told you," Micki says to me. "He doesn't hate Halloween." She hands him a foam pumpkin. "Knock yourself out."

Leo takes it but doesn't move. He looks from her to me, a smile lighting up his already bright blues. "You've been talking about me?"

Crap. I take my time finishing tying a stalk to the table leg and stand up. "Only to tell her I'll be winning our bet since you don't care for the holiday." *Nice save.*

"Ah." He reaches for a popsicle stick, glue, and felt. "Dream on."

I take a step closer to him. "I don't have to. My position is firmly anchored in reality, thank you very much."

He mimics my stance, and now there are only feet separating us. I've been close to him in the car before, but face-to-face like this, a weird tension forms between us—like a tether. It makes me want to hook my fingers through his belt loops and tell him all about my favorite memories from childhood. The mild, chalky-sweet scent of the open glue stick he's holding ties the past and present together.

He looks down at me. "And mine's not?"

I pull my gaze off his and direct it toward Canine King where Jaz is waving through the window. "You have one sorry pumpkin outside your store. Winning!"

He scoffs. "Maybe I have plans you don't know about."

An alarm goes off in my head. Maybe he does. I should prepare. I cannot let him win.

"I could seriously watch you guys do this all day," Micki says with a giggle from the other side of the table. "You're too much, both of you."

I take a step back, the bubble we were just in now burst. "Hey, you're supposed to be on my side."

"Which is why I interrupted that whole thing." She waves her arm in a circle to encompass Leo and me. "We don't have a ton of time here."

Leo has dived into his crafting as if our exchange never happened, so I settle for side-eyeing Micki on my way back into the store. "I'm going to get the tape."

Back in the storage room, I sink down onto a box by the

door, my hand pressed to my chest. What was that even? When Leo looked at me like that, challenged me, it was like a powerful surge knocked me into overdrive. I usually back down from situations like that. What a rush.

"There. Done," he says when I return. He holds up his pumpkin as if it's a rare painting.

"Look at that. You made Cholula," Micki exclaims. "It even has her dangly tongue."

The resemblance is uncanny—if we inflated Cholula and turned her orange that is—and as much as I don't want to be, I'm impressed.

"Admit it, you're impressed," Leo says as if he can read my mind.

I scoff. "No." I take the Cholula pumpkin from him. "It's average at best."

"So cruel." He feigns a shot to the heart.

I pull off a piece of tape and excuse myself to put it up on the window inside. When I return, Leo stares at me with a mix of humor and befuddlement.

"Let me guess, you have an opinion about the placement of your masterpiece." I don't have time for this. We open in thirty minutes.

He blinks a few times. "Not at all. I'm just...You put it up."

I look at the largely empty window with the lone foam pumpkin. "That's the whole point. All of them are going up. Did you want to take it home?" I ask this in the tone of voice I'd use with a small child. "Put it on the fridge?"

"I think it looks great there," Micki chimes in.

"Yeah, no. I'm good." Leo digs his teeth into his lower lip as if to stifle another smile. It's futile. His eyes give him away every time.

The whole display does something to my stomach I haven't felt in a good, long while.

He hikes his thumb over his shoulder. "I'll let you get to it. I have some decorating to do. Really looking forward to seeing you in a Canine King apron when you lose."

He strides confidently back to Canine King, leaving, I admit, a bit of a void there on the sidewalk.

"Leo and Cora sitting in a tree…" Micki sings in a low voice.

I throw a popsicle stick at her.

I don't have time for climbing trees, and if I did it with him, he'd probably make it a race to the top.

Jaz comes darting out of the store as soon as Leo's disappeared into it. "I told him I had to run to the pharmacy real quick," she pants, ducking down behind the table. "Come on, cover me."

Micki and I do, though it's a pathetic excuse of an attempt that wouldn't fool anyone who was actually looking.

"What's going on, sis?" Micki asks.

"I saw it. I saw the letter. Or at least I think that was the one. He had me bring Tilly upstairs yesterday when we got busy, and it was sitting right there on his kitchen table."

I lower my voice. "Tell me you didn't take it."

"Of course not. What do you think of me?"

"What do I think… You literally told me you were going to steal it last we talked about this."

"Okay, okay. Well, I didn't. But…"

Micki and I both lean in.

"What?" Micki asks impatiently.

"It's from someone named Samantha. Real pretty handwriting."

"And?" I hold my breath.

"That's it."

"No, but where was it sent from?"

"I'm not sure. I only looked at the name."

"You only...?" Micki stands back. "That tells us nothing."

"Be nice, it's not nothing," I try. To Jaz I say, "Thanks for looking. I appreciate it. Stay alert, okay?"

"Roger that." Jaz grins. "This spying stuff is fun. Okay, gotta go."

Micki's arms are crossed, and her toes are tapping the ground. "I mean, Boris would make a better sleuth."

"It's not a ton of info," I concede. If anything, it adds questions about him to my already long list. Is Samantha the woman who took the #honeymoon photo of him? And if so, are they still a thing? Is she a family member? A friend? A secret baby mama pressuring him for alimony?

"Maybe you should ask him," Micki says. "I bet he'd tell you."

"Except then it would seem like I care."

She watches me a long moment. "Yeah, we wouldn't want that."

24

Living History Illinois Flockify DM, Monday 12:15 PM

AlCaponesGhost25: Just checking in. Getting a lot done?

SingerQueen: Tons. You ever get 'in flow' and lose hours?

AlCaponesGhost25: God, I forgot about that feeling. I played football when I was younger, and some games were magical like that.

SingerQueen: But not since?

AlCaponesGhost25: I guess not.

SingerQueen: Sounds like you need to reevaluate your life. *winky face emoji*

AlCaponesGhost25: Working on it.

Wednesday afternoon drags, the hours leading up to training longer than is polite. I keep checking the clock and being disappointed. I don't know what's changed, but I'm not dreading spending time with Leo anymore. I frown, glancing across the street. Am I looking forward to it?

When six o'clock finally rolls around, I hurry to close out the system and register, round up the pack, and head across the street.

The lights are on inside Canine King, but Leo is nowhere to be seen. Tilly greets us alone.

"Hello?" I call. "Anyone here?"

No answer.

"Where is he?" I ask Tilly. "Upstairs?" How irresponsible of him to leave the store unlocked and unattended. Out of character, even.

I'm about to call for him again when there's a loud ruckus in the back.

I tell the dogs to stay put and go to investigate.

"Stay where you are," I hear Leo say in a tight voice. "No. Stay."

Is he talking to me? "Leo?"

Silence.

Is there someone in there with him? What if he's being robbed? I look around for something to use as a weapon but come up short. My heart is racing as I tiptoe the last few steps to his storage room. I peer around the corner, and there's Leo, alone on top of a hay bale. No intruder. I relax and enter the room. "What's going on? Who were you talking to?"

He waves at me to stop. "Shh. Don't move." His eyes roam the floor beneath him.

"Why are you up there?" I can't believe I didn't think to incorporate hay bales into my decor. I'll have to rectify that. You're not supposed to bring them inside though. Sometimes they have fleas and other critt—

"Ah!" Leo shouts, pointing at the floor. "There."

A tiny mouse runs out from under a shelf and disappears beneath another. I look from the floor to Leo's colorless face and back again. The mouse comes back out and sniffs the air.

"Aw, so cute." I crouch down to get a closer look, and it doesn't seem scared at all.

"No, not cute." Leo shudders from his high perch. "It's disgusting."

I straighten and assess the situation, trying my best not to smile. "I take it you don't like rodents."

"You wouldn't either if you'd woken up one night when you were five with a mouse inside your pajama shirt. Can you get it out of here? Tilly was no help at all."

Yikes, that would do it. Still, I pretend to think about it. "Not sure if I should. You were pretty smug about the spider in the mailbox."

"I'm sorry, okay? Just please." Leo looks down, another shudder making him adjust his stance on the bale. "I going to stay here until it's gone, so unless you want to miss training…"

"Yeah, no. That seems unnecessary. Do you have any peanut butter upstairs?"

"I do."

"Okay give me your keys."

Leo hesitates. "You're going into my apartment?"

His reluctance is intriguing. He let Jaz up there. What is it he doesn't want me to see? "Do you want me to get rid of the mouse or not?"

He digs his key out of his pocket and tosses it to me. "Please be quick."

Opening the door to his place feels exactly like entering my parents' bedroom when I was little. I wasn't allowed in there unless there was an emergency, so it was forever a place shrouded in mystery where possible treasures might be hidden. I snuck in once in fifth grade and went through Mom's jewelry chest. I lived on that high for a while.

The space smells like Leo but in more concentrated form. I inhale deeply and make my way to his kitchen cabinets. I would have expected to find a stash of health foods on sparsely stocked shelves, but the offerings are surprisingly normal. A package of Oreos sits next to a box of granola. There are English muffins and white rice. His fridge has yogurts and eggs but also beer and takeout leftovers. Yeah, I know the peanut butter isn't likely to be in the fridge, but despite the saying, I'm not sure curiosity ever has killed the cat. I may never get this chance again.

Satisfied with my findings, I grab the peanut butter and an empty Tupperware container and set course for the door. I almost miss the letter, but my gaze snags on it at the final moment. Like Jaz said, it's sitting in the middle of the table. Calling my name. A quick look, that's all.

Careful not to disturb the envelope, I read the full address of the sender. It's from a Samantha Salinger, and the postal address is in Seattle. "Maybe he has a sister?" I mumble. If not, the last name takes on a whole different meaning.

The stairs outside creak, and I jump back. Time to get out of here.

Leo hasn't moved when I return.

"Took you long enough," he says, jaw tense.

I ignore him and get down on the floor. *Who is Samantha?* "Where did you last see it?"

He points, and I smear a dab of the sweet and savory spread on the floorboard. "Here, mousy, mousy," I coo. "Got you a treat."

It doesn't take long before the little critter emerges, whiskers shivering. It heads straight for the food, and once it's there, I lower the container over it. I slide a piece of cardboard beneath it, and, voilà, the mouse is airborne. "There. You're safe," I tell Leo.

"Thanks," he says, tightly, finally stepping down. "Let's get going."

I don't argue. We've already lost a half hour of our time.

"Sorry you had to see me like that." Leo doesn't look at me as we walk into the field.

I shrug. "Everyone has their quirks. I only swim in pools where I can see the bottom. You'll never catch me in the ocean or a lake." I shudder. "Those pesky sharks…"

"Still. Not my finest moment."

"At least you got some decorations. I forgot about hay bales."

"You can have them. I'm not touching those things."

"You could put them outside."

"Not worth it." His mouth pulls into a wry smile. "You'd be doing me a favor. Another one," he corrects.

"You'll lose the bet."

He grimaces. "Let's face it. I was never going to win at Halloween decorating. At this, on the other hand…" He points to the training area ahead. "Tilly and I will take you guys down."

"Yeah, how's that recall coming along?"

"We're slow on the uptake, that's all. Dark horses always are. And then—surprise ending." He claps his hands together, startling both me and the dogs. Cholula circles back toward us, growls at Leo, and runs away again. "Speaking of surprises…"

He jogs to the shed and returns with two blue canvas circles. "I had these shipped here. They're tunnels to practice with."

He ordered one for me, too? Dark horse, indeed. "That's amazing. Cho's never seen one of those."

"Neither has Tilly." He tilts his head, lips pursed, thinking. "Care to make things interesting?"

"What do you have in mind?"

"Ten bucks on the dog that goes through the tunnel the most times."

Hell, I just won a bet not five minutes ago. I'm game.

What ensues is a frenzy of cajoling, bribery, begging, and encouragement. Shouts of "Good girl," "Wrong way," "Yes, you've got it," and "Again!" ring out in the evening air. Leo and I are getting as much exercise as the dogs, if not more, and despite the cool temperatures, we both soon discard our jackets on the fence post.

Twenty minutes in and Tilly and Cholula have made it through their tunnels only one time each. They're fired up and fully invested in the game, but neither cares for the tunnel. I don't know how many times Cholula has gone halfway through only to turn around and come back.

"I think that should count," I say. "Two halves of a tunnel still make a whole even if it's the same half twice."

"No dice." Leo shakes his head at me. Behind him, Tilly runs straight through his tunnel.

"She did it!" I point. "You missed it."

He turns in time to see Cap also going through. We both cheer, and at the sound, the beagle mix gladly runs back through it, pivots, and makes a third run.

"That's one for Cho, two for Tilly, and three for Cap," I summarize.

"Cap wasn't in on it."

"Sure, he was. You said, 'the dog.' No names were specified."

"No."

"Yes."

"Agree to disagree."

I shake my head. "Why do you always say that?"

"Maybe I don't feel like arguing."

"Said the person scared to lose the argument."

Leo lifts his finger as if to correct me, but then lets it fall. "Damn, I've got nothing."

"That's what I thought. Now, are we doing this or what?"

"Oh, you're on. Tilly, let's get 'em."

"Come on, Cho," I call. She's over by the fence, sniffing. When she hears my voice, she barks loudly and sits down. What now? As I approach, she circles the area and starts whining. "What is it? We've got a bet to win, girl."

Then I see it. Boris's leash, but no Boris.

25

How far can a blind, geriatric dog get in ten minutes?" Leo asks as we make our way through the cornfield, flashlights in hand.

Boris was still there when we took off our jackets, so he couldn't have gone that far. Footprints in the mud lead us in this direction, but outside our pockets of light, it's pitch-black and not a little like a horror movie before the alien serial-killer children attack. He could be anywhere.

"Boris," I call, echoed by Leo several rows over. "Where are you, buddy?"

"He must have caught the scent of some animal," Leo says. "Wolfhounds are great hunters."

I'd laugh if I wasn't so worried. "Yeah, that's what I think of when I see Boris—a great hunter…"

"Instinct never goes away."

I put my hands up like a cone and yell his name again. Far behind us, the aunts do the same. They stayed back, volunteering to search closer to the house while keeping tabs on the other dogs.

"What if he's hurt?" I shine my flashlight through the cornstalks. "What if we can't find him?"

"Don't worry." Leo's voice is soft. "We'll keep searching until we do."

A few minutes later, we're crossing a dirt road to the next field when Leo grabs my sweater and pulls me to a stop. "Shh, what was that?"

We freeze and listen. At first there's nothing, but when I call Boris's name again, there's a sharp yelp coming from somewhere on our left.

"That's him!" I take off running, almost tripping over the uneven wheel tracks. "Over here."

Boris is in a shallow ditch, muddy up to his neck, but he's alert and happy to hear my voice. He licks my face profusely. "What's going on, buddy?" I run my hands across his body, and when I get to one of his back legs, he whimpers. His foot is stuck in what looks like a small drainage grate. "You poor thing."

Leo leans forward. "Here, I'll hold it still, and you get his leg."

As gently as possible, I free Boris from the trap.

"I think it's a tractor footstep," Leo says, examining the metal piece. "Weird."

Whatever it is, it hurt him. "Aww bud, you're shivering." I stroke Boris's head in my lap.

"I've got him." Leo puts his flashlight down, and before I have time to protest, he pulls off his gray Henley and wraps it around Boris. "That should keep him warmer until we get back."

I'm speechless. He gave up his shirt. For my dog. In the ambient light from the flashlights, it looks like steam is rising off Leo's bare chest. It's the pool photo all over again, only better because it's live.

"Won't you…um, be cold?" My tongue is like sandpaper. I haven't seen a male torso quite so erotic since Hugh Jackman poured a bucket of water over himself in the movie *Australia*. A voice in the back of my head tells me to look away, but there's no chance. I don't even care if he notices my gawking. Leo Salinger is fi-ine.

"Nah, I'll have to carry him back anyway," Leo says. "It'll keep me warm."

That snaps me out of my drooling session. "But he's over a hundred pounds."

"I bench two fifty."

"I bet you do." My face heats. I did not mean to say that out loud.

"Was that a compliment?" He flexes his arms, playfully illuminating them with his flashlight. "You like these?"

Thank God it's dark out, because I really do, and I'm sure it shows.

Leo chuckles. "Help me get him up so I can get a good hold."

Boris lets us manhandle him into Leo's arms like a swooning lady, and then we start our trek back through the field with me in the lead. Behind me, Leo walks in silence, his breath coming in rhythmic huffs. I don't care what he said, Boris is heavy. I'm not sure how I'll be able to repay him for what he's done tonight.

Back at the house, Diane gives Boris a bath and administers first aid. She assures me nothing is broken—a scratch on his foot and more adventure than he bargained for, that's all. "He should be fine with some rest," she says. "And I'd get a sturdier leash when you're out here. Lots of wild animals to tempt an old tracker."

Leo comes downstairs, having showered and changed. No more bare chest. *Boo.*

"Did you want to get cleaned up, too, before we head back?" he asks.

My jeans are ruined from kneeling in the ditch, and I'm sure I look a sight, but it's late, and I can't in good conscience borrow yet another outfit here. "I'll sit on a towel in the car if I have to, but we should get going."

He nods. "I'll bring Boris out."

For the second time tonight, he lifts the shaggy beast into his arms, blanket and all. I stare after him as he heads out the door.

"You okay?" Dawn asks sidling up to me. "You look a bit shell-shocked."

Is that what I am? "Yeah, no, I'm ... fine. He's—" I nod in the direction Leo disappeared, but I can't finish my sentence.

"He's a good guy," Dawn fills in with a smile. "I know. See you in a few days."

Damn it. He is, isn't he?

This is going to make not liking him so much harder than it already is.

26

The hay bales are outside my store when I get downstairs the following day. To be honest, I'm surprised Leo had it in him to touch them at all after yesterday, but they'll look great next to my pumpkin display, so I have nothing but gratitude.

Canine King is still dark and made all the more so by its lack of a festive front step. Leo has clearly given up on our bet, and while I fully intend to claim my prize, I also feel a little bad. I tell myself the sympathy has more to do with the costumed kids being met by this sad, un-Halloweeny sight than with Leo, but even I know that's not entirely true. I don't want anyone to be left out, not even him. Before I can change my mind, I load a cart up with three pumpkins and set off across the street.

Jaz arrives as I'm unloading the first one. "What are you doing?" she asks.

"Decorating." I sprinkle a bagful of cinnamon-scented pine cones around the pumpkins and stand back to admire my work.

"I don't understand. Are they booby-trapped?"

"No."

"Then what's the catch?"

"No catch. He gave me hay bales, so I'm reciprocating."

Jaz stares at me a moment. Then she taps the side of her nose with her finger. "Ah. You're biding your time. Gotcha."

I'm about to set her straight but decide against it. In a way, her perspective is correct. Nothing has changed. Leo is still here, and I still want Canine King gone. I'm just not sure how to explain that the once black-and-white situation suddenly is morphing into a kaleidoscope of complex colors.

"Anyway, I need to get back. Don't tell him it was me."

"He'll know." She calls after me. "You're the only one around with a serious pumpkin problem."

She's right. He texts me shortly after I open.

Thanks for the pumpkins, he says. **It looks great. Can't believe you did that.**

I look up, and there he is inside his store, smiling at me. He has his phone in one hand and a round broom in the other, bristles up as if he's channeling his inner witch.

Me: Thanks for the hay.

Leo: I'll have no choice but to dress up now, won't I?

Me: Aren't you already?

He sends me a question mark.

Your current witch cosplay, I clarify. **Or what's with the broom?**

His response takes a few seconds. **In case something needs sweeping obviously.**

The bristles need to face down for that to work.

The three dots appear then stop.

I knew it. You're worried Cinderella's little helper will decide to return to the scene of the crime, aren't you?

No, he texts right away. Then, A little. How far away did you set the mouse loose?

Far enough, I reassure him. And I'm only a stone's throw away should you need my bravery once more.

Okay fine. I'm putting it down. He looks at me across the street, places the broom on the floor right inside the doors of his store, and backs away as if I've disarmed him. Then he's back to typing. How's Boris doing?

"Changing topics, are we?" I say out loud. Tired, but moving around again. No great harm done.

> That's a relief. I might stop by with a treat for him later if that's okay.

My stomach does a weird loop the loop, but before I can respond, Customer—gotta go pops up on my screen, and sure enough, I look up to catch a party of four entering Canine King. I don't have time to mope about it though because, a moment later, I'm busy with customers of my own.

After closing, I finish putting in orders while eating instant ramen at the table upstairs. All my seasonal pumpkin-flavored foods and treats have flown off the shelves as if the obsession with pumpkin spice lattes extends to include the family pooch, and there's still another week to go before October 31. I've just closed my laptop when there's knocking on the front door of the shop. For once I remembered to close and lock up on time, and I get stragglers?

I move gingerly down the stairs in my sasquatch fuzzy socks, speeding up when I see Leo outside.

He must see my quizzical look because he holds up a small bag. "Treats for Boris."

I unlock and open the door. "I didn't think you were actually going to come."

"Why not?"

"Come in." I head upstairs, and he follows. Cholula is perched, teeth bared, at the landing, so I scoop her up and place her on a cushioned chair by the table. "Be quiet. We don't growl at our friends." I turn to Leo. "I guess I figured you're busy. People say things."

"If I say I'll bring treats, I'll bring treats." He hands me the bag and moves out of the way as I clear a pile of dog capes off a chair. After he sits down, he does a not-so-stealthy inspection of the space I currently call home.

"What do you think?" I ask, observing him carefully. His place is a luxury penthouse compared to this. I've strung up fairy lights behind the curtains to add ambiance, but that only goes so far.

He does a floor-to-ceiling sweep again. "It's nice."

I purse my lips. "You don't have to lie. It's a tiny hole of a place. A supply closet basically."

"Yeah, okay, it's a little cramped. I think Diane's truck could fit everything in here."

"It's like an airplane bathroom and a storage bin had a love child together."

"But the bed alcove is cute." His eyes glitter. "If you're a hobbit."

"Good one."

"No, but seriously. It isn't bad for one person. Kind of cozy in a wintery, cabin-nook type of way."

"A nook with three dogs, lest you forget."

"Right." He points to the treat bag between us. "They're all made from scratch, organic, healthy. The big one is apple—that's for Boris since it's his favorite."

I squint at him. "How did you know that?"

"You told me, remember? The first time we went out to the farm. Apple pie…"

I pause my unraveling of the bag. "I can't believe you remember that."

"Where is he anyway?"

"He and Cap are sleeping over there." I indicate the hallway, and, as I do, Boris appears with major bedhead even for someone whose normal state is "disheveled galore."

"Hi, bud. How are you doing?" Leo asks.

Boris limps to his side and puts a heavy head on his thigh.

My heart instantly turns more puddle than solid. "Aww, he wuvs you now," I coo. "He usually only does that with Pop. Here." I hand him the cookie.

"Want a treat, bud?"

Boris devours it in two bites and then rests his head against Leo again. Leo strokes two fingers between the big dog's bushy brows until Boris lets out a pleased huff. There's something so tender and unguarded about the pair that makes me choke up a little, and I don't know why.

"Penny for your thoughts?" Leo says, catching me watching him.

"Nothing." I pull the cover off my sewing machine that's sitting off to the side and start changing the spool of thread to have something else to look at.

"That's the most complicated thing I've ever seen. I didn't know you could sew."

"You didn't?" I choose a moss-green fabric from the pile on the chair next to me and find a matching thread from the tin. "I post my pet costumes on Insta all the time. You've seen them."

Leo gapes. "You make those?"

"We sell a lot this time of year. Those capes next to you will be gone in a week."

He picks one up. "Hey, maybe I should get one for Tilly. Someone told me we have to dress up."

I stop short. "What happened to 'Halloween is for kids'?"

"Another terrible impression of me, but yeah. You win. The decoration bet, the costume... You are the rightful queen of Halloween."

"Wow." I pretend to be confused. "But, if I'm the winner, then that must mean that you're... What's the word again? The... the... I think it starts with an *L*."

"The *loser*," Leo grunts, his lips twisted with wry humor.

"I'm sorry, what's that?"

"I'm the loser," he says, louder, putting his hands behind his head and stretching. "Enjoy it now, because we both know what's coming."

"You mean when you'll be wearing a Happy Paws shirt to work and post about it online? Yes, I do know that." I give him my best megawatt smile.

He shakes his head in mock disappointment. "I should have known better than to stop by. What was I thinking?" Despite his words, he stays seated, fingertips tapping the tabletop.

"You were thinking of Boris."

His eyes lock with mine. "Yes... That must have been it."

A long moment follows when Boris's breathing is the only

sound around us. Leo's gaze makes me want to lean forward, closer, but thankfully my machine is between us. I press my palms to the cool metal and sit back instead. "It'll be fifty bucks even for the cape," I say, looking away. "I'll let you know when it's ready. Those over there will be too small for her."

"Deal." After a brief pause, he stands. "I should go. Like I said, I just wanted to check on the big guy."

The way he says it makes me feel bad, like I'm kicking him out in the cold when he deserves better. I scramble for something to say to make the feeling go away. "It was very sweet of you—how you carried him back and everything. Thank you. I mean it. I'll try to be nicer."

"You're welcome. But for what it's worth, I already think you're nice." He moves toward the stairs. "And I actually *do* like your place. Especially what you've done with the lights around the window. They make you look like a Renaissance painting when you sit there, half lit among your fabrics."

I peer over at him, afraid to move. My heart pounds unevenly against my ribs.

He lifts his hand and is just about to head down the stairs when he spots something in the murky hallway that makes him flinch. "Oh God, that scared me. For a second, I thought it was a person."

I go over there to look. "It's just my dress form." I pull it out from the wall, and the blue silk of the half-finished gown I'm working on glints in the light.

"That's pretty. Is it for you?" Leo asks, stepping around it to see the back.

"Nah. Sometimes I take commissions from people online."

He stops and looks from the dress to me and then back. "Oh?" The word catches and comes out like a small croak.

I run my hand across the pinned-together bodice. "This one is actually for the Lincoln masquerade ball, so it'll be pretty tight to finish it. It's currently sucking up every spare moment I have."

Leo pulls in a quick breath that ends in a cough. "Ah." He bangs his fist against his sternum twice. "Got something…" He coughs again. "Stuck."

I squint at him. "You okay?"

He backs away a step, eyes still on the dress. "Yeah. Uh-huh." A quick smile, another step back.

"You sure? You seem a little…off." If I didn't know any better, I'd say he's still unnerved by the dress form.

Finally, he meets my eyes again. His are wide like he's just noticing me there. "No, sorry. I'm just…I should go."

"Okay. Well, thanks again." I take hold of the dress to stay put. The air feels weird. Charged with undefinable undercurrents.

He nods slowly and presses his lips together. "Okay, I'll see ya." A moment later, he's gone.

And so, it would appear, is my common sense because, in a turn of events only Micki could have predicted, I wanted him to stay.

I think I like Leo Salinger. I think I like him quite a bit.

27

Living History Illinois Flockify DM, Saturday 9:55 AM
@AlCaponesGhost25

SingerQueen: What sits at the bottom of the sea
and twitches?

Living History Illinois Flockify DM, Tuesday 07:49 PM
@AlCaponesGhost25

SingerQueen: Did I stump you with that one?

Living History Illinois Flockify DM, Thursday 11:55 AM
@AlCaponesGhost25

SingerQueen: Hello?

In the week leading up to Halloween, I'm too busy to do much besides run the store and sew. I squeeze in a visit with Harvey who's making progress with his walking, but training is a no-go. It almost feels like Leo and I are avoiding each other. My only interaction with him for the week is a wave or two through the windows and a comment he leaves on my Instagram post featuring Boris snoozing at my feet.

Did you register him as a lethal weapon yet? he writes. ***Winky face emoji.***

It's probably for the best that that's all I get, but it also doesn't feel like enough. His visit at my place still lingers in my mind like a cliffhanger at the end of a chapter where I've yet to turn the page.

The day before Halloween, however, I am done with all the preparations, most of my customers have picked up their costume orders, I've delivered the masquerade ball gown, and all I have left to do are the last few touches on my Belle dress.

Micki texts me as I'm finishing up the hem.

Be ready at 8. No excuses.

The last thing I want after this week is a night out, but one of the breweries nearby has an annual fall event the last weekend of October with apple-themed brews and all-you-can-eat BBQ that we always go to. A promise is a promise. Jaz will be there, too, as well as a couple of Micki's colleagues from the salon who I've met before, so I know it's a fun crowd. As long as I can muster up enough energy, it'll be a good time.

"That's what you're wearing?" Micki frowns when I let her and Jaz in a little before eight. "You do remember what it's like to go out, right?" She heads straight for the closet and opens the door, shaking her head. "I've neglected you. This is what happens when they flee the nest," she complains to her sister. "A complete hermit."

"What's wrong with this?" I look down. Cozy knitted sweater, my favorite corduroy skirt, thick leggings, and combat boots. Perfect for a chilly, beer-filled fall evening.

"Nothing. If you were headed for the mall…" Micki turns around, a black off-the-shoulder top in her stretched-out hands. "Put this on. Keep the rest, but no grandma sweaters tonight."

Jaz checks the time. "We have fifteen minutes."

"Okay, okay." I do what Micki asks, then return from the bedroom and give them a spin.

"And earrings." Micki points me back to where I came from. "And run a brush through your hair, please. God, I can't wait to get my hands on that tomorrow."

Micki has persuaded me that, if I'm dressing up as Belle, I need princess hair to complete the illusion, so tomorrow I'm sitting my butt in her chair next door for a trim and style before trick-or-treating begins.

Jaz stomps her feet by the door. "Come on, people. Let's go."

"Schnitzel and Brew" has a long line of people waiting to get in, but with reservations, we pass the line and are seated without delay. Roderick and Donna from the salon are already there, so the first few minutes are a flurry of hugs and catching up.

"The first round's on me," Roderick says. "Prost!"

I tip back my Honeycrisp ale, and when the fizzy brew hits my system, the demands of the week finally drain away.

There's live music, five different kinds of brats, ribs, slaw, laughter, and more beer. For the first time since I took charge of the store, I'm able to let go. One night. I've earned it.

"I hear you're competing at Winter Fest this year," Donna says when we're in line for the bathrooms during a break from eating. "With the little one."

"Cholula. Yeah."

"Can she really balance on another dog?"

I could slap Micki. She wasn't supposed to talk about that. I have no idea if Cho is going to pull it off in the end. So far, I've only been able to get her to climb onto Cap when he's lying down. "We're working on it," I say. "I'm trying different things."

We're finishing our second round of drinks when Micki puts her hand on my arm and points to the entrance. "Look who's here."

I direct my attention to the crowd at the door, and there's Leo accompanied by a slightly shorter version of himself and a redhead with an expensive blow-out.

"You should go say hi." Micki nudges me.

Roderick leans forward. "Who are we talking about?"

"The king is here," Micki says under her breath.

"He is?" Roderick's head spins toward the door.

"The king?" I ask Micki. "You'd better not let Leo hear that or his head will explode."

"I heard from a client that he was fired from his fancy Wall Street job, and there's a lawsuit," Donna says.

"No way," Jaz says.

"Yeah, the king is no crook," Roderick counters. "Look at that honest face."

Honest or not, I am looking at Leo's face. I feel like I haven't looked at it in forever. The way it animates when he laughs, that thing he does with his eyebrows when he listens, the curve of his lips.

"We can add a few chairs," Jaz says, seemingly having forgotten that he's not supposed to know that I know her.

What? "No, I'm not sure that's a…" But she's already half-way across the room when I finish my sentence. "…good idea."

And now they're talking. She's shaking Leo's companions' hands. They're looking at me. I smile and wave. There's something tentative in Leo's movements as he lifts his hand in response, but then he nods at whatever Jaz is saying, and they all head our way. By the time he reaches us, he's his regular, confident self.

"So you guys know each other?" he asks in greeting. "And your hair is blond, Jaz."

Jaz's face falls. "Shit. Sorry, Cora. I wasn't thinking."

"She's my sister," Micki volunteers. "Ta-da!"

"Really?" He cuts a glance from Micki to me. "Should I be concerned at this little undercover operation?"

I smile sweetly. "Depends. Do you have a bunch of skeletons in your closet I'll be able to use against you?"

"You wish." He grins, and I turn the proverbial page to the next chapter.

Finally.

"Cora, this is my brother, Bennett, and his wife, Courtney." There are handshakes all around, more introductions, and a scramble to find more chairs for our table. We commandeer two, but a third one is not in the cards.

"That's okay, you squeeze in next to Cora on the bench," Micki says to Leo.

"You sure?" He looks to me.

Micki nudges my arm. "Come on, make room."

What choice do I have?

Once we're all seated, Bennett orders another round of drinks and appetizers for the table. If I understand him right, this is a rare night off for him and his wife. The kids are with the aunts, and they're all staying the night there to take part in the festivities tomorrow. I only pick up snippets of the conversation after that—I'm too distracted by Leo pressed up against my side. Every time he goes to take a drink, his arm brushes mine. When he laughs, it reverberates from his muscular thigh, up my hip, and through my core and chest. The warmth from his body becomes my warmth.

The truth dawns on me halfway through Courtney's story about some trip they went on last year to Sweden or Switzerland or someplace like that: I've missed seeing him this week.

"You okay?" Leo asks, his voice a murmur beneath the din of the room. "You're quiet tonight."

I have another sip of my beer before I turn to look at him. He's so close that I see the dark blue star closest to his pupil. His lips part, and I look away.

"I'm good. I'd forgotten your brother was visiting."

Another silence stretches between us. I smile and nod to something Bennett says without knowing what it was. My skin tingles, hyperaware of only Leo. His movements. His breathing. Does he want more space? Should I move closer to Micki? I fold my arms tightly, clasping one hand in the other.

"What do you do, Cora?" Courtney asks suddenly. Everyone turns to me.

"Um, I…" I reach for my beer but change my mind before picking it up.

Leo's knee presses into mine. It's subtle, but I'm not imagining it. *I'm here*, it says. *Relax*. Little does he know his body heat is the main reason I'm strung this tightly. At least that last move serves as confirmation that he doesn't mind my proximity.

Finding my nerve, I flex my leg his way in return and take a deep breath, relishing the full-femoral contact. "I run a small pet shop," I say.

"How quaint."

"Or it's my grandpa's, but he's recovering from a broken hip at the moment. Usually I'm more of a helper, but right now it's just me."

"Ah." Courtney turns and flags down a server, having already lost interest. Maybe that's what happens when you've married into the Canine King conglomerate.

I bite down on the inside of my cheek. "What about you?" I ask. She doesn't hear me.

"They're both lawyers," Leo says, close enough to my ear that his breath teases goose bumps out of my skin. "Busy, busy, right guys?"

Bennett pulls his attention from his phone to Leo. "What's that?"

"Work keeping you busy?"

"Always. Speaking of which, when's this little suburban sabbatical over? I bet the city misses you."

Leo runs a hand through his hair. "Yeah, no, I've still got… um…some time." He glances at me, a strange expression flitting across his face.

"Man, I wouldn't know what to do with myself. All that time off."

Time off? What's he talking about?

Donna's voice cuts through the silence at the table. "I knew the gossip about you being fired wasn't true. Didn't I tell you that?" she asks Roderick. She puts another piece of pretzel in her mouth and leans forward. "But doesn't opening a store defeat the purpose of a sabbatical? And what are you going to do with it when you go back to New York?"

Leo has become immobile at my side, and that's when I put two and two together. His brother doesn't know about the store. Bennett thinks Leo is here temporarily.

Is he?

28

I look at Leo's profile. Will someone else take over the store once he's got it up and running? I don't want that. I want his jaw to unclench, and his shoulders to relax. I want him to challenge me to another bet.

"How about another round of drinks?" he asks. "Cora, another ale? Micki, Jaz, what are you having?"

Bennett scrutinizes Leo, forehead creased. "What the fuck, Useless? You started your own firm? Here? Why?"

Useless? Firm?

Leo forces a smile. "Um, sort of. How about I tell you all about it later? More drinking, less talking."

There's enthusiastic agreement all around the table except from Courtney. She looks at her shiny wristwatch. "I don't know." She faces Bennett. "When did you tell Diane we'd be back?"

He finishes the rest of his lager in two gulps. "Yes, we should probably head out."

Next to me, Leo leans back as he exhales. "Are you sure? The night's still young."

"Yeah, man. We'll see you for lunch tomorrow, though." Bennett pulls the chair out for Courtney, and they gather their jackets.

They take their leave, and for a long moment, no one at our table speaks. Finally, Micki grabs her drink and moves to one of the now-empty chairs. Reluctantly, I scoot away from Leo to give us both more space.

Micki looks at us above the rim of her glass. "Fine, I'll be the one to address the elephant, then." The glass thumps when she sets it down. "You." She points a finger at Leo "Your brother doesn't know you opened a branch of Canine King here?"

"I thought I was the only one who picked up on that," Roderick says. "Yeah, what's the deal there? And nice going, Donna—you almost outed him."

"What? I didn't know," she protests.

"You shouldn't be ashamed of it," Jaz says. "It's a good store."

Leo puts his hands up. "It's fine. I was going to tell him tomorrow anyway. That, or he'd find out when they come trick-or-treating."

"Why haven't you told him?" I ask. "Or do you not want to talk about it?"

He fiddles with the signet ring he always wears on his right hand and glances toward the others. "Yeah, maybe not."

His unwillingness to share stings. I know he doesn't owe me any explanations, but I want to know what's going on in his head. He's always so reluctant to talk about his life before he moved here. Is there something to the rumors Donna heard after all?

When the chitchat resumes, Leo leans closer to me. "I forgot to tell you there'll be more people at lunch tomorrow. If you want to skip out on training, I'll totally understand."

I scrunch up my nose. "Actually, it's my bad. Micki is doing my hair before the Halloween extravaganza starts, so I can't come. I should have told you sooner."

He reaches out as if it's an everyday thing and runs his fingers through a strand down my back. "She's not cutting it, is she?"

My insides jolt at his touch, but I force myself to be still. Everything is cool. Nothing to see here. When I think I have control of my voice again, I turn my head his way. It's not lost on me that his hand still lingers low on my back.

"Only a trim," I say. "It's overdue."

"Like years overdue," Micki chimes in.

Leo's hand twitches against my back at the intrusion into our private sphere, but before he can pull away, I scoot a few inches closer to him and lean into his touch. He stills again, seeming to get my message.

"I don't mean to alarm you," Micki continues to Leo, "but you're not going to recognize her when I'm done. That rats' nest will be a thing of the past." She gestures to my head. "Pearls before swine."

Jaz and Donna nod.

"I'd give anything for hair like that," Donna says.

As the three of them continue their rant about people not taking care of their tresses the way they should, I finish my third beer and set it down.

"I like it, too," Leo says beside me, and now his fingers start moving. They tug softly at the ends of my hair, each pull sending electric sparks across my scalp.

Between his touch and the alcohol warming my blood, I'm melting in my seat. If I was a cat, I'd be purring. I steal another glance at Leo, and this time I don't look away when his gaze catches me. Because I am caught. A little bit against my will, and definitely against my better judgment. I want Leo. I want to talk to him, to touch him, to kiss him, to ride next to him in the car, to chase dogs through tunnels with him. I'm not sure when this happened, I just know that it did.

I'm stupidly lost in him until a pointy boot hits my shin, reminding me we're not alone at the table.

"Didn't you say you had to get up early tomorrow to finish your dress?" Micki asks me, her voice one hundred percent failing at hiding how much she's dying to stand up and shout "told you so" in front of everyone in the brewery.

I do have to get up early. But it's not that late and—

"I'll walk you home if you need to go," Leo volunteers.

"That's so nice." Micki sighs. "Isn't that nice?"

I send her a faux-icy glare. She's not even trying to be subtle. "Sure. I still have to settle my bill, though. Are you sure you don't want to stay for another round?" I ask Leo.

He shakes his head. "I'm good. And I've got the tab. I'll go tell the bartender."

He's halfway across the room before I can voice a protest at his chivalry. The bench is instantly colder with him gone.

"You're welcome," Micki hisses across the table. "Now, take him home and do nasty things to him. For your sake. End the drought."

"Charming."

"You know you want to. He wants to."

Leo is waiting for the bartender to return with his check. He's leaning against the bar counter, his fingers drumming an impatient rhythm. He glances my way, catching me gawking, and the corner of his mouth turns up.

Micki looks like she's about to start clapping her hands in celebration.

"Chill," I tell her, putting on my jacket. "I'm not sleeping with him. He's walking me home."

She pouts. "But you'd make such beautiful babies."

"Okay, you weirdo. I'll see you tomorrow. Bye guys," I say to the others.

Micki blows me a kiss.

"Ready?" I hand Leo his jacket.

He finishes signing the receipt and slides it across the bar. "Ready."

He steers me out of the brewery with a hand on my back, but when we get outside, he lets go. We walk for a minute without speaking.

"It was nice to meet your brother," I say eventually. "Were you guys close growing up?"

"In some ways. It gets competitive between boys, though."

"You competitive? No way."

He chuckles. "Can you believe it?"

Another arm touch. I bet if I flex my hand, it will touch his. I'm working up the nerve when the backs of his fingers graze mine. He holds still there, waiting for me.

"I believe it," I say, letting my fingers interlace with his. His warm palm against my cool one is like stepping inside after being caught in the rain. Every touching point radiates comfort and something more urgent, and when he squeezes tighter, the pressure resonates deep in my stomach.

"I didn't mean to be cryptic earlier by the way." Leo looks at me. "About Bennett and the store. When I said I didn't want to talk about it, I meant in front of the others. I don't mind telling you."

My chest expands. "No?"

He shakes his head. "It has to do with people I don't want to let down."

"Like your dad?"

"You know about my dad?" It comes out sharp.

Whoa there. "Not really, but I figured since Canine King is a family business…"

"Oh." He pauses and nods. "Right. Well, my father and my uncles have relied quite a bit on my position in New York for contacts, so this"—he gestures around us—"is not what they want from me."

"Are you sure? Maybe you'd be surprised—"

"I tried," Leo says. "I suggested something like this to my father before I left the city, and he laughed."

"But you are here. I don't understand."

"They don't know I opened this branch because I'm financing it myself. I wanted it to be profitable before I told them."

I stare at him. That's ballsy. And I can't imagine entirely legal. "And Bennett will tell your dad?"

A wry smile. "He'll relish it. It'll give him a leg up."

"But you're both adults now. Why does it matter?"

He's quiet for a while. Shrugs. "Maybe because it's always mattered. No one wants to disappoint their parents. And my mom is…" His voice trails off.

I finally dare the question I've been wanting to ask for a long time. "Dawn told me she was in an accident?"

He sucks in his lips. Releases them. "My senior year of high school. She fell off her horse—cracked her skull when the helmet flew off and broke her back. Still needs assistance round the clock."

The pain in his voice reaches out and squeezes my heart. "That must have been so hard."

"For everyone. My dad, too. The brain injury erased skills everyone else takes for granted. But she has a great assistant, and I know she's still herself inside, if that makes sense.

Stubborn, curious, passionate about animals…You'd get along great." He smiles. "I should try to see her more often."

I nod. "She sounds wonderful. Sorry, I didn't mean to pry."

"I don't mind. Everyone has something."

"Yeah. Maybe you could talk to Bennett tomorrow and tell him to keep it to himself?"

"Nah." His grip on my hand tightens. "I should be able to stand up for what I want to do, right?"

"Don't ask me. My parents still think I'm going to be a dentist one day."

"Why?"

"Long story." I give him a tight smile as we stop outside Happy Paws' back door. "Some other time."

He faces me without letting go of my hand. "I'll hold you to that."

I look up at him, at his curved lips, half shaded in the weak light from an old, rusted sconce. Is this it? The moment?

I wait, knowing his hands will soon be firm on my waist, not demanding but sure. They'll find their way beneath my black sweater where they'll caress the sensitive skin at the bottom of my spine and make me shiver, not from the coolness of the night but from a longing that's alive and urgent at my core.

Then he'll pull me closer. Slowly. He'll savor the approach in that meticulous way of his so that only the greatest self-control will keep me from charging him. His hands will run up my sides and down the length of my arms, circling my wrists where I'm sure my racing pulse will call to his skin.

Maybe he'll stop there, smirk at me, and lean in close, his breath a gossamer caress against my ear as he murmurs something like "I bet I want you more than you want me right now." And he'd lose that bet, too, because there's no chance.

Then, finally, I'll get a taste, and his flavors will be vibrant life and sweet hops. A case of it would not be enough. I know that for certain.

My mouth waters as his eyes skirt the edges of my face before settling on mine. He blinks. His lips part.

"I'm glad I got to hang out with you guys tonight," he says, letting my hand go and taking a step back. "I'll see you tomorrow."

What the hell?

29

Micki pulls open the door to the salon as if she's been waiting for me to show up all morning. "Tell. Me. Everything." She pulls me inside and takes the jacket off my shoulders.

The place is empty—they're closed on Sundays—but soothing music still plays over the speakers, and Micki has lit the candle on the front desk. Her eagerness to find out what happened last night only worsens the sinking pit of quicksand in my stomach. Not even a peck on the cheek?

"There's nothing to tell." I take a seat in the chair she points to and undo the scrunchie keeping my hair in a bun.

Micki stops what she's doing with the tray of scissors, combs, and brushes. "What do you mean?"

"I mean, nothing happened." I force myself to meet her gaze in the mirror.

"Nothing?" She frowns.

"Nothing." I sigh. "I thought he was going to kiss me, but then…he didn't."

"Huh. Maybe he thought you didn't want to?" She pulls out a big brush and starts detangling my hair.

"I mean, I held his hand on the way back." And I wouldn't be surprised if I was drooling.

"Okay, okay." She considers this. "So there was hand-holding at least—that's good. Maybe you had sauerkraut breath? Or did you say something weird?"

I glare at her. "Why would I do that?"

She shrugs. "Sometimes you're a bit... I don't know."

"Is that supposed to make me feel better?" Is that why Al has been MIA too? Because I'm *a bit*... what? Man repellent? Human repellent even?

She tugs at a knot at the base of my skull. "I'm sure you were fine. Maybe he wanted to take things slow. Some guys are like that, you know. No guy I've ever dated, but he could be the unicorn."

Just my luck then. My phone dings with a message. It's a picture of Tilly at the farm. With the morning mist in the background, she looks like a movie dog sent to rescue innocents from peril. **Halloween Dog**, Leo writes. And that's it. I turn my ringer off and put it away. "But now what do I do?"

Micki rests her hands on my shoulders and looks at me in the mirror. "You sit back and relax and let me work my magic. When I'm done, he won't be able to resist you."

"Pretty confident, huh?"

"You know it. And I've been wanting to get my mittens on this for ages." She holds up a long strand. "A trim, a few accent pieces around the face, a mask, big wavy curls, half updo. You're dressing up as Belle, so I'll be giving you princess hair. I don't even care that it'll be back up in a bun tomorrow."

To my surprise, I'm not opposed to her plans. Princess hair sounds good. The costumes I've made for the dogs and me are ready and waiting at home, and I couldn't be more thrilled with how they turned out. I have a cauldron with dry ice set up right inside the doors of Happy Paws, and enough candy for several busloads of kids should it be needed. I'm ready for the trick-or-treaters. Hopefully, Micki's expertise will also get me ready to see Leo again.

"Then work your magic, fairy godmother."

"There." Micki dusts the makeup brush across my nose and stands back.

I've been in her chair for hours, and she's finally done. A cloud of hair spray lingers in the space, tickling my nose, and my neck is sore from holding still, but my reflection in the mirror is worth it. I get out of the chair and study my new self closer.

My daily beauty routine involves little more than mascara and, on occasion, blush, which is why Micki insisted on doing a full face today. "I want you to *be* Belle," she said when I tried to protest. "That means shaped brows, lashes, lips, all of it."

At that point in the process, she'd already plied me into compliance with a lengthy scalp massage, so I didn't have it in me to say no. I am not sorry.

"I've never worn fake lashes before." I angle my face this way and that.

"They're magnetic. Super easy to take off. You like?"

I smile at her. "I do."

Micki hands me a stick of lip gloss. "Put this on after you get dressed."

"'Pucker-up Pink,'" I read on the wand.

"Foolproof." She winks. "What do you think about the hair?"

"What can I say? You're a magician. I thought you cut it, but it looks longer."

"It looks healthier."

I shake my head so that the long waves bounce around my shoulders. "I could be in a shampoo commercial."

Micki laughs. "Now, that's a compliment. Does that mean you'll let me do this on the regular?"

"Do I have to pay?"

She snorts and reaches out to fix a curl caught in my neckline. "I suppose it's open for discussion. Maybe you make me a dress instead."

"Deal." I pull her into a hug. "Thank you for this. I can't remember the last time I felt this pretty."

"What are you talking about? You're always pretty."

"Not like this. Anyway, I should go get the dogs out before it's time to get ready."

"I only have this." She picks up a witch's hat from the shelf behind her. "There, ready."

"Smart."

"Donna is coming over in a bit, and she's dressing as Dorothy. We're pretending we're coordinating."

"Without the green face?"

"Too much work."

"Says the person who just spent three hours getting me ready."

"Yeah, yeah. Go, princess. Go get your prince." She shoos me out the door with a promise to stop by the store later because her salon isn't participating in the candy-giving.

I don't think she knows the story of *Beauty and the Beast* very well. Belle doesn't go get the prince. They have to fall for each other in order to turn him into one.

Trick-or-treating goes from four to six, and the streets are packed. Boris, Cholula, and Cap play their parts as my furniture sidekicks as well as can be expected, monitoring each child who enters for runaway treats. We pose for photos, admire costumes, and hand out candy until my cheeks hurt from smiling. When the flow of people finally subsides, I've been called a "real princess" by at least two dozen adorable kids. Micki will get a kick out of it.

For the first time during the event, I step outside the store for some fresh air. I wave to the little Sleeping Beauty who now has a dragon-bedecked golden retriever courtesy of me. It's nice outside, cool but not freezing, and the skies are clear. Since there's not a lot of time left, I drag out my fake cauldron with candy and a chair to sit on.

I've been too busy until now to think about Leo, but from this vantage point, Canine King is in my direct line of sight. The lights are on inside, and several people crowd the entrance. Maybe I should have texted him back when he sent the picture of Tilly this morning, but I didn't know what to say. *Why didn't you kiss me?* Hardly.

The crowd leaves Leo's store only for another family to show up at mine. There's a fairy, an octopus, and a baby in a stroller dressed as an old lady in a curly wig and glasses.

"Are you a real princess?" the octopus asks.

"I am tonight," I say, placing candy in their bowls.

The fairy looks me up and down. "Are you going to marry the prince?"

"Alas, no prince has visited in many moons," I say, adding some affect to my voice.

"He's right there." The octopus points across the street.

I look up, and sure enough, there's Leo standing outside Canine King with a crown on his head.

"Come on, kids. Let's move on." The dad gathers his brood with a quick "thank you" to me.

"Sure," I mumble. Leo is staring at me, a baffled look about him. I try a small wave.

He glances down the street and back at his store. Then he seems to make up his mind. All I can do is stand there, statue-like, as he approaches.

"Wow." He shakes his head slowly. "You look..."

"Like a princess?"

"Gorgeous."

Oh. "Thanks. It's all Micki." I indicate his head. "You dressed up, too. Kind of thought you'd drop the ball on the whole thing."

He touches his crown. "Looking at you, I feel like this doesn't count."

I smirk. "It's an understated costume, I'll give you that. But the kids still knew you're a prince."

"I was going for king, actually. Because of..." He points to his store.

"Yeah, that makes more sense. Nice one."

He shakes his head again. "I told you I'm terrible at this stuff."

"You did." I chuckle. "I should have believed you."

"But you." His eyes do that sparkly thing again. "You made that dress, too? It's very impressive."

My stomach summersaults. His attention is bringing back last night. His palm against mine, the high before the disappointment. "Come on, you have to see the dogs." I lead him inside where the three of them are sleeping.

Leo laughs. "Poor Boris looks miserable. I don't think *candlestick* is his color. Here, let me get a picture. You sit there."

He positions me behind Mrs. Potts, Lumiere, and Cogsworth and snaps a few shots. "You need to frame one of these for the store."

"Yeah, send me one." I want to say more, but all the words that come to mind sound so needy.

His gaze jumps past my shoulder. "Shoot, there are people at the store." He turns in a hurry, but halfway out the door, he stops. "Hey, we're almost done with this, right? Do you want to go over to the park for some cider after?"

My belly warms again. "For sure."

30

Once the kids go home, the celebrations continue along the Riverwalk with live music, food trucks, and fire pits for the adults reliving their childhood dress-up games. There are elaborate Star Wars costumes, a Thor who could be Chris Hemsworth's body double, mummies, Wonder Women, and zombies. My dress is partly covered by an old stole I found among my grandma's things, but Leo and I still turn heads in our matching crowns.

We've just entered the park when Micki and Donna catch up to us.

"No way" is the first thing Micki says. "You guys coordinated? Look at you." She spreads her hands as if presenting us.

"It wasn't intentional. Where've you been? I thought you were stopping by the store?"

"I tried once, but it was too crowded, and then we ran into some other friends. You're not mad?"

I assure her I'm not.

"There's a beer tent at the end of the walk that has karaoke. You guys should join us," Donna says.

"Oooh, that would be fun." I turn to Leo. "I hereby challenge the king to an epic karaoke battle."

"Seriously, did you know she was going to be Belle?" Micki asks Leo. "Or was this a serendipitous accident?"

"I didn't know," he says. "About the costume or the karaoke. My people neglected to pass on that information."

"But you'll come?" Micki asks me. "It'll be fun."

I glance at Leo. "Maybe in a bit," I say. "We're going to grab some food first."

Micki looks from me to Leo and back, a sly smile pulling at her cheeks. "You do that. See you guys later." She backs away. "Or not." She winks at me.

When they're gone, I nudge Leo's elbow with mine as we head toward the food trucks. "So, you and me, a sing-off. What's the bet going to be?"

"Ah, I don't know."

In the distance, music spills out of the beer tent—a terrible rendition of Def Leppard's "Pour Some Sugar on Me." "Come on. I'm positive you can do better than that."

He gives me a self-deprecating smile. "Unfortunately, we will never know. This is one bet I'm afraid I'll have to forfeit."

I feign shock. "You? Forfeiting?"

"I don't do singing. Or stages. And especially not singing on stages."

"Are ya' scared?" I make a chicken noise.

"Well…"

"Afraid people won't take you seriously anymore?" *Cluck, cluck.*

"Ah, ha, ha." He scratches his tilted head, peering at me. "Sorry. Salingers work hard. We're not as good at playing."

He means it. I'm more disappointed by this than I should be, even though a forfeit technically means another won bet for me.

Leo gets us hot cider and elephant ears that we eat on a bench not far from where we first ran into each other.

"I meant to ask, how was lunch? Did you do any training?" I pull off a piece of fried dough and chew carefully, trying to avoid getting powdered sugar all over Leo's jacket that he loaned me when I got cold. Grandma's stole is not as warm as I'd thought.

"Ha! Tilly refused. I think she missed Cholula. The food was great as usual, though." His lips press together briefly. "Bennett stopped by the store earlier—not sure if you saw."

"I don't think so. What did he say?"

"*You're in for it now, Useless,*" he says in a mocking tone. "Wouldn't let me explain."

I resist the urge to reach out and touch his arm. "That bites. Um, why does he call you *Useless*? He did it last night, too. Seems rude."

Leo hesitates but then acquiesces, tipping his crown to me. "John Leopold *Eustace* Salinger the third. Nice to meet you."

I try not to laugh, but I can't help it. "No way."

"Laugh all you want. It's a family name—oldest son gets it. To Bennett's great joy."

"And the third...Very regal. Fitting tonight."

"I think so. Cheers to that." He clinks his paper mug to mine.

The pieces of him are slowly coming together. Of his background. But there is still so much I don't know.

"You know, you've told me you were in finance before this, but you've never actually explained how you ended up back here."

He takes another sip of his cider and looks off toward a group of laughing teens.

I had to open my mouth. I already know this is a touchy subject for him. "Sorry, it's none of my business. We can talk about something else. How did Tilly like her cape?"

"No." He rests the mug against his leg and turns back to me. "I'll tell you. I don't mind." He pauses as if considering where to start. "The first thing you should know is that I grew up knowing exactly what the expectations were for me. If at any point Bennett or I strayed from that path, we felt it. My dad is not a bad person, but he's very traditional. His word was law."

"What would he do?"

He must hear the concern in my voice because he hurries to say, "He's not physically abusive or anything. Let's just say he's turned the silent treatment into an art form." A wry smile. "Anyway, success was always important. Grades, sports, what have you. Good college, impressive job."

"And you did all that."

"Without questioning. I mean, I enjoyed the status that came with it, and I didn't mind the work, at least in the beginning. Investment banking can be exhilarating if you're good at it, and I was."

"But?"

"But I was working all the time. My relationships suffered, my health…"

At the mention of relationships, I suppress an urge to cover my ears. He probably had a string of glamorous, uber-intelligent girlfriends. I want to know, and I don't.

"Last year, I started having weird physical symptoms. I was dizzy, my mind felt foggy, I could never get enough sleep—and I nearly lost a client millions of dollars. It would have been bad. Lawsuit bad. Fortunately, my boss caught the mistake." He lifts his shoulders high and releases them. "That was it. I quit. I was burned out, my wife left me, and I came out here to rest. Diane's farm was the first place I thought of when everything fell apart. I have some of my happiest childhood memories there."

I blink at him, wanting to make sure I heard him right. "Your wife?"

His lips pop open. "Um, right." He runs a hand across his forehead. "Shit, I didn't mean to...Yeah, I was married. Her name's Samantha. But I'm not anymore. We signed the divorce papers not long ago."

Samantha. The letter. The pieces fall into place. Still, getting it confirmed is a doozy. He had a whole life somewhere else before this. A grown-ass life. And here I am with nothing to show for myself. Is that why he didn't kiss me?

His fingers brush my hand for the briefest of moments. "What are you thinking?"

"That that's a lot."

"I didn't mean to pile it all on you."

"No, I mean a lot for you to deal with. A lot of change. Are you doing better now? The physical symptoms are gone? That must have been hard."

"It was, but Diane and Dawn totally nursed me back to health. I needed space and quiet. Being out there with them and the dogs—it was the smartest decision I ever made."

Something dawns on me. "So Tilly is your emotional support dog."

"For all intents and purposes." He smiles.

"And you don't regret giving up any of it? Your life before this, I mean."

He shakes his head. "No. There were perks, of course, but they're not worth everything else. The sacrifices."

"And your marriage?"

He puts his arm up on the backrest of the bench so his hand comes to rest near my shoulder. "I won't lie—that was rough. Samantha and I met at Yale, got married at twenty-five—Martha's Vineyard, the whole shebang. I meant my vows. She felt differently and moved on."

He emphasizes the word *meant*, and that earnestness alone makes me want to reach out for him and rest my hand where his shoulder meets his neck. "And what about now? Do you still—"

His gaze latches on to mine, making the rest of my words catch. It's as warm and heady as it was last night. "No. Now I'm moving on, too."

I give the smallest of nods before I shift forward slightly. My lips part in anticipation as his fingers flex near my arm and make contact. I can almost feel his breath against my skin.

But then he stops, a pained expression chasing across his face. "Cora, wait."

I've misread him. In an instant, I am as sure of that as I was of the opposite a moment ago. I scramble back and start bumbling an apology. "I didn't mean…God, it's this night, and the dress and…Ha. Why would you want to—"

"No, stop." Leo gets up from the bench and spins to face me. "I do want to." He takes off his crown and musses his hair with a hand, leaving it on end.

He does want to… I frown. "Then what is it?"

He sits back down, rolling back his shoulders. "Okay." He blows out a breath. "Okay fine. I have to tell you something."

"Clearly." I try a smile, but he doesn't reciprocate.

"And please believe me when I say, I didn't know."

A shiver runs up my spine. "You're starting to freak me out. Didn't know what?"

He extends his hand as if to introduce himself to me for the second time that night. When I take it, he says, "I'm AlCaponesGhost25. It's nice to officially meet you SingerQueen."

31

I can't move. I think I heard him say what he said, but it's simultaneously not possible.

"I'm sorry what?" I stare blankly at him.

"I didn't know you were you," he says. "Not until I saw the dress you were making, the Lincoln ball one, and then everything fell into place. Diane also has a Singer sewing machine—I had just never noticed it before. I would have told you sooner, but I honestly didn't know how you would react, and I didn't want to piss you off or string you along or pretend I didn't know so I—"

"Just stayed away from the server this week," I fill in, pulling myself free from his grip. That explains the absent Al mystery. I lean forward and rest my head in my hands. "But how? Why?" I look up again. "You were listed as an international member." It comes out as an accusation.

He makes a pinched grimace. "Because I'm a 'ghost.' Ghosts can go anywhere."

I sputter a baffled laugh despite everything. "Pfft, that's...I don't even...But you're not twenty-five either. How do you explain that one?"

"My birthday is February fifth. And don't forget you said you're a clothing designer. That you travel for work."

I snap my mouth shut. He's right, I did. We both did what people do online—embellish, withhold, dream. *This* was not supposed to happen.

"Cora, it's not the end of the world, right? It's like a freak coincidence."

But I was complaining about him to "Al." As our conversations return to me in snippets, I realize he was complaining about me. What else have we said that we shouldn't have?

My phone rings in my pocket before I can go down that path. "Sorry, hold on."

My first thought is that it's the nursing home. I don't know why—I have no reason to think something would have happened to Harvey, but that's why I pull it out in the first place. Turns out, it's my mom.

"It's okay. Take it." Leo gets up and walks away a few steps.

"Thanks. I'll be quick." I turn away from him. "Mom?"

"Hi, hon."

"What's going on?"

"Not right now, Martin, I'm talking to Coralynn. Yes, put the paints in the bin over there. Did you get batteries?"

I sigh. "Mom?"

"Sorry, we're packing up here in Montana. We'll be driving through Yellowstone and Grand Teton the next few days with a stop to visit with friends we met in Florida a couple of years ago, so I thought I'd give you a call to say Happy Halloween and happy early birthday. I'm not sure where we'll be on Wednesday, so this seemed easier."

"My birthday is *next* Wednesday, but okay…" You'd think

with only one kid she'd know when my birthday is. But maybe it's hard to keep track of the days when you're on the road.

She disappears again. "No, the other one. Martin—the one to the left. The other pillow is too soft."

I glance toward Leo and make a spinning motion with my finger indicating the conversation is dragging on.

No worries, he mouths.

"Coralynn, are you still there?" Mom asks, as if I'm the one having two conversations at once.

"I'm here."

"We'll owe you a present when we see you next. I didn't have time to ship anything."

"Or you could transfer some money instead." I say the words quickly, both hoping and not hoping she'll hear them.

Mom scoffs. "Where's the fun in that?"

"I suppose."

Leo shoves his hands deep into his pockets. He must be freezing.

"Was there anything else, Mom? I've got to go."

"No, no, that's it. Dad says hi."

"Hi to Dad. Drive safely."

"Always do."

We hang up, and I put the phone away. "Sorry. Parents."

"You don't have to tell me."

"So…" I stand up.

"So."

His hair is still messy, and the tip of his nose glints in the streetlight. For a long while, neither of us speak. The sparkling tension from earlier has solidified into a concrete block, awkward and rigid. It sits between us like an obstacle we have yet to figure out how to scale.

"Micki and the others are probably waiting for you," Leo says, eventually. "I think maybe you should join them."

My teeth let go of my lip. "And you?"

"I'm going to head home."

I nod slowly. "Oh, your jacket." I start shrugging it off.

Leo puts a hand up. "No, keep it. You need it more than I do. Maybe you give it back tomorrow?" A tinge of hope tilts up the last syllable.

I know what he's really asking. Will we move past this? The truth is, I need to think.

"I'll make sure you get it," I say. It's the best I can do in the moment.

"Where did Leo go?" Micki asks, when I've elbowed my way to their table in the tent.

"He had to get home."

She scrutinizes me over her beer. "You okay?"

"Yeah." I suck in a deep breath. *Shake it off.* "Yeah, I'll be fine. I'll tell you later. Have you put a song in yet?"

"We've narrowed it down to 'Waterloo' by ABBA or 'Torn' by Natalie Imbruglia," Donna says. "Got a preference?"

"Definitely 'Torn,'" I say. I can think of no better word to encapsulate my feelings in this moment.

32

'm hoarse and a little hungover when I wake up the following morning. Linda Ronstadt's "You're No Good" still plays on repeat in my head. I might have leaned into man-bashing songs a little hard in my song selection last night, but needs must.

My mind is still grappling with Leo being Al because what are the chances? I can't help but feel that this is the universe trying to tell me something. I flash back to how he looked at me the day we met in the park. How I was nothing but a nuisance to him. I know he's ambitious, and if there's still a part of him that sees me like that—like my needs are secondary—we'll never work out anyway. And that's not taking into account that I now know he's recently divorced, recovering from burnout, and in the midst of an elaborate scheme to decide his future for himself—a scheme that, I'd be foolish to forget, is still causing me quite a bit of financial strain. Maybe allowing something to happen with him would only cause unnecessary complications when I have enough on my hands already.

"That sounds like a weak-bellied cop-out," Micki says when I tell her as much over lunch. She's come over so I can quiz her on muscle names. "You're saying that because this nice guy you talked to online is the same person as the nice guy across the street, you should cut your losses and run?" She throws a balled-up paper towel my way.

I duck and pout. "Well, when you put it like that…"

"What other way is there to put it?"

"You're saying I'm overthinking things with him."

"One hundred and ten percent."

I groan. "But he called me a *grouch* to a supposed stranger online."

"You've called him worse to his face." She cocks an eyebrow. "And haven't you both come to your senses since?"

I nibble the inside of my cheek as I look through the window toward Canine King. Leo has stayed deep in the store today, sending Jaz out with Tilly for her walks. I've barely caught a glimpse of him, and I don't like it. Maybe Micki is right.

I hold up the illustration of a skinless human body and indicate the leg. "Okay, show me what you've got?"

"Sartorius, rectus femoris, vastus medialis." She points. "So? What will you do?"

"I'm going to make sure you pass your class."

She awards me a pointed glare. "With Leo."

I lower the illustration to the table with a sigh. "I really don't know, Mick. What would you do?"

She shrugs matter-of-factly. "Just text him. Start with *Hi* and take it from there."

"Simple as that?"

"Simple as that."

I do start several texts to Leo after Micki leaves, but none of them make it past her proposed beginning. He doesn't reach out, either, and his apartment is dark all evening. For all I know, he's fled to the farm to avoid me.

When noon rolls around on Tuesday and there's still no sign of him, I finally text Jaz who I know is at the store. Just an innocent **Are you guys having a good day over there?**

It takes an hour before she responds. **It's nuts. Leo is sick so I'm alone. How do you answer the phone, take payments, and keep the store tidy without going completely bonkers?**

He's sick? With a pang of guilt, I glance at his jacket that's still hanging on a hook by the back door. I knew he'd get too cold.

Sorry it's hectic, I text Jaz before I pull up my thread with Leo. Things between us may be awkward, but it's not going to stop me from checking in. **Hear you're sick. Anything I can do?**

Soon after, I get busy with the afternoon shoppers, and when I look at my phone again, he's still not responded. I'm getting genuinely concerned now.

What kind of sick is he? I ask Jaz. **Have you been in touch with him?**

Bad cold I think, she responds. **I talked to him at lunch and he sounds awful.**

Okay. That calms me somewhat. At least he's not dead with Tilly chewing on his bones over there.

I lock up for the day at five and send him another text: **Let me know if I can pick up some meds.** My fingers hover above the screen for a moment before I add, **And let me know you're okay.**

I find it hard to focus on my sewing that evening. My gaze constantly goes to the dark windows of his apartment, wondering, worrying. Why isn't he texting back? Maybe something really has happened. Lunch is now almost twelve hours ago, and pondering it further, I'm not at all sure Jaz's assessment was even right.

I reach for my phone again. Sorry to keep texting, but I'm a little worried. Okay medium worried. So here's the deal, if I don't hear back from you by 10 am, I'm calling the police. Or the aunts.

I jump into a straighter position when, finally, the moving dots appear. He's alive!

> I'm here. Sick and gross. I've basically been sleeping since yesterday afternoon.

I let out a breath. Impressive. Sorry you're so sick, but at least you're not kidnapped or lying in a pool of blood somewhere.

> That's where your mind went?

I send back a shrug emoji.

I'll be fine, he types. Fluids and rest, right? You'll have to train alone tomorrow, though. Sorry. Say hi to the aunts from me.

I suppress the disappointment and refocus—more training is always more training. It might give me another leg up. At least that's what I'm supposed to think.

> Will do. Get some more rest and I'll check in tomorrow. Keep your phone on! G'nite.

G'nite, he types. And thank you for worrying about me.

I'm not sure what to say to that, so I turn my phone off. With any luck, he won't remember my excessive concern tomorrow.

33

Cholula is unhappy. She does what I ask of her at training but with more frequent evil glares than usual. She weaves through the cones and then looks at me over her shoulder in disgust. She comes when I call but at a petulant pace that would impress no one. *Look at me obeying your stupid commands,* she seems to say. And I kind of agree. It does feel stupid today.

"I'm sorry Tilly isn't here, too," I say. "Now, let's show this tunnel who's boss."

We cut our session short after ten successful tunnel runs, two of which came directly following a cone weave. She's definitely getting better. My ugly little dog is a genius who's going to save us all.

Diane brings me a container of chicken soup to take home to Leo, and she confirms my assessment. "I was watching from the window," she says. "Cho *is* a smart dog."

For the first time since we arrived, Cho looks alert. Sometimes she scares me a little.

It's almost eight when I get back, so I head across the street as soon as I've cleaned and fed the dogs. There's TV noise coming from Leo's apartment, which is encouraging, but I knock hard in case he's sleeping again. Instantly, Tilly starts whining inside, followed by a raspy voice telling her to go lie down.

"Hold on," the voice says next.

The door opens, and there's a disheveled Leo in pajamas and with a blanket wrapped around his shoulders. When he sees me, he glances down as if to double-check he is, in fact, wearing pants. "Hi."

"Hi." I hold up the soup and his jacket. "I come bearing gifts. Can I come in?"

"Um…" The temperature has dropped, and a shiver rattles his shoulders. "You're not worried about getting sick?"

"Eh." I shrug. "It's not like I'm going to kiss you."

He startles, but then a first sign of life materializes. "Pity. I guess I'll settle for your company then." He opens the door wider and shuffles back to the couch.

Me and my brainless mouth. "So, how are you feeling?"

He runs a hand through his hair which doesn't help one bit. "Well, let's see. I'm going through half a box of tissues an hour and Olympic amounts of decongestant. My body aches, and my throat feels like I've swallowed a zester. So pretty good, I'd say."

"At least the virus didn't impair your sense of humor. That's always something." I gesture to the food. "Diane made chicken soup. Do you want me to heat some up?" Maybe the answer to moving forward is to pretend the online stuff never happened.

His stomach growls as if it's never wanted anything more. "That would be amazing." He pulls the blanket up to his chin. "I've had nothing but peanut butter for the past two days."

I put a bowl in the microwave and glance over my shoulder while it spins. "You do look pretty terrible," I say. "No offense."

"None taken. All jokes aside, I don't feel awesome either. But better now that you stopped by. How was training?"

"No one ran away." I smile, ignoring his compliment. "Spoon?"

"Second drawer. Well, that's a success then."

I set the soup down on the coffee table next to him and then help myself to a portion as well.

We eat in a silence that stretches with the clang of metal against ceramic. Our eyes meet occasionally, but suddenly words seem to have escaped us both. So much for pretending.

When I can't take it anymore, I spit out the first thing that comes to mind. "Cholula did good with the tunnel today. Cap too."

His brow lifts, and he nods. "That's good." I think he's going to leave it like that, but then he asks, "Are you having second thoughts about which one of them to show?"

I chew and swallow. "No. Cap had one of his spacey episodes afterward. Maybe he got overexcited."

Leo finishes his soup and sets the bowl down. "If I wasn't so exhausted, I'd worry about falling behind." He leans back against the cushions and closes his eyes.

"You'll catch up."

Again the room falls quiet. Tilly is dreaming on the floor next to us, her tiny yips the only interruption to latch on to.

"Aww, so cute," I say.

Leo turns to look and hums in agreement.

We both watch her as if she's the most fascinating creature. A sleeping dog. Leo is not usually at a loss for words, and I keep hoping he'll dive in and launch us out of our stalemate, but he doesn't.

My fingertips find a loose thread at the hem of my shirt that I pull on until it frays, and when the knit threatens to unravel, I give up the wait. I reach for Leo's bowl and bring it to the sink. "Anything else I can get you before I go? More water? Tea? Another blanket?"

He peers up at me, dark shadows marring his face. For a second, he looks as if he can't believe I'm here. As if he doesn't want me to go. Then he closes his eyes again. "No, I'm okay. But thank you."

I look out the window toward Happy Paws. The store is dark, but I've left a light on for the dogs upstairs. *That's* where I'm supposed to be, I remind myself. Preventing the man in front of me from edging me out of business. Maybe this is for the best. "Okay, well…then I'm going to head out." I pull on my knitted cap and reach for my jacket, pausing for a moment in the middle of his room. "I'll check in again tomorrow, but let me know if you need anything before that, okay?"

"Okay. Hey, Cora?"

I turn, my hand on the door handle. "Yeah?"

He rubs a hand across one eyebrow. Pauses. "Never mind. See you tomorrow."

I know he's watching me as I leave, and I feel his eyes on me as I cross the street.

I can still see him through the window when I get up to the apartment. He has his laptop open at the table, and in a flash, an idea sparks.

With shaky hands, I pull out my phone and navigate to Flockify. My last message to Al still sits unanswered, but I don't let that stop me. Maybe SingerQueen and AlCaponesGhost25 are better communicators than Cora and Leo.

Living History Illinois Flockify DM, Wednesday
09:34 PM

SingerQueen: Can I ask you a question?

Here in the dark, I have a front row seat to him reacting to the message alert. There's a split second where I worry he'll read it and leave me hanging again, but this time, he responds right away.

AlCaponesGhost25: Of course, hotdog girl.

SingerQueen: We talked about that …

AlCaponesGhost25: How about hot *dog* girl?
winky face emoji

SingerQueen: Aren't you supposed to be sick?

AlCaponesGhost25: Just had an invigorating
visit … What's your question?

SingerQueen: Were you telling the truth about
when you realized this was me?

AlCaponesGhost25: Yes.

SingerQueen: You had no idea before that?

AlCaponesGhost25: If you're asking would I string
you along and pretend to be a stranger in order
to surreptitiously learn information about you, the
answer is no. Would never.

SingerQueen: That's very specific and on point.
Mind reader?

AlCaponesGhost25: Not last time I checked.

SingerQueen: Phew.

AlCaponesGhost25: Can I ask you a question?

SingerQueen: Only fair.

AlCaponesGhost25: Did I ruin things by telling you?

Did he ruin… There's a flutter at the pit of my stomach at the implication. I bite my lip before I let my thumbs touch the screen.

SingerQueen: I hope not.

34

This is fulfilling almost all my nurse fantasies," Leo jokes when I bring him some bread and milk to go with his peanut butter for breakfast. "Are you actually a fever dream?"

I laugh and throw one of Tilly's plush toys at him. "Behave. We'll be having no sponge baths today."

"Aw," he whines. "Not even if I say please?"

"Even then. But it's good to see you're feeling a little better." My face is threatening to change color, so I busy myself pouring him a glass of milk and then putting the carton back in the fridge. Should I bring up our online exchange at all? I'm desperate to know what *things* he was worried he had ruined.

"I slept like a rock thanks to a full belly last night," he says, and the moment passes.

"You should still take it easy today. Jaz has things covered."

He wrinkles his nose at me and cocks his head. "Did you really place her as a spy in my store?"

I lick a dab of peanut butter off my finger. "I had nothing to do with it. And even if I did, you should know she's about as cunning as a...um...whatever is the opposite of a fox. Here you go." I set a plate down in front of him.

"Thank you. Will you keep me company?"

I look at the time. I have a few minutes before I have to get the store ready to open, so I take a seat at the table.

He munches in silence, occasionally pausing to have a sip of milk. His complexion is not as pallid today, and there's life back in his eyes.

"Think you'll be able to train this weekend?" I ask.

"I have to or Tilly will lose everything she's learned so far. Saturday probably, if that works for you. Maybe Sunday, too."

"What's her talent going to be? In the show?"

"I can't tell you that." He says it so matter-of-factly.

"Oh, really? Are you getting scared because I'm three-for-three so far?"

"Queen of Halloween was one. And the karaoke forfeit. What's the third?" He wipes crumbs off his fingers with a napkin.

"The tunnel runs."

"No, hold up. We never finished the tunnel runs because of Boris."

"Cap had the most runs. That means I won, and you...what was that word again?" I finger-gun him. "Lost."

His eyes narrow. "Fine. I'll make my comeback when it counts."

"Or not."

He suppresses a laugh that threatens to turn into a coughing fit, so I go to fill up his glass with water.

"You're pretty full of yourself this morning," he says between gulps. "Feeling emboldened by my measly state?" He wipes his mouth. "I guess we'll see what happens."

I smirk. "I guess we will."

I pick Micki up after work. She's coming with me to see Harvey, and she's not the only one. Cholula is snoozing in the back seat because I have a plan. Every time I've talked to Pop the past two weeks, he has asked about the dogs over and over. It's not that he doesn't think I'm capable of caring for them, but he's used to them being around. Dogs fill your space with a certain kind of energy that combats loneliness like no other, and without it, there's only empty space.

"You're going to smuggle her in?" Micki asks when I tell her as much. "Isn't that against the rules?"

"Oh, most definitely."

Micki laughs. "Got to say, I'm kind of liking this side of you."

When we park at Dalebrook, I tell Cholula to get into the large canvas tote bag I brought and then I hoist the handles of it onto one shoulder. "Be a good girl," I tell her. "No barking."

Micki shakes her head. "This will never work. She's going to give us away."

There's a sign on the front door banning dogs from the premises unless they're licensed guide dogs, but that doesn't stop me. "Walk on my right so you cover the bag," I whisper to Micki as we hurry past the front desk.

Halfway through the lobby, the receptionist calls out, "Excuse me."

We stop short. *Shit.*

"You forgot to sign in." The receptionist smiles. "Who're you seeing today?"

We step up to the counter, me clutching the top of the bag closed with my elbow, willing Cho to stay still. "Harvey

Morton," I say as casually as I can. "Do you mind signing?" I ask Micki. "On account of my, um, wrist."

"Oh, of course." She springs into action, scribbling our names on a list.

Cholula isn't liking the dark, it seems. The bag wriggles against my hip.

"Thanks." The receptionist takes the clipboard from him. "Have a great visit."

I set a faster pace than is probably inconspicuous down the hall while trying my best to shield the bag from view. It works. We reach Harvey's room without incident.

"I thought for sure she knew," I pant. "Okay, come on out, girl." As soon as I open the bag, Cholula's head pops out like a jack-in-the-box.

"Cora," Harvey exclaims from his bed. He puts his book away on the side table. "And Michaela!"

"And a special visitor today." I bring Cholula to the bed.

"No…" Harvey's astonishment is priceless as Cholula attacks him with kisses. "Aww. Hello, my friend." He laughs. "Yes, I've missed you, too. Aww. Yes, we're so excited."

Micki leans closer to me and says under her breath, "Okay, this reunion definitely makes the sneaking around worth it."

"I thought she'd break up the monotony," I say. "How are you doing?"

We chat for a bit about his rehab, the store, Halloween, and who didn't get a rose on *The Bachelor*.

"They say I might be able to come home early December," Harvey says. "I can't wait to sleep in my own bed."

Micki has been standing guard near the door, but now she looks at me as if she senses the flicker of concern Pop's words have triggered. It means my window to prove myself is running out.

I put on a brave face. "You've had enough of being waited upon already? There are no bells to ring at home. No cute nurses to chat up."

He waves me off. "I'm aging twice as fast in here. Don't get me wrong, everyone's fantastic, but a man wants his own."

Micki cranes her neck toward the doorway. "Cora, someone's coming. Maybe put Cholula away in case."

"Yes, yes," Harvey says, getting in a few last pets.

"Hurry," Micki whispers, as footsteps approach.

Cholula gets in the bag at the same time the door opens.

"Well, good morning, gentlemen," a stout, silver-haired nurse says. "And visitors. You must be Harvey's granddaughter," she says to me. "He talks about you all the time."

"Morning," I say, moving away from the bed, closer to Micki.

"How was physical therapy?" the nurse asks Harvey.

"Excellent as always." He sits with his hands properly in his lap, but every so often he glances at my bag. Like Jaz, he'd make a terrible spy.

"Now let's get you comfortable," the nurse says to Charles in the bed next to Harvey. The man is awake this time but hasn't said a word so far. "Is your sister coming in later?"

Charles doesn't respond, but Harvey perks up. "Not until one. Sylvia's getting a new washing machine delivered between ten and noon."

Micki and I look at each other. Harvey knows a lot about Sylvia.

"Dog."

The sound startles all of us. It sounded like a honk, and it takes me a moment to realize it came from Charles.

"You're talking!" Harvey exclaims. He turns to us. "He hasn't spoken since his stroke, and now Sylvia missed it."

That's exciting and all, but did Pop not notice what word was said?

"Dog," Charles says again.

The nurse raises the back of his bed farther and takes his hand. "That's very good, Charles. Do you miss your dog?"

Charles turns his head slowly to look at Harvey. "His dog."

"Yes, Harvey has three dogs. What are their names again, Harvey?"

"Um...I have Boris, Cap, and—" Panic rises in Harvey's eyes, and next to me, Micki is stiff as a board. My bag is moving.

"Dog," Charles says in a louder voice.

"And Cholula," Harvey finishes.

As soon as her name is spoken, Cholula pokes her head out of the bag and lets out a happy bark.

The nurse spins, mouth round like an O. "What on earth?"

Charles sags back against his pillow, one corner of his mouth turning up.

The color on the nurse's cheeks is darkening. "Harvey, is this your dog?"

"I wanted to cheer him up," I say, stepping between them. "He didn't know."

The nurse huffs and puffs. "And it's an awfully ugly little thing, too."

Harvey's features harden. "She can't help how she looks any more than you or me."

"Dog," Charles mumbles.

"At least she made him speak," I try.

The nurse whips around and looks from Cholula to me and Micki. "Be that as it may, we have rules here at Dalebrook. I'm going to finish in here. In the meantime, I suggest you take that dog outside." She looks at her watch. "I will meet you in the lobby in ten minutes."

Uh-oh. Called to the principal's office again. Leo will get a kick out of this.

At least I wasn't the one to get you in trouble today, he responds when I text him later.

This is true. I'm choosing to look at it like we helped Charles regain his speech. Not that he was especially appreciative.

I'm sure he'll come around. Maybe Harvey ate one too many of his puddings or something.

I chuckle. That would do it. This was definitely a personal vendetta carried out with more determination than I've ever seen. At least I wasn't banned from the premises this time.

Leo: Ouch.
Me: You know what I mean.
Leo: On that topic, I told Dianne and Dawn we'll be there Saturday. Good with you?

I type my response but hesitate before I send it. Then I do it anyway. **Can't wait.**

35

Living History Illinois Flockify DM, Friday 09:15 PM

AlCaponesGhost25: Did you decide yet?

SingerQueen: Decide what?

AlCaponesGhost25: Whether you judged the "showoff at your work" unfairly?

SingerQueen: Leaning toward yes.

AlCaponesGhost25: He might get a second chance then?

SingerQueen: Does he want one?

AlCaponesGhost25: Very much.

That's good to know. I'm also surprised at his straight answer. What is it about this medium that makes it so much easier to spell things out? But maybe that's something to take advantage of.

SingerQueen: If that's the case, I have another question.

AlCaponesGhost25: Shoot.

SingerQueen: When you walked me home from Schnitzel & Brew, I thought you were going to kiss me.

AlCaponesGhost25: Pretty sure that's not a question. *winky face emoji*

SingerQueen: Smart-ass. Was I wrong?

It takes a few moments before he responds.

AlCaponesGhost25: No. I wanted to very badly.

SingerQueen: But?

I hold my breath.

AlCaponesGhost25: But I knew what I knew, and I was worried you'd feel tricked into it once you found out. I didn't want to start something then risk ruining it.

The flutters are back. I press a palm to my stomach.

SingerQueen: Define *something* please.

AlCaponesGhost25: You'll know it when you see it.

SingerQueen: Promise?

AlCaponesGhost25: Promise.

I'm still jittery the next morning. The prospect of heading out to the farm again with Leo for the first time in over a week—and after everything that's happened—feels big. To take my mind off it, I start work on a couple of Christmas sweater orders from Etsy between customers, and that helps. By the time the workday rolls to a close, I've almost forgotten to be nervous.

Leo lets us into Canine King with a cheerful "Come on in." He's almost back to normal and as put together as always in dark pants and a soft, knitted, dove-gray V-neck with a white button-down underneath.

My stomach lurches at his smile, but I inhale deeply and push the feeling away.

Cholula barks and backs up a step at the sight of him.

"Cho, come on." I snap the leash. "When are you going to learn?"

"You should have dressed her up as Cerberus instead of Mrs. Potts," Leo says. "It would have been more in character."

He's not wrong. I usher the small guardian of the underworld past me, and as soon as she sees Tilly, she's placated.

I finally look up at Leo. My hair is down today so I push it out of my face. "Hi."

"Hi." His voice is warm, and his expression even more so. There's a long silence that contains plenty more than a greeting. "You look very pretty today," he says eventually. Bashful almost.

I look down at my brick-orange cardigan and blue jeans. "You don't miss the princess getup?"

"Nah. This is more you."

It is absolutely the right thing to say.

"Want to get going?" He snaps his fingers, and Tilly goes to him.

"Impressive. You guys have been practicing." It's the reminder I need. The dog show is just over a month away, and there's still a lot of work to do.

"How come you're only bringing Cholula today?" Leo asks in the car.

"I just want to be able to focus for once to make up for lost training hours, and considering Boris might be starting a late-in-life career as an escape artist, I figured I'd give him and Cap a break. I'll bring them next time."

"Makes sense. Do you think Cholula and Tilly will remember what to do?"

"Let's hope so."

"I've missed it." Leo glances at me.

"Me too." I hesitate, but then I reach out and place my hand on his where it's idling on the gear knob. As soon as my palm makes contact, the fine hairs on my arms rise.

Leo's jaw flexes.

"Is this okay?" I ask.

In response, he turns his hand so our fingers can weave together.

Diane is outside with the dogs when we pull up. In boots and an oversized oil cloth jacket, she looks ready for a fox hunt in the British countryside, but the illusion dissipates when she tells us there's a mac-and-cheese bake still warm inside if we're hungry.

"Training will be better on full stomachs," she insists.

I let Leo decide, so food it is.

"I could get used to having someone else cook for me on a regular basis," I say after stuffing myself. "My clothes would no longer fit, but it would be worth it if I didn't have to come up with dinner ideas ever again."

"You don't like cooking?" Leo asks.

"Nope. Do you?"

"I don't mind."

"Did you hear your brother has hired a housekeeper?" Dawn interjects from her chair in the adjacent sitting room. "For cooking and cleaning?"

"No, he didn't tell me that."

"Sounds amazing," I say, chewing.

Dawn pushes off her seat and joins us in the kitchen. "Seems like a waste of money to me. How hard is it to clean your own house and put food in a crockpot?"

"They both work a lot." Leo clamps his lips together around the words. I get the feeling he's been no stranger to hiring help in the past.

Dawn purses her lips. "Lots of people work a lot. You work a lot."

"Come on, now," Diane says, filling up her wife's mug with coffee.

Dawn's expression softens. "Sorry, I'm a tired grumpus today. The week after Halloween is always a lot. Kids stuffing themselves with sugar every chance they get—it takes the wind out of me. You'd think high schoolers would have gotten past the novelty, but nope."

One last piece of the puzzle finally clicks into place. Of course—Mrs. McInnis! Dawn is Jaz's old history teacher who started the history server. That's why Leo/Al said he was there "doing someone a favor." He must have meant he was helping Dawn out moderating the group.

Before I can voice my epiphany, Dawn continues. "All I'm saying is, I'll never understand that lifestyle. They're off to Hawaii for Thanksgiving, New York for Christmas, and I think Courtney has to be in Dallas for a week in December. I couldn't keep up."

Leo hums something noncommittal in response.

I watch as he stabs a few remaining pieces of bell pepper onto his fork and puts them in his mouth. He's far away in thought before he looks up.

"You miss it," I say, the words feeling truer than I want them to be.

His lips part as if he's about to deny it, but then he relents. "Part of me does. Not because it's better; it's just different. There's a certain rush in the anticipation of knowing something's always around the corner—an event, a trip, a party. It's easy to get addicted to that lifestyle."

I nod as if I know what he's talking about when nothing could be further from the truth. There's a wistful note in his voice that rubs me like steel wool would—in no way pleasant. I push my plate away and stand. "I'm stuffed. Ready to train?"

His eyes narrow. "Something else is on your mind, I can tell. Spit it out."

I pull on my boots and pause in the doorway after letting Tilly and Cholula run out ahead of us. "I guess I'm wondering if you'd turn it down if it was offered to you again. Sounds like a pretty cushy life." I jog down the steps and he follows.

"The perks are, but you pay for it with a pound of flesh. I've told you what it did to me."

"So that's a no?" We've reached the edge of the field.

He reaches for my arm, forcing me to stop and look at him. "If you're asking if I'm planning on staying here, the answer is yes."

I'm in no position to want that, I know. In fact, I should technically want the opposite. And yet, his *yes* makes everything a little bit lighter.

"Not saying that's what I was asking, but okay." I turn to face the field. "Cholula, come here."

Leo gets a crease between his brows. "You said your parents left when you were in high school, right?"

The lack of an obvious segue startles me. "You want to talk about that now?"

He shrugs. "I guess I'm trying to understand you. Are you guys close?"

"Well, my mom can't remember what day my birthday is, and I haven't talked to my dad since Christmas, so no, I wouldn't say so. My dad was almost fifty when they had me. Mom's a decade younger, but I don't think I was planned."

"I'm pretty sure Bennett wasn't planned—at least not that close to me. It happens."

"Yeah, it's not the same." I look at him, drawn in by irises that run a dusky dark blue in this light. "Look, I know you struggle with your dad's expectations and what not, but at least he always cared—still cares, obviously, even if it's in an overbearing sort of way. I've always been a footnote in my parents' lives." Saying it out loud brings with it a rush of tiny stabs across my skin, and I wrap my arms around me. "For a while, I thought that if I followed in their footsteps, they'd care more."

"Dental school," he says.

"Yeah." I kick at a tuft of grass as I step over it. "But you're not the only one keeping secrets from your parents." In response to his querying gaze, I continue. "I dropped out of college. My final year. It wasn't a good fit, and I ended up partying too hard to make up for it. Throw a bad breakup in the mix, and when time came for graduation, I told them I had a job interview out of state so they wouldn't come. Five years later, they still don't know."

Leo considers this. "And you're worried they'll be disappointed even though it's been a long time?"

That would make the most sense, but... "No. I'm worried they wouldn't be. That it wouldn't matter." I've never said the words out loud before. But if my grandest failure in life doesn't elicit more ire than a flat tire on I-90, what does that say about me? I'd rather not know.

His face falls. "That's messed up."

"Families—screwing you over since the beginning of time," I say, aiming for levity. "Except for Pop. He and my grandma were always good to me."

"So, Harvey knows?"

"He knows I'm not saving up for grad school like I told my folks. Not about dropping out."

"Then why does he think you're here?" Leo's forehead is creased as if he's trying to figure me out. I'm not used to this level of scrutiny, so I look away.

"To help him. I don't know. He doesn't ask, and I don't tell. Maybe he hopes I'll take over the store one day."

"Is that what you want? What about your designs?"

Damn. I give a quiet laugh and stop walking. "Do you always ask this many questions?"

"Sorry, I'm just interested. You're interesting." He smolders at me the way only he can. It pulls me in, and before I know it, my cheeks are twitching.

In that moment, I want to share all my hopes and dreams and fears. He'd tell me to go for it. That he believes in me. Look at what he's doing for himself, how he's reinvented his life.

The problem is that I'm not him, and I have Harvey to think about.

"Okay, I think that's enough about me for one day," I say, reaching out to playfully push him away. Of course, he doesn't budge.

"Fine." Leo grins beneath his gray knitted cap. "Then let's train."

36

We run through recalls, tunnels, and cones, and today the dogs do everything we ask of them. Leo stops intermittently to check his training book and mutter to himself.

"What does *The Plan* say?" I joke. "Wouldn't want to stray from *The Plan.*"

"Wouldn't you like to know." He pretends to hide the book from me, so naturally I try to grab it.

Soon Tilly and Cholula join us, adding happy barks to the game. It's not fair—all he has to do is hold the book over his head, and I can't reach it. I also think he's enjoying me trying to climb him a little too much, but that's when I have an idea. I stop jumping and still, one of my hands lingering on his chest. My breath is like a cloud between us.

"You really won't tell me?" I ask, batting my lashes. I fiddle coquettishly with one of the buttons on his coat.

It works. Leo's jaw slackens, and his arms drop to his side. Before he has time to react, I snatch the book from his hand and run toward the barn with a triumphant hoot. "I win again!"

Leo tilts his head back and snorts before strolling after me at a leisurely pace. "Come on. Let's focus."

"Or what?" I stop. "You'll make me run behind the car the whole way home?"

He smirks. "That would be cruel."

"Hmm…tell Diane and Dawn on me?"

He steps into my space, prowling closer. "I'm not a child."

"You'll…throw me up against the wall and ravage me?" My words come out of left field, a scenario I may or may not have conjured in my dreams last night.

His eyes widen almost imperceptibly as he takes one final step my way. We're only a foot apart. "That depends," he says, his gaze not leaving mine.

My breath catches, and I make two attempts before I manage a sound. "On?"

"On what you want." A devilish smile. "I think you know I'd be game. For any of the above." He extends his hand, palm up. "May I have my book back, please?"

I hold it out, and he takes it, his fingers brushing mine. *The last one*, I want to say. *I pick the last one!*

He uses the book to point to the barn doors. "But while you're thinking that over, we need to get a bit crafty. Make some jumps. There should be things we can use in there. Want to take a look?"

No, I don't want to take a look. I want him to touch me, for his hands to push under my shirt, his fingers making my nipples even harder than they already are. I want to grind into him, and have him strip me down, and—

"You've seen this contest before," Leo says. "What kinds of obstacles do they have?"

I also want him to never have opened his stupid store here, and I definitely don't want him to win the show.

Damn it.

I clench my legs together and steel myself. I can do this. "Other than the tunnel and the cones, nothing too complicated. There's a low jump and a seesaw. A small one."

"Easy to make."

"And the dogs usually start out sitting on a raised block."

"Like a table."

"Yeah. But most of the dogs are pets, not show dogs or agility pros, so as long as they don't completely botch the course, it's fine."

"That's good for us."

"What do you mean?"

"I don't know about you, but I'm setting my standards a bit higher than 'won't botch the course.'"

"Obviously."

He cocks his head sideways and studies me. "You've changed," he says. "You're different than when we started out. Hungrier. Good for you."

I blush at his words, even as I acknowledge that he's right. And he doesn't even know the extent of my starvation.

"But so we're clear," he continues, "just because I want to kiss you, doesn't mean I'll go easy on you in the show."

My stride falters. He says it so easily. Maybe it's payback for how I duped him into dropping his guard with the book earlier. Well, I won't give him the satisfaction of seeing how his words affect me. "Cholula, here," I call. The tiny dog turns on a dime and comes hauling back to us. "Good girl," I praise, crouching low, before I turn to Leo again. "Oh yeah, golden boy? I think we both know Cholula and I will smoke you."

He looks down at me, and I know desire when I see it. His voice is heady when he counters. "I guess we'll see."

Leo invites me to come train with him for a second day in a row, but I'm forced to turn him down. Not because I don't want to, but I'm behind on accounting and I've promised Micki a half day at the mall to get Christmas shopping out of the way. She's been deep in her books since Halloween cramming for finals, and I know she needs a break.

As nice as it is to have a girls' day out, there's a constant thrumming inside me that increases in intensity every time I think of Leo. Something is building between us and I'm past the point of trying to stop it.

After we get back, I keep an eye on his apartment from my kitchen table while I'm wrapping a book and a sweater for Harvey and a pair of earrings Micki picked out for herself, insisting that come Christmas she'll have forgotten all about them. The dogs are resting at my feet but look up every time I move as if they're worried I'm going to leave again. They probably miss Harvey as much as he misses them.

Finally, just after seven, the light inside Leo's place turns on, and I spot him moving into the kitchen. I wrestle with several pieces of tape that are stuck to my fingers to get them off, and then I reach for my laptop.

Living History Illinois Flockify DM, Sunday 07:12 PM

SingerQueen: What do ghosts want for Christmas?
AlCaponesGhost25: Is that a riddle? Boo-ts?
Boo-ze? A boo-merang?
SingerQueen: No, I meant you.

AlCaponesGhost25: Or if it's a pervy ghost, boo-bs and boo-ty...

SingerQueen: Lol stop. It was purely a wish list question.

AlCaponesGhost25: Because you thought of me today?

He caught me there.

SingerQueen: Yes.

AlCaponesGhost25: Interesting. What exactly were you thinking?

What wasn't I thinking? After his teasing yesterday, my mind's been stuck on a loop playing a scenario where nabbing his notebook ended very differently. His lips on mine, naked skin, his hands in...places. My cheeks flush hot.

SingerQueen: I can't tell you that.

AlCaponesGhost25: Sure you can.

My eyes flick up above the screen, and there he is, watching me through his window. Even across the distance, his gaze burns hot, igniting my blood.

SingerQueen: I think you *are* a pervy ghost.

AlCaponesGhost25: Never said I wasn't. Tell me something real.

SingerQueen: Real?

AlCaponesGhost25: Pretend we're still anonymous. What are you thinking now?

I let out all the air from my lungs. Close my eyes.

> **SingerQueen:** I'm thinking of a man who once took off his shirt in the middle of a cornfield at night.
> **AlCaponesGhost25:** I didn't realize I'd made an impression.
> **SingerQueen:** Come on. False modesty doesn't become you. You know you're hot.

Through the window I see his lips stretch into a smile. Then he looks at me again.

> **AlCaponesGhost25:** All you have to do is say the word. If it was up to me, you'd be a lot closer than you are right now.
> **SingerQueen:** Wouldn't that ruin our budding friendship?
> **AlCaponesGhost25:** Is that truly all you'd call it?
> **SingerQueen:** Really truly? No.

37

The farther we get into November and the holiday season, the more daily foot traffic and more online orders I see. I'm up at the crack of dawn every day and sew any moment I get between customers. Still, I'm busy well into the night, and from the look of things, so is Leo across the street. He texts me Wednesday morning asking if it's always like this this time of year, and I confirm. It's been only four days, but I already can't wait to see him at training again.

Micki shows up at lunch with soup, sandwiches, and cupcakes from my favorite bakery.

"Happy, happy birthday," she hollers, even though I still have customers in the store. She's the only person I know who keeps a list of birthdays and anniversaries for her friends. It's the sweetest thing.

I finish ringing up the customer before I flip the OUT TO LUNCH sign on the door and let Micki give me a hug.

"Big twenty-eight!" Micki pretends to stick a microphone in my face. "How does it feel? Do your hips hurt? Any new wrinkles?"

"Shut up." I take the bag of food from her and proceed up the stairs. "Just because you're a year younger."

Micki grabs two plates from the cupboard while I pull out sparkling, nonalcoholic cider from the fridge where it's been chilling. It's a tradition her ex started that stuck around even when he didn't—special drinks for special days. This one is apple pomegranate.

"Fancy." She nods as I pour two wineglasses full.

I sit down and light the candle I keep on the table. "Thanks for bringing food."

"It's the least I can do. I don't have a present. Things are a bit tight right now. Turns out Jaz isn't much more reliable than you when it comes to rent."

I finish chewing my first mouthful of herby focaccia. "Oh no. Sorry."

She waves off my concern. "I'm fine. I'm holding her goldfish hostage until she coughs it up. I know she's good for it. Also, I'm taking on a few more hours at the salon."

"Won't that affect your study time?"

"No, I think I'm ready. I swear I dream about joint anatomy and body systems at night."

"Well, let me know if you need any more quizzing."

My phone vibrates with another text from Leo:

Diane is wondering if we want to eat there tonight before training. Something about the flank steak being too big for two.

Not having to make dinner—count me in. **Sounds good, I** text back.

He sends a thumbs-up.

"Leo?" Micki asks, mouth full of bread.

She knows we've gotten past the awkwardness of Halloween

night and that nothing of significance has happened, and she's been admirably restrained about not giving me a hard time about it, but I can't help the smile currently plastered across my face. "Mm-hmm."

She has a sip of her drink, watching me continuously. "It must be exhausting," she says after setting her glass down. "You've got it as bad as anyone I've ever seen, and...nothing? I mean, I know he's Mister Bad Guy and all, but still. A girl's gotta butter that biscuit."

A deep gulp of cider sends bubbles fizzing up my nose. "That's...colorful," I wheeze in the middle of a coughing fit that brings all three dogs to my side.

Cholula jumps into my lap, but not to make sure I'm okay—in two seconds, she's hauled half my sandwich into her retreat beneath the bed.

"You stinker," I scold when I'm able to talk again. I attack the rest of my sandwich before someone else steals that, too. When I look up, Micki is watching me, eyes narrowed. "What?" I ask.

"No other reaction?" She points at me with the tip of her spoon. Two splats of soup land on the table. "You're thinking about it."

I glance out the window toward Canine King where two customers are exiting. Leo doesn't close for lunch like I do. Maybe I shouldn't either if that's what success requires. "Only around the clock." I sigh. "But like...what if I don't win the show? Or what if he decides he misses his old life and someone even worse takes over? What if we lose the store? How could I not blame him?"

"Someone worse than Leo?" Micki asks with exaggerated horror. "Not possible."

"Ha, ha."

"Dude, I'm telling you, you are overthinking this. Enjoy him. He's here now, you'll figure the other stuff out, and for what it's worth, I don't think he's going anywhere. He's very into you."

That, finally, brings a real smile back to my lips. "I know."

"Well, there you go."

"Okay." I shimmy the gloom away and raise my glass. "To friends who make other friends see reason."

A quiet smile plays across Leo's lips off and on during our drive into the countryside. With a playlist of random hits on in the background, the rush of the day slowly fades. After my lunch with Micki, the afternoon was a constant stream of customers. Unfortunately, I had to turn two of them away without making a sale. We're out of one of our bestselling dry foods and more should have been delivered last week at the latest. I'll have to get to the bottom of that in the morning.

"You good?" Leo asks as we stop at a light.

"Yeah, it was a hectic day." I lean my head against the headrest and turn it his way. "You're in a good mood."

He presses his lips together briefly. "I suppose I am."

"Any particular reason?"

"No."

His answer is too quick. I squint at him. Something's going on. "Let me guess, Tilly learned a new trick?" Which reminds me, Cholula and I need to practice the talent portion of the pageant. That's the one thing I don't want to do in front of Leo, and I still haven't figured out how to progress her balancing act.

"No, no new tricks. I don't know why I even bothered training on Sunday when Cholula wasn't there." Leo's grip tightens as he turns off the main road onto the bumpier country one. I think he's going to explain himself better, but instead he says, "We'll eat first, train later. I didn't take a lunch today."

"Yeah, I noticed."

His face lights up as he puts the car in park. "Did you now?"

"Not in a creepy way. Micki was over, and I happened to look out the window, and there were customers."

He stops me by nudging my thigh with the back of his hand. It's a split-second touch, but I'm already wound so tightly that it triggers a ripple of heat up my spine. "You don't have to explain," he says. "I'm glad I was on your mind."

Once at the house, we walk into a cloud of heavenly sweet and savory smells. Something warm and sugary drifts behind more demanding scents. There's a glow coming from the kitchen, and some eighties band sings about not being able to fight a feeling anymore over the built-in speaker system. How apt.

Leo takes my jacket and hangs it up. I turn to follow the dogs into the interior of the house, but he takes my hand and holds me back. "One thing first," he says, eyes shifting away from me. He smiles to himself but hesitates.

"Yeah?"

He takes a deep breath. "If this is too much, promise you won't get mad."

"What are you up to?"

"In here." He leads me through the doorway, not to a mid-week dinner, but to a feast.

"Surprise!" Diane calls out, coming at me with outstretched arms.

I stare in awe at the scene before me. The table is set with fancy china, flowers, candles, cloth napkins, and decorative confetti. There's a balloon tied to one of the chairs, and on the counter sits a two-tiered chocolate cake.

"Happy birthday," Leo says in a low voice next to me.

I force my jaw shut and blink at the scene before me. "How ... I mean, I didn't ..."

"I overheard you on the phone with your mom that night." He looks suddenly nervous. "It is your birthday, right? If not, I'll feel like a total jackass."

"No, it is." I take another step into the room, a lump forming in my throat. "But this is ..."

"Too much?" He scratches his neck. "Sorry. I just love birthdays and I wanted you to have a good one."

Tears well up even as astonished laughter spills out of me. No one has ever done something like this for me. Not my parents, and certainly not past boyfriends. I want to jump into Leo's arms right then and hold on for dear life. "It's perfect," I say instead. "Better than perfect."

Leo beams.

"I hope you're hungry," Diane says. "When you get to be our age, the desire fades to celebrate yet another year gone by. This is a rare occasion for us."

I hug her and Dawn again. "I can't believe he roped you into this. This is amazing."

Leo pulls out the chair with the balloon for me, and I sit.

"I know it's late," Leo says once we've polished off three courses and several glasses of wine. "But there's one more thing."

I put my napkin down and wish yet again I could unbutton my pants. After generous helpings of salad, bread, steak with béarnaise sauce, twice-baked potatoes, sautéed mushrooms, and cake, I suspect I won't need to eat for another week. If I make it home that is. I may have to roll out the door.

Leo stands and pulls out my chair. "Cap and Boris can wait here but bring Cholula." He grabs my jacket and hands it to me.

"What about dishes?" The kitchen counter is overflowing.

Dawn titters. "Don't be silly. No chores on birthdays."

"Go." Diane smiles. "Both of you."

"No point in arguing," Leo says, close to my ear. "They never lose."

He leads me to the barn and pulls open the heavy door with a creak.

I try to adjust to the impenetrable dark. The moon doesn't reach more than a yard into the space. "What did you do?"

"Hold on." He aims the flashlight at the wall and finds the light switch. "Ready?"

He turns on the light, which floods the front part of the barn, a space roughly forty feet square. The floor is lined with wood chips, and the boards, wheelbarrows, tires, shovels, and old windows that used to litter the space have been moved to the back of the building. The tunnels and cones we use for training are set up as are several new obstacles—three jumps of different heights, a seesaw, and two raised platforms. It looks like a real agility space.

He returns to my side. "As far as birthday presents go, I realize this is pretty lame, but I had limited time to work with."

I take several steps into the space. "It's not lame. At all." It is the absolute opposite.

"You like it?" Leo rests his hand on the top horizontal bar of one of the jumps. "I figured, with temperatures dropping, it might be nice not to have to train outside anymore. Even though this isn't heated, it at least offers some protection from the elements."

Tilly and Cholula are running laps around the obstacles, a physical manifestation of the giddiness bubbling inside me. Leo is vastly underestimating the thoughtfulness of this gift and the veritable earthquake it's set off inside me.

Enough thinking.

I don't know how I get to him, whether I run or walk, all I know is that suddenly I'm in his arms with mine wrapped around his neck.

"I need to..." I say, trying to find more words. I run my palms down the front of his jacket and up again as if I've only just discovered he's there. "I more than like it. I..." I look up, willing him to understand what I want. And of course, he does.

His lips crash down on mine, and it's everything I've wanted for a while now. If kissing Leo has been a quiet thrill in my imagination, reality is a thunderous torrent that reverberates deep in my core. His hair and skin are cool from the air, but his lips are warm and supple as they explore mine with a hunger that makes me lose any sense of where I end and he begins. I'm equally ravenous and help myself to plenty of him—fistfuls of cotton, greedy pecks along his jaw, and always, *always* one more kiss. His hands cradle my neck and my shoulders, skim lower over my breasts, and grip my waist. I pull him down to me, and it's almost like a tug of war—he gives, then I give, while we both hold on for dear life. Fortunately, this particular contest can be enjoyed whether on the winning or losing side.

I'm dizzy when we pull back, out of breath and unmoored. He looks as wild as I feel.

"I think we need to stop," he says while exhaling before he kisses me again.

I smile against his lips and then graze them with my teeth.

"You are very good at birthdays," I say between licks and nips. "Did anyone ever tell you that?"

Leo caresses my hair and groans, pulling away again. "No, we really need to stop, now. You're so..." His eyes roam my face, like he's drinking me in.

I lean my cheek into his palm. "So?"

"Alive."

That's a first as far as compliments go, but the wonder in his voice stifles my laugh. "And you're not?"

He smiles. "Not like you. But being with you makes me think I could be."

His words make my throat tighten. Shame on me for pegging him as a one-dimensional snob when we first met. The more he shows me, the more I want to know.

"For the record," I say, once again nudging my lips near his, "I like you just fine the way you are right now."

"Yeah?" His arms encircle me, lifting me closer.

"Mm-hmm." The only thing that would make this full body embrace better is less clothing, but considering where we are, I'm thankful for the obstacle. Lord knows what would happen otherwise.

"Want to get out of here? We could train twice this weekend to make up for lost time if you want."

Training... Who cares about that?

He can bet his sweet ass I want to get out of here.

38

The car smells of food from the containers of leftovers Diane insisted we bring along as we drive home. One of the dogs yawns in the back of the car, and shortly thereafter, I do, too. It's nearing 10:00 p.m., but I don't want the night to end. Not yet. Not when he looked at me the way he did in the barn.

Leo's fingers tighten on mine when we pull into the courtyard behind his place.

"Good birthday?" he asks, turning to me.

"Best ever." My thumb strokes the back of his hand.

"I think I'm going to have to work on raising your standards. I barely did anything." A small smile tugs at his lips as he opens his car door. "Let's get these guys inside." He indicates the dogs in the back.

Is that truly how he feels? Like he didn't do enough for me tonight? I join him in the back and gather my leashes, but then the urge to set him straight is too strong. I grab hold of his sleeve to bring us both to a stop. He looks down at me, his eyes immediately going tender.

"You thought of me," I tell him, adding weight to my words. "You remembered it was my birthday when I hadn't even told you directly." I look down at where our hands have found each other. "You always remember." I bring his hand to my lips. "I need you to understand how amazing that felt."

After a beat, he simply nods, placing his hands on either side of my face and pressing his lips to mine. It's a soft kiss and over too quickly with the dogs tugging around our legs.

"I'll walk you home," he says. "Come on."

We're slow-moving on account of Boris, but eventually we reach my door where he holds all four pups at bay while I unlock it. My time is running out. How to know if he's thinking what I'm thinking?

"Are you tired?" I ask. "It's only ten o'clock. Do you want to have some tea?" The words spill out of me in a rush that I'm sure gives my state of mind away, but he doesn't bat a single lash.

"I've got cookies in the car," he says in that low, sexy voice of his. "From Dawn. If you don't mind coming back to, um, my place."

Thank God he's smooth like that. "Let me bring the dogs upstairs, and I'll be right back." I don't wait for his response before I head inside and rush through evening procedures. Cholula paces behind me when I put up the gate, hopeful, but she sits when I tell her to. "No more play for you tonight, girl." I reach over the barrier to scratch her ears. "You're going to be good?" She yawns, and I take that as a yes.

Leo is pacing outside when I open the door. "Ready?" he asks.

As ready as I'll ever be.

Inside his door, he takes my coat before disposing of his own. "Make yourself at home," he says, moving deeper into the apartment.

I follow him, the angles and shapes of his space now familiar rather than forbidden. "It smells good in here. I'm trying to fig-ure out what it is."

"Food from the restaurant next door." He sets the bags of leftovers on the counter and starts rearranging the fridge.

I step up to his kitchen table and lean against it. "That's what it is. I couldn't place it last time, either. You know, I used to picture you living in a fancy magazine spread—cold, sterile, immaculate. It's nice to have been proven wrong."

He closes the fridge. "That's interesting."

"What is?"

"You, picturing where I live." He stalks a few steps closer to me.

"I'm sure you did the same."

"Maybe, maybe not. Can I get you some tea?" He gestures toward the counter without looking away.

I push off the table and meet him in the middle of the floor. "That was the plan, right?" My palms come to rest on his chest, his heartbeat reverberating underneath his shirt. It's solid and urgent, matching mine.

"Plans change," he murmurs, running his fingers up my sides.

The muscles beneath my skin ripple in response. I let out a sharp breath. "Yeah? What are you gonna do? Throw me up against the wall and ravage me?" It's meant to be funny, a tongue-in-cheek nod to the other day in the barn, but even I hear the need in my voice.

He steps up close, thigh to thigh, chest to chest, a sultry continuous contact that makes my whole body vibrate with anticipation. I cling to him as his caress moves to my neck. "Do you want me to?" he whispers, placing a kiss just beneath my earlobe before pulling back to look at me.

His dark pupils probe for an answer, and all I can do is nod before he lifts me up and carries me the few steps to the doorway leading to his bedroom. With my back to the wide doorjamb, I lock my legs tighter around him as he presses closer. He's hard, and the knowledge that I'm the reason makes me grip the fabric of his shirt tighter.

"Like this?" he asks, kissing his way up my neck. One of his hands slides lower to grip my ass.

"I don't know…that I…feel ravaged enough…yet," I pant, urging his mouth to mine.

He grinds his hips into me. Our mouths hover open against each other as if neither one of us knows how to get close enough. His breath is damp and hot. Demanding in the best way.

Leo lets out a low growl and spins me away from the wall and into the bedroom. A moment's freefall and my back hits the sheets. I yank the bottom of his shirt out of his pants and push it up. He understands and sits back, tugging it over his head, and there it is, my favorite torso.

"I have a request," I say, unbuttoning my jeans and shimmying them down my hips.

"Anything." His gaze widens at the sight of my lace panties. "Oh, those are nice." His hand sweeps across the fabric, which makes my hips buck up involuntarily.

"Will you flex for me?"

He stills, a sputtered little laugh interrupting his admiration for my undergarments. "Flex? As in…? He bends his arm, making his biceps and triceps dance.

"Mm, but like both." I pull off my top and lean back on my elbows. "All of it."

"Like this?" He steps off the bed and proceeds to do his best impression of Schwarzenegger, posing this way and that. His pecs swell, and his six-pack tightens in a way that makes my fingertips—and other places—tingle.

"God, yeah." Dear Lord, he is a specimen of rare caliber.

"This does it for you?" he asks, turning his back to me to display his back muscles. "I'm not even that built." He looks at me over his shapely shoulder, and I can't help myself. My hand trails down across my stomach and between my legs to where I most want him.

His eyes pop open wide, and he's on me a second later, pinning my arms above my head. "Oh no, you don't."

I laugh when he nibbles my neck. "But you make me so hot."

He rolls me on top of him, unsnaps my bra, and rolls us again. I want to touch him, but by some kind of sorcery, he still has my arms locked in place.

"Good," he says with a quick glance up before he takes one of my nipples in his mouth.

My shoulders rise off the bed toward him at the deep thrill caused by his deft tongue. Finally, he releases my arms so I can touch him, too, and I bury my fingers in his hair as he kisses wet trails across my chest.

"I don't know why you're always hiding beneath oversized sweaters," he says, his palms dragging down my sides to my hips where his fingers hook around the lacy waistline of my panties. "You should be naked all the time." He crawls down the length of my body, baring me completely.

"You'd like that." My eyelids half-close in delirium at what will come next.

He pulls down his pants and boxers in one go and reaches into the nightstand for a condom. I watch him roll it on, and the way he palms his rigid length makes my insides clench.

I beckon for him, and he obliges, but instead of blanketing me with his fine body, he rolls me onto my side and slides up behind me. It's a new sensation, how the fine hairs on his chest tickle my back, how his hardness presses into my butt cheek, how his hand now reaches everywhere…

I turn my head as far as I can to allow for a kiss, and as our tongues dance, he rakes his nails down my chest, all the way past my ribs, my navel, and lower. He uses one finger to part me, and when it sinks in deep, I push back against him with a small yelp.

He holds still, his lips skimming my shoulder. "You good?" he whispers.

Good is an understatement. I feel like I'll blow if he so much as exhales too hard. Heck, maybe I'll go for it. "Give me more," I say, moving my hips a little.

He's quick to oblige, adding another finger, and now I couldn't stay still if my life depended on it. The position we're in has the flat of his hand pressed up against my entire sex so when he starts working his fingers, every last sensitive nerve ending joins in a chorus of pure elation. I come hard and fast, my hips quaking beneath his grip, and all the while he whispers encouragement against my neck—how sexy I am, how beautiful, how hard I make him. I'm ready for more before the first orgasm has completely subsided.

"I want you," I pant. "Come here."

I don't have to ask him twice.

39

It's still early when I'm startled awake by the insistent ring of a phone somewhere in the room. I groan and flop onto my back. "Make it stop."

Leo is already out of bed, searching the pile of our clothes for the intruding disturbance. I think he's about to turn it off, but instead, his form grows tense, and he mutters something that sounds like "Get some more sleep. I'll be right back."

I doze for a little, the cave beneath the covers warm and lush. My pillow smells like Leo, and that makes me smile in my half-gone state. I'm tired to the bone. Not a lot of rest was had here last night.

At some point, I become more aware of his absence and also of low talking in the kitchen. I wrap the comforter around me and tiptoe across the cool wood floor to the door. It's open a crack, and I peer out, careful not to intrude.

"Respectfully, I fail to see how this reflects on the family at all," Leo says. "No one knows I'm here. The store's been open since early October and even you just found out. Thanks to Bennett. *And* it's doing well." He has his back to me, and one of his hands is resting lightly against the tabletop. "Who's they?" He pauses to listen. "I don't know any of them."

Whoever is on the other line must be raising their voice because Leo pulls the phone away from his ear. When the other person stops talking, Leo hangs his head. "Mom would like me doing this." He listens again and then slams his palm down on the wood. "You know that's not true!" His words ring out in the dim room.

I push the door open and pad across the floor, a deep need to make things better rising. Leo startles when he sees me but doesn't object when I take hold of his arm. The man before me is not the same one who fell asleep spooning me last night. This version is rigid and edgy, the tendons in his neck taut, his brow low.

"I can't talk to you right now," he says into his phone before disconnecting the call. He throws it down on the table and runs a hand through his hair. It was already on end before, and it makes me want to smooth everything down. Settle him.

"What's going on?" I ask, my thumb gently massaging his forearm.

He tries but doesn't succeed in adjusting his expression. "Nothing." He inhales quickly through his nose. "My father."

Uh-oh. That can't be good. "What did he say?"

"Apparently, I'm humiliating the family by being here." He frees himself and goes to the faucet. "I don't want to talk about it. Sorry I woke you up."

Maybe I was wrong. Maybe having parents who care too much isn't better than having parents who don't care at all. I go to him and place a hand on his back, unwilling to let him slip away to a dark place. Little by little, he relaxes under my touch.

"It's not true." I make him face me. "You couldn't humiliate anyone. You're the most determined person I know. Look at you—you're ambitious, goal-oriented, and hardworking. You inspire loyal customers, and your organizational skills would make any neat freak drool. All of those are admirable qualities. Ones I wish I had. Why does it matter what your dad says?"

"Because he's my dad."

"But it's your life."

He pulls away from me again. "You wouldn't understand."

I cross my arms. "Try me."

"No." He looks about him like a trapped animal searching for escape. When he can't find one, he finally meets my gaze, and the fight goes out of him. "I'm sorry, okay? I know I'm being a dick, and believe me, this is not how I wanted this morning to go."

The apology is sincere, and since I had other hopes for this morning, too, I stop pushing. "Parents," I say instead, shaking my head.

That brings a cursory smile to his lips. "You can say that again." He rolls his shoulders and shakes out his arms. A loud sigh. Then he bridges the gap between us and places his hands on my shoulders. "I'm sorry." He pulls me to him and inhales deeply. "Did you at least sleep okay until all this?"

I nestle close to his chest. "You've seen Harvey's alcove bed, right? Do you really have to ask if your memory foam wonder did it for me?"

"Ah, so you were in it for the mattress? Ouch, my ego."

I smack his arm lightly and tilt my face up. "Honestly after such a thorough ravaging, I could have slept anywhere. Always knew you'd be an overachiever in your time off, too." I smirk. "No, the bed was a bonus. You were the prize."

A shadow flickers behind the contentment at that, but he blinks it away instantly and leans in to kiss me. His lips are cool like the air in the room this morning, but they warm beneath mine, as does my skin where he touches me. Our lips linger and tease while, outside, the sky brightens.

"What time is it anyway?" I ask as we part.

He glances toward the microwave. "Seven thirty."

"Damn." I look down at our bare feet. "I should get going. The dogs…"

He nods but doesn't let me go. "You know, I swear, when I got up for water last night, Cholula was in your window, silently judging me and plotting revenge for taking you away from her."

"I'm so sure."

"No, it's true. She was totally…" He points two fingers to his eyes and then one forward in the universal I'm-watching-you sign. "That dog has it in for me."

"Maybe sex makes you hallucinate?"

"That would have had to be some fantastic sex, then." His hands glide down my backside and squeeze. "Mm. Mind-blowing even. Will I see you later?"

I should work tonight. The Etsy store is generating more orders as holiday shopping picks up, and I have sewing to do. But when he looks at me like that—like he needs me—how can I say no? Maybe I can multitask. "Dinner at my place?"

He caresses my face. "Of course." He still doesn't let me go.

I laugh. "I'm going to have to get my clothes."

He kisses my nose. "Uh-huh."

"Which is easier without a man attached to me."

"I see." The scruff on his cheek tickles as he nestles into the crook of my neck.

A giggle bubbles up my chest. "Leo, come on. I *have* to go."

He groans and finally lets his arms drop. "Fine." He takes a reluctant step back. "I'll note my dissent, though."

"Noted."

It still takes me another twenty minutes to get out the door.

40

We quickly settle into a routine of working during the day and training the dogs or hanging out at night. I'm treated to Leo fresh out of the shower, curled into a ball sleeping at two in the morning, and chasing me around the kitchen with peanut butter on his finger, ready to dab my nose. I don't have the urge to be anyone but me, and I think he feels the same. Consequently, AlCaponesGhost25 and SingerQueen are on hiatus. Now if I want to tell him something, I just do.

A few days after my birthday, the florist down the street enters Happy Paws with an armful of peach-and-cream roses in a vase.

"Oh, those are darling," my customer says. "Someone must think you're very special."

I don't have to look at the card to know who that someone is. One glance across the street at the grinning man in the window tells me everything I need to know.

As soon as I'm alone again, I send him a text. **Believe it or not, but I've never gotten flowers before.**

He responds, **You must have hung around the wrong people.**

The crisp-sweet scent makes me smile every time I pass the

counter, and when I go upstairs, I bring the vase with me. I would take it to bed if I could.

Leo knows exactly how to get my attention and hold it. Little by little, my sewing pile grows. I vow to spend my days off catching up, but then he invites me to go ice-skating or to go listen to a band downtown, and it's so easy to say yes to him. I sleep over at his place as many nights as I sleep at home. My back is thanking me for it, but the dogs are not. In the back of my mind, I know I should slow things down, but I also haven't felt like this since…I don't know when.

When more than two-thirds of November has passed, Micki enters the store with my mail in her hand one day and a wrinkle above her nose. "You forgot to bring this in again," she says. "Ugh, it smells like a funeral home in here."

I shove the rest of my turkey sandwich into my mouth and take the stack of envelopes and mailers from her. I probably should throw a few of the bouquets Leo's given me away. Some are definitely past their prime.

I finish chewing. "It's not that bad."

"Because you're living in it. I'm telling you, it's too much."

As she says so, the door opens, and the florist enters again, carrying another bouquet. My heart sinks. The first one with the roses was a romantic bull's-eye, but Micki is right—the daily offering is a little much.

Micki purses her lips but doesn't say anything until the woman is gone. "It's sweet and all, but please tell him to stop. This isn't you."

I unwrap the pink-and-burgundy arrangement and throw an old bouquet into the trash so I can use the vase. "But he likes doing it." I pick up the tiny envelope that's attached to one of the buds.

"Another note, too? It's like he's read a manual on how to be the perfect boyfriend and is determined to top it."

That's when I realize why the flowers no longer make me giddy and warm. He's trying to impress. And while I loved the first thoughtful gesture, being showered in gifts isn't what makes my heart go boom. Not like a home-cooked meal for my birthday or a genuine compliment. He's doing this for him. But why does he think he has to court me like this?

"Yeah, maybe you're right," I tell Micki.

"You should talk to him. Maybe no one's ever told him try-hards are a turnoff."

God, I'm so stupid. This is Leo we're talking about—the guy who's never been allowed anything but excellence. He's just falling into old patterns.

"I'm going to throw some of these out," Micki says, shrugging out of her coat. "Flower corpses scare away customers."

While she wanders the store, I sort through the stack of mail. One envelope in particular stands out. It's from our landlord. I did pay the rent, didn't I? I tear it open, and praise be, it's not an overdue notice. *Dear tenants*, etc., etc. I skim the text until I get to the final paragraph where reality smacks me across the head so hard that tiny dogs flutter around me like stars. The rent increase…I knew about this, have known since early spring. And I forgot. Come the new year, the whole block is being rezoned, and the cost will be incorporated into our leases. Fuck me all the way to the Emerald City.

"What is it?" Micki stares at me while wiping a rotted leaf off her hand.

I sink onto the stool behind the counter and show her the letter. My stomach is solid lead. "I haven't planned for it." I bury my face in my hands. When I open them, the first thing I see is the next envelope in the pile—another notice for the electrical bill. To the right of me is my sewing machine that's gone largely untouched since my birthday. And behind Micki, the store is devoid of customers. A glance out the window tells me Leo is having no such woes.

"I think I've messed up," I say.

Micki's eyes rest on me, dark and serious. "Nothing you can't fix, right?"

"I don't know." It's like waking from a dream, a fluffy pink mist dissipating to reveal concrete blocks and smokestacks. Now I smell the decay in the air. It's making me nauseous. "I have so much to do." I never even followed through with that vendor who didn't deliver my dry food.

Micki leans over the counter and places a hand on my arm. "You can do this. How can I help?"

Where do I start? I can't believe I dropped the ball like this. Because of a guy. "Would you mind feeding the dogs? And then finding the holiday signs in storage?"

"On it." Micki takes off up the stairs.

Okay, what's next? My pulse is a palpitating mess that sends flashes of heat up my neck. How could I let myself forget what's at stake here? When Harvey is discharged, do I want to hand back the place in worse condition than it was before he fell? No. Tell him he and the dogs will be out on their asses come January first? Hell no.

"Eyes on the prize, Cora," I mutter. And I was wrong; Leo isn't the prize. The prize is $15,000, and Cholula, Boris, and Cap living out their full natural lives with us, the people who love them most. Don't get me wrong—I'll lose myself in Leo's arms tonight, too—but he can't be my priority right now. I'm going to have to tell him I need to take a step back. A small step. Temporarily. I need to focus.

I call the vendor first, and after being patched through from customer service to vendor service and billing, they insist my order was delivered as agreed.

"And I'm telling you, I never received it."

They put me on hold once again to a discordant version of "Santa Baby." I rub my forehead where tiny elves wield sledgehammers on my skull.

"Ma'am?" The service rep sounds as tired as I feel. "I have your delivery confirmation right here." She rattles off the number of boxes, which is twice what I ordered. "Delivered October 29."

"No, my order was for six boxes, and I never got them," I say again, getting out of my seat and pacing toward the window.

She starts responding, but at the sight of Canine King, I stop listening. What if…?

"Sorry," I interrupt her. "What's the address on the delivery slip?"

She tells me, and while the street name is right, the number isn't. She has Leo's address. "I'm going to have to call you back," I say and hang up as she asks if I'd like to place a new order.

Leo answers on the second ring, his voice warm in the way that makes me want to purr when I'm with him. Not today. I get right to it. "Hey, did you get a delivery from Pet-Pet Foods a while back that was bigger than usual?"

He looks up, finding me across the street. "How did you know?"

Damn. "They bundled our orders. I've been looking for those boxes ever since."

"That's a bummer."

Bummer? It's a little worse than that. How many customers have gone elsewhere because I haven't been able to deliver? That food is our bestseller. I crack my neck. *Not his fault*, I remind myself. "At least I figured it out. Would I be able to come get them now? Micki can cover here."

"Um, hold on." He disappears from view. "I only have two boxes left. I assumed Jaz had placed a duplicate order again, so I did a promotion. This stuff flies off the shelves."

"Okay, but I paid for them." It sounds snippier than I intend.

"Obviously, we'll settle that. I'm not trying to rip you off. I honestly didn't know."

Micki returns from the depths of storage with two signs that she holds up for me. I nod.

"I know," I say to Leo. "I'll be right over."

"There should be two more signs," I tell Micki after hanging up, grabbing my jacket from its hook. "The snowflake one we always put in the window and that old easel blackboard. Harvey always does a deal of the day on that for December."

"Are you going somewhere?"

I explain the situation and ask her to watch things while I'm gone.

"Wait, so he had your boxes? And sold them? Wow, if you guys weren't a thing, one could almost suspect he's still trying to take out the competition."

I stare at her, my insides chilling.

"Which, obviously, he's not," Micki hurries to add. "Right?"

"Right." I swallow. *He's not. He didn't know.*

41

Leo is busy helping yet another customer when I enter through the back door where I park the red wagon I've brought for the haul. Tilly greets me with her whipping tail, but when it's clear Cholula isn't with me, she backs off. While I wait, I chat with Jaz who's bringing out empty cardboard boxes, but we're interrupted when her cell rings. Judging by the inflection of her voice, it must be a new beau.

After that, I browse the shelves inside. At first, I can't put my finger on what's different, but then I see it. With a subtle repositioning of goods, Leo's managed to change the rustic chic color scheme to red and green, and, paired with a faint smell of cinnamon in the air, he's ushered in the holidays more than any of my signs and displays ever could. I thought he was supposed to be bad at decorating. What gives? That also reminds me he owes me a day in Happy Paws teal.

The doorbell chimes as the customer leaves at the same time Leo says, "Hi."

I tear my gaze from the snow spray at the base of the windowpane. "Um, hi."

"Are you all right? I haven't seen *that* expression since we first met."

Damn my horrid poker face. He's allowed to decorate his store. With a conscious effort that probably comes off as a spastic grimace, I attempt to put my features in order. "I'm fine. Just need to get those boxes. Pretty swamped today."

He's about to respond when his phone rings. He sighs and pulls it out of his pocket. I have time to see "Dad" flash across the screen before he rejects it.

"You don't need to take that?"

His jaw has tightened. "No. I'm done letting him mess with my mind. Once this branch is profitable, he'll come around. He needs to understand I make my own decisions." They're the right words, but rather than coming off self-assured, he sounds like he's trying to convince himself.

But then he relaxes again. "I'm sorry about that. And about the boxes. If I had known..."

"You couldn't." I point to the back of the store. "Back there?"

He follows me. "You sure you're okay?"

I'm definitely not. I'm fucking everything up. Like I do. And seeing how well he's doing isn't helping. "Yup. Totally."

He turns the light on in his storage space. "It's these two. I'll help you load them." He hesitates "But first..." He takes a step closer and forces me to look at him. "Cora, I know something's going on. Talk to me."

Why am I being such a jerk about this? He's going to pay me back for the boxes. *But you'll lose the mark-up for this month*, the voice in my head reminds me. *You might have lost more customers.* Leo's hands on my hips muddle everything. I want to lean into him and have his arms block me from the stress of the world. I should tell him about the bills, how behind I am. *Baring all your weaknesses to your rival*, the voice says. *Smart.*

"Come here." He pulls me closer, and despite my snarky

inner narrator, I let him. A moment passes, then another, and eventually, his warm breath trickling down the top of my head eases the tension in my shoulders. "Whatever it is, I'm sorry," he mumbles into my hair. "If there's anything I can do— Make you dinner? Foot massage? Cookie Monster impression?"

A smile fights its way to the surface, and I grab on to him tighter. The voice is silent again.

"Thank you," I say, looking up at him. "I'm having a bit of a day." The words are on the tip of my tongue—rent, everything else—but when I look into his eyes, there are other things I'd rather say. Other things I want to do. The best distraction.

I press my mouth to his in a soft kiss, ending with a pull on his lower lip. The move elicits a gruff noise in his chest and a tighter hold on my backside. He leans his forehead against mine and lets his fingertips run the length of my jaw to the nape of my neck.

"You know what that does to me," he says, the words caressing my skin.

"I do." I press my hips to his.

He glances over his shoulder out the door. "There might be customers," he whispers.

"Can't Jaz handle them?" I run one of my hands down his arm and encircle his taut glute. "We can be quick."

He spins me around so he can reach the door and pushes it shut. Another half spin and I find myself pressed up against it. "Like this? Here?"

I nod eagerly. Then I grasp his shirt and bring him to me for another kiss.

He pushes closer so that I can feel just how excited this makes him. His lips are greedy now. He's not as in control as he wants me to think, and that turns me on even more. Gone are any thoughts of misplaced orders or difficult parents—his touch erases all that, leaving desire as the sole focus of both my body and my mind.

Leo's hands go to the buttons of my top, but give up before long, instead pushing under the fabric, lifting it.

"You're wearing too many layers," he mumbles, lowering himself so he can get his lips on my belly. His tongue leaves wet trails across my skin, and I shiver when his thumb skims the lace of my bra. Somewhere in the distance, the bell to the front door jingles, and the urgency of what we're doing ratchets the heat up another notch.

"Leo," I breathe.

"Don't worry, I've got you." He grasps a handful of my skirt and hoists it up my legs. The pad of one of his thumbs brushes the sensitive skin on the inside of my thigh. The other is edging closer to the hem of my panties. My knees quiver, and I reach out and grab hold of the shelf next to me for support just as his head disappears underneath the fabric. A moment later, he's pulled the flimsy lace down my legs. I lean my head back against the door in anticipation.

He steadies my hips with both hands and places a soft kiss at the top of my thigh before finally tasting me. A low moan escapes my throat, and my hand grips the shelf tighter. The pulsing low in my stomach grows with each lush lick, and it's only the awkward angle that allows me enough self-control not to come instantly. My hips want to move but can't, and I need more to get to where I want.

"Come on," I plead, my free hand pawing at my skirt to unearth him. "I need you."

With one last peck, he straightens and presses his mouth

against my neck instead while his hands make quick work of his belt buckle and fly.

He hesitates, hungry eyes searching mine. "Damn, I don't have a condom here."

I shake my head rapidly. "No, we're good. I've been on the pill forever. Just..."

I reach for him, and the indecision becomes resolution in a flash. He shoves his pants down, his cock springing free against my leg.

There's a rush of movement where he lifts me, I wrap my legs around him, and we both shove at my clothes to get the skirt out of the way, but then, finally, he's perched where I most want him.

"Don't stop," I grunt, digging my fingers into his shoulders, and he doesn't.

With one smooth stroke, he buries himself inside me, and for a split second, we both tense on a gasp.

Then he sets a rhythm, and, oh my Lord, I will never bash quickies again. The threat of discovery only serves to heighten the sensation, making my body hyperaware of every firing nerve ending.

"You feel so good," Leo says with a quiet moan in my ear. He moves as if I weigh nothing, doing all the work. I'm just along for the ride.

"Think you'll be able to stay quiet when you come?" I tease, my breath punctuated by his thrusts.

His low chuckle sends delicious vibrations through my core. "I'm more worried about you." He gives me a devilish smile and picks up the pace.

With lush strokes of his tongue against mine, he matches the rising thrum at my center, chasing my arousal ever higher. It's not long before he pushes me over the edge, triggering a shock wave of pleasure as I orgasm around him. I bury my face against his shoulder where any noise I make will be muted and hold on tight until he follows me, his climax making him shudder and gasp. Together we ride out the aftershocks, slumped against the door. His breath is jagged, his neck slick with perspiration, but his grip on me never falters.

Slowly, my surroundings come back into focus.

"I might need a nap after that," he says, setting me down gently.

On the other side of the door, the doorbell jingles again. "Yeah, I don't foresee that in your immediate future." I smile and lean down to pull my panties back on. "You'd better not service your other customers like this, though."

"Nuh-uh. Only you." He zips himself up. "Do I look okay?"

I run my thumb next to his mouth. "You look like you just had sex."

"Damn."

His phone buzzes again in his pocket, but this time he ignores it.

Maybe it's my spent state lowering my inhibitions, but the question is out before I can stop it. "Hey, you don't regret moving out here, do you?"

His chin pulls back. "Why would you ask that?"

I shrug. "When we did those rapid questions, you said you preferred city over suburb. Wondering if there's anything to what your dad is suggesting. That you belong there. Not here."

He sputters something unintelligible. "I like it here. I'm happy here." When I don't respond, he reaches for me again. "I feel like good things are going on here, don't you?"

I nod. Dog food order mishap notwithstanding. When he kisses me, he tastes like peppermint and chance. The faintly perilous undertones make me tighten my hold on his shirt. He's right, we do have a good thing going, but I'm also very much aware that he never answered my question.

"Good." He runs his hand over my hair, smoothing flyaways. "Did you get my flowers today?"

I practically hear Micki's stern voice in my head telling me to nip that display of affection in the proverbial bud. "Yeah, thanks. About that, though." I scrunch up my face while I search for a way to say what I need to say without hurting his feelings. "It's sweet and all, but I think... I'm not..." *Aargh, what are words?* "I'm actually allergic, um, to many flowers." My skin prickles at the lie spilling out of me.

"Oh." His face mirrors mine. "Oh, shit. I'm sorry."

Shame stings my throat. "Yeah... Yep. I had forgotten."

"I wish I'd known. I guess I'll have to think of something else."

"Or not." At his quizzical expression, I elaborate. "You're sweet, but I don't need gifts."

His brow lowers. "Then what should I do?"

"What do you mean?"

"Well, to show you how I..." He looks down. "That I care about you."

Something warm and fizzy spreads through my limbs. He's so dense sometimes. "I already know that, silly. You don't have to do anything other than be you."

He looks skeptical, so I kiss him instead. Maybe that will convince him that he doesn't have to give me things to earn my affection.

This time, it's my phone that interrupts us. Micki is wondering where I am.

Did you drown in his eyes or something? You need a lifeguard?

"I should get going," I tell Leo. "Micki thinks I abandoned her."

"Will I see you tonight?" he asks, his lips pink from my attention.

Desire coils tight in my belly again, but across the street are responsibilities that outweigh this want. "I need to work on Cho's talent. The show is only a few weeks away." It's at least part of the truth.

42

Usually, Micki and I do Snacksgiving and movies at her place for Thanksgiving, but this year Harvey has invited us both to the holiday meal Dalebrook puts together for residents who aren't going home for the weekend. When we arrive, the lobby is decorated with leafy garlands, turkey crafts, and pumpkins, and in the common room, two long tables have been covered in checkered, rust-red tablecloths with centerpieces in cardboard that spell out GIVE THANKS.

Micki and I help ourselves to some apple cider while we wait for Pop to join us. He's changing into the button-down shirt and tie he insisted I bring him for the occasion. I also think he wants to show off his newfound independence. While he's still using a walker, he is no longer requiring someone at his side when he moves around.

"Pretty festive for a rehab home," Micki says, nodding toward the table.

There are about thirty other people in the room, not including the staff, and everyone is dressed up and in good spirits. Sylvia and Charles are already seated, and I wave and nod to her when she raises her eyebrows in question and gestures to the chairs next to them.

"Come on," I tell Micki. "Let's grab seats."

"Happy Thanksgiving," Sylvia says when we reach them.

Charles says nothing. According to Harvey, his roommate hasn't spoken again since the Cholula incident, though his overall health seems to be improving.

"To you as well." I sit down a chair away from her, saving a spot for Pop. Micki sits down on my right.

We've made small talk for a few minutes when Micki calls out, "Harvey, over here!" She waves to Pop, who has paused in the doorway.

He grins when he spots us, and, if I'm not mistaken, his smile widens further at the sight of Sylvia.

I get up to help him into his chair. "Saved you a seat," I say with a wink.

"Thanks, kiddo." He adjusts his tie.

Sylvia nods in approval at Pop. "You're looking very snazzy today."

"As do you," he responds. "That is a lovely scarf."

Micki and I exchange a knowing look but don't have time for much else before a man I've never seen before introduces himself as the director of the facility and invites everyone to the table. Once the commotion settles, he calls a toast to family, friends, and the food service staff and wishes everyone a festive night before he disappears out of the room.

Before long, the din of conversation mutes as everyone dives into heaped plates of roasted turkey, stuffing, buttered corn, mashed potatoes, gravy, and more. Even Micki, who is not a huge fan of the holiday, admits it's a great meal, and when Harvey points out that there's also a dessert table loaded with cookies and pies, she groans out a wish that she'd worn bigger pants.

"Why don't we all say something we're grateful for," Harvey suggests after I pour him a cup of coffee. "I'll start." He gathers himself up, shoulders straight, and then he pats my hand. "Cora, I'm so thankful for everything you're doing. Not just picking up the slack at the store through all this, but taking care of the dogs, preparing for the contest, being here tonight… You are truly one of a kind."

I'm not prepared, so for a moment I just blink at him while trying to dislodge the words that stick in my throat. I want to tell him I don't deserve the praise, but before I can say anything, he pulls me in for a hug and then keeps going.

"Michaela, thank you for being here tonight and for being such a good friend to Cora."

Micki clutches her chest. Then she reaches out to squeeze Harvey's hand. "You're the best, Harv," she says. "I'm grateful for you."

"And Charles," Pop continues, "we may not have known each other long, but I am thankful for your quiet companionship, nevertheless."

"And for the extra puddings," Micki whispers so only I will hear.

I suppress a snort.

Harvey faces Sylvia. "And finally, I'm very grateful for your company, dear Sylvia, which has been vital to my improvement and day-to-day morale." He nods. "What a blessing. Oh, and the food. Can't forget the food."

We all laugh, but I also can't help but notice the flush of color on Sylvia's cheeks.

I go last, and because there's a real risk that I'll crack if I delve too deep into what Pop means to me, I keep it generic by proposing a toast to the people and things I appreciate most.

"To this lovely evening, the bountiful food, our dogs, Micki, and the best grandfather a girl can have. Our health! Cheers!"

I almost get away with it, but when Pop and Sylvia resume their conversation to my left, Micki breaks a snickerdoodle in half and nudges my elbow. "Not Leo?" she asks.

"What do you mean?"

"You didn't mention him in your toast. I would have thought you were grateful for him, too."

The word *complicated* blares in my head. I will it to quiet down. *Things are fine. All fine.* "Of course, I am. But tonight feels more like it's about family."

"But I'm not—"

I cut off her protest. "Oh, you are definitely family."

It works, and instead of pushing it, she hugs me tight. "Right back at you."

Again, I think I'm in the clear, but when I return a few minutes later with slices of pecan pie for us both, she returns to the topic. "Leo asked about you when I cut his hair the other morning, by the way."

I pause with my fork halfway to the dessert. "What about? Not asking for gift suggestions or anything like that, I hope. I told him to give that a rest."

"No, he seems to think you're stressed about something. He said you're distracted."

He's noticed then. "What did you tell him?"

She pops a pecan in her mouth, which she chews with studied care as if she's stalling. "I may have let it slip that you're behind on orders, so you have a lot to do."

I put a finger to my lips and glance over my shoulder to make sure Harvey didn't hear. No need to worry—he and Sylvia are deep in conversation. *Phew.*

"Sorry," she whispers. "You are, though. I figured Leo would already know that, as much time as you two spend together."

I shrug.

She leans back in her chair. "Is something else going on?"

Her question triggers a montage in my head. Leo in his crown, Leo carrying Boris, Leo scared of a mouse, Leo with his hands on me in his bed. But also Leo as a hotshot Wall Street guy jet-setting around the world in his spare time. Leo looking down his nose at Happy Paws. Married Leo. Leo, larger than this life.

"Hello? Earth to Cora."

I shake my head and focus on my friend. "Sorry."

She frowns and then lowers her voice again. "Why do you look like life has shoved a bushel of extra-sour lemons down your throat? We're talking about your new squeeze. The best sex you've ever had. Do not tell me you're having second thoughts already."

I sigh and brush a stray crumb off my sleeve. "No, of course not."

She rolls her eyes. "But?"

"But I don't know." I don't want to do this now. I am happy about Leo. I'm *thankful* for him. When he looks at me, I feel like I'm the only person in the room. When he touches me...

No, putting words to the worry-weevil in my belly will bring nothing good. I push the unwelcome images out of my mind and hold on to the ones that matter. "It's fine. I'm just in my head. The show is coming up, and I'm nervous."

"If it makes things any better, I told him there's no way he'll beat you." She pulls out her phone. "And did you see his Insta today?" She shows me his feed, and there he is in the doorway of Canine King wearing my Happy Paws T-shirt. The teal color makes his irises pop in a mesmerizing way. The caption reads: *When engaged in friendly competition, don't lose.*

I smile even though the heaviness inside me still lingers. I know that, for him, there's truth to those words. "No matter what you told him, he's not going to give up without a fight."

"Neither are you." Micki squeezes my arm. "And from where I'm sitting, you're consistently one step ahead of him."

"I don't know about that. Did you see the town newsletter? Best New Business nomination?"

She shakes her head. "But I also don't see you wearing a Canine King apron. And now that Jaz has given her notice, there'll be one available."

"Never. I can't believe she's moving back in with her ex."

"She seems happy about it, even though Leo probably isn't."

She's right. I suppose I'm not the only one with my plate full. No pun intended. I look down at my dessert, suddenly certain that, if I eat even one more bite, bad things will happen.

"What's with the serious faces, girls?" Pop asks on my left. "Everything okay?"

I conjure up a smile. "Yes, fine. Just so full. Do you want this pie?"

"Oh no, I'm all right."

Behind him, Sylvia pushes her chair back and stands. "I'm going to bring Charles back to the room. Again, happy holidays to you both."

"I'll follow shortly," Harvey tells her. Then to me, "It's going to take a good night's sleep to digest all of this, eh?"

And man, he sure is right about that.

43

I'm still full the next morning as I ready the store for Black Friday shoppers, and my thoughts still attempt to backtrack into the Murky Swamp of Complicated Feelings. Fortunately, channeling Micki helps. With her voice in my head, I try to remind myself that it's good that Leo is being recognized professionally because that will lessen the sting for him when I win the dog contest. I also revisit his Instagram where seeing him in Happy Paws teal brings the first smile of the day to my face. The next few are courtesy of customers, of which there's a steady stream all day. My buy-one-get-one-free promotion for holiday-themed pet treats is doing its job.

As it turns out, Micki's slip of the tongue must have made an impression on Leo because he's extra considerate about giving me space and doesn't linger after bringing me dinner the way he usually does. He just kisses me goodnight and tells me he can't wait to see me for training tomorrow.

I text Micki before bed to apologize for being a downer the night before. Life is full of ups and downs, I tell myself, and now things are looking up again, both with Leo and the store.

But then I wake up to a scathing Etsy review where someone is complaining about something that's not even my fault, and my resolve to be optimistic turns out to be as wobbly as the Jell-O mold from Thanksgiving dinner. What if I really can't do this?

There's snow in the air when Leo and I drive out to the farm after work on Saturday.

"Only two weeks left," Leo says when I reach over to flip through the radio stations for the third time to get away from everything golden oldies. Boris is in a singing mood, and I can't deal with his howling today. "Feel prepared?"

I glance back at the dogs. "We're still working on Cho's talent. How is Tilly doing?"

"I thought we agreed not to talk about that."

I scoff and look at the passing landscape outside. "Okay."

"Hey." He puts his hand on my knee. "What's going on?"

His touch relaxes me somewhat, and I relent. I tell him about the review. "They said the sewing was poor quality, and that it fell apart after the first wash. I included instructions—that outfit was handwash only."

His tone is light when he responds. "Don't worry about it. It's one review."

I glare at him. "Don't worry? Do you know how much it pulls down the ratings when you only have a handful of reviews?"

"Can you respond?"

"That looks defensive." I rest my elbow against the door and lean my head in my hand. "It doesn't matter. It's not your problem."

"But I want to help."

"And I want to quit." He's quiet at that, which makes me feel even worse. "Sorry. It's not your fault. Let's talk about something else."

Large snowflakes have begun swirling in the air outside. It's not supposed to stick, but I'm relieved to see Leo has both hands on the steering wheel all the same. On the dash, his phone rings. He declines it right away.

"Your dad again?" I ask.

"Yeah. He's nothing if not persistent. He's called Diane, too, trying to get a hold of me."

"And you don't think it would be easier to let him say what he has to say? Maybe then he'll go away."

"With all due respect, you don't know my father. No one does guilt better than old-school Catholics. I don't need that in my life."

I watch his profile for a moment. To me, he's such a self-reliant man that this side of him makes little sense. "I guess I don't understand why you can't shrug it off. You're an adult so he shouldn't have a say."

"Like I said, he's still my dad." We stop at a light, and he bumps the back of his head against the headrest before looking at me. "I still respect him. He raised me. Taught me about hard work, success, the meaning of family. The way he's loved and cared for Mom throughout everything…Still does." He pauses. "What if…" Something's churning behind his troubled gaze.

The realization hits in his lingering silence. "Oh my God. You believe him. You think you're disappointing people by being here."

His jaw works at my words. "No," he says at first. He runs the windshield wipers once to get rid of a few heavier flakes. "Maybe. I don't know. I want to be here. But I am uncomfortable knowing he disapproves."

"But you said he'd come around," I remind him. "If the store is what you want, tell him that."

He scoffs. "You make it sound so simple. But I don't see you going after your dreams of being a designer."

My mouth snaps shut. "It could be a hobby and nothing more."

"I think you lying about already being one says differently."

I sink farther into the seat as if deflating. "Yeah, I know I'm not being fair. It's just hard, you know. Things aren't going super well for me, and here you are nominated for Best New Business by the Chamber of Commerce."

His head whips my way. "I am?"

"It was in the town newsletter."

He seems to take in this news with a mixture of confusion and pleasant surprise. "When do they announce the winner?"

"The end of the year." I look down at my hands resting in my lap. "I'm happy for you."

He touches the brake pedal lightly as we come to a stop at an intersection. The roads are slushy, but his SUV handles well. "Are you? If you ask me, it doesn't quite sound like it. I'm trying to be supportive. Getting a bit of that back would be great."

"Yes, it's super supportive to open a competing store across the street," I mutter.

His hands tighten on the steering wheel. "I thought you'd stopped seeing us as rivals."

"It's kind of hard not to when we did fine every year until you got here."

"Harvey has been out of the picture."

My face flares. "So it's because I'm in charge?"

"No, that's not—"

All my self-doubt and worry that have been building over the past few days boil over. "What do you need from me? A pat on the back? Here." I tap his shoulder. "Well done. There, is that better?"

He grinds his teeth together around a rebuttal I no doubt

deserve but that he's too much of a gentleman to say out loud. The seething silence drags out until, finally, he speaks in a measured tone. "You like that I work hard for things. You've said so yourself. That I set goals and reach for them. That I'm ambitious. Don't you see? I want to be the best, not just for me, but for people I care about, too. For you. My dad may not be father of the year, but at least he's always been that person for my mother."

Hot tears of shame and frustration threaten behind my lids. "But I don't need you to be the best. I'd still like you if you messed up completely. And right now, it's hard not to feel like you're—or whatever, the universe—is rubbing it in. I'm failing, you're not."

He takes a moment. Then he nods. "You know what the only difference between us is?" he asks, gently. "I want to be here and do this. You don't. That's it. If design is truly your passion, go for it."

"Who's making things sound easy now?"

"Well, it is."

"Not to mention if Happy Paws goes away, Canine King will do even better."

He huffs out a sharp breath at my snide remark. "Now you're deliberately looking for a fight. You know that's not what I'm after anymore, and I still think we can coexist."

"Either way, I can't leave Harvey and the dogs."

"I'm certain he'd find a good place for them. He wants you to be happy." He gestures with an open hand to the landscape outside our little bubble. "All I'm asking is that you also consider your life. You could do something of your own that will be a great success and that makes you happy."

"Or it would be a great flop. I'm good at those." I tilt my head back. "I'm sorry. I'm just in a terrible mood today."

He puts the car in reverse and backs up to the house to park. It's snowing heavier here. After fifteen seconds of immobility, the hood of the car is already turning white. He twists in his seat to face me and reaches out a finger to push my too large, knitted cap up above my brow. "You do look a bit like a petulant gnome in this," he says with a smile. "Please. Let's not fight."

I rest my cheek against his hand. A lone tear trickles across my left temple.

"I'll make you a deal, okay?" he says softly, as if worried about rousing the beast again. "I'll tell my dad to shove it, and you tell Harvey you two have to make a plan that involves you pursuing *your* dreams."

I inhale deeply and nod. "Okay. I'm sorry I'm being such a B."

He pushes a strand of hair behind my ear. "It's not me, it's you?"

That pulls a soft laugh out of me. "Totally. I didn't mean it."

His fingers slide into my hair and pull me closer. "What part?"

"All the mean stuff."

"Ah, that."

He covers my lips with his, and we're finally done talking.

44

Living History Illinois Flockify DM, Wednesday
8:15 PM

AlCaponesGhost25: I saw someone in the general
channel ask about costumes, so I told them to DM
you. And if you have a pic of the ballgown, I could
pin it to the top of the period clothing channel?
SingerQueen: I thought self-promo wasn't really
allowed. But thanks for the referral!
AlCaponesGhost25: See, I'm not a threat to your
livelihood.
SingerQueen: ...
AlCaponesGhost25: ?
SingerQueen: I mean...
AlCaponesGhost25: Do you think you'll ever fully
get past me opening my store?

The snow doesn't stop. Over the next week, the temperature
drops further, and layer after layer of white reshapes the
town.

We wake up to muted winter light falling through Leo's curtains. I stretch and roll into him. It's our first morning together in a while. He's been as busy as I've been it seems. I've missed him, but it's also allowed me to catch up at the store. Holiday decorations are up, December promotions are underway, the guy who's installing the stairlift for Harvey is coming tomorrow, and I'm only a few orders behind on sewing. Judging by the slowed speed of new Etsy orders, I do think that bad review hurt me. But like Micki says, I have no choice but to move forward. She's also the one who told me to get over myself about the Best New Business thing.

"Happy Paws can't be nominated for that anyway," she said. "The council has like three stores to choose from. Don't you agree it should go to Leo?"

And I do. I wrap my arm around his shoulder beneath the covers and rest my forehead on the spot at the base of his neck. He takes hold of my hand and brings it to his lips.

"Did you sleep?" he mumbles.

"Like a rock. I wish I didn't have to get up."

He turns to face me, a pillow indent marring his beautiful face. I run my fingertips across it, and his lashes sweep low. "I'd ask you to stay," he says between little sighs of pleasure as I paint featherlight trails across his features, "but I know you've got a full plate."

He's mentioned that several times this past week and has given me time and space. I appreciate it, I do, but there are moments, like right now, when I wish his restraint didn't come quite so easily. A vain part of me wants him to claim my time because he can't help himself. If letting go after a night like the one we just had evokes no stronger emotion than "you do what you have to do," then what's to say he won't tire of me before the year is up? Or, say, pack up and leave town?

"Do you want me to go?" I whisper, nestling into the crook of his throat.

"I want you to do whatever is best for you." He kisses my head.

I roll away from him and sit up. My toes tentatively try the floor, and I shiver as the chill creeps up my legs.

"What does it look like outside?" Leo asks.

I pull the curtains open and take in the winter wonderland before me. "The good news is it stopped snowing." I let the curtain fall closed again. "The bad news is we got another eight inches or so overnight."

"Probably best not to drive out to the farm today, then."

"Yeah, I don't care how well your car handles. I'm not risking it." I sit down on the chair next to the bed and pull on my jeans. "And to be honest, I think Cho is as good as she'll get. At this point, she either has it or she doesn't. I'm going to focus on her talent this week."

Leo nods to himself. "Probably a good idea. Plus, if you're not going to train, there's no point in me doing it either since Tilly won't do a thing without Cholula nearby."

I grimace. "What can I say? They love each other."

His expression lightens. It's like hearing the L-word spoken jolts him out of whatever rigid fist has him in its grip, whatever idea of "correct behavior to please Cora" he's operating from.

"Something on your mind?" I ask, breathless, as an inner flame animates his face. For once, I want him to let himself go without any careful planning, without weighing each word in gold. *Say it even if it's perfectly imperfect.*

He blinks. Then his lips tip up in a half smile. "Nothing." He pulls the covers back and gets out. "Brr, it's freezing in here. Can I make you some coffee before you go? Breakfast of champions."

The muscles on his bare back play beneath his skin as he reaches for his shirt. It transports me to that night in the fields looking for Boris. I still think his naked torso deserves to be cast in bronze and put on display somewhere. Too soon it disappears behind soft cotton.

"Coffee would be great."

"Stay," I tell Cap hours later after I've cleaned the store, stuffed three new orders into their mailers, and talked to Harvey. I have Cap lying in the middle of my living space, the promise of a treat in my hand keeping him at attention. "Cho, your turn. Hop on."

She jumps onto his back, and I praise them both. They've got this down now, but it's time for the next step. I make him stand and repeat my commands. "Cap, right here. Stay."

I tried this a few weeks back when they weren't ready, which led to Cap avoiding Cho like the plague for a few days. Can't say I blame him. If someone unexpectedly jumped onto my back, I'd be terrified of her, too. But, little by little, we've worked toward this moment. Fancier treats associated with my new command to "hop on" have made Cap more amenable to the circus act. This is the moment.

"Cho, hop on."

The tiny dog sits back for leverage, pushes off, and lands gracefully on her brother's back. It's a dog tower. We did it!

"Yeah!" I laugh. "You guys!" I hand out treats and throw one

Boris's way, too, even though his contribution is limited to staying out of the way. For him, that's still an accomplishment.

Each dog in the show has only two minutes to show off a skill. My plan is to have Cholula balance on a number of different items and end with Cap's back. If I had more time, I might have attempted an exercise ball like Harvey suggested, but this will have to do. I feel...okay about it. The outcome will depend on the other contestants. Last year, the most exciting skill was a mini goldendoodle who spent the full two minutes on his hind legs like a meerkat. Cholula would have beaten that easily. The year before that, however, someone brought in a spaniel who could jump through a burning hula hoop. If they come back, we're toast. Pun intended.

I snap a picture and send it to Harvey. Five minutes later, he calls.

"How did you do that?" he asks.

"Lots of patience."

"Cho looks well-pleased with herself. Aww, I miss my girl. And you too of course," he hurries to add.

"They'll be happy to have you home again. What time are you coming on Thursday?" Mom has arranged an accessible transport through Dalebrook to take him home, and for that I'm grateful. The roads have been salted, but Harvey's car predates even basic safety measures like airbags. It's better for everyone that I welcome him here.

"Some time midday, I believe. Hold on."

Someone speaks on the other end of the line, muffled words I can't make out.

"Sylvia says the transport picks up at noon. She says hi."

"Hi, Sylvia. Okay, then I know when to expect you."

"And you are sure you'll be all right at your place again? Didn't Michaela rent out your room?"

"To her sister, but she'll be moving out soon." Lucky for me, or I'd have to call the little couch my home a lot longer. "Don't worry about anything other than getting ready to break out of that joint," I say. "I'll be fine. I'm always fine. Are you excited?"

The day is almost gone outside, streetlights casting yellow circles on the plowed snowdrifts. Canine King's interior is lit up even though they're closed. I lean closer to the window when I spot Tilly bounding across the floor. What are they doing? My breath makes the pane fog up, and I wipe it off with my sleeve as Harvey recounts his recovery and what he'll miss about the nursing home. He makes it sound like he's been on vacation.

A projectile goes flying through the air inside Leo's store, followed by Tilly jumping up and catching it in her mouth. Leo becomes visible, and the two of them roughhouse with the toy between the displays. I can't help but smile. Leo backs up again, and it looks like Tilly barks in excitement before she catches the toy again. She's good.

Oh…

They're practicing her talent. That means good is bad.

"How does that sound?" Harvey asks.

I've completely tuned him out. I move away from the window and take a steadying breath. Many dogs can catch, fewer can balance on their brother's back. I've got this. When I win, Leo will be happy for me. "Sure, yeah, that's great."

"Leo is welcome, too, of course."

Um what? "Welcome to—?"

"You okay, kiddo? I was saying Sylvia might be stopping by this weekend for a meal. I've talked so much about the store. She wants to see it."

He's got my full attention again. "I knew it! You and Sylvia." I make a melody out of her name.

He tuts at me. "No, no, we're only friends."

Right...Finally, something good has come out of this fall. Geriatric *lurve.* "I'm happy for you, Pop."

"Psht," he huffs, but I hear him smiling. "Happy that I have made a friend, okay? Everyone needs a social life. It's important for keeping the mind young. Life can't only be about work."

At the mention of that, I throw another glance across the street. The lights are off downstairs now, but it feels like Leo is watching me. I haven't forgotten our deal. Maybe I should rip the Band-Aid off. At least this way, I don't have to see the disappointment in my grandpa's eyes.

"I actually wanted to talk to you about that," I say, sitting down on the bed. Cholula jumps up next to me and curls against my side.

"One sec, kiddo." He covers the receiver so his voice garbles. When he returns, he says, "Sylvia was leaving. Charles spoke again by the way."

"That's great." My hands have started to sweat. This is taking too long—I need to get it out. "So, I was saying...I've been thinking about the future and stuff, and I know I've said I'll always be here, but— Um..."

"But you want to do other things," Harvey fills in, his voice soft.

For a moment I sit there in a stupor. He knows?

"I won't lie. I had hoped we'd continue together. It's been such a joy. But then this happened, and you got thrown in the deep." He pauses, and I hold my breath until he speaks again. "I guess what I'm saying is, during my stay here, I've realized I never asked you what you wanted. And when Sylvia showed me your intergram—"

"Instagram."

He brushes off my correction and continues. "With your cre-ations and how people react and comment, everything came together. That one picture of you at the sewing machine...your smile..." He pauses. "You're not happy being a store clerk. Like I said at Thanksgiving, I will be forever grateful to you, my granddaughter, for giving me these years, but you should do what you want."

A shallow sob escapes my throat. "You're not upset?"

"Not a bit."

Fifty tons of dread lift from my shoulders and flitter off.

"Just have to keep the place afloat for now, but we'll figure the rest out," Harvey says.

Just. That's still plenty of responsibility. Twenty-five of the recently departed tons return to perch. My stomach tightens. If I'm not going to stay on at the store, I'll at least make sure to leave Harvey in good shape and able to afford reliable help.

"You have to win," I tell Cholula after I hang up. "Everything depends on it."

45

The snow sparkles in the early morning sunlight as I bring in the mail. After over a week's snowfall, the icy coating is still pristine most everywhere you look, and in the distance, frost-heavy branches dip toward the Fox River where the shallows sport a crisp layer of ice. December has started off dressed in its wintriest shroud.

Leo and I are both doing inventory this morning—I am well on my way to digitizing Happy Paws—but we're meeting up for lunch later after my long overdue dentist appointment. I can't wait to tell him about my conversation with Harvey. For the first time in a while, that trapped feeling that's lurked in the background for so long has subsided.

I hum to myself as I make coffee and fill up the dogs' bowls. Then I sit down to do my social media posts for the week. I upload one of Boris in a Santa hat captioned *Getting in the spirit of the season* and click post. Maybe Leo had a point about there being benefits to competition after all. I have come a pretty long way.

Dr. Bartelli's office is running behind, so by the time I have my sugar-free sucker in hand, I'm nearly late for my lunch date. I walk into the café, breathing heavily, and look around, but it seems like I have nothing to worry about. I still beat Leo here. If I can only keep up this winning streak for the show in a few days, that would be splendid!

I find a table in the back that's tucked into a small alcove decorated with watercolor paintings by local artists. The place has multiple little nooks like this one, each with its own mismatched furniture and decor. It smells like coffee beans and old wood. **Want me to order?** I text him. Five minutes pass and no response.

At first, I shrug it off. He's probably running late and is hurrying across the street right now, soon to pull open the door. I stare at it intently. Any minute now its bell will jingle and announce Leo's arrival.

I surf my phone mindlessly until, finally, I hear the bell and look up. It's not him.

Where is he? We were supposed to meet fifteen minutes ago.

I get a sandwich and a cup of soup, thinking he'll for sure show up by the time my food is ready, but again I'm wrong, and now I'm starting to worry. What if something happened or…? No, it wouldn't be like him to forget.

I have a few bites of my food and then I dial his number. Several rings go through. Four. Five.

"Hey," he says, his voice low and quick. "I'm so sorry."

Relief courses through me. "Where are you? We said noon, right?"

"Yeah, I'm…" He pauses. "I've been, uh, waiting for a delivery at the store for an hour now."

The relief is replaced by something more caustic. "And you couldn't call me? I've been at the café for thirty minutes already."

"I know, I know. I'm so sorry. I was on the phone with shipping and time slipped by."

I think he's going to keep talking, fix it, but he doesn't. Something is off. Why is his voice so hushed? "Well, are you coming now? You're not the only one with things to do."

A beat passes. Two. "I wish I could, but I'm still waiting for the guy to, uh, show up. I'm really sorry. I'll make it up to you, okay? Tonight?"

I take a deep breath. My options are to pick another fight or roll with it. One of the two will suck more, and I have no reason to think he's avoiding me. "Fine. You're sure there's nothing else going on?"

"A slip of the mind, that's all." He clears his throat. "So, I'll see you tonight?"

"Tonight. You cook. It's the least you can do."

"Definitely." He sounds relieved.

I hang up, the pang of having been stood up still echoing inside me. Things happen, I tell myself. These are busy times. On my way out, I order another sandwich for takeout. He has to eat one way or another.

I know I've been lied to as soon as I find Jaz alone inside Canine King and no sign of Leo out back, either. I'm about to throw his food in the garbage when raised voices reach me from upstairs. I gingerly navigate the narrow wooden staircase on the exterior that leads to Leo's front door. A little ice and those steps are a lawsuit waiting to happen.

There are two voices, both male, coming from inside Leo's apartment. They rise and fall like a duet, going from barely audible to loud enough that I'm able to make out the words. I take a few steps closer on the landing.

Suddenly, there's a loud ruckus as if a chair has toppled over, and a voice yells, "Bennett is not the one who carries my name!"

The outburst is followed by Tilly barking, and that's the intermission I need for the truth to settle in.

Leo's dad is here, and he is not happy.

I knock hard, and everything on the other side quiets down. I take off my hat and wait.

I'm about to knock again when Leo opens the door enough for me to see him and nothing else.

"Hey..." He's pale, his shoulders tense.

I squint at him. "What's going on?" I try to get him to make eye contact, but his gaze doesn't settle. "I looked for you at the store."

"I can explain."

"Explain what—why you didn't tell me your dad is here?"

His surprise is visible. "I..." He hangs his head and pushes the door open wider.

A movement in the kitchen draws my attention away from him. I step inside, and at the kitchen table is an older gentleman I recognize from my web search of Royal Equine. Unlike in that photo, though, today he's not smiling.

"Cora, meet my father, John Salinger. Dad, this is Cora Lewis." Leo remains a step behind me, his voice strained.

My bravado fizzles at the sight of Mr. Salinger's imposing presence. "Nice to meet you," I say.

"Likewise." Mr. Salinger smiles briefly, and as he does, his face transforms into a vestige of Leo. Charismatic command runs in the family, it seems, along with the blond hair and steel-blue eyes. At sixty plus, he's still as broad-shouldered and towering as his son. I suppose a life of working with horses will do that. Only the creases lining his face and the grays at his temples betray his age.

"I didn't know you were visiting," I say. "I didn't mean to interrupt."

"You're not." Leo sweeps up next to me, his hand at the small of my back. "Come on in."

The scene looks highly domesticated—like I've interrupted a gentlemen's conference over a civilized cup of coffee. There's even a bowl of sugar sitting out and a plate with what looks like gingersnaps. But the atmosphere is completely different. The tension in the room is suffocating. Tilly must agree with me because she vigilantly follows every move of the people present.

I glance up at Leo, waiting for him to take charge of the situation with his usual confidence, but nothing happens.

"So, is this why you want to stay?" his dad says eventually, nodding to me.

Excuse me?

Leo's arm drops to his side, releasing me.

Whatever is going on here, I'm no longer sure I want to be a part of it. "Maybe I should…" I hitch my thumb in the direction of the front door.

"That would be best." His dad doesn't take his eyes off Leo as he speaks. It's a dismissal of proportions I'm not used to.

I'm about to turn when Leo grips my hand. "No." His Adam's apple bounces twice as he swallows. "Anything you have to say, you can say in front of Cora."

I know this sort of gesture should make me feel flattered, but at the moment, it's hard to tell if his insistence that I stay is a vote of confidence or a need for a shield. I can't read him when he's jittery like this.

Mr. Salinger turns to me, the trace of a smile now completely gone. "You do know he's married?"

"She knows I'm divorced," Leo spits out.

His dad's eyebrows arch. "You finalized it, then? Took your time."

A knot lodges in my gut. It was that recent?

"Respectfully, that's between Samantha and me. We've both moved on."

His dad studies me again, and his disapproval could not be clearer. "So I see."

"What's that supposed to mean?" I hear myself say.

Leo's hand tightens around mine. "I think it's time for you to leave, Dad."

"Very well." Mr. Salinger looks about him as if making sure he's not leaving anything behind. "But your mother and I look forward to seeing you this weekend."

Leo glances toward the door. "She's here?"

"Don't be ridiculous."

At Leo's quizzical expression, his dad reaches into the inner pocket of his sport coat and produces a business card that he slides toward us on the table. "I've arranged an interview for you with Silverton Financial. Thursday afternoon. A fantastic opportunity *in your field*. I've known Spencer for ten years now—stand-up guy, a real shark. You'll like him."

Leo picks up the card, and I crane my neck to see the fine print, but all I can make out is the company name and beneath it in bold, NEW YORK.

46

My tongue lodges itself against the roof of my mouth in indignation. Who does this man think he is?

Next to me, Leo sways slightly before he tosses the card back onto the table. I don't know if I should take hold of him or try to blend in with the wallpaper. I know he asked me to stay, but I can't imagine he would have if he thought I'd get this earful.

"This branch will be profitable by March," he says in a clipped voice. "I've worked hard to make it so."

"Behind my back."

"You wouldn't listen. It wasn't possible for me to stay."

Mr. Salinger huffs. "*Possible.* Of course it's possible. Giving up is a coward's choice. Goddamn it, what is wrong with you, son? Everything you've worked so hard for. All the money I've invested. This is not who I raised you to be."

"I'm not one of your horses!" Leo snaps. "And Canine King is our family business. I thought you'd be..." His hands open and close at his side. "Does Mom know? What does she think?"

His dad's complexion darkens to a deep red. "Leave your mother out of this. Like I would burden her with your folly in her state." He snaps his mouth shut, at the same time letting out a shuddered breath through his nose as if overcome with emotion. "She's doing well right now. So well. We mustn't…" He shakes his head quickly as if to shrug off a persistent fly. Then he squares his shoulders again and lifts his chin. "Even if we did absorb this branch, you would most certainly not be managing it. Salingers rise above. We hold the strings. You are more than this." He gestures around us with a scowl. "More than gimmicky photos advertising the competition."

And that would be me. He must have seen the photo of Leo in my Happy Paws tee.

Leo is practically vibrating with fury but so is his dad. Chests heave, nostrils flare. It's a Wild West standoff, sans guns.

"I will not let this go, Leopold," the older cowboy says. "Four o'clock Thursday. Wear a suit." He sidesteps his son.

Leo follows him into the hallway. "I won't do it."

His dad spins around, a finger cocked and ready to fire at his chest. "You will if your family and your inheritance mean anything to you. My secretary is forwarding your plane ticket as we speak." He rests a heavy hand on Leo's shoulder. "I know you won't let us down."

He leaves without acknowledging me, and as soon as the door closes behind him, Leo returns to the kitchen and sinks into one of the chairs. "Fuck!" He slams his fist on the table, making Tilly and me jump. "I'm sorry," he says. "I've told you what he's like."

I don't know where to start. My brain is still processing. "So, an interview in New York?" I ask, eventually.

At the table, Leo fiddles with the business card, turning it over and over in his hand. "Three blocks from my old job."

"Your dad has a lot of nerve. Scheduling an interview for his adult son." I scoff. "I'm so sorry."

"Yeah, well…"

When he doesn't continue, a chill makes its way from the base of my spine upward. I sit down across from him. "Hey." I force him to look up. "Tell me you're not considering it."

Leo rubs the side of his nose with one finger and looks out the window. "You heard him. If I don't go, I'm no longer welcome home…"

"But you said you don't want to go back. You've created something for yourself here."

His shoulders slump, and his eyes are weary as they connect with mine again. "My father didn't get to where he's at because of his listening skills. And either way, he won't let me keep the branch."

This conversation feels more and more like a downhill sled ride after the brakes have given out. It's going nowhere good, very quickly. "But you can't go. The show is Saturday."

He blows air out of his nostrils. "Fuck," he says again.

That's when I realize that he's already made up his mind. I choke back the lump forming in my throat. "That's it? You're giving in just like that?"

"Don't."

"I thought…We've been working so hard. What about…" *Me*, I want to say. What about us? A traitorous tear swells and runs down my cheek, but I wipe it away before he sees it. "You said you were done with that life. That it wasn't good for you."

"He's my dad." Leo's voice is louder now. "They're my family. My mom…" He scrubs a hand across his face. "You don't know what it's like. Anyway, it's only an interview."

"And you think he'll stop at that? If not this job, there'll be another."

Leo doesn't answer.

"You know I'm right."

"I don't know that." His gaze is hard when he looks at me. A carbon copy of his father's. That's who he'll become if he goes down this route. I want to grab him, shake him, make him see reason, but there's no point. His dad has thirty years of whispering in his ear on me.

"And isn't this what you wanted all along anyway?" he asks snidely. "No more competition?"

My heart drops like a frozen rock. We're back at the park again—like the past few months never happened. Like I'm still nothing but a nuisance to him.

I lift my chin and push the chair back to stand, the wetness behind my eyelids magically gone. "Fuck you," I mutter, turning toward the door.

"Cora..."

"No." I stop and give him my best glare. "We had a deal. I'd talk to Harvey about what I want, you'd do the same with your dad. Well, I held up my end of the bargain. That's what I was going to tell you at lunch today. And yeah, it was scary, but I did it. If you can't do your part, you're a coward, and if you want to pretend you don't know what I'm talking about, you're an asshole. But then I guess New York deserves you. Don't bother with dinner." I storm out, almost slipping on the stairs.

He doesn't chase after me.

Thank God for Micki. All it takes is one sputtered voice mail, and she shows up after work, loaded with fried rice, ice cream, and a six-pack of hefeweizen. I haven't moved from my bed all afternoon where I've binged poorly aged sitcoms from the early

2000s on my laptop. All three dogs are at my side, sensing, like dogs do, that their comforting presence is needed. Cholula is tucked at my elbow, Cap at my feet, and Boris is on the floor next to us.

"Let the man bashing begin," Micki says as she sets her offerings on the table. "I'm here for it. I'm prepared." She holds up a box of Kleenex. "See—I'm like a freaking Girl Scout."

In spite of myself, I smile. "I'll have a beer first, thanks."

"Good thinking. I'm going to have some food because some of us worked today and are starving." She hands me a bottle and then pulls out two plates for us.

After a deep swig from the bottle, I push the blanket off my legs. Micki digs into her rice, and my stomach growls.

She peers at me between bites. "Are you going to keep sighing or do you actually want to tell me what happened?"

Careful not to step on Boris, I join Micki at the table and reach for the takeout box. "Fine. Men are stupid."

My statement catches her in the middle of a swig and makes her sputter around the bottle neck. "Tell me something I don't know." She scrunches up her face. "Ow. It got in my nose."

"Sorry." I finish another bite, and then I relay in detail what happened earlier in the day. When I get to the part where Leo is throwing away the work he's done for the show and going back on his promise to me, new tears well and spill down my face. "It's like it's meant nothing to him, you know? Like, what have we been doing all this time if all it takes for him to go back is his dad snapping his fingers?"

"Maybe it is just an interview, though—like he said."

I shake my head. "He'll be gone by Christmas if not sooner. His dad will see to it." I scoff and wipe my cheeks. "It's extortion.

What kind of parent does that? And I can't believe Leo's letting him." There's a sharp twang in my chest at those words because my real fear here is that, deep within, Leo doesn't mind.

Micki lowers her fork. "Why is your face melting?"

I rest my head in my hand and sniffle. "What if I was right and he misses his old life? Maybe this whole thing with his dad is a convenient excuse for him to go back."

To my surprise, Micki doesn't contradict me right away. She moves a piece of broccoli around on her plate, and the fact that she takes my concern seriously for once is more alarming than anything else. "Yeah, it's a tough nut to crack," she says eventually. "Because on the one hand, he's put a lot of time and money in the store here, but on the other, I assume the same could be said for his condo in New York."

My head jerks up. "His what?"

Micki digs her teeth into her bottom lip.

"Well, that's fucking great," I rant. My hands fly out in a wtf-universe move. "He made it sound like he'd made a clean break."

"Not completely it seems." Micki's voice is full of sympathy.

"How do you know?"

She hedges but not for long. "We got on the topic of wealth when I was cutting his hair. I asked him if he's rich basically." At my visible disapproval, she tuts. "I was curious, okay? He said he wasn't, and that his 'assets' were mostly tied up in the store and his place in New York. But you know, I hear real estate is a good investment. Maybe that's why he hasn't sold yet?"

"Don't make excuses for him."

She holds up her hands. "Not my intention. I'm on your side. Men are stupid."

I take another sip of my beer. "So stupid," I mutter. The bottle clangs loudly when I set it back on the table. Anger feels better than sadness. I cling to it with everything I have because, oh my God, he's leaving. I let him in. I thought I mattered to him.

I should have known better.

I never matter enough for people I love to stay.

47

Leo calls and texts me several times that day and the next, but I don't respond. Micki's revelation about his condo and the ease with which his dad convinced him to go back have me questioning everything, and I'm not ready for more excuses yet. I do my best to focus on preparing for Harvey's homecoming to avoid dwelling, but it's not easy.

A couple of days after Mr. Salinger's visit, I'm jolted awake early by a rhythmic thumping coming from outside. At first I pull the covers up over my head and squeeze my eyes shut, attempting to will sleep to return, but soon the sound of dog feet pattering about makes that an impossible pipe dream.

I pull the curtains aside, open the window to the street, and look down to identify the source of the ruckus, and there's Leo, shovel in hand and his face turned skyward as if he's catching his breath. We got dumped on again yesterday, so the street and sidewalks are an ocean of white. The snow is about half-a-foot deep on the sidewalk closest to the building, deeper near the plowed snowbank, and when the temperature drops suddenly overnight, a crust forms on top of it, making clearing it hard work. Leo has unzipped the top of his jacket, so he's been at it for a while. From the look of things, he's already shoveled up past the salon toward the park and back to my front door, and now he's working his way in the other direction.

"What are you doing?" I call down.

"Thought I'd help."

Fine way to do it—waking me up…

He shades his eyes against the cornea-shredding morning sun to see me better. "Can we talk?"

A brisk gust of wind sends icy prickles across my skin. The thermometer on my windowsill announces seventeen degrees. I can't say I'm in the mood for this, but he did shovel my sidewalk. "Hold on," I say, and close the window. I snatch my grandma's threadbare old robe from a hook on the wall and slip my feet into Harvey's slippers. Cholula and Cap follow me down the stairs.

As I approach the front door, Leo sticks his shovel into the snowbank and steps in under the awning. At first, he's smiling, but when he sees my expression, he stops.

"What is it?" I ask, opening the door. "I was up until two o'clock working." The dogs are sniffing around my slippers, so I close the door a little and use my foot to keep them back. "No guys, you stay there."

Leo wipes his gloved hand across his nose. Looks at his watch. His face falls. "I didn't realize the time," he says. "Sorry. I didn't want you to have to clear the snow by yourself."

It sounds genuine. Like he woke up and thought of a good deed to do, but also, there's no way he's not hoping to get something out of it for himself. I sigh and shift my stance. "Leo, come on."

The color in his cheeks darkens. "Come on what? I'm trying to do a nice thing here."

"What do you want me to say?" I shrug a little, both from

exasperation and from the cold air creeping up my bare legs. "Thank you?" I scan the length of the sidewalk. "Looks like a lot of work. Is that what you wanted to talk about? My gratitude for your services?" Is this what we've come to—communicating in platitudes? My throat feels tight again. With him standing in front of me like this, sad, blue eyes resting on my face, hands idle at his sides, it would be so easy to go to him and wrap my arms around his solid body. I know exactly what it would feel like. If only we could rewind time and make his dad never show up.

"I miss you," he says, echoing my thoughts. "This is ridiculous. I've tried calling you."

My mind sorts through possible responses. *I miss you, too. I didn't know what to say to you. I wish this never happened.* In the end, I settle on, "Are you still going to New York?"

He adjusts his hat on his forehead. "Yes. Tomorrow."

His words are as disappointing today as they were last time. I nod, my head bobbing slowly up and down as I shove any tenderness back down. "Goodbye, Leo."

I start closing the door, but he's faster.

"No!" He puts his boot between the door and the frame to keep it open. "Why does it have to be goodbye?"

Does he really not get it? "Because you've made your choice. And it's the wrong one." He starts to object, but I cut him off. "You know it's the wrong one. You don't want to do this, but instead of fighting, you're letting your dad decide. I can't watch you do that to yourself." As the words pour out of me, I lose some of the carefully conjured control I've managed so far, and my voice breaks.

"Oh, Cora…" He pushes the door open wider and takes one step toward me, and as he does, a flurry of brown shoots past me outside.

"Cholula, no!" I yell. I shove Leo aside and take off after my little beast who's jumped headfirst into the snowbank, mouth open wide. It's a buffet of juicy ice. "Cut her off over there," I call to Leo as I circle around Cholula's right side. "Come on, Cho. Let's go back inside."

Cho pauses her digging and looks at me long enough that Leo can get closer on her other side.

"Gotcha." He scoops her up, and she yelps. Her tiny teeth dig into his jacket but don't seem to pierce all the way through the layers. "After all these months, she still can't stand me." He hands her to me.

"Cho, no. Bad dog. We don't bite." I clutch her close to my chest. "You're a complete popsicle now, silly girl."

"Glad I was able to grab her," Leo says.

I shuffle back inside in slippers that now are more like sponges. "Would have been even better if you didn't let her out in the first place."

"Cora, I—" He cuts himself off, pointing instead to my sleeve. "Shit, she's bleeding." He takes two steps closer.

I glance down to see a rapidly growing red stain on the sleeve of my robe. Dread courses through me as I turn Cholula in my arms to see where it's coming from. There's an oozing wound on one of her paws. "She must have cut it on the snow crust."

"Can I do anything?" Leo's voice is tinged with regret.

"No, I've got it. I think it looks worse than it is." I move to head back upstairs but pause near the register to look back at him, disappointment and longing warring inside me. "Please close the door after you," I say. "And safe travels."

By the time the stupid sun rises next, he's gone. A leaden sky would be a much more appropriate illustration of the gloom that's taken up permanent residence inside my head, but no such luck. Its rays reflect in Canine King's dark windows, but I can't help myself. I still look for Leo every time movement outside draws my gaze that way.

That's why I nearly jump out of my skin behind the counter when, around noon, Canine King's front door opens. I'm in the middle of helping a customer pick out the right size collar for their cat, and I cut myself off midsentence to stare as Jaz steps out onto the sidewalk with Leo's A-frame.

"Everything okay?" the customer asks.

I assure them it is and hurry to close the transaction.

I thought you quit, I text Jaz as soon as I'm alone again. I'm standing by my door watching as she picks up her phone. A moment later, she looks my way.

I did. But he needed someone at short notice and I don't start my new job downtown until Monday so . . . She adds three cash wad emojis to explain the rest.

Gotcha.

Micki says he's being a moron, she types next. Sorry. Need me to do any spying? Put some cheese in the storage room? *Mouse emoji.*

The corner of my mouth quirks.

Last chance, she says. His aunts will be here tomorrow.

No cheese, I text. But maybe . . . I hesitate, thumbs at the ready. Should I? But maybe let me know if you hear anything. It's the masochist in me—what can I say?

She sends me a thumbs-up.

The doorbell jingles, and Mrs. Callihan comes inside with her Pekingese in tow. I put my phone down but turn up the ringer.

I fully expect Leo to ace his interview, and the sooner I know he's gone for good, the sooner I can start the process of moving on.

48

"You got it, Pop?" I stand with my arms stretched out, pre-paring to catch Harvey if he falls coming down the ramp of the transport that's brought him home from Dalebrook. He walks with a cane, no wobble in his step, but I'm not taking any risks. The cobblestones behind our building are precari-ous on any given day, and right now they're covered in snow as well.

"I'm fine." He takes the last step onto the ground and smiles. "Ah, it's good to be home."

"The stairlift guy was here finishing up earlier, so every-thing is ready."

"You've had a busy morning then."

I have. Small blessings. I'll take what I can in the form of distractions to keep me from thinking about where Leo is right now and why. Nope, there I go again.

"Where are my pups?" Harvey asks as we head inside.

"Upstairs. I didn't want them knocking you over."

He stops at the bottom of the stairs, mouth falling open. "The store." He turns to me, excitement sparkling. "It looks fantastic. You did all this yourself?"

I try to see what he sees. The space is better organized these days, not as chaotic. And the lower tables in the front offer a good overview of in-season items. "Micki helped."

He steps up to the counter and runs his fingertips over the display of tags. When he looks at me again, his eyes are red-rimmed and glistening. "You're the best damn granddaughter a man could have, kiddo."

I stand cemented to the ground. I've never seen Harvey cry, and it's jarring.

"Forgive an old man." He sniffles and dabs at his crow's feet with his sleeve. "Nothing like being bedridden for two months to remind you of your mortality."

That sets me in motion, and I all but rush him and wrap my arms around him. He smells like bar soap and wool, and I inhale deeply. It takes a beat, but then he hugs me back.

"There, there. You've worked hard." He pats my back but then holds me at arm-length's distance. "You did good, Cora. And I'm here now."

I nod, the lump in my throat blocking my words. Yes, he's here now. Not sure about me "doing good," though. Unless Saturday goes my way, we're still in a precarious situation.

A duet of whines rises above our conversation, making us turn our faces upward. Cap and Cho are looking at us through the gate at the top of the stairs, pacing with impatience.

"You'll have to show me how that contraption works," Harvey says, nodding at the lift.

I take a second to refocus before pulling my features into a smile. "Nothing to it. You sit down, strap in, and move this switch."

He lowers himself into the seat, and I point to the seat belt.

"Amazing!" Pop exclaims when the lift starts moving slowly up the track.

I walk next to him, carrying his bag and cane. "It does the trick."

Cap bounces up and down on his bowed legs the closer we get.

"Almost there, buddy." Harvey chuckles.

The dogs give him a warm, slobby welcome as expected, and even Boris is up and wagging his tail. Cho respectfully stays on the floor instead of jumping into his lap once he's seated, either because she knows he's more fragile than usual or because the bandage I've wrapped around her paw makes graceful leaps impossible, but Harvey scoops her up all the same and starts scratching her neck as if no time has passed.

I grab a yogurt from the fridge and sit down. I should have enough time to finish it before I have to open the store again. "I'll fill you in on everything later," I say. "You should get some rest this afternoon. Will you need help unpacking?"

Harvey shakes his head. "If you put the bag on my bed, I should manage."

"No heroics, though. Promise?"

Harvey chuckles. "Promise. I could live without another stint in a facility."

"I thought you liked Dalebrook."

He grunts in a noncommittal way. "It wasn't all bad, I suppose. Which reminds me—tonight is the night that Sylvia is bringing over dinner." His face lights up when he says her name. Someone is smitten.

"Any day I don't have to cook is a good day."

"Will Leo join us?"

The knife slides in farther, and I focus intently on my yogurt cup, so Harvey won't see the pain plastered across my face.

"He's in New York," I say, hoping it will suffice as explanation for now. "But are you sure you wouldn't rather it be just the two of you?"

"No way. I've missed you, kiddo."

At least one person wants me around. "Then dinner for three it is."

49

You're snoring."

"Huh?" I jolt awake the following morning to find Micki seated at the foot of the couch I'm calling home for a few more nights until Jaz moves out.

"Like a logger with a deviated septum." Her recently coral-streaked tresses are on end, bringing to mind the villain of some animated fairy tale or other.

"What time is it?"

"Time for you to wake up so I can get a couple more hours of snooze. Were you always this annoying of a roommate?"

I throw my pillow at her and pull the covers up again.

"Oh no you don't." She yanks the blanket off me and backs away. "You're getting up, and on your way home tonight, you'll pick up a pack of earplugs for me and some nose spray for you. That way I won't have to kill you." She tosses the blanket in a chair off to the side and stalks back to her room.

"But I'm tired," I call after her. "And I do have a deviated septum," I mutter to myself. "Some of us are born that way."

I reach for my phone to get my bearings straight. It's Friday, December 10. "What the hell?" I whisper when I notice the time. Five thirty in the morning. I give Micki's closed door a glare and swing my legs off the side of the couch. How odd not to have the dogs under my feet first thing. Here there's no movement, no noise at all.

The winter fair opens tomorrow, which means showtime, which means do or die for Happy Paws. Now that Harvey is back to run the store, I should spend some time today making sure Cholula and Cap are ready. I've made a cape for my little star, similar to Tilly's, and I know she'll be perfect. The question is—will it be enough?

There are no messages from Leo, and he hasn't updated his social media or posted on the server. My fingers hover over the keys. I want to know how the interview went yesterday. Want to know how he's doing. As much as I still want to slap some sense into him, I'm not a robot. I can't simply turn off what we had together. If only this was his apartment, his couch, his . . .

No. Stop. It.

Leo has made his choice.

I push off my seat and pull a clean shirt out of my suitcase. If I'm not allowed to sleep, I might as well get a head start on my day. Look forward. If Leo is gone, that means one less distraction.

It's quiet and dark upstairs when I enter the store through the back door thirty minutes later. Harvey is typically an early riser, but who knows how long Sylvia stayed after I left. The two of them have a never-ending vault of conversation topics it seems, and as much as I know I was a welcome third party, I don't think either of the two were sad to see me go once we'd finished our burgers and truffle fries. Yes, burgers. Fancy ones. She knows her way to Pop's heart, that's for sure. I like them together.

I tiptoe to the front desk, grab my sewing machine, and bring it into the storage room. It's not an ideal workspace, but I don't want to wake anyone up. It's odd that not even Cholula has stirred. She's a light sleeper and normally hears the mail truck at the end of the block. She must be extra tired, too, from having Harvey back.

Around seven forty-five, I'm caught up on Etsy orders and pat myself on the back for not lingering on Micki's couch this morning. I stretch and yawn. Then I wrap my coat around me to go get the paper since I know Harvey is going to want that with his breakfast.

As I step outside, Dawn unlocks the front door of Canine King to do the same. She sees me and waves. "How are you, hon?" she calls, stepping closer to the curb.

A car goes by between us, then another. This is no way to have a conversation. I look both ways, and when the coast is clear, I jog gingerly across the salted roadway. She gives me a hug when I reach her.

"Jaz said you'd be taking over today," I say. "You'll have to let me know if you have any questions or anything I can help with."

"He left a list." Dawn smiles, but it doesn't reach her eyes.

I nod. "Of course, he did."

For a moment, neither one of us seems to know what to say, but then Dawn puts her hand on my arm. "If it makes you feel any better, Diane and I told him in no uncertain terms he's acting a fool and then some. All the work he's done since he came to stay with us—for nothing."

"Yeah..." I pinch my coat tighter at the neck. "I don't get it."

"Have you heard from him?" she asks.

I shake my head. "I don't expect to. We didn't leave things in a great place."

"Aw, hon." Another hug. It makes me want to cry again.

"Have you?"

"He texted Diane last night to check in on Tilly. Sounds like the interview went well, or whatever you want to call it. Said he has a second one today at some fancy restaurant."

I was wrong, having it confirmed does not make it better. "Well, there you have it."

Dawn's face pulls into an apologetic grimace. "I'm sorry. But don't lose heart yet. As much as he tries to hide it, he does have a good head on his shoulders. He could come to his senses."

I'm not holding my breath. I wave the newspaper in front of me. "I should bring this to Harvey," I say. "Good luck today."

"And to you, tomorrow. We'll come cheer you on."

"You don't have to do that."

"Nonsense." A genuine smile now. "We'll be there."

I enter the store, cold both of body and heart, but now there's life upstairs—Harvey's cane-supported gait and the pitter patter of doggy toenails. My stomach rumbles. I find Harvey at the table with a fresh cup of coffee in his hands. "You're up early," he says. "Couldn't sleep?"

"Something like that." I get myself a mug and sit down. Boris is in his old favorite spot near Harvey's feet, and Cap sits next to him, following Harvey's hand from table to mouth as he eats his English muffin. "Where's Cho?" I ask, not seeing her.

"On her bed. Still snoozing."

I squint at the shaded hallway. That doesn't sound like her. I get up to have a look. Sure enough, she's still curled into a ball in the middle of her blankets, but when I crouch down next to her, she lifts her head slightly and looks at me through heavy lids. A low whine escapes her, and her head drops back onto the pillow.

"What's wrong, girl?" I ask, running my fingers across her head. Then I see it—the paw she cut on the snow is twice its normal size.

Our regular vet isn't open yet, so the pet ER it is. I cradle Cholula in my arms as we wait our turn and tell her what a good girl she is and how the doctor will make everything better. She tries to lick my face but doesn't have the energy to reach all the way, so instead her tongue flops limply against my jacket. "I know," I whisper. "I've got you."

The fact is, I haven't got her. I let Leo distract me, and Cho ran out and got hurt. I'm responsible for this. I swallow against the knot in my throat. She'll get better, she has to. I stroke Cho's side and inspect the angry limb. Her foot is shiny and distended, a balloon ready to pop. Poor thing.

"We're ready for Cholula," the assistant says from the doorway.

My phone buzzes in my pocket, but I ignore it. I've got my hands full.

After the vet does a thorough examination, I brace for the verdict.

"It's a pretty nasty infection," she says. "We'll administer an antibiotic shot today and send you with an oral round that she needs to finish. She should start improving after the weekend. You'll also have to clean and rebandage the foot regularly until it's healed. The tech will show you how."

"But you think she'll be okay?"

"Yes. I'm glad you brought her in today." She scratches Cholula's ear and pauses to look at her pupils. "Tell you what— bring her back in tomorrow so we can make sure she doesn't get worse. That will let us change the bandage, too."

I nod, resisting the urge to hug this stranger for her kindness. "Thank you."

My phone buzzes again, and I pull it out of my pocket. It's Harvey. Two missed calls. I frown.

"We're going to get her all cleaned up if you want to take that," the vet says. "We'll come get you when she's ready."

I nod a thanks and head outside. It rings only once before Harvey picks up.

"How's she doing?" he asks. He must love the dog even more than I thought. I relay what the vet told me, and he sighs in relief. "When do you think you'll be back?"

"They're bandaging her up now. Thirty to forty minutes? Why?"

"Well"—Harvey pauses—"there's a bit of a situation."

Panic rises inside me. He'd better not have fallen again. He doesn't sound like he's in pain. "Are you okay?"

"Sure, sure." Another pause. "Except, I'm stuck in the stairlift."

"You're what?"

"It seems like...well...the power went out."

"And you're..."

"In the lift. I probably could make my way down. There's about six steps left, but—"

"No, don't risk it." Fucking hell, this morning. "I'll call Micki. She might be at work by now. If not, I'll be home as soon as I can." A nauseating tide of shame builds within me as I look at the clock, at the clinic, at my car. I never paid the overdue bill at the end of the month. Amid everything else, it slipped my mind. Now Harvey, too, will know just how much of a screwup I am.

It's at that moment that the greater implication of the situation slaps me across the face with a resounding whack!

Cholula won't be able to walk for some time.

We can't do the show.

And with no way of winning the money, everything is lost.

50

My feet are leaden as I walk up the stairs carrying Cholula. The store is dark, the CLOSED sign up on the front door. Thanks to Micki coming to the rescue, Harvey has been liberated from the lift and is doing a crossword puzzle in the overcast daylight coming through the window.

"How is she?" he asks, getting out of his chair.

"Lethargic. They gave her fluids and antibiotics. She should be fine." That's what matters most, I tell myself. Winning the show was always a long shot anyway.

I place her on the bed, and Harvey strokes her between the ears. "My poor girl."

"I'm so sorry." Releasing the words does little for my inner peace, but what else is there to say? "I messed up. You thought you could trust me, but—" My voice cracks.

"But you said so yourself—she'll recover."

I blink at him. "Not Cho. The store. I'm mortified. I've been so focused on training and…and other…I didn't stay on top of things." A sob rolls up my chest.

"Hey, now." Harvey shuffles over to me and puts an arm around my shoulder. "I've made some calls. Your mother has agreed to wire enough to cover immediate bills, and the power company will flip their magic switch as soon as payment is posted. This is not the end of the world. You think this is the first time we've been behind on bills? One time, Martha had to pawn her mother's bracelet until we were back in the black. Oof, did I hear about that for a good long while afterward." His crow's feet deepen with a lopsided smile. "Come on, let's have some tea. We'll get through this, kiddo. I can feel it in my bones."

Ever the optimist.

I make us tea and heat up leftovers from a couple of nights ago on the gas stove while Harvey fusses over Cho.

"Now," he says, after adding milk and honey to his cup, "will you tell me what's going on with Leo?"

I suck my lips in to hold more tears at bay. "He left." I tell him about Mr. Salinger's visit and Leo's subsequent departure. "Kind of feels like he showed up here for no other reason than to mess with me. With us."

"Ha!" Harvey barks. "As if I can't spot a lovesick puppy when I see one. Give the man some credit. Parents can be a hard nut to crack." He raises a brow. "As you well know."

"Yeah, but—"

He shakes his head. "I can't tell you he'll make the right choice in this. Only he knows that. But you can't convince me for a moment his intentions with you were in the wrong place. And for what it's worth, I think you know we were already having our worst summer since you moved here before he came around. This"—he gestures to the darkened light fixture above the table—"isn't his fault."

I let that sink in for a moment. My tea has turned dark amber and is probably too bitter to be palatable by now. Still, I stir it with my spoon. Take a sip. "Forget what I said the other day,"

I say eventually. "I'll stay here. Design school can wait. Maybe with better marketing or new promotions—"

Harvey leans forward and puts his hand on mine to stop me. "This changes nothing. You need to live your life, Cora."

"No, I won't back down. I'll stay until Happy Paws does well enough that you can hire someone else to help you, no matter how long it takes. That's final."

"I meant what I said yesterday. You're the best granddaughter." His eyes twinkle and crease. "But this most certainly isn't final."

Errands and dog care help the afternoon pass, and after making sure Cholula is comfortable, and with a promise to be back in the morning to assist with opening the store before I take her back to the vet, I hug Harvey good night and head out.

The windows of Canine King are dark opals in the gleam of the streetlight, and I wonder what will happen to it now that Leo will be leaving. Will he sell it? Will his dad make it an official Canine King with new management? Will it go away completely, with a comic book store or shabby chic antique dealer popping up in its place?

As much as that last thought should relieve my qualms about Happy Paws, a wave of regret comes over me. Did I drive him away? His words linger in my mind: *I want to be here and do this. You don't.* For all my pigeonholing Leo as the culprit in Happy Paws' decline, I know Harvey is right—we were already doing poorly before Canine King opened. And if my heart was in it, we'd be better off, which means I'm to blame more than him for our struggles. Going forward, I'm going to have to muster up enthusiasm and work harder than I have been to pull us through. No more distractions.

"You look like shit," Micki says after I've shrugged out of my jacket at home. She watches me warily and points to an open bottle of wine on the table. "Want some?"

"Please." I grab a glass and sit down next to her. "Thanks for helping Harvey earlier."

"No biggie. How's Cho?"

I fill her in, and we sink into a drained silence. I don't notice I'm crying until Micki hands me a tissue.

"She'll be all right," she says.

I snicker. "And the store will be all right, and Leo, and Harvey, and my whole fucking life." I take a deep gulp from my glass. "What is it about me that makes everything turn to shit?"

"You know that's not a thing, so don't get me started." Micki folds her legs up under her on the couch. "What you need is a good night's sleep, and in today's amazing news, Jaz packed up early, so you can have the room back. I already put new sheets on the bed."

I blow my nose and sit back against the cushions. "As sad as it may sound, that is probably the best thing I've heard all week."

Micki smiles. "Then wait until you see this." She pulls up her phone and shows me the screen. "I passed my finals! See—you help good things happen, too."

"Aww." I hug her. "I'm so proud of you."

"Couldn't have done it without you. So shake off this mood, okay? We're looking forward now." She stretches her arms above her head. "What happens tomorrow? What do I need to know?"

Micki has agreed to work the booth at the fair while I take Cho back to the vet.

"I've got the boxes in my car. Setup starts at eight, and I'll do that with you before I open the store. We have a good spot." I get my phone from my purse to check the exact location of our booth and show her the layout. "Cho's appointment is at eleven, so I should be back around twelve, twelve thirty."

"Perfect. I don't start my shift until two at the salon."

"Thank you. Again."

She studies the schedule for the day in silence. "I'm sorry you won't be able to do the show."

I nod, my eyes stinging. "Me too. Ugh, you're going to make me cry again."

"No, no more crying. Here, have some more wine."

I cover my glass. "I'm good. I should get to bed." Dog show or not, the first day of Winter Fest is always a big one. I grab my things and put my glass away.

"Hey," Micki says when I'm almost to my room. "Everything will be fine. Try not to worry."

I wish I was as certain as she is.

51

The salted road crunches under the tires as Cholula and I leave the vet's office. It's a gorgeous winter day—perfect for the fair—but here we are, heading in the opposite direction.

"It wasn't meant to be, huh?" I tell the poor pup in the seat next to me.

She lifts her head and looks at me solemnly. She's being so good, leaving the bandage alone, and according to the vet, the fever is gone. She'll make a full recovery.

"We're back," I call, carrying Cho into the back hallway of Happy Paws twenty minutes later.

No one answers.

I shrug out of my jacket—no easy feat with a lax twelve pounds in my arms—and make my way through the store. "Pop?" I look up the stairs. Still nothing. At least nothing human—only Boris lifts his head on the landing above and licks his snout.

I ascend the stairs, trepidation filling me at what I might find. "Where is he?" I ask Boris when I pass him, searching. But the place is empty. Cap is gone, too.

As I stand in the middle of the room trying to make sense of this, my eyes land on the idle stairlift that's been left in the downstairs position. I didn't notice that earlier. Could he have taken Cap for a walk?

I leave Cholula on her bed and jog back down. No, he couldn't have. He's not reckless, and he'd never leave the store closed on a Saturday for something as mundane as that. This doesn't make any sense.

I'm scratching my head, searching the space for clues, when my phone rings in my purse. Micki's name flashes on the display.

"Harvey is missing," I answer in a rush. "I don't know where he is."

"Hello to you, too," Micki says, lightly. "He's here with me."

At the fair? I pace toward the windows. This is so confusing. "But we agreed he wasn't going to work the booth this year. Why is he…? Is something wrong?"

"He's fine." Micki laughs. Behind her, the crowd cheers. "Dude, you need to get your butt over here stat."

"Why?"

"I'll show you. Hang up and I'll FaceTime you."

What is she talking about? I do as she asks, and when she calls back, my screen fills with a shot of the agility course in the Winter Fest barn.

"Pair number eight is next," the MC's tinny voice says over the PA system. "And boy, these two are something—Captain Spots von Puppington handled by John Leopold Eustace Salinger the third. My mouth is going to need a nap after that."

There, on my tiny screen, are Leo and Cap in the lineup of competitors waiting their turn, and I think I must be hallucinating.

Micki's exuberant mug returns. "Can you believe it?" she hollers. "He showed up at the booth an hour ago looking for you, ran off when I told him what had happened, and now he's doing this." She gestures to the arena where I see several jumps, a tunnel, posts to weave through, and a seesaw.

"With Cap?" My slack jaw barely forms the words.

"Something about Tilly not cooperating unless Cholula is around?"

That's right! But instead of giving up, he's taking a chance on the improbable. For me.

"They're up," Micki says. "Can you see okay?"

I don't know how to stop shaking my head as I watch the slow-moving disaster that is Cap in an agility course. He barrels straight through the first obstacle instead of jumping over it while Leo runs beside him shouting orders. The audience laughs. And Leo, who hates making a spectacle of himself...

"It's a sprightly performance by Captain Puppington and his handler," the MC says. "Oof, there goes another jump. This pup must have a steel plate in his forehead."

"Oh my God." Micki giggles. "I can't."

Somewhere next to her, I hear Harvey's deep guffaws, too. At least he's okay.

Cap is in the tunnel now, but Leo can't seem to make him come back out. He tries both ends, but not until he pulls out a treat, does Cap obey.

"Come on, bud," I whisper. "You can do it." Something between a chuckle and a sob fights its way up my chest. Leo is back. And he's... Yes, what exactly is he doing?

On my screen, the crowd cheers as Leo and Cap run the last stretch toward the finish, Cap, to my surprise, nailing the slalom obstacle.

The camera flips, and Micki's face fills the screen again. "Did you see that?" she shouts. "Get. Over. Here. Now! Gotta go."

She hangs up, and I waste no time. My tires spin against the slushy pavement as I peel out of the parking lot.

Between freeway congestion and the general haze of misfortunes that's surrounded me like an ominous cloud lately, I'm convinced I'm going to miss the talent show until the moment I pull into the parking lot and Micki calls me again yelling about how they're about to go onstage any minute.

The fairground is teeming with people dressed in winter coats and scarves, hats and mittens. Kids wear Santa hats and reindeer headbands with antlers, and the sun shines on it all, making the white ground sparkle.

The archway at the entry is clad in pine branches wrapped with a wide red ribbon, and two volunteers dressed as Christmas elves are handing out maps of the grounds. At regular intervals, the backdrop of cheerful voices is interrupted by the sound of sleigh bells coming from the pony-riding event to the far right of the parking lot.

"Candied nuts and pretzels!" a vendor calls out as I pass the first booth heading into the maze of festivities.

Dodging sugared-up children, bargain-hunting grandmas, and heart-eyed couples, I weave down the main lane past homemade ornaments, baked goods, and antique knickknacks like a gladiator through a gauntlet. The red barn rises like a friendly colossus in the distance, getting closer by the moment. I can do this. I can make it.

"Our favorite polyonymous pair is up next," the MC calls, as I push through the doors and search the crowd nearest me for a familiar face.

"Cora, over here!" Micki is three sections away, halfway up the temporary stadium seating, waving like a maniac.

"'Scuse me. Sorry, I'm just gonna…" I squeeze up the risers and make my way to her. In my peripheral vision, Leo and Cap walk onto the stage.

"You made it." Micki squeezes my arm.

I unravel my scarf and tuck it in my lap. "Don't ask me how."

"Let's see what Captain Puppington has in store for us, shall we?" the MC muses.

"Why is he calling him that?" I ask Micki. "I registered him as 'Cap.'"

"I may have elaborated." Micki smiles. "Now shush. Things are about to get interesting."

"You don't actually think they stand a chance? Cap doesn't have a talent."

Micki shrugs. "The crowd loves him."

We turn to the stage where Cap and Leo both look like they've stared too long at Medusa's face. When the music starts, their rigid forms look even more out of place.

"He didn't," I gasp as the first few lines of Leo's chosen song resound over the loudspeakers, and we all hear how they're too sexy for my love.

Leo scans the crowd and runs his hand through his hair several times.

"Why aren't they moving?" Micki asks.

"He's freaking out." I shove my knuckles between my teeth. "Shake it off," I mumble. "Let your overachiever freak flag fly."

Just then, Leo squares his shoulders and turns to Cap. He says something I can't hear and gestures for Cap to sit.

Nothing happens.

"Oh no," Micki whispers.

Leo tries again, this time using the hand signal to lie down, but Cap still doesn't move. A snicker travels through the audience and hits my very core. This is painful. Leo's stage fright is going to be quadrupled after this—it's exactly what he wanted to avoid.

Leo's face gets redder and redder as he tries, in vain, to get Cap to do even one of the tricks we've worked on at the farm with Cho and Tilly. And the more embarrassed he gets, the more my heart melts because he's much too concerned with appearances to be doing this for fun. He's doing it for me.

No sooner has this revelation sunk in than Micki leans forward, her hand coming down hard on my leg.

"Ow. What was that for?" I ask.

"Look at Cap."

I do, and what I see brings me to my feet. His head has started twitching—incidentally in time with the music—and one of his legs moves in and out. He's having one of his episodes.

I'm torn between running up on stage and calling out to Leo, but before I can react, Leo looks from Cap to the audience, sees me, smiles, puts a finger up as if to pause me... and starts dancing.

One of his shoulders goes up, the other goes down, then his arms bend at the elbow, and his feet move sideways as if pulled by an invisible string.

"You never told me Leo knows how to pop and lock," Micki hisses next to me. "He's not bad, actually."

A sigh goes through the audience before the first cheerful "whoop" rises into the air.

"Ah, here they go," the MC says quietly. "Had me worried there for a while."

Leo makes his way around Cap, seemingly matching the pup's

movements with his, and the crowd goes ballistic. There are chest pops, hip gyrations, and even a poor moonwalk attempt before Leo bends his elbows ninety degrees and wiggles forward on stiff legs like a musically inclined C-3PO. Fully in the zone now, he links eyes with me, cocks his head to the side, and lets the movement travel down his joints to end with a flick of his foot before scooping Cap up into his arms and accepting the audience's standing ovation.

I have never loved a man more.

52

Micki and I hold hands as we wait for the verdict. The MC starts in fifth place and makes his way up.

"And finally—in an upset no one saw coming—a tie to be settled between Jessie the wheaten terrier and Captain Spots von Puppington, the, um, beagle mix. What's he mixed with anyway? A robot?" He laughs self-indulgently at his own quip.

"How does that guy live with himself?" Micki mutters at my side before joining the chorus of cheering and applause.

"What does this mean?" I ask, my pulse racing. On the one hand, we're still in it, but on the other, Jessie is clearly a trained pooch. If this pageant was scored traditionally, Cap wouldn't stand a chance. Fortunately for him, crowd enthusiasm seems to have carried him through.

I look to Leo on the stage, side by side with Jessie's handler. He looks as confused as I feel, and when our eyes meet, he shrugs.

"Folks, we're going to let all the dogs have a short break before we crown our champion," the MC says. "The tiebreaker will be the ultimate game of fetch. Each dog must retrieve five balls shot out of this here ball machine. Winner takes all."

Cap knows fetch. It's the game he loves most. He's never done it with Leo, though.

"I have to get down there," I tell Micki. "I know Cap better." Another idea strikes. "There are capes at the booth, right? Can you go get one?"

"On it."

We push our way through the still-seated audience, but when Micki heads outside, I set a course for backstage.

Leo and Cap are on their way out a back door when I get there, but Leo stops in his tracks when I call his name.

I slow and approach with some trepidation, not sure how to bridge the last few days in the right way.

"You're here," I say. "I mean, not *here* here, but you know… Although *here* here is also unexpected, I guess." *Stop talking, Cora.* To hide my red cheeks, I squat down to greet Cap. He licks my face as I praise him for being such a good boy.

When I stand, a jumble of emotions is playing across Leo's face. "I wanted to make it up to you. All of it—leaving, letting Cho out, being a jerk…"

I nod. "Yeah, this week has not been great." Cap pulls toward the door, but Leo holds his leash tightly. I take my chance to ask the question most on my mind. "What about your dad?"

His jaw ticks. "We'll see. But I talked to Mom through her assistant, so I know she's on my side at least."

"That's great." I shove my hands in my pockets but then take them out again. "Right?"

"Yeah." He scratches his temple and motions toward me. "Cora…"

I hold my breath. "Yeah?"

"I came back to tell you—"

"Got it," Micki calls, almost running into me. She shoves a

blue-and-white cape into my arms before she bends at the waist, hands on thighs, panting for air. "Hey, there," she says peering up at Leo. "Nice dance routine. Can I call you Mr. Robot from now on?"

The moment is gone. I'm going to have a talk with Micki about her timing.

"Very funny." Leo presses his lips together. "Honestly, I'm not sure what happened up there." He nods toward the stage. "I think I blacked out when he refused to sit. I really hope he'll fetch for me."

"No, no. I'm taking over." I drape the cape over Cap. "You got us this far, but he knows me better."

"Of course." Leo hands me the leash. "Not to get ahead of myself or anything, but thanks for saying *us*."

"Five minutes," the MC calls over the speakers.

I let out a sharp breath.

"We'll talk after?" Leo asks, intent on me.

The belly butterflies I torched earlier this week rise from the ashes like tiny phoenixes. "Yes."

He nods. Then, after a moment's hesitation, he leans forward and kisses my cheek. "Break a leg."

"This is it," I tell Cap at the edge of the arena. I rub his flanks and adjust the cape. "You look very snazzy. Like a winner. Okay?"

He pants, tongue hanging out. If he understands, he's not letting on.

"The ball machine will shoot one ball at a time," the MC announces in a voice that brings to mind Super Bowl commentary. "Each dog will be timed from launch to retrieve, and an average of the five rounds will be calculated for each. Are we ready?" He looks from the other handler to me, lowering the microphone. "Who are you?"

I make myself as tall as I can. "Cap's owner. I was in the original paperwork."

For a moment, it looks like he might protest, but then he shrugs and raises his arm in the air. "Cue music."

Jessie is a fantastic dog, and she runs like the wind after the first three balls. Cap isn't bad, either, his awkward gallop surprisingly speedy today. The cape flies behind him, creating exactly the kind of eye-catching effect I intended.

"A dog with many names already, but I think we might need to give him another after this," the MC says. "He's like a tiny Captain America with his superhero cape. *Marvel*-ous. See what I did there?"

The crowd forgives the terrible dad joke and seems to agree. I don't want to get my hopes up, but surely they cheer louder for Cap than for Jessie?

At the fourth ball, Cap is swept up in the general elation rising toward the ceiling and does an extra lap before returning to me. The prize money takes wings in my mind, fluttering away, but as I find Leo in the audience and see his grin, I'm reminded that giving up isn't an option.

"What's that?" the MC asks, pretending to hear something in a nonexistent earpiece. "It's practically a tie again, you say? Well, we can't have that. Let's hear it from our fabulous audience—who are you rooting for today?"

"One left," I tell Cap. "You're such a good boy."

Around us, the audience chants.

Jessie's final ball shoots out of the canon, but this time, she doesn't move.

"Come on, girl," her owner cajoles. "Last one."

Jessie pants, clearly exhausted, but with the promise of a treat, she takes off again and returns seconds later with the ball.

"Come on, Captain America!" the MC shouts. "This is it."

I have time to think the guy isn't exactly being impartial, but then the ball goes flying, and so does Cap. I jump up and down as he races, faster than I've ever seen him go, the cape like a sail behind him.

"Cap! Cap! Cap!" rises from the audience.

"Well, I'll be damned," the MC narrates. "Don't judge a book by its cover, folks, that's all I have to say. Here he comes. Whoo—and the final ball is in. What. A. Show."

Cap jumps into my arms, as riled up as I am, his little heart pounding against his ribs.

"You did so good," I say with a laugh. I hug and squeeze him, craning my neck to get away from the sloppiest kisses. "Here, let's get some water in you."

"We're going to take a minute to do the math. Don't go any-where," the MC says.

A couple of people in volunteer vests show him their notes in a brief deliberation. One of them hands him a blue ribbon.

"Will the two finalists please join me onstage?" The MC makes his way up the stairs while a jolly Santa lumbers up the steps stage left carrying an oversized check.

The audience has sat back down, but Micki and Leo are still standing. So are two other figures on the opposite side. Diane and Dawn wave to me.

The MC starts by thanking all the participants today, and

the sponsors who make the show possible. "These two dogs are both champions in their own way," he says. "But only one can take home the grand prize of fifteen thousand dollars."

The crowd claps, randomly at first and then in a steady, united rhythm that drives excitement to new levels. *Clap. Clap. Clap, clap, clap.*

"Today," the MC says, his voice reverberating over the speaker system, "the winner of our annual Winter Fest's dog show is..." He looks from Jessie to Cap, pausing to further heighten the suspense. "None other than Captain Spots von Puppington!"

The audience erupts, and my whole body goes numb. All sound disappears, and I'm only vaguely aware of Micki pushing through the crowd and running toward me, Leo on her heels.

"Well deserved. Ho ho ho," Santa says, handing me the oversized check. There are flashes going off, and someone attaching the ribbon to Cap's collar, but my mind is still blank.

"You did it!" Micki hollers, body slamming me into a bear hug. "You fucking won!"

Finally, my senses start working again. "We won," I mumble, shaking my head. Then louder, "We won." Happy Paws is safe for now.

Leo steps onto the stage, a wide grin stretching ear to ear. *Well done*, he mouths, sauntering toward me.

A giggle trills up my throat. Because it's true. But while I do acknowledge that I brought it home on the final stretch, none of this would have been possible without him.

I hand Micki the check, and half walk, half run straight into Leo's arms. I don't care that we're on a stage or that I should possibly still be mad at him—I only know I need to kiss him.

His lips are soft and inviting, as hungry for me as I am for him. A low grunt escapes him when I wrap my arms around his neck and pull him even closer, and he responds quickly, lifting me so I can wrap my legs around his waist. He might have to carry me home like this.

"Get a room, people," Micki teases a few yards away.

After one last smooch, I reluctantly pull back, but only so far that our foreheads still touch. "Hi."

"Hi." His hands flex against my jean-clad bottom.

I bite my lip to stifle the elation floating inside me. "Seems like we won."

"Never doubted you would."

"We," I correct him.

"Agree to disagree." He smirks.

"Come on. You danced and everything. On a stage."

He rubs the tip of his nose against mine. A soft stroke that sends shock waves all the way to my toes. "Cap won. That's as far as I'm willing to go."

"Fine." I press my lips to his again and linger there for an extended moment that holds all of the past few months, good and bad. Leo opening Canine King, training, lunch with his aunts, Cholula and Tilly going nuts together, his dad, my parents, Halloween night, my birthday...

He sets me down but doesn't let go of my hands. For a long while, we just look at each other, oblivious to anything and everything around us.

"What did you come back to tell me?" I ask eventually. "Micki interrupted you earlier." As I say the words, there's a pinprick of fear deep within that it's going to be bad news. He's taken the job. He's leaving. But it's gone as soon as his fingers tighten around mine.

He clears his throat. "I came home to tell you that I'm sorry. So sorry. I made a huge mistake, and I'm not going anywhere.

Because…" His lips curve up. "I love you. Very much. And I don't want to be anywhere you're not."

My knees tremble, but I still push myself up to kiss him again. And again. If it wasn't a lie, I'd say I don't even care about the prize money in this moment, but more than that, I'm plain happy. Happier than I've ever been before because, for the first time in forever, things are looking up.

"I will make it up to you, I promise," Leo mumbles near my ear. "This whole past week. My stupidity."

I push away from him. "You don't think you already did that today?"

He shakes his head. "Not nearly enough."

"You did plenty."

He laughs. "Another fight? Bring it on. It's what we've always done best."

"I don't know about that." I thread my fingers with his and bring them to my lips.

His eyes darken and glimmer. "I really do love you," he says, letting his thumb caress my cheek.

"I know." I lean into his hand. "I love you, too."

Epilogue

Seven months later

C ome on, we're going to be late." Leo and Tilly are at the door. He's been ready for a while, always on top of things as he is, but I'm still making last-minute tweaks to Cholula's outfit.

"I forgot to move the snap." I rush into the hallway, the fabric of my strapless, royal-blue dress, made special for the occasion, swishing around my legs. I hold up the floral tutu I'm referring to. "It was way too big on her the other day, but now it's perfect." I lean forward to tie my heeled espadrilles, smiling up at Leo as I balance.

"Can't have anything less than that." He offers me his hand to stand. "You have everything? Purse, phone, gum? Your hair looks amazing by the way. Reminds me of Belle."

"That was the plan." I give him a flirty pat on the behind. "Now let's mosey."

We stroll arm in arm down the street to the park and down the Riverwalk, joining a throng of equally dressed-up folks heading in the same direction. Some I recognize, others I don't.

"There's Pop and the dogs." I call his name and speed up, dragging Leo along.

The gazebo at the end of the narrow peninsula that stretches into the middle of the river is clad in wisteria and birch branches, and the chairs set out on the lawn before it are wrapped in white tulle. It's not fancy or elaborate but highly effective.

"How are you doing?" I ask Harvey. "Ready?"

He glances toward the gazebo and then buttons and unbuttons his linen jacket. "Sure, sure."

"It's a beautiful day for a wedding," Leo says, shaking Pop's hand.

"That it is. Did you lock up the store?"

"Of course. And I put up the sign. But I think every single customer this week already knew about today. Good news spreads fast."

Harvey pats Leo's arm. "Good man."

Canine King is no more. Rather than letting his dad absorb it and put someone else in charge, Leo sold off his inventory at a steep discount to yours truly and ended his lease early. I know he took a loss, but he wouldn't hear of it when we offered to pay cost in installments. All he wanted in return was a chance to turn Happy Paws around, and how could we say no to that? With him in charge, we've never been doing better.

Leo is right—it is a beautiful day. July heat, sunshine, blue sky, bare shoulders, sandals. Personally, I'd prefer a fall wedding beneath red foliage and a huge party in a barn decked out in maroon, gold, and dusty pink, but so far, that remains a purely hypothetical fantasy. Although, come to think of it, Leo has been dropping hints about our upcoming trip with Diane to see his mom in New York next month, so maybe there's a chance my dreaming will manifest into something tangible sooner than I think.

"I have Cholula's outfit." I push my romantic visions aside and squat down to pull the tutu over Cho's tail end. I also fasten a white lace collar around her neck. "Do you have the ring?"

"I do." Harvey pulls a small box from his pocket and hands it to me so I can attach it to the collar with a bow.

"There. Should we head over to the gazebo?"

"I'll take the dogs." Leo holds out his hand for the leashes. Then he wishes Harvey good luck.

Harvey winks at him. "Good luck has nothing to do with it, son. When it's right, you know it. You feel it in your bones."

My eyes narrow at the silent understanding that seems to be passing between them, but I don't ask. There's no time, and if they're in cahoots about something, I will eventually find out about it.

Leo holds my hand tightly throughout the ceremony, which is brief but sweet and officiated by Dawn who was already ordained from a previous wedding.

"You did a great job with her dress," Leo whispers to me when Sylvia walks down the aisle on her brother's arm. Charles has regained his ability to walk, but his speech is still a work in progress. More importantly, he's also forgiven Harvey for stealing his puddings.

Cholula prances proudly ahead of them and stops next to Harvey as if she's trained for this moment her whole life. I guess she missed out on the audience back in December.

"Thanks, I'm happy with it."

"You made that?" my mom asks on the other side of me. She and my dad are in town for the weekend, though I'm still not convinced they'll actually stay for the picnic later. If they hauled away in the RV right after the happy couple is pronounced husband and wife, I'd not be surprised. Consequently, I'm not holding my breath, but instead focusing on the warm, solid fingers gripping mine. Some people have awesome, close relationships with their parents. Others have grandfathers, bonus aunts and grandmothers, and boyfriends who treat them like the princess they once dressed up as for Halloween.

"Yeah, it's part of my portfolio from class," I tell her. My Christmas present from Leo was a design class at a fashion studio in downtown Chicago. After winning the money, and then having Leo, and Sylvia for that matter, step onto the stage as major players at Harvey's side, I'm not needed at the store much anymore.

"Maybe you can make something for me some time," Mom says.

It's the closest thing to a compliment I'll get from her, so I'll take it.

"Have you thought of doing it professionally?" Dad asks, leaning forward on Mom's other side.

"Martin," Mom says sternly and slaps his arm. "Look alive, will you. She's starting classes at the Art Institute this fall. I told you this already." She shakes her head discreetly so only I can see. *Getting old*, she mouths.

I smile indulgently.

"Very good." Dad nods to me. "Good for you."

They do end up staying for the picnic, which is a rustic affair with blankets, baskets, barking dogs, and finger foods provided in large part by Diane.

Sylvia has a big family, and after the newlyweds cut a cake the size of a small horse, the younger crew breaks out lawn games and kites. As far as perfect afternoons go, it is a solid ten—I don't know how else to describe it.

Leo lounges next to me, his six-foot-two frame stretched out languidly in all its glory, feet bare, sleeves rolled up. Cholula is curled up next to him, drilling her dark eyes into his every time he stops feeding her ice cream from the carton in his hand.

"Should I be jealous?" I ask, my smile tilted to the sun. "Or are you just making amends for old times?"

The boombox someone brought is playing retro hits in the background, and my toes keep the rhythm while I wait for him to answer. When he doesn't, I use my hand as a shade and look at him.

His gaze is a caress, playing across my face.

"What are you thinking?" I ask.

"Nothing." He feeds Cho another spoonful. "Sometimes you still take my breath away, that's all."

That lightness only he evokes fizzes inside me. "Good answer. I shouldn't be jealous then?"

"Definitely not."

The steady piano beats of a Dolly Parton song ring out over the speakers, and Boris's tail starts wagging on the blanket next to ours where Sylvia and Harvey have been whispering sweet nothings to each other going on a couple of hours now.

I want that. And I want it with Leo. One day.

"Here he goes again," Leo laughs, echoing the lyrics as the wolfhound starts singing along.

Leo puts the spoon down and pulls us both to our feet, sweeping me into his arms so that we move together in a slow shuffle.

"I never told you this, but I once saw you dance with Boris in the store, and it made me jealous. I think that's when I knew I was in trouble."

I tilt my head back to look at him. "Really? Jealous of a dog? Never heard of such a thing."

"Strange huh?" He kisses my nose and then tucks me close as the song plays.

"Come on, Boris. You're kind of ruining the moment," I say, as if that will have any impact on the howling coming from yards away.

"I don't blame him for singing along. He's got great taste."

A low hum starts deep within Leo's chest, becoming clearer by the moment as we move. Is he…singing?

"You and me, Boris—let's take it away," Leo says before launching into a pitch-perfect rendition of "Here You Come Again" for my ears only, every word hitting a bull's-eye at my heart.

It's a serenade for the history books—man and dog in perfect harmony—and when the final chord fades, we come to a stop.

"Of course, you sing, too," I say. "I suppose that means I should be thankful you forfeited that karaoke challenge way back. Kept me on a winning streak." I place a soft kiss on his lips. "In fact, if I'm not mistaken, you lost every single one of our bets. You know what that means, don't you?" I sneak a hand up to my forehead in the shape of an L.

Leo laughs and takes hold of it. Braids his fingers with mine. "Are you kidding?" he says, squeezing me to him. "If you ask anyone here, watching us right now, they'll tell you I'm the real winner. Have been this whole time."

I get up on my toes and lean in, my lips almost touching his ear.

"Agree to disagree."

Another year later…

Living History Illinois Flockify Post, Period Dress Channel

RenaissanceMom Saturday 06:16 PM
@SingerQueen Looking to have another costume made for Halloween. Are you available?

SingerQueen Monday 08:32 AM
Sorry, I'll be busy through October. Getting married!

AlCaponesGhost25 Monday 08:40 AM
Yeah you are. *heart emoji*

Acknowledgments

I was never going to have a dog. Don't get me wrong—I've always liked other people's dogs—I just didn't want to be responsible for one myself. We even chose soft-species hardwood floors to replace the existing five different kinds of carpet in our house when we moved into it because there was no chance whatsoever that we'd ever have a pet.

Fast forward eight years, and now this book is dedicated to the stage-five clinger-doodle responsible for the steady decline of those same floors. Ha! I guess it's true what they say—the only certainty is that nothing is certain. So, thank you, Archie, because without you this book would never have been written. And the floors don't matter when your hilarious zoomies, boopable nose, biiig stretches, and cuddly snuggles bring us so much joy.

Second to my dog in this one instance only, I want to thank my agent, Kimberley Cameron, for always championing my stories whether they're of the lighthearted and sexy variety or the emotional and suspenseful one. Your belief in me helps me believe in myself.

Thank you also to the whole team at Forever for everything from brilliant cover design and editing to PR and marketing, but especially to my editor, Alex Logan, for championing this

2212

story the whole way through. I'm so thrilled to be working with you and seeing what more we can do together.

As always, I'm grateful to my early readers whose vocal support, thoughtful questions, and insightful feedback helped make the story the best it could be. Thank you so much to Megan McGee, Melissa Wiesner, Amy Jones, and Erica Gick! Also, a shout-out to my Rompire peeps who keep holding my hand through this roller coaster of a journey and to my family both for continuously inspiring fictional hijinks and for keeping me grounded in what really matters. I love you so much!

Lastly, I'm forever grateful to my readers who keep picking up my books and asking for more and to everyone who has mentioned this book on social media, posted reviews, and generally spread the word. It is truly one of the best feelings in the world to know that, somewhere out there, someone else might find a moment of escape in a world that was once a mere fragment of my imagination. Thank you for letting me keep writing, and thank you, always, for reading!

About the Author

ANNA E. COLLINS is an award-winning Seattle-area author of contemporary romantic comedies and women's fiction. She was an RWA Golden Heart finalist in 2019, a WFWA Star Award finalist in 2023, and won the PNWA Nancy Pearl Book Award in 2023. Her work has earned praise from *Kirkus, Publishers Weekly, Booklist*, and *Library Journal*, as well as coverage in *USA Today, Woman's World*, and PopSugar, among other outlets.

Once upon a time, Anna was a high school teacher in Sweden, but after moving to the US with her American husband and two children, she realized she had stories to tell. Consequently, she put her master's degree in educational psychology on the shelf, picked up the proverbial pen, and ventured into uncharted fictional waters. When not writing, reading, or raising teens, Anna can be found exploring other creative pursuits such as drawing and singing, as well as snuggling with her mini goldendoodle, Archie, who is a Very Good Boy.

You can find her at:

aecollinsbooks.com

Instagram: @aeccreates

Facebook.com/aecollinsbooks

X: @AEC_Writer

TikTok: @aeccreates